SHOCK

SHOCK

robin cook

BOOKSPAN LARGE PRINT EDITION

G. P. PUTNAM'S SONS   NEW YORK

This Large Print Edition, prepared especially for Bookspan, contains the complete, unabridged text of the original Publisher's Edition.

G. P. Putnam's Sons
Publishers Since 1838
a member of
Penguin Putnam Inc.
375 Hudson Street
New York, NY 10014

ISBN 0-7394-1913-7

Printed in the United States of America

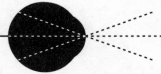

This Large Print Book carries the
Seal of Approval of N.A.V.H.

In memory of my good friend
BRUNO D'AGOSTINO
We miss you

For my fissioned nuclear family
Jean and Cameron
with love and appreciation

SHOCK

The human egg cell, or oocyte, that was snared by the slight suction exerted through the blunt end of the holding pipette was no different from its approximately five dozen siblings. It was merely the closest to the end of the tiny glass rod when the rod came into the technician's view. The group of oocytes was suspended in a drop of culture fluid under a thin layer of mineral oil beneath the objective of a powerful dissecting microscope. The oil prevented evaporation. It was vitally impor-

tant that the environment of these living cells stay in an appropriate steady state.

Like the others the fixated oocyte appeared healthy with an appropriate granularity of its cytoplasm. Also like the others its chromatin, or DNA, fluoresced under ultraviolet light like miniature fireflies in a pea-soup fog. The only evidence of the cell's earlier rude aspiration from its developing follicle were the ragged remains of its corona radiata of granulosa cells adherent to the comparatively dense envelope called the zona pellucida. All of the oocytes had been yanked from their ovarian nest prematurely and then encouraged to mature in vitro. At that moment they were ready for spermatic penetration, but that was not to be the case. These female gametes were not to be fertilized.

Another pipette entered the visual field. This was a more lethal-appearing instrument, particularly beneath the microscope's strong magnification. Although in reality only twenty-five millionths of a meter in diameter, it looked like a sword with a tip beveled to needlepoint sharpness. Inexorably it closed in on the hapless, immobile gamete and indented the cell's zona pellu-

cida. Then with a practiced tap by the experienced technician on the pipette's controlling micrometer, the end of the pipette was plunged into the cell's interior. Advancing to the fluorescing DNA, a slight suction was applied to the pipette's interior and the DNA disappeared into the glass rod.

Later, after ascertaining that the gamete and its sisters had withstood the enucleation ordeal as well as could be expected, the cell was again immobilized. Another beveled pipette was introduced. This time the penetration was limited to the zona pellucida, sparing the oocyte's cell membrane, and instead of suction being applied, a tiny volume of fluid was introduced into what's known as the perivitelline space. Along with the fluid came a single, comparatively small, spindle-shaped adult cell obtained from a buccal scraping of an adult human's mouth.

The next step involved suspending the gametes with their paired adult epithelial cells in four milliliters of fusion medium and placing them between the electrodes of a fusion chamber. When the gametes were all appropriately aligned, a switch was *thrown sending a ninety-volt electrical pulse through the medium for fifteen millionths of a second. The result was the same for all the gametes. The shock caused the membranes between the enucleated gametes and their adult cell partners to dissociate momentarily, fusing the two cells.*

Following the fusion process the cells were placed in an activation medium. Under chemical stimulation each gamete that had been ready for fertilization prior to the removal of its DNA now worked magic with its adopted full complement of chromosomes. Following a mysterious molecular mechanism, the adult nuclei forsook their previous epithelial duties and reverted to their embryonic roles. After a short period of time each gamete began to divide to form individual embryos that would soon be ready for implantation. The donor of the adult cells had been cloned. In fact, he'd been cloned approximately sixty times . . .

prologue

APRIL 6, 1999

"Are you comfortable?" Dr. Paul Saunders asked his patient, Kristin Overmeyer, who lay on the aged operating table clothed only in a backless hospital johnny.

"I guess," Kristin answered, although she was not comfortable at all. Medical environments never failed to evoke a level of anxiety in her that was tolerable but not pleasant, and the present room was particularly disagreeable. It was an ancient operating theater the decor of which was the absolute opposite of the sterile utilitarianism of a modern medical facility. Its walls were surfaced in bile-green, cracked tile with dark splotches presumably from old blood staining the grout. It looked more like a scene in a gothic horror movie set in the nineteenth century than a room currently in use. There were also tiers of observation seats that disappeared up into the gloom beyond the reach of the overhead surgical light. Thankfully the seats were all empty.

" 'I guess' doesn't sound too convincing," Dr. Sheila Donaldson said from the side of the operating table opposite Dr. Saunders. She smiled down at the patient, although the only observable effect was a crinkling at the corners of her eyes. The rest of her face was hidden behind her surgical mask and hood.

"I wish this was over," Kristin managed. At that moment, she wished she hadn't volunteered for the egg donation. The money would provide her with a degree of financial freedom that few of her fellow Harvard students enjoyed, but that seemed less important now. Her only consolation was that she knew she'd soon be asleep; the minor procedure she was about to undergo would be painless. When she'd been offered the choice of general anesthesia or local she chose the former without a moment's hesitation. The last thing she wanted to be was awake while they pushed a foot-long aspiration needle into her belly.

"I trust we are going to be able to get this done today," Paul said sarcastically to Dr. Carl Smith, the anesthesiologist. Paul had a lot to do that day and had scheduled only forty minutes for the upcoming procedure. Between his experience with the operation and his facility with the instruments, he thought he was being generous allotting forty minutes. The only holdup was Carl; Paul couldn't begin until the patient was under, and minutes were inexorably ticking away.

Carl didn't respond. Paul was always in a hurry. Carl concentrated on taping the precordial stethoscope's head onto Kristin's chest. He already had the IV running, the blood pressure cuff positioned, the EKG leads attached, and the pulse oximeter in place. Satisfied with the auscultatory sounds he heard through his earpiece, he reached over and pulled his anesthesia machine closer to Kristin's head. All was ready.

"Okay, Kristin," Carl said reassuringly. "As I explained to you earlier I'm going to give you a bit of 'milk of amnesia.' Are you ready?"

"Yes," Kristen said. As far as she was concerned, *the sooner the better.*

"Have a good little sleep," Carl said. "The next time I'll be talking with you will be in the recovery area."

Such was Carl's usual comment to his patient just before beginning anesthesia, and indeed it was the usual course of events. But on this occasion it was not to be. Blithely unaware that disaster was imminent, Carl reached for the IV line where he had the anesthetic agent piggybacked. With practiced ease he gave the patient a predetermined amount based on her weight, but on the low end of the recommended dosage. It was the Wingate Infertility Clinic's policy for outpatient anesthesia to use the least amount appropriate of any particular drug. The goal was to ensure the patient's same-day discharge, since the clinic's inpatient facilities were limited.

As the induction dose of propofol entered Kristin's body, Carl dutifully watched and listened to his monitoring devices. All seemed in order.

Sheila chuckled beneath her mask. "Milk of amnesia" was Carl's humorous sobriquet for the anesthetic agent propofol, which was dispensed as a white liquid, and the term never failed to tickle her funny bone.

"Can we start?" Paul demanded. He shifted his weight. He knew he couldn't begin yet, but he wanted to communicate his impatience and displeasure. They shouldn't have called him until all was ready. His time was too valuable for him to be standing idly while Carl messed around with all his toys.

Continuing to ignore Paul's peevishness, Carl concentrated on testing Kristin's level of consciousness. Satisfied she'd reached an appropriate state, he injected the muscle relaxant mivacurium, which he preferred over several others for its rapid spontaneous recovery time. When the mivacurium had taken effect, he skillfully slipped in an endotracheal tube to ensure control of Kristin's airway. Then he sat down, attached the anesthesia machine, and motioned to Paul that everything was set.

"It's about time," Paul mumbled. He and Sheila quickly draped the patient for laparoscopy. The target was the right ovary.

Carl settled back after making the appropriate entries into the anesthesia record. His role at that point was to watch his monitors while maintaining anesthesia by carefully titrating the patient's state of consciousness with a continuous propofol infusion.

Paul moved quickly, with Sheila anticipating his every move. Along with Constance Bartolo, the scrub nurse, and Marjorie Hickam, the circulator, the team worked with metronomic efficiency. At this point there was no conversation.

Paul's first goal was to introduce the trocar of the insufflation unit to fill the patient's abdominal cavity with gas. It was the creation of a gas-filled space that made the laparoscopic surgery possible. Sheila helped by grabbing two bites of skin alongside Kristin's belly button with towel clips and pulling up on the relaxed abdominal wall. Meanwhile, Paul made a small incision at the umbilicus and then proceeded to push in the nearly foot-long Veress insufflation needle. In his experienced hands two distinct pops could be felt as the needle passed into the abdominal cavity. While holding the needle firmly at its serrated collar, Paul activated the insufflation unit. Instantly, carbon dioxide gas began to flow into Kristin's abdominal cavity at a rate of a liter of gas per minute.

As they waited for the appropriate amount of gas to enter, disaster struck. Carl was preoccupied, watching his cardiovascular and respiratory monitors for telltale signs of the increasing intra-abdominal pressure, and failed to see two seemingly innocuous events: namely a fluttering of Kristin's eyelids and a slight flexion of her left leg. Had Carl or anyone else noticed these movements they would have sensed that Kristin's level of anesthesia was becoming light. She was still unconscious but close to waking, and the discomfort of the increasing pressure in her belly was serving to rouse her.

Suddenly Kristin moaned and sat up. She didn't get all the way up; Carl reacted by reflex, grabbing her rising shoulders and forcing her back down. But it was too late.

Her rising off the table forced the Veress needle in Paul's hand to plunge deeper into her belly, where it penetrated a large intra-abdominal vein. Before Paul could stop the insufflation unit, a large bolus of the gas entered Kristin's vascular system.

"Oh my God!" Carl cried as he heard in his earpiece the beginnings of the ominous telltale mill-wheel murmur as the gas reached her heart; a threshing sound like the agitation cycle of a washing machine. "We've got a gas embolism," he yelled. "Get her on her left side!"

Paul yanked out the bloody needle and tossed it to the side, where it clanked against the tile floor. He helped Carl roll Kristin over in a vain attempt to keep the gas isolated in the right side of her heart. Paul then leaned on her to keep her in position. Although still unconscious, she fought back.

Meanwhile, Carl rushed to insert, as aseptically as possible, a catheter into Kristin's jugular vein. Kristin resisted and struggled against the weight on top of her. Inserting the catheter was like trying to hit a moving target. Carl thought about increasing the propofol or giving her more mivacurium, but was reluctant to take the time. At last he succeeded with the catheterization, but when he drew back on the plunger of the syringe all he got was a bloody froth. He did it again with the same result. He shook his head in dismay, but before he could say anything Kristin briefly stiffened, then convulsed. Her body was racked by a full-blown grand mal seizure.

Frantically Carl dealt with this new problem while he battled the sinking feeling in his own gut. He knew all too well that anesthesiology was a profession marked by numbing, repetitive routine occasionally shattered by episodes of pure terror, and this was as bad as it got: a major complication with a young, healthy person undergoing a purely elective procedure.

Both Paul and Sheila had stepped back with their sterile, gloved hands clasped in front of their gowned chests. Along with the two nurses, they watched as Carl struggled to terminate Kristin's seizure. When it was over, and Kristin was again on her back motionless, no one spoke. The only sound other than the muted noise of a radio coming through the closed door to the sterilizer room was the anesthesia machine breathing for the patient.

"What's the verdict?" Paul said finally. His voice was emotionless, and it echoed in the tiled space.

Carl breathed out like a balloon deflating. Reluctantly he reached forward with two index fingers and pulled back Kristin's eyelids. Both pupils were widely dilated and did not react to the brightness of the overhead light. He took his own penlight from his pocket and shined the beam into Kristin's eyes. There was no reaction whatsoever.

"It doesn't look good," Carl croaked. His throat was dry. He'd never had such a complication.

"Meaning?" Paul demanded.

Carl swallowed with difficulty. "Meaning my guess would be that she's stroked out. I mean, a minute ago she was light, now she's gorked out. She's not even breathing on her own."

Paul's head bobbed up and down perceptively as he pondered this information. Then he snapped off his gloves, tossed them on the floor, and undid his mask, which he allowed to fall forward onto his chest. He looked at Sheila. "Why don't you continue with the procedure? At least you'll get some practice. And do both sides."

"Really?" Sheila questioned.

"No sense being wasteful," Paul said.

"What are you going to do?" Sheila asked.

"I'm going to find Kurt Hermann and have a chat," Paul said as he untied and pulled off his gown. "As unfortunate as this incident is, it's not as if we haven't anticipated such a disaster, and at least we've planned for it."

"Are you going to inform Spencer Wingate?" Sheila asked. Dr. Wingate was the founder and titular head of the clinic.

"That I don't know," Paul said. "It depends. I prefer to hold off and see how events play out. What do you know about Kristin Overmeyer's arrival today?"

"She came in her own car," Sheila said. "It's out in the parking lot."

"She came alone?"

"No. As we advised her, she brought a friend," Sheila said. "Her name is Rebecca Corey. She's out in the main waiting area."

As Paul started for the door his eyes locked onto Carl's.

"I'm sorry," Carl said.

Paul hesitated for a moment. He felt like telling the anesthesiologist what he thought of him, but changed his mind. Paul wanted to keep a cool head, and getting into a conversation with Carl at that point would have gotten him all worked up. It had been enough that Carl had kept him waiting for so long.

Without even bothering to change out of his surgical scrubs, Paul snatched a long white doctor's coat from the room that served as the surgical lounge. He pulled the coat on as he descended the metal stairs in the stairwell. Passing the first floor, he exited out onto the lawn, which was showing the first signs of spring. With the coat clutched around himself against the blustery early April New England wind, he hurried down toward the clinic's stone gatehouse. He found the chief of security behind his scarred and worn desk, hunched over his department's schedule for the month of May.

If Kurt Hermann was surprised by the sudden arrival of the man who ran the Wingate Clinic, he didn't show it. Other than looking up, his only acknowledgment of Paul's presence was a slight questioning elevation of his right eyebrow.

Paul grabbed one of the straight-backed chairs that lined the sparse office and sat down in front of the security chief.

"We have a problem," Paul said.

"I'm listening," Kurt said. His chair squeaked as he leaned back.

"We've had a major anesthetic complication. Catastrophic, actually."

"Where's the patient?"

"Still in the OR, but she'll be out shortly."

"Name?"

"Kristin Overmeyer."

"Did she come alone?" Kurt asked as he wrote Kristin's name down.

"No. She came by car with a friend named Rebecca Corey. Dr. Donaldson said she's in the main waiting room."

"Make of the car?"

"I have no idea," Paul admitted.

"We'll find out," Kurt said. He raised his steely blue eyes to meet Paul's.

"This is what we hired you people for," Paul stated tersely. "I want you to handle it, and I don't want to know anything."

"No problem," Kurt said. He laid his pen down carefully as if it were fragile.

For a moment the two men stared at each other. Then Paul stood up, turned, and disappeared out into the gusty April morning.

one

"So let me get this straight," Joanna Meissner said to Carlton Williams. The two friends were sitting in the dark inside Carlton's Jeep Cherokee in a no-parking zone on Craigie Street alongside the Craigie Arms apartment building in Cambridge, Massachusetts. "You've decided that it would be best for us to wait to be married until after you finish your surgical residency some three or four years from now."

"I haven't decided anything," Carlton

said defensively. "We're having a discussion here."

Joanna and Carlton had been out to dinner in Harvard Square that Friday evening and had been enjoying themselves until Joanna had brought up the sore subject of their long-term plans. As usual, from that moment on, the tone of the conversation had deteriorated. They had been over this thorny issue many times in the past as a consequence of their engagement. Theirs was a quintessentially long affair; they had known each other since kindergarten and had been dating each other exclusively since the ninth grade.

"Listen," Carlton said soothingly. "I'm just trying to think of what's best for both of us."

"Oh, bull!" Joanna blurted. Despite her vow to herself to stay calm, she could feel anger brewing in her gut as if she were a nuclear reactor about to go critical.

"I'm serious," Carlton said. "Joanna, I'm working my tail off. You know how often I'm on call. You know the hours. Being a resident at the MGH is a hell of a lot more demanding than I'd ever guessed."

"What difference does that make?"

Joanna snapped, unable to keep the irritation she felt from being painfully obvious. She couldn't help feeling betrayed and rejected.

"It makes a lot of difference," Carlton persisted. "I'm exhausted. I'm no fun to be with. I can't have a normal conversation outside of what's going on in the hospital. It's pathetic. I don't even know what's happening in Boston, much less the world."

"That kind of comment might have some validity if we were dating casually. But the fact of the matter is we've been seeing each other for eleven years. And up until I broached this delicate issue of setting a date tonight, you were enjoying yourself, and you were perfectly fun to be with."

"I certainly love seeing you . . ." Carlton said.

"That's reassuring," Joanna interjected sarcastically. "What I find particularly ironic about this situation is that you're the one who asked me to marry you, not vice versa. The trouble is, that was seven years ago. I'd say that suggests your ardor has significantly cooled."

"It hasn't," Carlton protested. "I do want to marry you."

"I'm sorry, but you're not convincing. Not after all this time. First you wanted to graduate from college. That was fine. No problem. I thought that was appropriate. Then you thought you should just get through the first two years of medical school. Even that was okay with me since I could get most of my Ph.D. coursework out of the way. But then you thought it best to put things off until you got yourself all the way through medical school. Are you detecting a pattern here or is it just me? Then the issue became getting the first year of residency behind you. Stupid me even accepted that, but now it's the whole residency business. What about the fellowship deal you talked about last month? And then after that you might even think it best to wait while you set up your practice."

"I'm trying to be rational about this," Carlton said. "It's a difficult decision, and it behooves us to weigh the pros and cons . . ."

Joanna was no longer listening. Instead her emerald-green eyes wandered away from the face of her fiancé who, she recognized, wasn't even looking at her as he spoke. In fact, he'd avoided looking at her throughout this conversation; as far as she could tell, he'd only intermittently met her glare during her monologue. With unseeing eyes she stared straight ahead into the middle distance. All at once it was as if she had been slapped across the face by an invisible hand. Carlton's suggestion of yet another delay in setting a marriage date had spawned an epiphany, and she found herself laughing, not out of humor but disbelief.

Carlton halted in midsentence while enumerating the pros and the cons of getting married sooner rather than later.

"What are you laughing about?" he asked. He raised his eyes from watching himself fumble with the ignition keys and gazed at Joanna in the car's dim interior. Her face was silhouetted against the dark side window by a distant streetlamp whose light fingered its way through the windshield. Her sleek and delicate profile was limned by her lustrous flaxen hair, which appeared to glow in the half light. Diamond-like flashes glistened from her starkly white teeth just visible through her slightly parted, full lips. To Carlton, she was the most beautiful woman in the world even when she was badgering him.

Ignoring Carlton's question, Joanna continued her soft, mirthless laugh as the clarity of her revelation sharpened. Precipitously, she'd come to acknowledge the validity of what her roommate Deborah Cochrane and her other female friends had been hawking all along, namely that marriage in and of itself should not be her life's goal. They'd been right after all: she'd been programmed by the totality of her suburban Houston upbringing. Joanna couldn't believe she'd been so stupid for so long and so resistant to question a value system she'd so blindly accepted. Thankfully, while treading water waiting for Carlton, she'd been smart enough to lay the foundation of a rewarding career. She was only a thesis away from a Ph.D. from Harvard in economics combined with extensive computer skills.

"What are you laughing about?" Carlton persisted. "Come on! Talk to me!"

"I'm laughing at me," Joanna said finally. She turned to look at her fiancé. He appeared perplexed, with his brows tightly knit.

"I don't understand," Carlton said.

"That's curious," Joanna said. "I see everything rather clearly."

She glanced down at the engagement ring on her left hand. The diamond solitaire sucked in the weak available light and threw it back at Joanna with surprising intensity. The stone had been Carlton's grandmother's, and Joanna had been thrilled with it, mostly because of its sentimental value. But now it seemed like a vulgar neon reminder of her own gullibility.

A sudden sense of claustrophobia gripped Joanna. Without any warning she unlatched the door, slid out, and stood up on the curb.

"Joanna!" Carlton called. He leaned across the car's center console and peered up into Joanna's face. Her expression was one of fierce resolve. Her usually soft lips were set in grim determination.

Carlton started to ask Joanna what was the matter, although he knew all too well. Before he could even get the sentence out, the car door slammed in his face. Pushing himself back upright, he groped for the passenger-side window button. When the window opened, Joanna leaned in. Her expression hadn't changed.

"Don't insult me by asking what's the matter," she said.

"You're not being very adult about this," Carlton stated firmly.

"Thank you for your unbiased assessment," Joanna retorted. "I also want to thank you for making everything so clear for me. It certainly makes it easier to make up my mind."

"Make up your mind about what?" Carlton asked. The newly found firmness of his voice vanished. In its place was a definite quaver. He had a premonition about what was coming, and it was accompanied by a sinking feeling in the pit of his stomach.

"About my future," Joanna said. "Here!" She extended her clenched fist with the obvious intention of giving something to Carlton.

Carlton reached out hesitantly with a cupped palm. He felt something cold drop into his hand. Glancing down, he found himself staring at his grandmother's diamond.

"What's this all about?" Carlton stammered.

"I think it's pretty clear," Joanna said. "Consider yourself free to finish your residency and whatever else your little heart desires. I certainly don't want to think of myself as a drag."

"You're not serious?" Carlton questioned. Caught completely off guard by this sudden turn of events, he was befuddled.

"Oh, but I am," Joanna said. "Consider our engagement officially over. Good night, Carlton."

Joanna turned and walked back along Craigie Street toward Concord Avenue and the entrance to the Craigie Arms. Her apartment was on the third floor.

After a brief struggle with the door release Carlton leaped from his Cherokee and ran after Joanna, who'd already reached the corner. A few deep red maple leaves, which had fallen from the tree that very day, wafted in his wake. He caught up to his former fiancée as she was about to enter her apartment building. He was out of breath. He was clutching the engagement ring in his fist.

"All right," Carlton managed. "You've

made your point. Here, take the ring back."
He extended his hand.

Joanna shook her head. Her grim determination had disappeared. In its place was
a tenuous smile. "I didn't give the ring back
as a mere gesture or machination. Nor am
I actually angry. You obviously don't want
to get married now, and all at once, I don't
either. Let's give it a rest. We're still
friends."

"But I love you," Carlton blurted.

"I'm flattered," Joanna said. "And I suppose I still love you, but things have been
dragging on for too long. Let's go our separate ways, at least for now."

"But . . ."

"Good night, Carlton," Joanna said. She
pushed herself up onto her tiptoes and
gave Carlton's cheek a brush with her lips.
A moment later she was in the elevator.
She hadn't looked back.

Putting her key in her apartment door
she noticed she was trembling. Despite her
airy dismissal of Carlton, she felt her emotions rumbling just below the surface.

"Wow!" her roommate Deborah
Cochrane exclaimed. She checked the task
bar on her computer to see the time.

"Rather early for a Friday night. Wussup?" Deborah was dressed in oversized Harvard-emblazoned sweats. In comparison with the soft, porcelain femininity of her roommate, she was mildly tomboyish with short dark hair, a Mediterranean olive complexion, and an athletic build. Her facial features contributed by being stronger and more rounded than Joanna's yet no less feminine. All in all, the roommates complemented each other and emphasized each other's natural attractiveness.

Joanna didn't respond as she hung up her coat in the hall closet. Deborah watched her closely as she came into their sparsely furnished living room and collapsed on the couch. She tucked her feet under herself and only then met Deborah's inquisitive eyes.

"Don't tell me you guys had a fight," Deborah said.

"Not a fight per se," Joanna said. "Just a parting of ways."

Deborah's jaw dropped. For the six years she'd known Joanna, from freshman orientation onward, Carlton had been a fixture in Joanna's life. As far as she was concerned there'd not been the slightest hint of discord within the relationship. "What happened?" she asked with astonishment.

"I suddenly saw the light," Joanna said. There was a slight trill to her voice that Deborah noticed instantly. "My engagement is off, and, more importantly, I'm not going to count on getting married, period. If it happens, fine, but if it doesn't, that's okay too."

"My word!" Deborah said, unable to keep the glee from her voice. "This doesn't sound like the 'butter cream frosting, silky bridesmaids' dresses' girl that I've come to love. Why the change of heart?" Deborah considered Joanna's march toward marriage almost religious in its unswerving intensity.

"Carlton wanted to postpone the wedding until after his residency," Joanna said. In short order, she recounted the last fifteen minutes of her date with Carlton. Deborah listened with rapt attention.

"Are you all right?" Deborah asked when Joanna fell silent. She leaned forward to peer more directly into Joanna's eyes.

"Better than I would have guessed," Joanna admitted. "I feel a little shaky, I suppose, but all things considered, I'm doing okay."

"Then this calls for a celebration," Deborah exclaimed. She stood up and bounced into the kitchen. "I've been saving that bottle of champagne cluttering up the fridge for months," she called over her shoulder. "This is the time to open it."

"I suppose," Joanna managed. She didn't feel much like celebrating, but resisting Deborah's enthusiasm would have taken too much effort.

"All right!" Deborah exclaimed as she returned with the champagne in one hand and two flutes in the other. She knelt at the coffee table and attacked the bottle. The cork came away with a resounding pop and caromed off the ceiling. Deborah laughed but noticed that Joanna didn't.

"Are you sure you're okay?" Deborah asked.

"I have to say, it's a big adjustment."

"That's an understatement," Deborah averred. "Knowing you as well as I do, it's the equivalent of Saint Paul falling on the way to Damascus. You've been programmed by the Houston social scene

toward marriage since you were nothing
but a twinkle in your mother's eye."

Joanna laughed despite herself.

Deborah poured the champagne too
quickly. Both glasses filled, mostly with
fizz, and spilled out on the table. Undeterred, Deborah snatched up the flutes
and handed one to Joanna. Then she
made Joanna clink glasses with her.

"Welcome to the twenty-first century social scene," Deborah said.

Both women lifted their stemware and
tried to drink. They coughed on the foam
and laughed. Not wanting to lose the moment, Deborah quickly took both glasses
into the kitchen, rinsed them, and returned.
This time she poured more carefully by letting the champagne run down the side of
the glass. When they drank, it was mostly
liquid.

"Not the greatest bubbly," Deborah admitted. "But it's not surprising. David gave
it to me way back when. Unfortunately he
was a cheapskate from the word go."
Deborah had broken off a four-month relationship with her most recent boyfriend,
David Curtis, the week before. In sharp
contrast to Joanna's, her longest relation-

ship had been less than two years and that was way back in high school. In many ways the two women couldn't have been more different. Instead of the affluent southern suburban social scene complete with debutante balls funded by oil money which Joanna had enjoyed, Deborah grew up in Manhattan with a bohemian single parent who was immersed in academia. Deborah had never known her father, since it was her imminent birth that had ended her parents' relationship. Her mother hadn't married until relatively late in life, after Deborah had left for college.

"I've not been much of a champagne fan anyway," Joanna said. "I actually wouldn't even know if it were good stuff or not." She twirled the glass in her fingers, momentarily mesmerized by the effervescence.

"What happened to your ring?" Deborah asked, noticing for the first time that the jewelry was gone.

"I gave it back," Joanna said casually.

Deborah shook her head. She was amazed. Joanna had loved the diamond and everything it stood for. She'd rarely taken it from her finger.

"I'm serious about this," Joanna said.

"I'm getting that impression," Deborah said. She was momentarily speechless.

The phone shattered the short silence. Deborah stood up to get it.

"It's probably Carlton, but I don't want to talk with him," Joanna said.

Over at the desk Deborah checked the caller ID screen. "You're right, it's Carlton."

"Let the answering machine get it," Joanna said.

Deborah returned to the coffee table and plopped herself back down. The two women eyed each other as the phone continued its insistent ring. After the fourth ring the answering machine picked up. There was silence while the outgoing message played. Then Carlton's anxious voice along with a bit of static filled the ascetically decorated room.

"You're right, Joanna! Waiting until I finish my residency is a stupid idea."

"I never said it was a stupid idea," Joanna interjected in a forced whisper as if the caller could hear.

"And you know what?" Carlton continued. "Why don't we go ahead and plan for this June. As I recall, you always said you wanted a June wedding. Well, June's fine by me. Anyway, give me a call as soon as you get this message, and we can talk about it. Okay?"

The answering machine made a few more mechanical sounds before the little red light on the front of the console began to blink.

"That shows you how much he knows," Joanna said. "There's no way my mother could put together a proper Houston wedding in eight months."

"He sounds a little desperate," Deborah said. "If you want to call him back and want some privacy, I can make myself scarce."

"I don't want to talk with him," Joanna said quickly. "Not now."

Deborah cocked her head to the side and studied her friend's face. She wanted to be supportive but for the moment was confused how best to play that role.

"This isn't an argument he and I are having," Joanna explained. "Nor is it some kind of lover's game. I'm not trying to be manipulative, and frankly, I'd feel uncomfortable if we did get married now."

"This is a total switch."

"Exactly," Joanna said. "Here he is trying

to move the date up and I'd be arguing to postpone. I need some time and space."

"I understand completely," Deborah said. "And you know what? I think you're being smart not to let this situation turn into a petulant debate."

"The problem is I do love him," Joanna said with a wry smile. "If there was any debate, I might lose."

Deborah laughed. "I agree. You're such a new convert to a more modern, sensible attitude about marriage, that you're vulnerable to a relapse. You definitely need time and space. And you know what? I think I have the answer."

"The answer to what?" Joanna asked.

"Let me show you something," Deborah said. She climbed to her feet and picked up the latest issue of the *Harvard Crimson* lying on her desk. It was folded lengthwise in the classified section. She handed the paper to Joanna.

Joanna scanned the page and read the circled ad. She looked up at Deborah questioningly. "Is this ad from the Wingate Clinic what you wanted me to see?"

"It is indeed," Deborah said enthusiastically.

"This is an advertisement for egg donors," Joanna said.

"Precisely," Deborah said.

"How is this the answer?" Joanna asked.

Deborah came around the coffee table and sat down next to Joanna. With her index finger she pointed to the offered compensation. "The money is the answer," she said. "Forty-five thousand dollars a pop!"

"This ad was in an issue of the *Crimson* last spring and caused a buzz," Joanna said. "Then it never reappeared. Do you think it's legit or some kind of college prank?"

"I think it's legit," Deborah said. "Wingate is an infertility clinic in Bookford, Massachusetts, out beyond Concord. That's what I learned from their website."

"Why are they willing to pay so much money?" Joanna asked.

"The website says they have some wealthy clients who are willing to pay for what they consider the best. Apparently these clients want Harvard coeds. It must be something like that sperm bank in California where the donors are all Nobel laureates. It's lunacy from a genetic point of view, but who are we to question?"

"We're certainly not Nobel laureates," Joanna said. "Technically, we're not even Harvard coeds. What makes you think they'd be interested in you and me?"

"Why wouldn't they be?" Deborah asked. "I think being grad students qualifies us as Harvard coeds. I can't imagine it's just undergraduates that they're looking for. In fact, the website specifies they're interested in women twenty-five and younger. We just make it under the wire."

"But it also says we have to be emotionally stable, attractive, not overweight, and athletic. Aren't we stretching reality a bit here?"

"Hey, I think we're perfect."

"Athletic?" Joanna questioned with a smile. "Maybe you, but not me. And emotionally stable. That's pushing the envelope, especially in my current state."

"Well, we can give it a go," Deborah said. "Maybe you're not the most athletically inclined female on campus, but we'll tell them we'll only consider donating as a pair. They have to take both of us. All or

nothing. And our SAT scores are appropriate."

"Are you truly serious about this?"
Joanna asked. She eyed her roommate,
who could be a tease on occasion.

"I wasn't at first," Deborah admitted.
"But then I got to thinking about it earlier in
the evening. I mean, the money is enticing.
Can you imagine: forty-five grand apiece!
That kind of money could give us some
freedom for the first time in our lives even
while we write our theses. And now that
you have so recently opted out of the eco-
nomic security of the marital goal, the idea
should be even more seductive from your
perspective. You need some equity besides your education to maintain your resolve and, frankly, to begin planning for the
life of a single individual. This kind of
money could be the start."

Joanna tossed the school newspaper
onto the coffee table. "Sometimes I can't
tell when you are pulling my leg."

"Hey, I'm not joking. You said you need
time and space. This kind of money could
provide it and more. Here's the deal: We
both go out to this Wingate Clinic, give
them a couple of eggs, and collect ninety

K. Of that, we take about fifty K and buy a two-bedroom condo in Boston or Cambridge, which we rent out to pay the mortgage."

"Why would we buy a condo to rent it?" Joanna asked.

"Let me finish," Deborah said.

"But wouldn't it be better to just wisely invest the fifty K? Remember: I'm the economist and you're the biologist."

"You might be getting a Ph.D. in economics, but you're a babe in the woods in relation to being a single female in the twenty-first century. So shut up and listen. We buy the condo to begin establishing some real roots. In the previous generation females looked to marriage for that, but now we have to do it for ourselves. An apartment would be a nice start as well as a good investment."

"My word!" Joanna exclaimed. "You're way ahead of me."

"You bet your sweet ass," Deborah said. "And there's more. Here's the best part: We take the other forty K and go to Venice to write our Ph.D. theses."

"Venice!" Joanna cried. "You're crazy, girl!"

"Oh yeah?" Deborah asked. "Think about it. When you're talking about having some time and space, what could be better? We'd be in Venice in some nice cozy apartment and Carlton's here doing his residency. We get our theses done and live a little at the same time without the good doctor breathing down your neck."

Joanna stared ahead with unseeing eyes while her brain conjured up images of Venice. She'd visited the magical city once, but only for a few days, and that had been with her parents and siblings when she'd been in high school. She could picture the sparkle of the water of the Grand Canal as it reflected off the gothic facades. With equally startling clarity she could remember the bustle of St. Mark's Square with the competing quartets from the two famous opposing coffeehouses. She'd told herself back then that she would return someday to that most romantic city. Of course that fantasy had included Carlton, who was not along at the time, but whom she was already seeing.

"And there's something else," Deborah said, interrupting Joanna's brief reverie. "Giving a few eggs, which by the way we have several hundred thousand of so they won't be missed, will provide a tiny bit of satisfaction to our procreative urges."

"Now I know you are teasing me," Joanna said.

"I'm not!" Deborah insisted. "Donating some eggs will mean that a few couples who couldn't have children will have them, and these kids will have half our genes. There'll be a few 'half Joannas' and 'half Deborahs' wandering around."

"I guess that's true," Joanna said. In her mind's eye she saw a little girl who looked something like herself. It was a pleasant image until she saw the little girl was with two total strangers.

"Of course it's true," Deborah said. "And the good part is that we don't have to change any diapers or lose any sleep. What do you say we give it a whirl?"

"Wait a minute!" Joanna said. She raised her hands as if to protect herself. "Slow down! Assuming we got accepted, which is hardly a sure thing given all the stipulations in the ad, I've got a few major questions."

"Like what?"

"Like how do we actually give the eggs?

I mean, what's the procedure? You know that I'm not fond of doctors and hospitals."

"That's a fine thing for someone to say who's been dating a doctor-in-training for the last half century."

"It's when I'm a patient that the trouble starts," Joanna said.

"The ad says there'd be minimal stimulation," Deborah said.

"Is that good?"

"Absolutely," Deborah said. "Usually they have to hyperstimulate the ovaries to get them to release a number of eggs, and the hyperstimulation can cause problems in some people like PMS from hell. The hyperstimulation is done with strong hormones. Believe it or not, some of the hormones come from menopausal Italian nuns."

"Oh, come on!" Joanna complained. "I'm not that gullible."

"I swear to God," Deborah said. "These menopausal nuns' pituitaries are cranking out gonadal stimulating hormones to beat the band. It's extracted from their urine. Trust me!"

"I'll take your word for it," Joanna said, making an expression of disgust. "But getting back to the issue at hand: Why do you think the Wingate people are not hyper-stimulating?"

"I suppose they're aiming for quality, not quantity," Deborah said. "But I'm only guessing. It's a reasonable question to ask them."

"How do they actually get the eggs?"

"I'm only guessing again, but I believe it would be by needle aspiration. I imagine they'd use ultrasound for a guide."

"Ugh!" Joanna voiced with a shudder. "I definitely don't like needles, and we'd have to be talking about a mighty long needle. Where would they stick it?"

"I imagine vaginally," Deborah said.

Joanna visibly shuddered again.

"Oh, come on!" Deborah said. "I suppose it wouldn't be a walk in the park, but it can't be all that bad. Lots of women do it as part of in vitro fertilization, and remember we're talking about forty-five thousand dollars. That's worth a bit of discomfort."

"Would we be put to sleep?"

"I have no idea," Deborah said. "That's another question we could ask."

"I can't believe you're serious about this."

"But it's a win-win situation. We'd get some serious money and a few couples would get children. It's like we'd be paid to be altruistic."

"I wish we could talk to somebody who's gone through it," Joanna said.

"Hey, we might be able to do that," Deborah said. "The egg donation issue came up in a biology 101 lab group discussion I was an instructor for last semester. It was back when the Wingate Clinic had their first ad in the *Crimson.* One of the freshmen said she'd been interviewed, accepted, and was going to do it."

"What was her name?"

"I can't remember, but I know how to find it. She and her roommate were in the same lab section, and both were terrific students. It would be in my grade book for the course. Let me get it."

While Deborah disappeared into her bedroom, Joanna tried to digest what had transpired in her life in the previous thirty minutes. She felt shell-shocked and a bit giddy. Events seemed to be transpiring at warp speed.

"Voilà!" Deborah called out from the bedroom. A second later, she appeared at the door with a soft-cover grade book open in her hand and made a beeline for the desk. "Where's the campus phone directory?"

"Second drawer on the right," Joanna said. "What's the name?"

"Kristin Overmeyer," Deborah said. "And her roommate was Jessica Detrick. They were lab partners, and I gave them the highest grades in the class." She got the phone book out and flipped to the appropriate page. "That's weird! She's not in here. How can that be?"

"Maybe she dropped out of school," Joanna suggested.

"I can't imagine," Deborah said. "Like I said, she was a dynamite student."

"Maybe the egg-donation ordeal was too much."

"You're joking."

"Of course I'm joking," Joanna said. "But it is curious."

"Now I have to get to the bottom of this or you'll use it as an excuse," Deborah said. She rapidly flipped through the phone book, found a number and dialed.

"Who are you calling?"

"Jessica Detrick," Deborah said.

"Maybe she can tell us how to get in touch with Kristin, provided the former room-mate's in her room studying on a Friday night."

Joanna listened after Deborah gave her the thumbs-up sign indicating that Jessica had answered. Joanna's interest peaked when Deborah's expression clouded over, and she started saying things like: "Oh, that's terrible," and "I'm sorry to hear that," and "What a tragedy!"

After concluding a rather long conversation, Deborah replaced the receiver slowly, then turned to look at Joanna. Deep in thought, she absently chewed the inside of her cheek.

"Well?" Joanna demanded. "Aren't you going to clue me in? What's the tragedy?"

"Kristin Overmeyer disappeared," Deborah said. "She and another freshman by the name of Rebecca Corey were last seen by a Wingate Clinic employee picking up an apparent hitchhiker just after leaving the clinic."

"I heard about two students disappearing last spring," Joanna said. "I never knew the names."

"What in God's name made them pick up a hitchhiker?"

"Maybe they knew him?"

"It's possible," Deborah said. Now it was her turn to shudder. "Stories like that give me the creeps."

"The women were never found? What about their bodies?"

"Just the car, which belonged to Rebecca Corey. It was found at a truck stop along the New Jersey turnpike. The women were never seen again. Nor any of their possessions like purses or clothing."

"Did Kristin donate eggs?"

"A half dozen, which her family sued to get possession of, but which the clinic turned over voluntarily. Apparently the family wanted to have some say in who got them. Such a sad story!"

"So much for having someone to ask about the donation procedure," Joanna said.

"We could always call the clinic and ask for the name of a previous donor," Deborah said.

"If we call the clinic we could ask our questions to them directly," Joanna said.

"If that goes well, then maybe we could ask for a referral."

"Then you're willing to give it a try?"

"I suppose there's no harm in getting more information," Joanna said. "But I'm certainly not committing myself, except for possibly a visit to the clinic."

"All right!" Deborah exclaimed. She stepped over to Joanna and high-fived her. "Venice, here we come!"

two

It was a beautiful fall day with a riot of bright foliage stretching away from both sides of Route 2 as Deborah and Joanna sped northwest out of Cambridge toward Bookford, Massachusetts. The sun was conveniently behind them, although there were occasional flashes of glare reflecting off the windshields of the mass of commuter cars heading in the opposite direction into Boston. Both women were wearing sunglasses and baseball caps.

There had been no conversation since they had rounded Fresh Pond. Each was engrossed in her own thoughts. Deborah was mainly marveling at how quickly everything had fallen into place as if the whole affair involving the Wingate Clinic had been preordained. Joanna's musings were more inwardly focused. She couldn't believe how much her life had changed in a week and yet how much at peace she felt. On Sunday, when she'd finally deemed herself emotionally capable of talking with Carlton and handling what she expected would be his insistence on getting married in June, he was in such a snit that he'd refused to talk with her. She'd called and left messages for several days without result. Consequently they'd not talked for the entire week, a fact which made Joanna more convinced her sudden epiphany concerning her attitude toward marriage in general, and to Carlton in particular, had been appropriate. After all the episodes she'd had to endure of what she had interpreted as rejection, it seemed inappropriate that Carlton would act negatively in this instance. As far as she was concerned, it was not a good sign. Communication had a high priority in Joanna's value system.

"Did you remember to bring that list of questions you wrote down?" Deborah said.

"I sure did," Joanna answered. They were mostly questions about what to expect after the egg-retrieval procedure and whether there would be any limitations concerning exercise, etcetera.

Deborah had been impressed at how responsive the Wingate Clinic proved to be. She and Joanna had called the number listed in the ad in the *Harvard Crimson* on Monday morning, and when they described themselves and their possible interest in donating eggs, they were connected with a Dr. Sheila Donaldson, who offered to visit them straight away. Less than an hour later the doctor had arrived at their Craigie Arms apartment and had impressed them with her professionalism. In short order she'd laid out the entire program and had effectively answered all the questions Deborah and Joanna had had up to that point.

"We don't feel we have to hyperstimulate," Dr. Donaldson had said early in the discussion. "In fact we don't stimulate at all. We call it our 'organic' approach. The last thing we want is to cause any problems with our donors, which synthetic or pooled hormones can do."

"But how can you be sure you'll get any eggs at all?" Deborah had asked.

"Occasionally we don't," Dr. Donaldson had said.

"But you'd still pay, wouldn't you?"

"Absolutely," Dr. Donaldson had said.

"What kind of anesthesia is used?" Joanna had asked. It was her major concern.

"That will be your choice," Dr. Donaldson had said. "But Dr. Paul Saunders, the individual who does the retrievals, prefers light general anesthesia."

At that point Joanna had given Deborah a thumbs-up.

The day following the interview Dr. Donaldson had called first thing in the morning to say that both women had been accepted and that the clinic would like to do the procedures as soon as possible, preferably that week, and in any case, they'd like to hear back from the women that very day. For the next several hours, the women debated the pros and cons. Deborah was heavily in favor of going ahead with it. Eventually her enthusiasm won Joanna over. A call back to the clinic resulted in an appointment for that Friday morning.

"Do you have any second thoughts about this?" Joanna asked suddenly, breaking a quarter-hour silence.

"Not in the slightest," Deborah said. "Especially thinking about that Louisburg Square apartment we looked at. I hope someone doesn't nab it before we have the money in our hot little hands."

"It's also dependent on the seller willing to give us a second mortgage," Joanna said. "Otherwise it's far beyond our means."

The women had contacted real estate agents in both Cambridge and Boston, and had seen a number of condo units for sale. The one on Louisburg Square in Beacon Hill had impressed them the most. It was one of Boston's finest addresses, centrally located, and close to the Red Line subway, which would whisk them over to Harvard Square in no time at all.

"To tell you the truth, I'm surprised the price is so reasonable."

"I think it's because it's a fourth-floor

walkup," Joanna said. "And because it's so small, especially the second bedroom."

"Yeah, but that bedroom has the best view in the whole apartment, plus the walk-in closet."

"You don't think walking through the kitchen to get to the bathroom is a problem?"

"I'd walk through someone else's apartment to get to the bathroom for a chance to live on Louisburg Square."

"How would we decide who gets what bedroom?" Joanna asked.

"Hey, I'll be happy with the smaller one if that's what you're worried about," Deborah said.

"Seriously?"

"Absolutely," Deborah said.

"Maybe we could rotate somehow," Joanna suggested.

"It's not necessary," Deborah said. "I'd be perfectly happy with the smaller bedroom. Trust me!"

Joanna turned her head to look out the passenger-side window. The farther north they went the more intense the fall colors became. The red of the maples was so bright it almost didn't look real, especially when surcharged against the dark green of pine or hemlock trees.

"You're not having second thoughts, are you?" Deborah questioned.

"Not really," Joanna said. "But it's dizzying how quickly everything is happening. I mean, if everything goes according to plan, by this time next week we'll not only be landowners, we'll be in Venice. It's like a dream."

Deborah had gone on-line and had found surprisingly inexpensive seats to Milan via Brussels. From Milan they would take the train to Venice, arriving in the middle of the afternoon. Deborah had also found a small bed-and-breakfast in the San Polo *sestière* near the Rialto Bridge where they'd stay until they could find an apartment.

"I can't wait!" Deborah exclaimed. "I'm psyched! *Benvenuto a Italia, signorina!*" She reached across and briefly tousled Joanna's coiffure.

Joanna leaned to the side, batted Deborah's hand away, and laughed. *"Mille grazie, cara,"* she said in a playfully sarcastic tone. She then bent her head back and ran her fingers through her shoulder-length

hair in hopes of returning it to some semblance of order. "I guess I'm a bit taken
aback at how quickly the Wingate Clinic is
making this all happen," she said as she
used the rearview mirror to inspect her efforts with her hair. Joanna was moderately
obsessive about her hair and general appearance, much more so than Deborah
who often teased her about it.

"It's probably the two clients who are
pressuring them," Deborah said. She readjusted the mirror.

"Did Dr. Donaldson mention that?"
Joanna questioned.

"No," Deborah answered. "I just assumed as much. She did say that the clinic
was only interested in two donors, so we're
lucky we called when we did."

"There's a sign that says Bookford is the
next exit," Joanna said, pointing ahead.
The sign was small and set in front of a
small clump of oak trees ablaze in lustrous
orange.

"I saw it," Deborah said as she put on
the directional signal.

After another twenty minutes of driving
along a narrow two-lane road bordered
with apple trees and stone fences that

wound across a countryside of rolling hills and rust-colored cornfields, the women entered a typical New England town. At the outskirts there was a large billboard that said WELCOME TO BOOKFORD, MASSACHUSETTS, HOME OF THE BOOKFORD HIGH SCHOOL WILD-CATS, DIVISION II STATE FOOTBALL CHAMPIONS 1993. The country road leading from the highway became Main Street and pro-ceeded to bisect the town in a north and south direction. It was lined with the usual bevy of turn-of-the-previous-century, brick-fronted stores. About midway a large white steepled church stood behind a green across from a granite municipal building. A swelling and noisy throng of schoolkids with bookbags were moving north along the sidewalks like migratory wingless birds.

"It's a cute town," Deborah commented as she leaned forward to get a better view through the windshield. She slowed to less than twenty miles per hour. "It looks almost too cute to be real, like it's part of a theme park."

"I didn't see any sign for the Wingate Clinic," Joanna commented.

"Hey, did you hear the one about why it

takes a hundred million sperm to fertilize one egg?"

"Can't say that I have," Joanna said.

"Because none of them are willing to stop and ask directions."

Joanna chuckled. "I suppose that means we're going to stop."

"You've got that right," Deborah said as she turned into a parking spot in front of the RiteSmart drugstore. There was angled parking up and down both sides of Main Street. "Do you want to come in or wait here?"

"I'm not going to let you have all the fun," Joanna said as she alighted from the car.

The women had to dodge children chasing each other along the sidewalk. Their taunting yells and screeches were just shy of the auditory pain threshold, and it was a relief for both women when the drugstore door closed behind them. In contrast, the interior of the store was engulfed in a relative hush. Adding to the calm was the fact that there were no customers. There weren't even any store personnel in sight.

After exchanging shrugs when no one appeared, the two women walked down the central aisle toward the prescription section in the back of the store. Positioned on the counter was a bell, which Deborah struck decisively. The noise was considerable in the comparable silence. Within moments a mostly bald, obese man in a pharmacist's tunic unbuttoned at the collar appeared through a pair of swinging doors like those leading into saloons in Hollywood westerns. Although it was relatively cool in the store, beads of perspiration stood out on his forehead.

"Can I help you ladies?" the proprietor asked cheerfully.

"We're looking for the Wingate Clinic," Deborah said.

"No problem," the proprietor said. "That's out in the Cabot State Mental Hospital."

"Excuse me?" Deborah said with surprise. "It's in a mental institution?"

"Yup," the proprietor said. "Old Doc Wingate bought or rented the whole damn place. I'm not sure which. Nobody really knows, not that it matters much."

"Oh, I understand," Deborah said. "It used to be a mental institution."

"Yup," the proprietor repeated. "For

about a hundred years or so. It was also a TB sanitarium. Seems that the people down in Boston were eager to banish their mentally ill and people suffering with tuberculosis. Kind'a locked 'em up in a fortress of sorts. Kinda outta sight, outta mind. A hundred years ago Bookford was considered to be way out in the sticks. Boy, times have sure changed. Now we're a Boston bedroom community."

"They just locked these people up?" Joanna questioned. "Didn't they try to treat them?"

"I suppose," the proprietor said. "But there wasn't much treatment back in those days. Well, that's not entirely true. They did a lot of surgery out there. You know, experimental stuff like collapsing the lungs of the people with TB and lobotomies on the crazies."

"That sounds awful," Joanna said. She shuddered.

"I imagine it was," the proprietor agreed.

"Well, there's no TB or mental patients anymore," Deborah added.

"Of course not," the proprietor said. "The Cabot, as we call it around here, has been closed for twenty to thirty years. I think it was in the seventies when the last patients were moved out. You remember: That was when the politicians began to seriously screw around with health care. It was a tragedy of sorts. I think they just bused the remaining patients back to Boston and let 'em loose in the Boston Common."

"I think that was a little before our time," Deborah said.

"Suppose you're right there," the proprietor agreed.

"Could you tell us how to get to the Cabot?" Deborah asked.

"Sure as shooting," the proprietor said. "Which way you headed?"

"North," Deborah said.

"Perfect," the proprietor said. "Head up to the next traffic light and hang a right. That's Pierce Street with the public library on the corner. From the intersection you can see the Cabot's brick tower. It's about two miles east of town, off Pierce Street. You can't miss it."

The women thanked the pharmacist and retreated back to their vehicle.

"Sounds like a charming environment for

an infertility clinic," Joanna said as she buckled her seat belt.

"At least it's no longer a TB sanitarium-cum-mental institution," Deborah said as she backed out into the street. "For a moment there I was ready to head back to Cambridge."

"Maybe we should," Joanna said.

"You're not serious, are you?"

"No, not really," Joanna said. "But a place having a history like that gives me the willies. Can you imagine the horrors it's witnessed?"

"I can't," Deborah said.

Paul Saunders put down the memorandum Sheila Donaldson had prepared for him and forcefully rubbed his eyes with the fingers of both hands, keeping his elbows on his desk. He'd repaired to his fourth-floor tower office after spending several hours in the lab checking his embryo cultures. For the most part they were doing reasonably well although not perfectly. He feared it was due to the age and quality of the eggs, a problem that he hoped to remedy shortly.

Paul was an early riser. His usual schedule was to get out of bed before five and be in the lab before six. That way he could get a significant amount of work done prior to the patients' arrival which generally began at nine. That morning he was starting his clinical day early because two egg retrieval procedures were scheduled. He liked to do retrievals as early as possible to ensure that the donors would have adequate time to recover from anesthesia to be dis-charged the same day. In-patient accom-modations were for emergencies only, and even then, Paul preferred to refer them to the nearest acute-care hospital.

Picking up the memorandum again and pushing back from the desk, Paul ambled over to the windows. They were triple-hung monsters that were considerably taller than Paul's diminutive five-foot-six stature. The view was the extensive lawn in front of the clinic that stretched down to the cast-iron, razor-wire-topped fence that encircled the entire grounds. Slightly to Paul's left was the stone gatehouse from whence came the macadam drive. It swept up toward Paul and then curved away before disap-pearing from view to the left where there was parking on the south side of the building. In the middle distance Paul could see the spire of Bookford's Presbyterian church as well as the chimneys of a few of the town's taller buildings poking up through the fall colors. In the far distance the foothills of the Berkshire Mountains were arranged along the horizon in the form of purple blips.

Paul reread the memorandum, pondered it for a moment, then looked back out at the view. He had every reason to be content. Things couldn't have been going better, and the thought brought a smile to his doughy face. It seemed incredible that only six years previously he'd been essentially run out of Illinois, having lost his hospital privileges and barely keeping his medical license. His lawyer at the time had told him it didn't look good, so he'd left, and migrated east, all because of a stupid fracas over his Medicare and Medicaid billing. He had, of course, pushed the envelope, but so had his ob-gyn colleagues. In fact, he'd merely copied and then refined a practice that another group that occupied the same medical building was using. Why the government came after him was still a mystery—one that could make him furious if he thought about it. But he didn't need to, not anymore now that things had turned out so rosy.

When he first arrived in Massachusetts and was concerned that he might have difficulty getting licensed if the Massachusetts Medical Board heard about his Illinois problems, Paul had decided to continue his training by taking a fellowship in infertility. It had been the best decision of his life. Not only had he avoided licensing problems, but he'd gained entry into a field that had no oversight to speak of, professionally or businesswise. On top of that, it was amazingly lucrative.

For him, infertility was a perfect match, especially since by sheer luck of being at the right place at the right time he'd come in contact with Spencer Wingate, an established infertility specialist, who was eager to semi-retire, lead the good life, rest on his laurels, do fund-raisers, and lecture. By now Paul was running the show in both the research and clinical realms.

Whenever Paul thought of the irony of his being a researcher, it never failed to bring a smile to his face, because he'd never imagined himself in such a role. He'd been last in his class in medical school and had never had any research training. He'd even managed never to take a single course in statistics. But it didn't matter. In infertility the patients were desperate enough to try anything. In fact they wanted to try new things. What Paul lacked in re-search experience he thought he made up for in imagination. He knew he was making real progress on a lot of fronts that would eventually make him famous as well as rich.

Turning back from gazing out over what he now thought of as his domain, Paul caught a fleeting glimpse of his image in an ornately framed mirror positioned between the two gigantic windows. Returning to peer directly at his reflection, Paul ran a hand up and down both cheeks. He was surprised and concerned by the pastiness of his skin, emphasized by his almost-black hair, until he realized it was mostly due to the harsh fluorescent light coming from the banks of fixtures mounted on the high ceiling. He laughed at his momentary concern. He knew he was pale; given his schedule, his skin rarely saw the light of day, much less real sun, but he knew he didn't look as bad as the mirror suggested. In his reflection, his complexion matched his signature white forelock.

Returning to the desk, Paul vowed to get down to Florida sometime during the winter, or maybe find an ob-gyn conference someplace in the sun where he'd present some of his work. He also thought that perhaps he should find the time to get some exercise since he'd gained weight—particularly around his neck, of all places. He hadn't exercised in years. Paul wasn't much of an athlete, which had caused him serious distress in his South Side Chicago high school, where athletics played a significant social role. He'd tried out for some of the teams, but it had never worked, and his efforts had only made him the butt of jokes.

"Let them see me now," Paul said out loud as he thought of the people who'd teased him. "They're probably bagging groceries." He knew the twentieth reunion was coming up that June, and he wondered if he should go just to flaunt his success in the faces of those bastards who had given him such a hard time.

Paul picked up the phone and dialed the

lab. When it was answered, he asked to speak to Dr. Donaldson. As he waited for her to come on the line, he reread the memorandum he had in his hand.

"What is it, Paul?" Sheila asked without a preamble.

"I got your memorandum," Paul said. "These two women who are coming in. You think they are good candidates?"

"Perfect," Sheila said. "Both are healthy with normal habits; absolutely no gyn problems; they're not pregnant; both deny drugs or any medications of any kind, and both are about mid-cycle."

"Are they both really graduate students?"

"That's affirmative."

"So they must be smart."

"Without doubt."

"But what's this about one wanting local anesthesia?" Paul asked.

"She's getting a Ph.D. in biology," Sheila said. "She knows something about anesthesia. I made some suggestions, but she didn't bite. I figure Carl can have a go."

"But you tried?" Paul persisted.

"Of course I tried," Sheila said irritably.

"All right, have Carl talk to her," Paul

said. He hung up the phone without saying good-bye. Sheila could annoy him on occasion with her obvious jealousy.

"That must be the tower the pharmacist was talking about," Deborah said, pointing through the windshield. They'd just made the turn onto Pierce Street from Main, and in the distance a narrow brick structure could be barely discerned poking up above its surrounding landscape.

"If that's two or three miles away, it's got to be one tall tower."

"From here its silhouette looks a little like the tower on the Uffizi Gallery in Florence," Deborah said. "How apropos."

Once they left the town behind, the trees lining the road blocked any further view of the tower or the Cabot complex itself until they'd passed a dilapidated red barn on the right. Around the next bend they came upon a sign for the Wingate Clinic on the left with an arrow pointing up a gravel road. As soon as they turned onto the unpaved road they caught sight of the two-story, gray granite gatehouse set back amongst the trees. It was a heavy, squat structure with small shuttered windows and a dark gray slate roof with elaborate finials at either end of the ridgepole. The trim was painted black. Stone gargoyles stuck out from the corners.

As they approached they could see that the road led under the house into a tunnel where it was blocked by a heavy chain-link gate. Beyond the gate they could see a recently mowed lawn, the only evidence the place was currently in use. An imposing cast-iron fence topped with razor wire was attached to both sides of the gatehouse and ran off into the trees on either side.

Deborah slowed, then stopped. "My word," she said. "That pharmacist wasn't joking when he said the inmates of the Cabot were locked up in a fortress. It almost looks like a prison."

"There's certainly nothing welcoming about it," Joanna added. "How do you suppose we get in? Do you see a buzzer, or do you think we have to call on a cell phone?"

"There must be a video monitor or something," Deborah suggested. "I'll pull up to the gate."

Deborah eased the car forward and

nosed it into the tunnel. The moment she stopped again, a heavy, paneled, window-less door opened and out stepped a uni-formed man clutching a clipboard. He ap-proached the driver's side window, which Deborah lowered.

"Can I help you?" the guard asked in a pleasant but no-nonsense tone. He had on a shiny, black-visored hat similar to a po-liceman's.

"We're here to see Dr. Donaldson," Deborah said.

"Your names, please?" the man asked.

"Deborah Cochrane and Joanna Meissner," Deborah said.

The man consulted his clipboard, checked off the two names, then pointed with his pen through the gate. "Follow the driveway to the right. You'll see the parking area. Someone will meet you there."

"Thank you," Deborah said.

The man didn't answer but instead touched the brim of his hat. With a screeching sound, the heavy chain-link gate began slowly to swing open.

"Did you see the gun the guard is pack-ing?" Deborah asked in a whisper when she had the window back up. The guard was still standing off to the left.

"It would be hard to miss it," Joanna said.

"I've seen armed police in inner-city hospitals," Deborah said. "But never at a rural medical clinic. Why on earth would they need so much security out here, especially at an infertility clinic?"

"It makes you wonder if they're more interested in keeping people out or keeping people in."

"Don't even joke like that," Deborah said. She started forward through the open gate. "Do you think they might be doing abortions, too? I've seen guards at abortion clinics in this state."

"I couldn't think of anything more inappropriate at an infertility clinic."

"I suppose you're right," Deborah agreed.

Emerging from the tunnel and rounding a copse of evergreens the women got their first unobstructed view of the Cabot. It was an immense red brick structure, four stories tall with a steeply peaked slate roof behind a crenelated cornice, small barred windows, and a soaring central tower. The tower had larger, multi-paned windows without bars.

Deborah slowed. "What a shock to see such a huge building sitting out here in the woods by itself. Curious design, too. Seeing the tower up close, I'd wager it's a deliberate copy of the Uffizi's. It's so similar, it can't have been by accident. If my memory serves me, it's even got the same style clock, although the one in the Uffizi works."

"I've seen other Victorian buildings like this around Massachusetts," Joanna said. "There's one out in Worcester that's stone, not brick, and almost as big. The difference is that it's deserted. At least this one is being used."

"The Wingate Clinic must be awfully busy to use this much square footage."

Joanna nodded.

Following the driveway around the right side of the building, Deborah drove into a parking lot with a surprisingly large number of cars in it. Both women were quick to notice that a number of the vehicles were not the usual Honda Civics or Chevy Caprices. One car stood out particularly among the

Mercedes, Porsches, and Lexuses. It was a burgundy Bentley convertible.

"Good grief," Joanna commented. "Do you see that Bentley?"

"Like with the guard's gun, it would be hard to miss." Its metallic paint was gleaming in the early morning sunlight.

"Do you have any idea how much that car costs?" Joanna asked.

"Not in the slightest."

"Over three hundred thousand dollars."

"Gadzooks! That's obscene, especially at a medical establishment."

Deborah parked in a plainly marked visitor's spot. As the women climbed from the car, a porticoed door facing the parking lot opened. A tall, chestnut-haired, white-coated female figure appeared. She waved.

"Now this greeting is the opposite extreme from what we experienced at the guardhouse," Deborah said. She waved back as she and Joanna started toward the door some fifty yards away.

"It looks like Dr. Donaldson."

"I think you're right," Deborah said.

"I hope we don't regret this," Joanna said suddenly. She was walking with her head down to watch where her feet were going. "I have an uncomfortable feeling we're making a big mistake."

Deborah grasped her friend around her upper arm and pulled her to a halt. "What are you saying? You don't want to go through with this? If that's the case, we should just turn around and drive back to Boston. I don't want you to think I'm putting any pressure on you, because I'm not."

Joanna squinted in the early morning sunlight at the slender doctor standing at the clinic's door. They were close enough now to be sure it was Dr. Donaldson, and they could tell the doctor was glad to see them. A broad, welcoming smile was fixed on her thin face.

"Talk to me, girl?" Deborah demanded, giving Joanna's arm an additional squeeze.

Joanna brought her attention around to Deborah. "Can you look me in the eye and say you're confident everything will be all right?"

"Absolutely," Deborah said. "Like I've said ten times: For us it's a win-win situation."

"I'm talking about these procedures," Joanna said.

"Oh, for goodness' sake. These re-trievals are small potatoes. Women under-going infertility treatment go through it mul-tiple times on top of enduring tons of hormones. For us it's no big deal."

Joanna hesitated. Her green eyes moved back and forth between Deborah and Dr. Donaldson as she mulled her em-barrassing medical squeamishness. She didn't even like getting a flu shot. After a sigh she cleared her throat and managed a smile. "All right, let's do it."

"Are you sure? I mean, you don't feel like you're being forced, do you?"

Joanna shook her head. "I'm all right. Let's get it over with."

The women started walking again.

"For a minute you had me scared," Deborah said.

"I scare myself sometimes," Joanna commented.

three

"I trust your ride out from Boston was without incident," Dr. Donaldson said as she closed the clinic door behind the women.

"It was fine," Deborah said as she eyed a large, unoccupied waiting room. The furniture appeared to be expensive modern Scandinavian, which stood in sharp contrast to the period Victorian architectural details. A large U-shaped receptionist's desk stood empty in the center of the room. Leather upholstered chairs and couches lined the walls. A generous display of current magazines were sprinkled around on coffee and side tables.

"I realized this morning that I'd failed to give you directions," Dr. Donaldson said. "I apologize."

"No need to apologize," Deborah said. "I should have asked. But we had no trouble. We stopped at the local pharmacy and asked."

"Very smart," Dr. Donaldson said. She clasped her hands. "Now, first things first. I trust that neither of you have had anything to eat since midnight."

Deborah and Joanna nodded.

"Excellent!" Dr. Donaldson said. "Let me give Dr. Smith, our anesthesiologist, a call. He'd like to speak with you. Meanwhile, if you'd like to take off your coats and make yourselves comfortable, we'll get things started."

While Dr. Donaldson used the receptionist's phone, Deborah and Joanna removed their coats and hung them in a cloakroom.

"Are you all right?" Deborah whispered to Joanna. In the background they could hear Dr. Donaldson on the phone.

"Yeah, I'm fine," Joanna answered. "Why do you ask?"

"You're so quiet. You're not changing your mind again, are you?"

"No! I'm just unnerved by this place," Joanna said. "Lots of little surprises like armed guards. Even that furniture out there in the waiting room bothers me."

"I know what you mean," Deborah agreed. "It looks like it cost a fortune but looks terrible in the environment."

"It's weird. Things like that usually don't bother me. I'm sorry I'm such a basket case."

"Just try to relax and think about having coffee in Piazza San Marco."

Returning to the main room, they allowed Dr. Donaldson to guide them over to a couch. Once seated, she informed them that Dr. Carl Smith was on his way down. She then asked if they had any questions.

"How long do you suppose this will take?" Joanna asked.

"A retrieval only takes forty minutes or so," Dr. Donaldson said. "Then we'll have you relax for a few hours to make sure the anesthesia has completely worn off. You'll be on your way before you know it."

"Will we be having the procedure at the same time?" Joanna asked.

"No," Dr. Donaldson said. "Miss Meissner, you'll be first since you'll be having the light general anesthesia. Of course, if Miss Cochrane would like to switch to general anesthesia, then you two could decide whom you would prefer to be first."

"I'm happy with the local anesthesia," Deborah said.

"Whatever you prefer," Dr. Donaldson said. She looked from one woman to the other. "Any other questions for the moment?"

"Does the clinic occupy this whole building?" Deborah asked.

"Heavens no. This building is huge. It used to house a large mental institution as well as a TB sanitarium."

"So we heard," Deborah said.

"The infertility clinic takes up two floors in this wing only," Dr. Donaldson explained. "We also have a few of the offices in the tower. The rest of the facility is empty except for the old beds and a lot of the old equipment. It's almost like a museum."

"How many people work here?" Joanna asked.

"We have about forty employees presently, but the number has been steadily increasing. For the exact count, I'd have to check with Helen Masterson, the acting head of personnel."

"Forty employees is a lot," Joanna said. "It must be a godsend to a small rural community like this."

"One would think so," Dr. Donaldson said, "but in actuality we have a chronic problem recruiting help. We're forever advertising in the Boston papers, mostly for lab technicians and experienced admin people. Are you ladies interested in jobs?" Dr. Donaldson smiled teasingly.

"I don't think so," Deborah replied with a laugh.

"The only department that isn't short-handed is the farm," Dr. Donaldson added. "We've had no problem in that arena since day one."

"The farm?" Joanna asked. "What do you mean *the farm?*"

"The Wingate Clinic has a large animal farm," Dr. Donaldson explained. "It's an integral part of our research efforts. We're interested in basic reproductive research in species besides homo sapiens."

"Really?" said Joanna. "What other species are you looking at?"

"Any species that are economically significant," Dr. Donaldson said. "Cattle, pigs, poultry, horses. And, of course, we're also very much involved with the reproduction of domestic pets such as cats and dogs."

"Where is this farm?" Joanna asked.

"On the property directly behind this main building, which we affectionately call the 'monstrosity,' and past a dense stand of white pine. The setting is rather idyllic. There's a pond, a dam, and even an old mill in addition to the barns, cornfields, hayfields, and paddocks. The Cabot Institution sat on over two hundred acres, with housing for its professional staff and its own farm to make it largely self-sufficient foodwise. Having the farm on the premises was one of the major reasons we leased the property. It makes our research a lot more efficient to have the farm adjacent to the laboratory, not to mention the housing."

"You have a laboratory here?" Deborah asked.

"Absolutely," Dr. Donaldson said. "A major lab. I'm particularly proud of it, probably because I'm mainly responsible for setting it up."

"Could we have a tour?" Deborah asked.

"I imagine that could be worked out," Dr. Donaldson said. "Ah, here comes Dr. Smith."

The women turned to see a large, heavy-set man dressed in surgical scrubs enter the room carrying a clipboard. Just then, the front door opened and a throng of employees swarmed in, abuzz with conversation. One woman headed for the receptionist's desk while the rest crowded into the hall that Smith had just exited.

Joanna felt herself stiffen. Seeing the anesthesiologist's operating room garb made the reality of the upcoming procedure more difficult to suppress.

After introducing himself and shaking hands with both women, Dr. Smith sat down, crossed his legs, and positioned the clipboard on his lap. "Now then," he said as he took one of the many pens from his breast pocket. "Miss Cochrane, I understand your preference is local anesthesia."

"Correct," Deborah said.

"May I ask why?" Dr. Smith questioned.

"I just feel more comfortable with it," Deborah answered.

"I assume you've been informed that we prefer light general anesthesia for egg retrievals."

"Dr. Donaldson said as much," Deborah said. "She also said the decision was mine."

"That's very true," Dr. Smith said. "At the same time, I'd like to tell you why we prefer to have you asleep. Under light general anesthesia, we do the retrieval under direct laparoscopic observation. With local, paracervical anesthesia the retrieval is done with an ultrasound-guided needle. Comparatively speaking it's like working in the dark." Dr. Smith paused and smiled. "Any questions about what I've said so far?"

"No," Deborah said simply.

"There's one more issue," Dr. Smith said. "Under local anesthesia we don't have the control of pain coming from intra-abdominal manipulation. In other words, if we have any trouble getting to either ovary and have to do some maneuvers to make it possible, you might experience some discomfort."

"I'll take my chances," Deborah said.

"Even considering the pain issue?"

"I think I can handle it," Deborah said. "I prefer to be awake."

Dr. Smith glanced briefly at Dr. Donaldson, who shrugged. He then went through a brief medical history with both women. When he was finished he stood. "That's all I need for now. I'll have you two get changed, and I'll see you upstairs."

"Will I be getting a sedative?" Joanna asked.

"Absolutely," Dr. Smith said. "It will be administered as soon as you get your IV. Any other questions for the moment?"

When neither woman responded, Dr. Smith smiled and left. Dr. Donaldson then escorted the women down the main hall and into a separate, smaller waiting room. On one side were several changing cubicles with louvered doors and on the other a bank of lockers. A rack of hospital johnnies, paper slippers, and bathrobes was next to the lockers. A pleasant-faced, petite nurse was restocking the patient apparel. Several gurneys were parked by the double swinging entry doors. In the middle of the room were a grouping of chairs, a couch, and a coffee table littered with magazines.

Dr. Donaldson introduced the women to the nurse, whose name was Cynthia Carson. She in turn supplied the women with sets of the in-patient hospital garb, gave each of them a key to a locker along with advice to pin the keys to their johnnies, and opened the doors of two adjacent changing cubicles. At that point Dr. Donaldson took her leave. A few moments later Cynthia also left, to get the IV supplies. She said she'd be right back.

"That was a rather hard sell for general anesthesia," Joanna called out from her stall.

"You can say that again," Deborah agreed.

The women stepped out from their respective changing rooms, each holding her thin bathrobe closed with one hand and clutching her street clothes with the other. They burst out laughing when they saw each other.

"I hope I don't look as pathetic as you," Joanna managed.

"I hate to break it to you," Deborah responded. "but you do."

They went to the lockers to secure their belongings.

"Why didn't you give in and take the general anesthesia?" Joanna asked.

"You're not going to start in on me, too, are you?" Deborah asked.

"The anesthesiologist's points made a lot of sense to me," Joanna said. "Especially when he explained about pain from intra-abdominal manipulation. It was enough to make me feel lightheaded. Don't you think you should reconsider?"

"Listen!" Deborah said as she slammed the locker door and yanked out the key. She faced her friend. Her cheeks had a sudden flush. "You and I have already had this discussion. I have this thing about being put to sleep. Call it a phobia. You don't like needles, and I don't like anesthesia, okay?"

"Okay!" Joanna said. "Jeez, calm down! I'm the one who's supposed to be unnerved by this, not you."

Deborah sighed. She closed her eyes briefly and shook her head. "I'm sorry. I didn't mean to snap at you. I suppose I'm on edge, too."

"No need to apologize," Joanna said.

At that moment Cynthia reappeared with an armload of paraphernalia, which she dumped on one of the gurneys. In her other hand she had an IV bottle, which she proceeded to hang on the gurney's IV pole. "Which one of you is Miss Meissner?" she called out.

Joanna raised her hand.

Cynthia patted the gurney's padded surface covered with a fresh bedsheet. "How about hopping up here on this contraption so I can start an IV? Then I'm going to be giving you a cocktail that will make you feel like it's New Year's Eve."

Deborah reached out and gave her friend's arm a squeeze as they exchanged a compassionate glance. Joanna then did as she was told. Deborah came around to stand on the other side of the gurney.

Cynthia went through the preparations of starting the IV with a practiced economy of motion. At the same time she kept up a distracting stream of conversation about the weather, and before Joanna had a chance to work herself up into a dither, Cynthia was already putting a tourniquet around Joanna's left arm just below the elbow.

Joanna averted her face and grimaced as the needle broke the skin. The next instant the tourniquet was gone, and Cynthia was applying tape.

"There, at least that's done," Cynthia said.

Joanna turned. Her face reflected her surprise. "Is the IV in already?"

"Yup," Cynthia said cheerfully as she drew up medication in two syringes. "Here comes the fun part. But, just to be one-hundred-percent sure: you have no allergies to any medication, isn't that right?"

"That's right," Joanna said.

Cynthia bent over the IV port and took the cap off the first syringe.

"What am I getting?" Joanna asked.

"You really want to know?" Cynthia asked. She finished with the first and started with the second.

"Yes!"

"Diazepam and fentanyl."

"How about in English?"

"Valium and an opioid analgesic."

"I've heard of Valium. What's the other stuff?"

"It's in the morphine family," Cynthia said. The nurse quickly cleaned up the wrappers and other debris and threw it all into a special receptacle. While she made an entry onto the clipboard that she'd pulled from beneath the gurney's pad, the door opened to the hallway and another patient walked in. She smiled at the women, went to the clothes rack for a set of the hospital patient clothes, then disappeared into one of the changing rooms.

"Do you think she's another donor?" Joanna asked.

"I've no idea," Deborah said.

"That's Dorothy Stevens," Cynthia said in a hushed voice as she went around to the head of the gurney and unlocked the wheels. "She's a Wingate client who's here for yet another embryo transfer. The poor dear has suffered a lot of disappointment."

"Am I going already?" Joanna asked as the gurney began to move.

"Yes, indeed," Cynthia said. "I was told they were eagerly awaiting your arrival when I went out to get the IV material."

"Can I go along?" Deborah asked. She'd taken hold of Joanna's hand.

"I'm afraid not," Cynthia said. "You stay and relax. You'll be going up yourself before you know it."

"I'll be all right," Joanna said with a smile

to Deborah. "I already feel that opioid stuff. It's not half bad, either."

Deborah gave Joanna's hand a final squeeze. Before the doors swung shut Deborah caught a glimpse of Joanna merrily waving to her over her shoulder.

Deborah turned back to the room. She walked over to the couch and sat down heavily. She was hungry from not having eaten anything since before going to bed the night before. She picked up several magazines but found she could not concentrate, not with her stomach growling. Instead she tried to picture where they were taking Joanna in the huge, old, white elephant of a building. Tossing the magazines aside, she glanced around the room. There was the same jarring disjuncture between the elaborate crown molding and trim and the furniture as there had been out in the main waiting room. Joanna had been right: The Wingate was a place filled with contrasts that were vaguely unsettling. As much as Joanna, Deborah was looking forward to having the egg retrieval procedures behind them.

One of the changing room doors opened and Dorothy Washburn emerged clutching her clothes. She smiled at Deborah before heading over to the lockers to store them. Deborah watched her and wondered what it was like to contend with continued infertility treatment and continual disappointment.

Dorothy locked the locker, then came over to the sitting area while pinning the locker key to her johnny en route. She picked up a magazine, sat down, and began to flip through the pages. Apparently sensing Deborah's stare, she raised her strikingly cerulean eyes. This time it was Deborah's turn to smile. She then introduced herself, and Dorothy did the same. For a few minutes the two women indulged in light conversation. After a pause, Deborah asked Dorothy if she'd been a patient of the Wingate Clinic for some time.

"Unfortunately, I have," Dorothy said.

"Has it been a pleasant experience?"

"I don't think pleasant is the right word," Dorothy said. "It's not been an easy road by any stretch of the imagination. But to the Wingate's credit, they did warn me. Anyway, my husband and I are not about to give up, at least not yet or at least not until we've used up all our credit."

"You're having an embryo transfer to-day?" Deborah asked. She was reluctant to admit she already knew.

"My ninth," Dorothy said. She sighed and then held up crossed fingers.

"Good luck," Deborah said sincerely.

"I could use some."

Deborah imitated the crossed-fingers gesture.

"Is this your first time to the Wingate?" Dorothy asked.

"It is," Deborah admitted. "For both my-self and my roommate."

"I'm sure you'll be satisfied with your choice," Dorothy said. "Are you both doing in vitro?"

"No," Deborah said. "We're egg donors. We responded to an ad in the *Harvard Crimson.*"

"That's wonderful," Dorothy said with unabashed admiration. "What a loving ges-ture. You are going to give hope to some desperate couples. I applaud your gen-erosity."

Deborah suddenly felt uncomfortably venal. She hoped to change the subject before her true motive for donating was re-vealed. Luckily she was saved by Cynthia's abrupt return. The nurse burst through the swinging doors without warning.

"Okay, Dorothy!" Cynthia called out with great enthusiasm. "You're on! Get yourself down there to the transfer room. They're all ready for you."

Dorothy stood, took a deep breath, and then headed out the door.

"She's quite a soldier," Cynthia remarked as the door swung shut. "I sure hope this turns out to be a successful cycle. If anyone deserves it, she does."

"How much does a cycle cost?" Deborah asked. Concern about her venality had brought the issue of economics to the fore.

"It varies quite a bit depending on what procedures are involved," Cynthia said. "But on average it's around eight to ten thousand dollars."

"Oh, my goodness," Deborah commented. "That means Dorothy and her husband have spent nearly ninety thousand dollars!"

"Probably more," Cynthia said. "That doesn't include the initial infertility workup or any ancillary treatments that might have been indicated. Infertility is an expensive undertaking for couples, especially since insurance doesn't usually cover it. Most couples have to come up with the cash somehow."

Two more patients entered, and Cynthia's full attention immediately turned to them. She took the women's paperwork, glanced at it briefly, got them apparel, and directed them into changing rooms. Deborah was surprised at the apparent age of one of them. She couldn't be sure, but she thought the woman looked old, like she was in her middle to late fifties.

Feeling restless, Deborah got to her feet. "Excuse me, Cynthia," Deborah said. The nurse was reading the patients' paperwork more thoroughly. "Dr. Donaldson mentioned that I could have a tour of the laboratory. Who should I see about it?"

"That's a request I haven't had before," Cynthia said. She thought for a moment. "I guess you could try Claire Harlow in public relations. She gives tours to prospective patients, although I don't know if that includes the lab or not. If you don't mind walking around in your robe, you can go out to the receptionist in the main waiting room and have her page Miss Harlow. You don't have a lot of time so I wouldn't go far. I imagine they'll be calling for you in an- other fifteen minutes or so."

Despite the warning about time, Deborah had to do something. Following Cynthia's suggestion, she retraced her steps out to the main waiting room and had the public relations person paged. While she waited for the page to be returned, she noticed that quite a few patients had ar- rived since she and Joanna had passed through. There was not much conversa- tion. Most of the women were reading the magazines. A few were blankly staring ahead.

Claire Harlow was a soft-spoken, gentle, accommodating woman who seemed pleased to take Deborah up a floor and show her the main lab. As Dr. Donaldson had suggested, it was huge, extending along the back of the building for almost the entire wing occupied by the Wingate.

Deborah was duly impressed. Having spent many hours in biology labs, she knew, for the most part, what she was looking at. The equipment was the newest and best available and included surprising things like automated DNA sequencers.

The other surprise was how few people were in the mammoth room.

"Where is everybody?" Deborah asked.

"The doctors are all doing various clinical procedures at the moment," Claire answered.

Deborah strolled along a long countertop supporting more dissecting microscopes than she'd seen in any one place before. They were also more powerful than the microscopes Deborah had had the pleasure of using.

"An army could work in here," Deborah said.

"We're always looking for qualified people," Claire said.

Deborah came to the end of the lab bench and glanced out the window. It faced out the back of the building and offered an impressive view. It was particularly expansive because the building sat on the spine of a hill, with lawn sloping away in both the front and the back. Northward through a tangle of orange oaks and red maples Deborah could make out stone buildings similar to the gatehouse but with white trim.

"Are those buildings part of the farm?" Deborah asked.

"No, those are some of the living quarters," Claire explained. Pointing off to the right in a southeastern direction to where the property sloped down even more dramatically than elsewhere, she directed Deborah's attention to a shimmering of light just visible through old-growth pines. "That sparkle is sun reflecting off the surface of the mill pond. The farm buildings are grouped around it."

"What's the story with the brick chimney spewing smoke?" Deborah questioned, gesturing toward a smokestack rearing up above the trees even farther to the right. "Is that part of Wingate complex as well?" The smoke was white as it left the chimney but faded to a dark purplish-gray as it trailed off in the distance toward the east.

"It certainly is," Claire said. "That's the old power plant for heat and hot water. It's a rather interesting structure. It was also the crematorium for the Cabot Institution."

"Crematorium?" Deborah sputtered. "Why on earth did they have a crematorium out here?"

"Out of necessity, I guess," Claire said.

"Back in the olden days I think a lot of the patients were essentially abandoned by their families."

Deborah cringed at the thought of an isolated mental hospital with its own crematorium, but before she could ask another question, Claire's pager went off. The woman checked the LCD window. "That's for you, Miss Cochrane. They're ready for your procedure."

Deborah was pleased. She was eager to get it over with so she and Joanna could be on their way.

four

OCTOBER 15, 1999
9:05 A.M.

There was no transition period. One minute Joanna was fast asleep, and the next she was fully awake. She found herself staring up at a high, unfamiliar, embossed-tin ceiling.

"Well, well, the sleeping beauty has awakened," a voice said.

Joanna turned in the direction of the voice and found herself looking up into an equally unfamiliar face. At the exact instant she was going to ask where she was, her momentary confusion was replaced by full comprehension of her situation.

"Let's get your blood pressure," the nurse said as he took his stethoscope from around his neck and put the earpieces into his ears. He was an impeccably groomed individual, close to Joanna's age, dressed in surgical scrubs. His name tag said MYRON HANNA. He began inflating a blood pressure cuff already present around Joanna's left upper arm.

Joanna watched the man's face. His eyes were glued to the pressure gauge while he pressed the stethoscope's bell against the crook of her elbow. As the cuff deflated she felt her pulse surge through her arm. The man smiled and removed the apparatus.

"Your blood pressure is fine," he said. He then reached for her wrist to time her pulse.

Joanna waited until he was through. "What about my procedure?" she asked.

"Your procedure is all done," Myron said as he recorded his findings on a clipboard.

"You're joking," Joanna said. She had no appreciation of the passage of time.

"Nope, you're all done," Myron repeated. "And it was successful, I assume. Dr. Saunders must be pleased."

"I can't believe it," Joanna said. "My roommate told me when you wake up from anesthesia, you're sick to your stomach."

"That's rare nowadays," Myron said. "Not with propofol. Isn't it great stuff?"

"Is that what I had?"

"Yup!"

"What time is it?"

"A little after nine."

"Do you know if my roommate, Deborah Cochrane, has had her procedure?"

"She's having it as we speak," Myron said. "How about sitting up for me on the side of the bed?"

Joanna did as she was told. Her mobility was limited by the IV still attached to her right arm.

"How do you feel?" Myron asked. "Any dizziness? Any discomfort?"

"I feel fine," Joanna said. "Perfectly normal." She was surprised, especially by the lack of pain.

"Why don't you sit there for a few minutes," Myron suggested. "Then, if you are okay, we'll yank the IV and send you downstairs to change back into your street clothes."

"Fine by me," Joanna said. As Myron

recorded her blood pressure and pulse, she glanced around at her surroundings. There were three other beds besides hers. None was occupied. The room was antiquated; it had clearly missed whatever facelift other parts of the Institute had received. Old tile lined the walls and floors, the windows looked old, and the sinks were made of soapstone.

The ersatz recovery room reminded her of the archaic operating theater where she'd had her procedure, and the thought gave her a shudder. It was the kind of OR in which she could imagine lobotomies being performed, against vulnerable patients' wishes. When she'd first been wheeled in, the setting had reminded her of a gruesome, several-hundred-year-old painting she'd seen once of an anatomy lesson. In the painting the tiers of seats disappearing up into the darkness were occupied by leering men gazing down at a skinned, ghastly pale corpse.

The door to the recovery room opened. Joanna turned and spotted a short man with a shock of dark hair. His pale complexion made her think again of the old anatomy lesson painting. She saw he'd stopped short, and his surprised expression quickly changed to irritation. He was attired in a long doctor's white coat over green surgical scrubs.

"Hello, Dr. Saunders," Myron said, looking up from the desk.

"Mr. Hanna, I thought you told me the patient was still asleep," Dr. Paul Saunders snapped. His eyes stayed glued to Joanna's.

"She was, sir, when we spoke," Myron said. "She just woke up, and everything is fine."

Joanna felt acutely uncomfortable under the man's unblinking gaze. Joanna had reflexive, visceral reaction to authority figures thanks in part to her emotionally distant, staunchly disciplinarian, oil-company-CEO father.

"Blood pressure and pulse are all normal," Myron said. He stood up and started forward but stopped when Dr. Saunders held up his hand.

The doctor advanced toward Joanna with his mouth set. His nose had a wide base that gave the false impression of closely spaced eyes. But by far his most distinguishing characteristics were irises of slightly different colors and a minute widow's peak of white hair that quickly lost itself in the rest of his mildly unruly coiffure.

"How do you feel, Miss Meissner?" Paul asked.

Joanna noticed his tone was devoid of emotion, similar to the tone her father had used to ask her how her day had been back when she was in elementary school. "Okay," she answered, unsure if the man cared particularly or even wanted her to respond. Marshaling her courage, she asked: "Are you the doctor who did my egg retrieval?" She'd been put to sleep before Paul's arrival into the operating room.

"Yes," Paul replied in a manner which discouraged further questions. "Would you mind if I had a look at your abdomen?"

"I suppose not," Joanna said. She glanced at Myron, who immediately came around the other side of the bed. He encouraged her to lie back supine and then pulled the sheet up to her waist to cover her legs.

Paul gently pulled up the johnny, being careful to keep the sheet covering Joanna's lower half in place, and gazed down at Joanna's exposed midriff. Joanna lifted her head to look herself. There were three Band-Aids. One was directly below her navel, and the other two were in the lower quadrants forming an equilateral triangle.

"No sign of any bleeding," Myron said, "and the gas has been absorbed."

Paul nodded. He pulled the johnny back to cover Joanna's abdomen and turned to leave.

"Dr. Saunders," Joanna called out impulsively.

Paul stopped and turned back.

"How many eggs did you get?"

"I can't remember exactly," Paul said. "Five or six."

"Is that good?"

"It's perfectly adequate," Paul said. A faint smile graced his heretofore grim expression. Then he left.

"He's not much of a conversationalist," Joanna commented.

"He's a busy man," Myron said. He pulled the sheet back to expose her legs. "Why don't you stand up and see how that feels. I think you're about ready to have that IV taken out."

"Does Dr. Saunders do all the egg retrievals?" Joanna asked as she sat up and dropped her feet over the side of the bed. Then she slid off to stand while holding the johnny closed behind her back with her left hand.

"He and Dr. Donaldson do them together."

"Do you think his coming in here means my roommate's procedure is done?"

"That would be my guess," Myron said. "How do you feel? Any dizziness at all?"

Joanna shook her head.

"Then let's get that IV out and get you on your way."

Fifteen minutes later Joanna was at the locker extracting her clothing, shoes, and bag. There were four other patients in hospital garb sitting on the couches and chairs and flipping through magazines. None of them paid her any attention. Deborah's locker was still locked up tight.

As Joanna entered the same changing room she'd used earlier, Cynthia arrived with Deborah in tow. Deborah's face lit up with a broad smile when she caught sight of Joanna, and she immediately rushed over to squeeze into the changing room. She closed the door behind her.

"How did it go for you?" Deborah demanded in a whisper.

"It wasn't bad at all," Joanna answered, unsure why they were whispering. "The anesthesiologist said I might feel a little burning in my arm when he gave me the 'milk of amnesia,' but I didn't feel a thing. I don't even remember going to sleep."

"Milk of amnesia?" Deborah questioned. "What the hell is that?"

"It's what the anesthesiologist called the medicine he gave me," Joanna said. "It was so rapid. It was like somebody just turned out the lights. I didn't feel a thing through the whole procedure. And on top of that, I'm happy to report I didn't have any nausea when I woke up."

"Not even a little queasiness?"

"Nothing. And I woke up the same way I went to sleep: really suddenly." Joanna snapped her fingers to emphasize her point. "The whole experience was benign. How was yours?"

"Truly a piece of cake," Deborah said. "No worse than a routine pap smear."

"No pain?"

"A little, I suppose, when the local anesthetic went in, but that was it. The worst part was the humiliation of being looked into."

"How many eggs did they get?"

"I haven't the slightest idea," Deborah admitted. "I assume only one. That's how many we women put out each month without hormonal hyperstimulation."

"They got five or six from me."

"Well, aren't we impressed," Deborah said in a playfully sarcastic tone. "How do you know?"

"I asked," Joanna said. "The doctor came by when I was in the recovery room. His name's Dr. Saunders. You must have met him, because he's the one who does the egg retrievals along with Dr. Donaldson."

"Was this Dr. Saunders a rather short guy with unusual eyes?"

"He's the one. I think he's also kinda strange as well as quiet. What was weird was that he seemed to act mad when he found out I was already awake."

"Get out of here!" Deborah blurted.

"I'm serious."

"The reason I'm surprised is that he acted mad with me, too."

"No kidding!" Joanna said. "Then he's

definitely got a problem, which is reassuring because I was wondering if I was making it up. You know me with authority figures."

"All too well," Deborah said. "And you think he was irritated because you were awake?"

"Yes," Joanna said. "He snapped at the nurse because the nurse had told him a few minutes earlier on the phone that I was still asleep. I suppose he had it in his mind to breeze in and breeze out. Instead, he had to relate to me, such as it was."

"That's absurd," Deborah said.

"The nurse excused his behavior by saying he was a busy man."

"He was equally inappropriate with me. Like everybody else he'd started in about wanting to use general anesthesia, and how much better it would be. But I just said no way. So he got mad. And you know what: It dawned on me why they had me suffer not eating or drinking since midnight. They thought they were going to talk me into it."

"You didn't have it, did you?"

"Hell no!" Deborah said. "I told them I was ready to get up and walk out, and I came close. If it hadn't been for Dr. Donaldson, who smoothed things over, I think I would have. But anyway, it all worked out."

"Let's get out of here," Joanna said.

"I'm with you," Deborah responded. She opened the louvered changing room door, winked at Joanna, and disappeared.

Joanna could hear Deborah out in the waiting room banging open her locker as Joanna peeled off the hospital clothing and tossed it into a convenient hamper. For a moment she gazed at herself in the changing room's full-length mirror. The thought of the small incisions beneath the Band-Aids made her shudder. They stood as minute reminders that someone had recently been looking into her innards.

The crash of the neighboring louvered door closing snapped Joanna back to reality. Fearful of keeping Deborah waiting, who was notoriously quick at dressing, Joanna concentrated on getting into her clothes. Once that was accomplished she began brushing out her hair, which she'd pulled back into a ponytail for the procedure but which was now a mass of snarls. Before she was finished, she heard

Deborah emerge into the waiting room. "How are you doing in there?" Deborah called through the door.

"Almost ready," Joanna answered. Her hair was giving her more trouble than usual, with loose ends dangling in her face. She'd had bangs in high school that she'd grown out in college. After a last check in the mirror, she finally opened the changing room door. Deborah rewarded her with an exasperated expression.

"I hurried," Joanna said.

"Sure you did," Deborah said as she got to her feet. "You should try short hair like mine. You'll save yourself a lot of grief; it's ten times easier."

"Never," Joanna said jokingly, but she meant it. Despite the difficulties, she treasured her long hair.

The two women called out a *thank you* to Cynthia, and she waved in acknowledgment. The women sitting on the couch and the chairs looked up, several smiled, but all had returned to their reading before Joanna and Deborah had passed through the swinging doors.

"I just realized there's something we forgot to ask about," Deborah said as they walked down the main hallway.

"Do I have to ask, or are you just going to tell me?" Joanna said with a sigh, when Deborah failed to complete her thought, she found it mildly irksome that Deborah had a tendency not to finish a thought unless prompted.

"We forgot to ask how or when we were going to be paid."

"It's certainly not going to be in cash," Joanna said.

"I know that!" Deborah grumbled.

"It will be by check or wire," Joanna said.

"All right, but when?"

"The contracts we signed stipulated we would be paid when we had performed our service, which we've now done. So they'll pay us now."

"You seem to be more trusting than I," Deborah said. "I think we should inquire about it before we leave."

"That goes without saying," Joanna said. "I think we should page Dr. Donaldson if she's not out in the main waiting room."

The two women came to the threshold

of the waiting room and glanced around the generous space. Nearly every seat was taken. There were spotty areas of hushed conversation but in general the room was surprisingly quiet for being so crowded.

"Well, no Dr. Donaldson," Deborah said. Her eyes swept the room once again to be certain.

"So, let's have her paged," Joanna said.

Together they approached the central desk. The receptionist was an attractive, young, amply endowed redhead. She had pouty, full lips like many of the women gracing the covers of the magazines displayed in the grocery checkout line. Her nameplate said ROCHELLE MILLARD.

"Excuse me," Joanna said to get the woman's attention. She was surreptitiously reading a paperback book cradled in her lap.

The book disappeared as if by magic. "Can I help you?" Rochelle asked.

Joanna asked for Dr. Donaldson to be paged.

"Are you Joanna Meissner?" Rochelle questioned.

Joanna nodded.

Rochelle's eyes switched to Deborah. "Are you Miss Cochrane?"

"I am," Deborah said.

"I have something for each of you from Margaret Lambert, the comptroller." Rochelle opened a drawer to her right and pulled out two envelopes with cellophane windows. Neither was sealed. She handed them to the surprised women.

After exchanging a covert, conspiratorial smile, the two women peeked inside their respective envelopes. A moment later their eyes met with new smiles.

"Bingo!" Deborah said to Joanna. She laughed. Then she turned to the receptionist and said: *"Mille grazie, signorina. Partiamo a Italia."*

"The first part means a thousand thanks in Italian," Joanna said. "The rest I'm not sure about. And forget about paging Dr. Donaldson. It's not necessary."

Leaving the confused receptionist, Joanna and Deborah started for the door.

"I feel a little like a thief taking this kind of money out of here," Deborah said sotto voce as they wended through the crowded room. Like Joanna she was clutching her envelope in her hand. She avoided eye contact with anyone, fearing she might be forced to face someone who'd had to mortgage her home to pay for infertility treatment.

"With this many patients here I think the Wingate can afford it," Joanna responded. "I'm getting the distinct feeling this business is a virtual money machine. Besides, it's the prospective clients who are actually paying us, not the clinic."

"That's just the point," Deborah said. "Although I suppose those people choosey enough to demand a Harvard coed's egg can't be hurting for cash."

"Exactly," Joanna said. "Concentrate on the idea that we are helping people, and they, in their gratitude, are helping us."

"It's hard to feel altruistic getting a check for forty-five thousand dollars," Deborah said. "Maybe I feel more like a prostitute of sorts than a thief, but don't get me wrong, I'm not complaining."

"When the couples get their children, they'll be thinking they got the better deal by a long shot."

"You know, I think you are right," Deborah said. "I'm going to stop feeling guilty."

They emerged into the crisp New England morning. Deborah was about to descend the stairs when she became aware that Joanna was hesitating. Glancing at her friend's face she noticed that Joanna was grimacing.

"What's the matter?" Deborah asked with concern.

"I just had a pang down here in my lower abdomen," Joanna said. She gestured with her left hand over the area. "I even felt a twinge in my shoulder, of all places."

"Do you still feel it?"

"Yes, but it's better."

"Do you want to go back and see Dr. Donaldson?"

Joanna tentatively pushed against her lower belly just in from the crest of her left hip. There was a mild degree of discomfort until she let go. Then she got another stab of pain. A whimper escaped from her lips.

"Are you all right, Joanna?"

Joanna nodded. Like the first spasm, the pain had been fleeting except for a remaining mild ache.

"Let's go page Dr. Donaldson," Deborah said. She grasped Joanna's arm with the intention of leading her back into the Wingate Clinic, but Joanna resisted.

"It doesn't feel that bad," Joanna said. "Let's go to the car."

"Are you sure?"

Joanna nodded again, gently extracted her arm from Deborah's grip, and started down the steps. At first it felt decidedly better to walk slightly bent over, but after a half dozen steps she was able to straighten up and walk relatively normally.

"How does it feel now?" Deborah questioned.

"Pretty good," Joanna asserted.

"Don't you think it would be a better idea to go back in and see Dr. Donaldson, just to be on the safe side?"

"I want to get home," Joanna said. "Besides, Dr. Smith specifically warned me about having the kind of pain I'm experiencing, so it's not as if it's unexpected."

"He warned you about pain?" Deborah asked with surprise.

Joanna nodded. "He wasn't sure which side I would feel it on, but he said I'd have a deep ache with some stabs of sharp pain which is right on the money. The surprise for me is that I didn't feel it until now."

"Did he have any suggestions for what to do for it?"

"He thought ibuprofen would suffice, but he said that if it didn't, I could have a pharmacist call him through the clinic's telephone number. He said he's available twenty-four hours a day."

"That's strange they gave you a warning about pain," Deborah said. "Nobody warned me, and I haven't had any. I think maybe you should have insisted on local anesthesia like I did."

"Very funny," Joanna said. "I liked being asleep through the ordeal. It was worth a bit of pain and the mild inconvenience of having to get three stitches removed."

"Where did you have stitches?"

"At the peephole sites."

"Are you going to have to come back here to get them removed?" Deborah asked.

"They told me any medical person could do it," Joanna said. "If Carlton and I are talking by then, he can do it for me. Otherwise I'll just stop in the health service."

They reached the car and Deborah went around to the passenger side to open the

door for her roommate. She even supported Joanna's arm as Joanna climbed in.
"I still think you should have had local
anesthesia," she said.

"You're never going to convince me,"
Joanna said with conviction. Of that, she
felt sure.

five

A shudder rippled through the plane signaling the start of a period of mild, clear air turbulence. Joanna lifted her eyes from the paperback book she was reading to glance around the cabin to make sure no one else was concerned. She didn't like turbulence. It reminded her that she was suspended far above the earth, and not being of a scientific mind, she didn't think it was reasonable that an object as heavy as a plane could actually fly.

No one had paid the few bumps and thuds any notice, least of all Deborah sitting next to her, who was enviably asleep. Her roommate hardly looked her best. Her now shoulder-length mane of almost-black hair was tousled and her mouth was slightly agape. Knowing Deborah as well as she did, Joanna knew she'd be mortified if she could see herself. Although the thought of awakening her passed through Joanna's mind, she didn't. Instead she found herself marveling at the transposition of their respective hairstyles. Deborah's was now long while Joanna had spent the last six months with her hair short, even shorter than Deborah's had been back when they had lived in Cambridge.

Switching her attention to the window, Joanna pressed her nose up against the glass. By doing so, she could see the ground thousands upon thousands of feet below, and just as it had been fifteen or twenty minutes ago, it was featureless tundra interspersed with lakes. Having consulted the map in the airline magazine, Joanna knew they were flying over Labrador en route to Boston's Logan Airport. The trip had seemed interminable, and Joanna was antsy and looking forward to their arrival. It had been almost a year and a half since they'd left, and Joanna was eager to set foot in the good old USA. She had resisted coming back to the States for the duration, despite her mother's recurrent pleading, which was particularly insistent during the Christmas holiday seasons. The holidays were a big deal in the Meissner household, and Joanna missed them, especially when Deborah had gone back to New York to be with her mother and stepfather. But Joanna had been unwilling to face her mother's constant harping about the unmitigated social disaster caused by her breaking off the engagement with Carlton Williams.

As they'd originally planned, she and Deborah had gone to Venice, Italy, to escape the humdrum aspect of their graduate student lives and to make sure Joanna didn't have a relapse into believing that marriage was a necessary goal. At first they lived for almost a week in the San Polo district near the Rialto Bridge in the bed-and-breakfast that Deborah had found on the Internet. After that they'd moved to the Dorsoduro Sestière on the recommendation of a couple of male university students they'd met on their second day while having coffee in Piazza San Marco. With a bit of luck and a lot of walking, they had managed to locate a small, affordable two-bedroom apartment on the top floor of a modest, fourteenth-century house on a square called Campo Santa Margherita.

As serious students, the women had quickly adapted to a strict schedule to facilitate their work. Every morning they made themselves get out of bed by seven regardless of the previous evening's festivities. After a shower they'd descend to the campo and take a short walk to a traditional Italian bar for fresh cappuccinos, which was particularly pleasant in the summer months when they'd sit in the shade of the square's plane trees. Then it was on to the Rio di San Barnaba to complete their *colazione* with fresh fruit purchased from the waterborne greengrocers, or *verduriere*. A half hour later they were back in the apartment at their respective workstations to write.

Without fail they wrote until one o'clock in the afternoon. Only then did they turn off their laptops. After washing up and changing clothes, they headed to the restaurant they'd picked out for that day's lunch, which often included a glass or two of white wine from Friuli. Then it was time to switch hats from committed doctoral students to tourists. Armed with a virtual library of guidebooks, they'd set out to visit the sites. Three afternoons a week they went to the university itself where they'd arranged to have Italian lessons as well as lectures on Venetian art.

The women's Italian sojourn wasn't all work and serious touring. Socially they had a *blast* dating almost exclusively Italian men who were associated in some way with the university. Deborah's first beau was a graduate student in art history who was also a gondolier in season. Joanna began seeing an instructor in the same department. But neither woman allowed herself to become terribly involved, maintaining, as Deborah described it, a decidedly male attitude toward dating: namely, treat it like a sport.

Joanna sighed when she thought of all the wonderful sights they had seen and experiences they'd had. It had been an extraordinary year and a half in every way, including professionally. Tucked in their carry-ons stored above in the overhead compartment were two completed Ph.D. theses. Thanks to E-mail, which had facilitated sending chapters and their revisions back and forth, the theses had already been accepted. All that was left were their defenses, which both women were confident would not be a problem. A week after they got back, both had interviews scheduled: Joanna at the Harvard Business School and Deborah at Genzyme.

Even Carlton had come for several visits. The first time it had been totally out of the blue, and it had made Joanna furious. Before leaving for Europe she'd tried a number of times to call him, but he had gone out of his way to avoid her and had staunchly refused to return her messages. After finding the apartment, Joanna had written a letter to give him the address so he could write to her when he felt he wanted to do so. Instead he'd just shown up and rung the doorbell one foggy, rainy winter day.

If it hadn't been for a sense of guilt over

how far Carlton had come to visit, Joanna wouldn't have seen him on that trip. As it was, she let him stew in his room at the Gritti Palace for a number of days before calling. They met for lunch at Harry's Bar, Carlton's choice, and although the conversation was painful at first, they managed to come to an understanding of sorts, which at least began a correspondence. The correspondence had led to two other visits by Carlton to La Serenissima, as the Venetians of old had called their fair city. Each visit was more pleasant than the previous for Joanna, yet not entirely comfortable. The perspective of her year abroad made her view Carlton as being progressively limited by the dedication medicine required. Yet the ultimate result of the contact was a truce in which they admitted they cared for one another but felt their current "unengaged" status was appropriate, enabling each to pursue their own interests.

Another series of bumps and thuds made Joanna again glance around the plane's interior. She was amazed that no one else appeared to be upset. Then the turbulence ended as suddenly as it had begun. Joanna looked out the window again but nothing had changed. She wondered how clear air could possibly make the plane behave as if it were a land vehicle driving over potholes.

As the flight grew calmer, Joanna couldn't dismiss the nagging feeling that her life was not complete despite all the gaiety, the traveling, and the intellectual stimulation.

Deborah was convinced that Joanna's restlessness had something to do with her rejection of traditional female goals: house, husband, children. But Joanna had located a different source. Seeing the Italians' con- tinual love affair with infants left her won- dering about the fate of her harvested eggs.

Increasingly, she was tempted to find out what became of them. For a long time, Deborah pooh-poohed her curiosity, but on the eve of their homecoming, her friend had surprised her with a stunning reversal.

"Wouldn't it be interesting to find out what kind of children resulted from our eggs?" she asked over their last Venetian supper.

Joanna had put her glass of wine down

and had looked into her roommate's dark eyes for some explanation. She was confused. She'd asked the same question a month previously, and it had evoked an angry reaction with Deborah accusing her of being obsessed.

"What do you think are our chances of finding anything out?" Deborah asked, seemingly oblivious to Joanna's reaction.

"It might be hard considering the contracts we signed," Joanna said.

"Yeah, but that was more to ensure our anonymity," Deborah said. "We didn't want anyone coming after us for child support or anything like that."

"I think it works both ways," Joanna said. "The Wingate Clinic certainly didn't want us coming after the kids and demanding maternal rights."

"I suppose you're right," Deborah said. "Too bad, though. It would be interesting even if it were only to be sure we can have kids. You know, there are no guarantees of fertility these days. I'm sure all those people we saw out there in the Wingate Clinic would attest to that."

"I can imagine," Joanna said, still bewildered by Deborah's turnaround. "I'd like to find out myself. So how about we call the Wingate when we get back and see what they say? There can't be any harm in asking."

"Good idea," Deborah had said.

That was a day and an ocean ago. Now the plane's intercom system crackled to life and brought Joanna back to the present. The captain's voice announced that they were soon to start their initial descent into Boston. He added that he was going to turn on the seat-belt light, and he wanted to make sure that everyone was buckled up.

Joanna checked her seat belt to make certain it was fastened. As a rule she always wore her seat belt during flights, whether the seat belt light was on or not. A quick glance at Deborah's revealed it too was secure. Returning her attention to the view out the window, she noticed there'd been a change. The tundra had been replaced by dense forest broken by widely spaced farms. She guessed they were over Maine, which was a good sign as far as she was concerned. It meant that Massachusetts wasn't that far off.

*   *   *

"Here comes my last bag," Deborah shouted. She dashed back to the baggage carousel from where she and Joanna had been searching through a pile of suitcases. She pulled the bursting bag free and lugged it over to where she and Joanna had amassed their others. Once they'd loaded them onto two carts, they stood in line for customs.

"Well, here we are back in Beantown," Deborah commented as she ran her hand through her long, thick hair. "What a great flight. It seemed a lot shorter than I expected."

"Not to me," Joanna said. "I wish I could have slept half the time you did."

"Planes put me to sleep," Deborah said.

"As if I couldn't tell!" Joanna said enviously.

An hour later, the two friends were in their two-bedroom apartment on Beacon Hill, newly vacated by the tenant they'd rented it to for their Italian sojourn.

"How about flipping a coin to see who gets which bedroom?" Joanna suggested.

"No way," Deborah responded. "I said

I'd take the smaller bedroom, and I'm fine with that."

"Are you sure?"

"Absolutely. For me a big closet and the view are more important than a space."

"It's the bathroom that's the problem," Joanna said. The bathroom had two entrances: one from the hall and one from the second bedroom. In Joanna's mind that made the second bedroom far superior.

"The smaller bedroom is fine by me. Trust me!"

"Okay," Joanna said. "I'm not going to argue."

An hour later the women had distributed the furniture, partially unpacked their luggage, and had even made their respective beds when, as Deborah put it, they "ran out of gas." Realizing it was after ten o'clock at night back in Italy, they collapsed on the sofa in the living room. The bright, mid-spring afternoon sun was still streaming in through the front windows to belie their exhaustion and jet lag.

"What do you want to do about dinner?" Deborah asked in a monotone.

"There's something else I want to do before thinking about eating," Joanna said. She pushed herself upright and stretched.

"Take a nap?" Deborah asked.

"Nope," Joanna said. "I want to make a call." She stood and walked across the room to pick up the phone from the floor. They had no phone table where the phone jack was located. They could have placed the desk there but had decided to put it on the other side of the room to keep glare from the window off the computer screen.

"If you are going to call Carlton, I'm going to throw up."

Joanna looked at her roommate as if she'd gone crazy. "I'm not going to call Carlton. What makes you even suggest it?" She brought the phone back to the couch. The phone was on a twenty-five-foot cord.

"I've been worrying about you backsliding," Deborah said. "I've been noticing how many letters you've been getting lately from that boring doctor-in-training, and it worries me, especially now that we're back here in Boston within a stone's throw of his hospital."

Joanna laughed. "You really think I'm spineless, don't you?"

"I think of you as insufficiently girded

against twenty-five years of maternal in-
doctrination."

Joanna chuckled. "Well, for your information, calling Carlton never entered my
mind. What I want to do is call the Wingate
Clinic. Do you have the number?"

"You're going to call already? We just
got home."

"Why not?" Joanna said. "It's been on
my mind for months, and yours, too, or so
you said."

"Toss me my phone book," Deborah
said without moving. "It's on the top of the
desk."

Joanna did as she was told, and while
Deborah looked up the number, Joanna sat
back down next to her. Deborah found the
number, put her finger under it, and held it
up for Joanna to see. Using the speaker-
phone button to get a dial tone, Joanna
punched in the numbers.

The call went through and was picked
up quickly. Joanna identified herself as a
previous egg donor and said she wanted to
speak to someone knowledgeable about
the program. There was no response.

"Did you hear me?" Joanna questioned.

"I heard you," the operator said. "But I

thought you were going to say something else. I'm not sure what you are asking. Are you interesting in donating again?"

"Possibly," Joanna said. She glanced at Deborah and shrugged. "But at the moment I'd like to speak with someone about my previous donation. Is anyone available?"

"Is everything all right?" the operator asked. "Are you having a problem?"

"No, not really," Joanna said. "I just have a few questions I'd like answered."

"Perhaps I should page Dr. Sheila Donaldson."

Joanna asked the woman to hold on and hit the mute button. She glared at Deborah. "What do you think? I was hoping for a secretarial type, not a doctor."

"I'd guess that secretaries would defer to Dr. Donaldson, so we might as well speak to her directly. I imagine it will save a step."

"I suppose you're right," Joanna said. She motioned toward the phone.

"Wait!" Deborah said. "Are you thinking about donating again?"

"Not at all," Joanna said. "But I figured

we might as well stay on their good side. Who knows, it might help."

Deborah nodded. Joanna pressed the mute button again and told the operator to go ahead and page Dr. Donaldson.

"Do you want to hold on or should the doctor call you back?"

"I'll hold on," Joanna said. A moment later, elevator background music emanated from the telephone.

"Maybe we should give the idea of donating again some thought," Deborah said. "I wouldn't mind being able to continue the lifestyle that I've become accustomed to." She smiled teasingly.

"You're joking," Joanna said.

"Not necessarily," Deborah said.

"I wouldn't do it again," Joanna said. "I've appreciated the opportunities we've had thanks to the money, but it's not been without an emotional price. Maybe I'd consider it after I have some children of my own, if that's going to happen. But of course, by then, I'd probably be considered too old."

Before Deborah could respond, Dr. Donaldson's voice interrupted the music. She identified herself with a degree of urgency and asked how she could be of assistance.

"I'm a former egg donor at your institution," Joanna said. "It was quite a while ago, but I have a question I'd like to ask . . ."

"What's the problem?" Dr. Donaldson demanded impatiently. "The operator implied there was a problem."

"I specifically told her there was no problem."

"How long ago did you donate?"

"Just about a year and a half."

"What is your name?" Dr. Donaldson asked, her voice decidedly calmer.

"Joanna Meissner. My roommate and I came in together."

"I remember you," Dr. Donaldson said. "I came in to visit you at your apartment in Cambridge. As I recall you had long blond hair, and your roommate had short dark hair, almost black. The two of you were graduate students."

"I'm impressed," Joanna said. "I'm sure you see a lot of people."

"What is it you'd like to ask?"

Joanna cleared her throat and then forged ahead. "We'd like to find out what happened to our eggs. You know, how many children resulted and maybe even their sex."

"I'm sorry but that information is confidential."

"We don't need names or anything like that," Joanna persisted.

"I'm sorry, all information, and I mean all information of that sort is strictly confidential."

"Can you at least tell us if children were born?" Joanna asked. "It would be reassuring just to know if our eggs are healthy."

"I'm sorry but we have stringent rules that preclude giving out any information whatsoever. I don't know how to say it any clearer."

Joanna made a look of exasperation.

"Hello, Dr. Donaldson!" Deborah called out. She leaned forward to speak directly into the speaker phone. "This is Deborah Cochrane, and I'm here as well with Joanna. What if the children need genetic information for some reason from the biological mother, or if they require a transplant—bone marrow or a kidney."

Joanna shuddered at the thought.

"We keep a computerized record," Dr.

Donaldson said. "In the unlikely event that something like what you are talking about were to occur, we might contact you. But that would be the only exception, and it is extremely unlikely. And even if it were to happen, the involved parties would still have the option of remaining anonymous. We would not give any of the information out."

Deborah threw up her hands.

"The only time the situation is different is when one of our clients finds their own donor," Dr. Donaldson continued. "But that is a completely different circumstance. It's called an *open donation.*"

"Thank you, Dr. Donaldson," Joanna said.

"I'm sorry."

Joanna pressed the speaker phone button to disconnect.

"Well, that's that," Deborah said with a sigh.

"I'm not giving up so easily," Joanna said. "The possibility that I've got progeny out there has eaten up too much emotional energy for me to just let it go." She pulled the phone wire out of the phone, put the phone on the floor and headed over to the computer on the desk.

"What do you have in mind?"

Joanna bent down behind the electronics unit of the computer and plugged the phone line into the modem. "Way back you told me the Wingate Clinic had a website, and that you'd gotten some information from it. Let's see what kind of firewall they have. Did you keep the web address?"

"Yeah, I put it into *Favorites,*" Deborah said. She got off the couch and came over to watch Joanna. Joanna was much more facile with every aspect of the computer than she. "What's a firewall?"

"It's software that blocks unauthorized access," Joanna said. Quickly she went onto the Internet and got the address for the Wingate. A moment later she was at the clinic's web page. Pulling up a chair, she tried to get into the clinic's files.

"No luck, huh?" Deborah said over Joanna's shoulder after a half hour.

"Unfortunately, no," Joanna said. "Of course I can't even be sure they have their web page on their own server."

"I'm not even going to ask what that means," Deborah said. She yawned and then made her way back to the couch where she stretched out full length.

Suddenly Joanna disconnected from the Internet, yanked out the phone line, and retreated back to where the phone was on the floor in front of the couch. When the phone was reconnected she called information to get the number for David Washburn.

"Who the hell is he?" Deborah asked.

"A classmate," Joanna said. "I took a couple of computer classes with him. A very nice guy, I might add, who actually asked me out a few times."

"Why on earth are you calling him now?"

"He's very computer-savvy," Joanna said. "And hacking was one of his sports as an undergraduate."

"Calling in the pros," Deborah commented with a wry smile.

"Something like that," Joanna agreed. Joanna had to go back to the desk for a pencil and paper to write the number down. Once she had, she dialed directly.

Deborah put her hands behind her head and watched Joanna's intent expression as the call went through. "Where are you finding the energy?" she asked. "You're all jazzed up, and I feel like death warmed over."

"This whole issue has been gnawing at me for too long," Joanna said. "I'd like some resolution."

six

"What time is it?" Deborah asked sleepily.

"Almost nine," Joanna said, checking her watch. "Where on earth is he?"

The conversation with David Washburn had gone well. After Joanna had explained to him what they were trying to find out, he was happy to help, but he insisted on coming over to use their computer to do it.

"I can't afford any electronic trail to my machine," he had explained. "I'm on informal probation after slipping some porno shots onto the Defense Department web page with the caption *Make love not war.*

Unfortunately, the Feds were less than amused."

Deborah yawned noisily. "Are you sure he meant tonight?"

"I'm positive," Joanna said. "I told him we'd be going out for a quick bite to eat, but then we'd be home. He said fine; it would give him a chance to finish what he was doing."

"I'm afraid I'm not going to stay awake," Deborah said. "Do you realize it's three o'clock in the morning back in Italy where our bodies think they are?"

"Why don't you turn in?" Joanna suggested. "I'll wait up."

"Aren't you tired?"

"I'm exhausted," Joanna admitted.

Deborah put her feet over onto the floor, pushed herself up to a sitting position, but before she could stand, a raucous buzz filled the room. Both women started. It had been the first time they'd heard the front doorbell, and it was considerably louder than they expected.

"No fear we'll ever miss that," Deborah said, collapsing back onto the couch.

Joanna got to her feet and moved quickly over to the door panel. "What do I do?" she asked in a minor panic. There were several buttons as well as a circular area of perforations through the metal.

"You're on your own."

Joanna pressed the first button. A crackling sound issued forth. "Hello, hello!" she said with her mouth close to the perforations.

"It's me, David!" a distant voice responded.

"Okay," Joanna answered back. She then pressed the second button while still holding the first depressed. She heard a distant buzz, followed by the faint sound of the front door opening and then closing.

"Well, that wasn't so difficult," Joanna said. She walked over to the apartment door, opened it, and stepped out. Bending over the railing, she looked down. The hall was like a chambered nautilus with the stair spiraling all the way down to the street level.

David bounded up the stairs with a broad smile baked on his face. He was a tall, athletic African American. After a moment's hesitation, he gave her a big hug. "How you doing, girl?" he said.

"Just fine," Joanna answered, hugging

back. Even though she'd not seen him for over two years, he appeared exactly the same; he had the same short, scruffy beard, the same laid-back manner, and the same casual clothes.

"Man, what a surprise to hear from you. You look good, real good!"

"You too," Joanna said. "You haven't changed one iota."

"Just a little older and a little wiser," David said with a laugh. "And I'm happy to report the old jump shot's still going down fine. But you look different. In fact you look younger. How can that be?"

"You're just trying to flatter me," Joanna said.

"No, really!" David persisted. He moved from side to side to view Joanna from slightly different angles.

"Come on!" Joanna protested. "You're embarrassing me."

"No need to be embarrassed," David said. "You look terrific. And now I know what it is. Your hair; it's short. I'm not sure I would have recognized you if I had bumped into you on the street. You look like you're sixteen."

"Oh, sure!" Joanna said. "Come in and meet my roommate."

Joanna took David's arm. She led him inside and introduced him to Deborah, who'd managed to get herself upright. Joanna then apologized for not having a thing to offer him to drink.

"No problem," David said. "We'll make up for it on another occasion. Now I know you ladies must be tired just getting back from Italy and all, so why don't we get right down to business." He peeled off his jacket made of black parachute fabric. From his pocket he produced a handful of floppy discs and held them up. "I brought along some tools, including my brute force password-guessing program. Where's your machine?"

A few minutes later David had the computer booted up and onto the Wingate Clinic's web page. With a rapidity that made Deborah blink, David browsed around the site. His fingers moved like a concert pianist across the keyboard. "So far so good," he reported.

"Can you tell me what you are doing?" Deborah asked.

"Nothing yet," David said as he continued his surfing. "Just checking things out and looking for obvious holes in their firewall."

"Do you see any?"

"Not yet, but they're there."

"How can you be sure."

"One of the roles of a website is to provide the world with access to the organization's network. Here you can see the Wingate Clinic has it set up for people to send in health-related data and to get information back. Any time there is such an exchange there's the possibility of unauthorized access. In fact, in general, the more interactive a site is, the easier it is to hack. In other words, the more traffic, the more holes."

Deborah nodded but she wasn't sure she understood. Her use of computers was restricted to her biological research work, using the Internet as a resource, and sending E-mail.

"But what about passwords?" Deborah questioned. Whenever she used the computer in the lab, she had to enter her password, which only she knew. "Don't those keep people out?"

"Yes and no," David said. "That's supposed to be the idea, but it doesn't always work like it should. A lot of network managers are lazy and they never change the manufacturer default passwords, so that narrows down what has to be tried. Also with a www. server there's no limit to how many attempts you can make, so we can try a brute-force password-guessing program like the one I brought with me."

Deborah rolled her eyes for Joanna's benefit.

"It's actually a lot of fun," David said, sensing Deborah's doubt. "It's like an intellectual arcade game."

"I can't imagine it's too much fun for the people being hacked," Joanna said.

"It's usually pretty innocuous," David said. "Most hackers I know aren't malicious. It's like an ongoing competition between them and the people designing the security. Or they're just doing someone a favor like me with you guys. You're not interested in doing anything other than getting the information that it seems to me you're entitled to."

"It would have been a lot easier if the clinic saw it that way," Joanna said.

All at once David stopped typing. He

stroked his beard thoughtfully. "Well, I have to give credit where credit is due. Seems like a pretty tight site. Certainly no glaring holes. In fact it seems to me to be fairly sophisticated. They've got an authentication server. Does this organization have a lot of bucks to throw around?"

"That would be my guess," Joanna said.

"I'm getting the feeling we're up against some pretty good security here," David said, "which means we'll have to get more sophisticated ourselves."

"What is it exactly that you would like to be able to do?" Deborah asked.

"I'd like the web server to recognize and authenticate us," David said. "Then we'd have the run of all their files. What I'm going to try now is to fill up the buffer on their new patient form and see if I can throw in some assembly-level commands in the space after the buffer to bypass the authentication. It's like riding in through the CGI on the patient-form coattails."

"Could you tell me that in English?" Deborah said.

David looked up to Deborah's face. She was watching over his left shoulder. "I was actually simplifying the process when I just described it."

"Fine!" Deborah said, pretending to be irritated. "If that's the case, then I'll take myself over to the couch and lie down. I'll let you two computer wizards attend to business."

David looked up at Joanna over his other shoulder. "I want to make sure you understand that if I do this, and it works, there will be an electronic trail through your Internet service provider to this machine. If the hack is picked up, they could come after you. Are you okay with that?"

Joanna mulled the question for a moment. She knew what they were doing was technically breaking the law, yet the information was important to her, even necessary for her peace of mind in view of the changes in her life. And what were the chances such an intrusion would be noticed if all they did was trace their own eggs? She thought the chances seemed small indeed.

"What do you think, Deborah?" Joanna asked.

"I'm willing to leave it up to you,"

Deborah said. "I'm curious, obviously, but not as curious as you."

"Then let's do it," Joanna said.

"Right on, baby!" David said gleefully as he rubbed his hands together in anticipation of the challenge. He cracked a few of his knuckles before bending to the task. Again his fingers flew over the keyboard. The sound was like a continuous clatter rather than individual strokes. Images flashed on the screen in rapid succession.

After more than thirty minutes of intense concentration, David halted. He took an exasperated deep breath while flexing his fingers in the air.

"It's not working, is it?" Joanna said.

"I'm afraid not," David said. "This is no Mickey Mouse setup, that I can assure you."

"What do you propose?"

David looked down at his watch. "This might be a long process. It's a more secure site than I would have imagined, and it's not letting me sneak in any commands whatsoever. I thought we were dealing with a Windows NT environment but it now looks like a Windows 2000 with Kerberos."

"Is Kerberos the authentication method developed at M.I.T.?" Joanna asked.

"You got it," David said.

"So what's your bottom line suggestion as the easiest way to get the information we want?"

David laughed. "Let me stay here for a week, and I'll try to bust in with stuff like the LophtCrack utility. Other than that, I'd suggest you find someone who works out there at the Wingate Clinic, who has access, and who would be sympathetic to your cause."

"Those are the only two choices?"

"No, there's something else. Get yourself or me into the server room." David laughed again. "Actually, that's the most efficient, foolproof way. Hell, it would probably only take less than ten minutes to create your own pathway. Then it would be a piece of cake, either from a workstation inside the network or even from offsite if you did it right."

Joanna nodded while her mind pondered the choices. She felt progressively committed, as if the more she hit up against barriers, the more she wanted to succeed, especially since she could picture a little girl somewhere nearby who looked like the photos she had of herself as an infant.

David glanced down at his watch, then back up at Joanna. "It's after ten. You want me to keep going here or what? I'm cool with it if you do, but like I said, I can't promise anything other than I'm sure I can crack this site eventually. I just don't know how long it will take."

"You've done enough," Joanna said. "Thank you." She stared off vacantly deep in thought.

David noticed the faraway look in her green, unblinking eyes. He waited for several beats, then stuck his hand up in her line of sight and waved it back and forth. "Are you with me, girl?"

Joanna shook her head as if waking from a trance and smiled. "Sorry," she said. "I was just wondering about what you said concerning getting into the server room. How hard would that be once you were in the building?"

"It all depends," David said. "Obviously if they care about security, it's not like you can just walk in anytime you want."

"But it is physically a room," Joanna

said. "It's not just computer jargon about something that exists in cyberspace."

"It's a real room all right," David said. "And it's got real hardware inside, which includes a keyboard and a monitor to access the central processor."

"How would you envision the room to be secured?"

"A locked door," David said. "All the ones I've seen have had a card swipe access. You know: like a credit card."

"Interesting," Joanna said. "If I were to get in there, what exactly would I do?"

"That's the easy part," David said. "You have some paper handy?"

Joanna pulled open one of the desk drawers and got out a fresh yellow legal pad. She handed it to David who proceeded to outline the steps that needed to be done. Joanna watched with full attention. At several points she asked for clarification, which David was happy to provide.

"And that's it," David said. He ripped off the page and handed it up to Joanna. She glanced over it again. Satisfied she had no further questions, she folded it and slipped it into her pocket.

"Thank you ever so much for coming over," Joanna said.

"Hey, my pleasure," David said. He scraped back the chair and stood up. "Any time for a former classmate."

"By the way, how's your Ph.D. thesis coming along?" Joanna asked.

"Now you're starting to sound like my mother," David said with a laugh. He gathered his floppy discs into a neat pile. "Unfortunately I'm running into a little writer's block along about the second chapter. How's yours?"

"Very well," Joanna said. "It's done."

"Done!" David squeaked before blowing out a lungful of air through pursed lips. He visibly sagged. "What a way to cut a friend off at the knees."

"I'm sorry."

"Hey, it's not your fault."

"Maybe you should think about changing your environment," Joanna suggested. "That's what Deborah and I did. She's finished as well."

"Maybe it's because I'm not so fired up about Stochastic Processes in the Commodity Markets of Third World Countries any longer. But then again, who would be?

Anyway, if I'm not being too personal, how are you and your fiancé getting along?"

"I'm no longer engaged," Joanna said.

David's posture improved. "Really? How long has that been?"

"A year and a half."

"Are you okay with that?"

"It was my idea."

"Cool. How about you and me having dinner some night?"

"I'd like that," Joanna said.

"I'll be in touch," David said. He pulled on his jacket and pocketed his floppy discs. On his way to the door he glanced over at Deborah's supine form. "Say good-bye to your roommate."

"I'm not asleep," Deborah said. She pushed herself up to a sitting position and blinked repeatedly in the light.

After another round of small talk David said his final good-byes and departed. Deborah, who was still sitting on the couch, watched Joanna go over to the computer to shut it down.

"No luck getting into the Wingate's files?" Deborah questioned. She yawned widely.

"Not yet," Joanna said. The computer

monitor went blank and the electronics unit fan went silent.

"Is David still going to try?"

"No, I am." Joanna walked past Deborah and disappeared into the bathroom.

"I'm confused," Deborah called out. "The reason you called David was because you couldn't do it. Did he give you some suggestions or advice that makes you think you can do it now?"

"We're moving to plan B," Joanna called out over the sound of running water.

Deborah stood up from the couch. She waited for a moment to allow a wave of queasiness to pass. Giddy with fatigue she made her way over to the open bathroom door and leaned against the jamb. Joanna was brushing her teeth.

"I'm afraid to ask, but what in heaven's name is plan B?"

"I'm going to get a short-term job at the Wingate Clinic," Joanna said through foam.

"You have to be joking," Deborah said.

Joanna spit loudly into the sink, then looked at Deborah in the mirror. "I'm serious. The only certain, expedient way of getting into the Wingate Computer files is to get into their server room, at least according to David."

"This is crazy," Deborah said. The sleepiness in her voice disappeared. "First of all, David doesn't seem to be the source of infallible information. When he got here he was sure he could hack into the Wingate computer, but he couldn't."

"He'd be able to do it, it just might take a long time. He knows what he's talking about. He gave me very specific suggestions once I get into the Wingate server room." Joanna went back to brushing her teeth.

Deborah made a gesture of exasperation with her hands then put them on her hips. She watched her roommate for several minutes before responding. "Won't this server room be locked?"

"Probably," Joanna said. She rinsed her mouth and plopped her toothbrush into the water glass business side up. "I'll just have to be resourceful. David thinks it will have a card swipe access. I'll just have to get one of those cards." Joanna started washing her face.

"Do you realize how insane this sounds?" Deborah said.

"I don't think it sounds insane in the slightest," Joanna said. "I want to know if there are children from my eggs, and I thought you wanted to know about yours as well."

"Of course I want to know, but that's not the point."

"I think it is the point."

"Let's be practical about this," Deborah said, trying to control her voice. "How are you going to get a job at the Wingate Clinic?"

"It should be easy," Joanna said. "Remember when we were out there they said they were always looking for people. They said that finding help was the downside of being in such a rural area. Well, I'm good at word processing. I'm sure I can find something to do."

"But they'll recognize you," Deborah said with a vehemence that bordered on anger.

"Calm down!" Joanna urged. She stared at her roommate who'd become red in the face.

"Don't you understand: They'll recognize you," Deborah repeated. "Probably most of the people we dealt with out there are still there, from the receptionist to the doctors."

"I don't think people would recognize me," Joanna said. "We were only out there for one morning a year and a half ago. Tonight David said he wouldn't have recognized me with my short hair if he bumped into me on the street, and he saw me at least three times a week for a number of years. And I won't use my real name."

"You're not going to be able to get a job without giving a Social Security number," Deborah said. "And the number and the name have to match. It's not going to work."

Joanna finished drying her face and stared at her image in the mirror. Deborah had a point she'd not considered. She'd need a name and a matching Social Security number. She thought maybe she could ask to impersonate one of her friends but dismissed the idea immediately. She couldn't knowingly implicate one of her friends in a scheme in which she'd be technically breaking the law.

"Well?" Deborah questioned.

"I'll get the name and Social Security number of someone who died recently,"

Joanna said. Vaguely she could remember reading something like that in a novel. The more she thought about it the more she thought it could work.

Deborah's jaw had dropped open at Joanna's latest suggestion. She pulled herself together. "I can't believe this. You truly are obsessed."

"I'd prefer to call it committed," Joanna said. She pushed past Deborah and walked into her bedroom. Deborah followed.

"I think you're going to be committed to Walpole Prison," Deborah said. "Either that or a mental institution. That's the kind of committed that's involved here."

"I'm not robbing a bank," Joanna said. She unbuckled her belt and stepped out of her jeans. "I'm just getting some information about my progeny."

"I don't know what kind of offense impersonating a dead person is," Deborah said. "But I know unauthorized access into computer files is a felony."

"I'm aware of that," Joanna said. "Nonetheless I'm going to do it."

Joanna continued undressing. When she was done she pulled a nightgown over her head. She arranged it so it draped evenly. Then she hung up her clothes. Finally she looked back over at Deborah who was still standing in the doorway. Deborah had not responded to her last statement other than to eye her with a combination of exasperation and disbelief.

"Well . . . ?" Joanna said, breaking the silence. "Are you just going to stand there or do you have more to say? If you do, out with it. Otherwise, I'm going to bed. Tomorrow is going to be a busy day."

"All right," Deborah said with angry resolve. She lifted a hand and poked a finger at Joanna. "If you insist on this crazy, idiotic plan, then I'm going too."

"Excuse me?" Joanna blurted.

"I'm not letting you go out there and get in all sorts of trouble without me. After all, it was my idea to do the egg donation in the first place. You're not the only one with a problem with guilt, and I'd never be able to live with myself if something happened to you that I could have prevented."

"You don't have to come with me just to be my protector," Joanna said with color rising in her face.

Deborah closed her eyes and extended

her hands palm down. "This is not an argument. The die has been cast. Obviously you're serious about this crusade, and now so am I." Deborah's eyes fluttered as if it had been difficult for her to open them.

Joanna came over and stared into her roommate's deep eyes. "Now I have to ask you if you are serious."

"I'm serious," Deborah said with a nod. "I'll get a job as well. With that huge lab out there, I'm sure they're as hungry for lab techs as they are for secretarial help."

"Then let's do it," Joanna said. She raised her hand with her fingers extended and high-fived with Deborah.

seven

MAY 8, 2001
6:10 A.M.

Still habituated to italian time, the women found themselves awake early despite their exhaustion. Deborah was the first to get out of bed. Believing Joanna was still asleep, she tried to be quiet as she passed through the kitchen into the bathroom. The moment she flushed the toilet the connecting door to Joanna's bedroom opened.

"You look like something the cat dragged in," Deborah said as she eyed her roommate.

"You've looked better yourself," Joanna said. "What time is it?"

"Quarter past six, but my pituitary gland thinks it's noon."

"Spare me the specifics," Joanna said. "All I know is that I had intended on sleeping late, yet I've been awake for at least an hour."

"Me too," Deborah said. "How about we go down to Charles Street for breakfast? I need coffee big time."

"Since the cupboard is bare we don't have much choice."

Three quarters of an hour later the women descended to the square and walked down Mt. Vernon Street to Charles. It was a fine spring morning with lots of bright flowers in the window boxes. Although there were few pedestrians until they got to Charles, the birds were out in full force. At the end of Charles Street fronting the Boston Common they found a Starbucks that was open. They went in and ordered cappuccinos and got some pastry as well. They carried their food over to a small marble table by the window. At first they ate and drank in silence.

"The coffee is good," Joanna said at length. "But I have to say it tasted better in Campo Santa Margherita."

"Isn't that the truth," Deborah agreed. "But it is reviving me."

"So you still want to go out to the Wingate Clinic and get jobs?" Joanna asked.

"Absolutely," Deborah said. "I'm psyched. But we'd better start brainstorming about specifics. How are we going to get names and Social Security numbers of dead people?"

"That's a good question," Joanna said. "While I was lying in bed this morning I was thinking about it. A few years ago I read about somebody doing it in a novel."

"How did he or she do it?"

"She had an *in.* She worked in a hospital and got the information from the hospital chart."

"What did she do with it?"

"It was a Medicare scam of some sort."

"Good grief!" Deborah commented. "That's interesting, but unfortunately it's not going to help us. That is, unless you were thinking of enlisting Carlton's help."

"I think we'd better leave Carlton out of this," Joanna said. "If he had an inkling of what we were up to, he'd probably turn us in to the FBI."

Deborah took another sip of her coffee.

"I think we should break the problem into two parts. First we get the names. After we have the names we worry about getting the Social Security numbers and whatever else we need, like birth date and maybe even mother's maiden name."

"Getting names won't be a problem," Joanna said. "At least that came to me while I was lying in bed. All we have to do is head over to the library and look at the *Globe*'s obituary pages."

"Good idea!" Deborah said. She sat forward eagerly. "Why didn't I think of that? It's perfect. The obituaries usually have ages if not birth dates. That will help picking out appropriate names since we should try to look for women about our age, as bizarre as that sounds."

"I know," Joanna said. "It's creepy. They also have to be women who have died relatively recently."

"Getting the Social Security number is going to be more difficult," Deborah said.

"Maybe I'll have to break down and ask Carlton for help," Joanna said. "The chances are, any woman our age who's passed away will have been a patient in a local hospital. If she'd been in the MGH, and if we could come up with some plausible reason why we want the Social Security number that won't make Carlton suspicious, maybe he'd help."

"That's a lot of ifs and maybes," Deborah commented.

"I suppose," Joanna agreed.

"I've got it," Deborah said. She slapped her palm against the tabletop. "A couple of years ago when my grandfather died, my grandmother had to get a death certificate to take his name off the deed to the house."

"How does that help us?"

"The death certificate is public information," Deborah said. She laughed at herself. "I can't believe I didn't think about this right off. The death certificate has the Social Security number."

"My gosh, that's perfect."

"Absolutely," Deborah said. "First we hit the library, then City Hall."

"Wait a second," Joanna said. She leaned forward conspiratorially. "We've got to make sure that the Social Security number hasn't been retired. Knowing government bureaucracy I'm sure it takes a while, but we have to be sure."

"You're absolutely right," Deborah said. "It would certainly blow our cover if we get out there to the Wingate and a background check turns up that one or both of us are dead." She laughed hollowly.

"I know what we can do," Joanna said. "After we go to City Hall, we stop at the Fleet Bank. We'll open up savings accounts with both names. As American citizens we'd have to supply the Social Security numbers, and they'll run a check on them straight off, so we'll know."

"Sounds good," Deborah said. "What time do you think the library opens?"

"My guess would be nine or ten," Joanna said. "But there's one other thing we should discuss. What about altering our appearances a bit more? I think our different hairstyles are quite effective and probably enough under the circumstances, but why not go a step further just to be sure."

"You mean like hair color."

"Hair color is one thing, but I'm also talking about our general style, our look. We're both rather preppy. I think we each ought to aim for another type."

"Well, I'm all for changing my hair color," Deborah said. "I've always wanted to be a blond. I've heard you guys have a lot more fun."

"I'm trying to be serious here," Joanna said.

"Okay, okay," Deborah said. "So what else do you have in mind: strategic facial piercings and a couple of wild tattoos?"

Joanna laughed in spite of herself. "Let's try to be serious for a moment. I'm thinking in terms of clothes and makeup. There's a lot that we could do."

"You're right," Deborah said. "Occasionally I've had a fantasy of dressing up like a hooker. I guess I have an exhibitionist streak; I've just never acted on it. This could be my big chance."

"Are you mocking me again or are you serious?"

"I'm serious," Deborah said. "We might as well make this fun."

"I was thinking about going in the opposite direction," Joanna said. "The prudish librarian stereotype."

"That will be easy," Deborah joked. "You're practically there already."

"Very funny," Joanna said.

Deborah wiped her mouth with her napkin and tossed it onto her pastry plate. "Are you finished?"

"I certainly am," Joanna said.

"Then let's get this show on the road," Deborah said. "On the way here we passed a grocery store. Why don't we stop in and get some staples so that we don't have to come out for every meal? By then the library should be open."

"It sounds like a perfect plan," Joanna said.

The women were standing on the front steps of the old Boston Library building gazing at the Trinity Church across the busy Copley Square when the library's custodian unlocked the front door. It was nine o'clock. Since neither of the women had been in the Boston Library before, they were, in Deborah's words, blown away by the grand architecture and the vivid John Singer Sargent murals.

"I can't believe I lived in the Boston area for six years and never came in here," Deborah said as they walked through the echoey, marbled halls. It was as if her head were on a swivel as it pivoted from side to side to take in all the details.

"I have to agree," Joanna said.

After inquiring where they could go to view old *Boston Globe* newspapers, the women were directed to the microfilm room. But once there they learned that there was a delay, sometimes as much as a year, before the papers were microfilmed. Consequently they were sent to the newspaper room. There they found the newspapers themselves.

"How far back should we go?" Deborah questioned.

"I'd suggest a month and then work backward," Joanna said.

The women got a stack of several weeks' worth of papers and carried them over to a vacant library table. They divided the stack in two and went to work.

"This isn't as easy as I thought it would be," Deborah said. "I was wrong about ages and birth dates. Few of the death notices have them."

"We'll have to just look at the obituaries," Joanna said. "They all seem to have the age."

The women went through the first stack

of papers without success and went back for another.

"There certainly aren't many young women," Joanna commented.

"Nor young men," Deborah added. "People our age are not supposed to die that often. And even if they do, they're usually not famous enough to have an obituary written about them. Of course we don't want the name of anyone famous either, so we might have a problem here. But let's not give up yet."

After three more trips to get fresh stacks of papers, they had success.

"Ah, here's one!" Deborah said. "Georgina Marks."

Joanna looked over Deborah's shoulder. "How old?"

"Twenty-seven," Deborah said. "She was born January 28, 1973."

"Right time frame," Joanna said. "Does it say what she died of?"

"Yes, it does," Deborah said. She was quiet while she scanned the rest of the article. "She was accidently shot in a shopping mall parking lot. Obviously in the wrong place at the wrong time. Apparently rival gangs were having a fight, and she

caught a stray bullet. Can you imagine being called up and being told your wife was
killed while she was out on a shopping trip
at the neighborhood mall?" Deborah shuddered. "To make it worse, it says here she
was the mother of four young children. The
youngest was only six months old."

"I think it is best if we don't obsess
about the sad details," Joanna said. "For
us, these should be just names, not
people."

"You're right," Deborah agreed. "At least
she wasn't famous except for the tragic
way she died, so it should be a good name
for our purposes. I suppose I'll be Georgina
Marks." She wrote the name and the birth
date down on a pad of paper she and
Joanna had brought.

"Now let's find a name for you," Deborah
said.

Both women went back to scouring the
obituaries. It wasn't until they'd perused six
more weeks of papers that Deborah came
across another name candidate.

"Prudence Heatherly, age twenty-four!"
Deborah read out loud. "Now that name
has an interesting ring to it. It's perfect for

you, Joanna. It even sounds like a librarian, so it will go with your disguise."

"I don't find that funny in the slightest," Joanna said. "Let me read the obituary." She reached for the paper, but Deborah moved it out of her reach.

"I thought we weren't going to obsess about the details?" Deborah teased.

"I'm not obsessing," Joanna said. "I want to make sure she's not a local celebrity in Bookford. Besides, I feel I have to know something about the woman if I'm going to be borrowing her name."

"I thought these were just names, not people."

"Please!" Joanna enunciated slowly as if losing her patience.

Deborah handed the paper over and watched her roommate's face while she read the obituary. Joanna's expression progressively sagged.

"Is it bad?" Deborah asked when Joanna looked up.

"I'd say it was just as bad as Georgina's story," Joanna said. "She was a graduate student at Northeastern."

"That's getting a little too close to

home," Deborah said. "What did she die of, or shouldn't I ask?"

"She was pushed in front of the Red Line subway at the Washington Street station." Now it was Joanna's turn to shudder. "A homeless man with no apparent motive did it. My word! What a tragedy for a parent getting a call saying your daughter was pushed in front of a train by a vagrant."

"At least we have the two names," Deborah said. She snatched the paper away from Joanna and refolded it. She wrote *Prudence Heatherly* down on the pad below Georgina, then busied herself restacking the papers. Joanna was motionless for a moment but then pitched in to help. Together the women carried the papers back to where they were kept.

Fifteen minutes later, first Deborah and then Joanna exited the library from the same entrance they'd entered. Although they were pensively subdued, they were pleased with their progress. It had only taken an hour and three quarters to get the two names.

"Should we walk or take the subway?" Deborah questioned.

"Let's take the subway," Joanna answered.

From the front of the library it was only a short walk to the inbound T stop on Boylston Street, and the Green Line took them directly to Government Center. When they emerged on the street level they were conveniently in front of the inappropriately modern Boston City Hall, which loomed out of its brick-paved mall like an enormous anachronism.

"Can you tell me where I'd find death certificates?" Joanna asked the receptionist at the information desk located in the building's multistoried lobby. Joanna had waited several minutes before speaking. The woman was involved in an animated but hushed dialogue with her colleague sitting next to her.

"They're downstairs at the Registry Department," the woman said without looking up and hardly interrupting her conversation.

Joanna rolled her eyes for Deborah's benefit. The two women set out for the wide stairs leading downward. Once on the lower level they found the proper Registry Department window without difficulty. The

only problem was there wasn't any personnel in evidence.

"Hello!" Deborah called out. "Anybody
home?"

A woman's head popped up from behind
a row of file cabinets. "Can I help you?"
she called out.

"We'd like several death certificates,"
Deborah answered back.

The woman ambled around the row of
file cabinets, rocking from side to side. She
was wearing a black dress that restrained
her ample flesh in a series of descending,
horizontal bulges. Reading glasses hung
around her neck on a chain and rested on
the nearly horizontal swelling of her
bosom. She came to the counter and
leaned on it. "I need to know the names
and the year," she said in a bored voice.

"Georgina Marks and Prudence
Heatherly," Joanna said. "And both passed
away this year, 2001."

"It takes a week to ten days for the certificates to get here," the woman said.

"We have to wait that long to get them?"
Joanna questioned with dismay.

"No, that's how long the death certificates take to get here to the registry after

the individual dies. I only mention it because if these people you're interested in have just passed away, the certificates won't be here."

"Both these people have been dead for over a month," Joanna said.

"Then they should be here," the woman said. "That will be six dollars each."

"We only want to look at the certificates," Joanna said. "We don't need to remove them from the premises."

"Six dollars each is fine," Deborah interjected. She gave Joanna a jab in the side to keep her quiet.

After writing the names down while eyeing Joanna skeptically, the woman leisurely disappeared behind the file cabinets.

"Why did you poke me?" Joanna complained.

"I didn't want you messing things up to save twelve dollars," Deborah whispered. "If the woman guesses we're here just to get Social Security numbers she might get suspicious. I think I would. So we'll pay the money, take the certificates, and get the hell out of here."

"I guess you're right," Joanna said reluctantly.

"Of course I'm right," Deborah said.

The clerk returned a quarter hour later with the forms. Deborah and Joanna had the money ready and the exchange was made. Five minutes later the women were back outside where each carefully copied down the respective Social Security numbers onto a piece of paper. They pocketed the death certificates.

"I suggest we try to memorize the numbers while we're on the way to the bank," Joanna said. "It might attract attention if we don't."

"Especially if we pulled out the death certificates by accident inside the bank," Deborah said.

Joanna chuckled. "I also think we should start addressing each other with our assumed names. Otherwise we'll forget in front of people and that could be a problem."

"Good point, Prudence," Deborah said with a chuckle of her own.

It was only a ten-minute walk from City Hall to the Charles River Plaza where the local branch of the Fleet Bank was located. For the most part the women were silent while committing the respective Social

Security numbers to their memories. When they turned into the Charles River Plaza, Joanna pulled Deborah to a stop.

"Let's discuss this for a moment before we go inside," she said. "We should open these accounts with just a token deposit because we're not going to be able to get this money back out."

"What do you suggest?"

"I don't think it really matters," Joanna said. "How about twenty dollars."

"Fine by me," Deborah said. "But I wouldn't mind hitting the ATM machine on the way in."

"That's not a bad idea either," Joanna said.

Each got several hundred dollars in cash before entering the bank proper. They then went directly to the service desk. Since it was in the middle of the lunch hour, the bank was busy with hospital people from the MGH, and the women had to wait almost twenty minutes before being helped. But setting up the accounts was accomplished quickly since the bank officer whose turn it was to help them was particularly efficient. Her name was Mary. The only minor problem was the lack of any

IDs, but Mary solved it by saying they could bring them in the following day. By one o'clock Mary had already excused herself to activate the accounts and get them receipts. Joanna and Deborah were sitting on vinyl chairs facing Mary's desk.

"What if she comes back and says we're dead?" Deborah whispered.

"Then we're dead," Joanna answered. "But that's what we're here for."

"But what are we going to say? We'd have to say something."

"We'll just say we must have been mistaken about the numbers. We'll tell them we'll check them and come back."

"I was enjoying myself a half hour ago," Deborah complained. "Now I'm nervous. We can't tell them a fishy story like that."

"Here she comes!" Joanna said in a forced whisper.

Mary came back clutching the deposit receipts. "I've got you all set up," she reported. "Every thing is just fine." She gave a receipt to each woman along with one of the packets of material sitting on her desk which she'd prepared earlier. "You're all set. Do you have a parking ticket?"

"No, we walked over," Joanna said. For

an address the women had given Seven Hawthorne Place, part of the Charles River Park apartment complex behind the hospital.

A few minutes later the women were back out in the May sunshine. Deborah was euphoric. "We did it!" she declared as they walked quickly away from the bank. "I had my doubts there for a minute, but apparently we've got good names and Social Security numbers."

"They're good for now," Joanna said. "But that's going to change sometime in the near future. Let's head back to the apartment, put in a call to the Wingate Clinic, and get the next step out of the way."

"What about a bit of lunch?" Deborah said. "I'm starved. That coffee and pastry we had a little after seven this morning is long gone."

"I could use some food myself," Joanna agreed. "But let's make it quick."

"Wingate Clinic," a pleasant voice said cheerfully. It came from the speaker phone in Joanna and Deborah's apartment. The telephone itself was on the couch between the women who were sitting on either side of it. It was two-thirty-five and sun was just beginning to spill onto the hardwood floor through the front windows.

"I'm interested in employment in your institution," Joanna said. "To whom should I speak?" The women had flipped a coin to see who should make the call. Joanna had won.

"That would be with Helen Masterson, Director of Personnel," the operator said. "Shall I connect you?"

"Please," Joanna said.

The same elevator music they'd heard the day before drifted out of the phone, but it didn't last long. A strong, deep, woman's voice preempted the Muzak. Both women jumped: "Helen Masterson here. I understand you are looking for employment."

"Yes, both myself and my roommate," Joanna said as soon as she'd recovered.

"What kind of experience do you and your roommate have?" Helen asked.

"I've had extensive word-processing experience," Joanna said.

"As a student or in a work environment?"

"Both," Joanna said. She'd worked summers during undergraduate school in a Houston law firm with whom her father did a great deal of business.

"Are you college graduates?"

"Yes, indeed," Joanna said. "I've a degree in economics. My roommate, Georgina Marks, was a biology major." Joanna looked over at Deborah who gave her a thumbs-up sign.

"Has she had any laboratory experience?"

Deborah nodded emphatically.

"Yes, she has," Joanna said.

"I must admit you both sound perfect for the Wingate Clinic," Helen said. "How did you hear about us?"

"Excuse me?" Joanna said while making a grimace of consternation for Deborah's benefit. It was a question she'd not anticipated. Deborah fumbled for the pad and pencil on the floor. While Helen repeated the question, she quickly wrote: "a friend saw an ad."

"Word of mouth," Joanna said. "A friend of ours saw an ad."

"Was that a newspaper ad or a radio ad?"

Joanna hesitated. Deborah shrugged.

"I'm not sure," Joanna said.

"Well, it doesn't matter except to know which is more effective," Helen said. "Do you live here in Bookford?"

"We currently live in Boston," Joanna said.

"So you are willing to reverse commute."

"That's the plan, at least for the time being. We'd be driving out together."

"Why do you want to work out here in Bookford?" Helen asked.

"We need to find work quickly," Joanna said. "We heard your organization was in need of help. We just got back from a rather long stay in Europe, and frankly we need the money."

"It sounds like we can help each other," Helen said. "I can either fax you or E-mail you employment questionnaires which you can fill out and send back the same way you got it. Which way would you prefer?"

"E-mail is fine," Joanna said. She gave Helen her E-mail address which conveniently had no association with her name.

"I'll E-mail forthwith," Helen said. "Meanwhile I think we should go ahead and schedule interviews. What would be a

convenient date for you and your roommate? Just about any day this week or
next week is available."

"The sooner the better," Joanna said.
Deborah nodded. "In fact, tomorrow would
be fine for us if it works for you."

"By all means," Helen said. "I applaud
your eagerness. Would ten o'clock be
okay?"

"Ten o'clock will be fine," Joanna said.

"Will you need directions?" Helen asked.

"I don't think that will be necessary,"
Joanna said. "We're quite resourceful."

"We look forward to seeing you tomorrow," Helen said before disconnecting.

Joanna hung up the phone.

"Very smooth!" Deborah commented. "I
think we're in."

"So do I," Joanna said. She unplugged
the phone and headed over to the computer. "Let's log on so we can get the
E-mail as soon as it comes in."

True to her word, Helen had sent the
E-mail within minutes of hanging up the
phone, and it popped up on the women's
computer screen just moments after they
logged on. Fifteen minutes later, Joanna
and Deborah had filled in their respective

employment forms directly on the screen and E-mailed them back to the Wingate Clinic.

"This almost seems too easy," Deborah commented as she shut down the computer.

"Don't jinx us," Joanna said. "You can call me superstitious, but I'm not going to say anything like that until after I get into the Wingate server room. There's too much that can still go wrong."

"You mean like one or both Social Security numbers suddenly going bad."

"Either that or someone like Dr. Donaldson recognizing us tomorrow morning."

"Let me guess," Deborah said. "You're back to thinking about the disguise idea."

"I've never stopped thinking about it," Joanna said. "And we have the rest of the afternoon. So let's do it. We can head over to the Galleria Mall in Cambridge and, without spending much, get ourselves some new outfits."

"I'm game," Deborah said. "The trendy tart . . . that's going to be me. Maybe I can find something with an exposed midriff that I can combine with a Miracle Bra. Then on the way back we can stop at CVS and get some hair coloring and extra makeup. Do you remember the receptionist when we were out at the Wingate doing the egg donations?"

"It would be hard to forget her," Joanna said.

"I'm going to give her a run for her money," Deborah declared.

"I don't think we should go overboard on this," Joanna said skeptically. "We don't want to draw attention to ourselves unnecessarily."

"Speak for yourself," Deborah said. "You don't want us recognized, and I'm going to make sure it doesn't happen, especially with me."

"But we want them to give us jobs," Joanna said.

"No need to worry," Deborah said. "I'm not going to go *that* far."

eight

MAY 9, 2001
8:45 A.M.

Spencer Wingate tossed aside the magazine he'd been reading and looked out at the countryside spread out below. Spring had finally arrived with its typical New England sluggishness. The patchwork of fields and meadows had assumed a deep, verdant green color although isolated patches of ice and snow were still visible in the deeper gullies and ravines. Many of the hardwoods were still without leaves, but they were covered with delicate yellow-green buds ready to burst, which gave the undulating hills a softness, as if they were upholstered in diaphanous green fleece.

"How much longer before we touch down at Hanscom Field?" Spencer called out, loud enough for the pilot to hear over the whine of the jet engines. Spencer was in a Lear 45; he owned a quarter share, although not of the plane he was currently in. Two years previously he'd signed on with one of the fractional-ownership companies, and the service had served his needs admirably.

"Less than twenty minutes, sir," the pilot yelled back over his shoulder. "There's no traffic so we'll be flying directly in."

Spencer nodded and stretched. He was looking forward to returning to Massachusetts, and the vista of the quaint southern New England farms fanned the fires of his anticipation. He'd wintered for the second year in a row in Naples, Florida, and this season he'd become bored, especially over the last months. Now he couldn't wait to get back, and it wasn't just because the Wingate Infertility Clinic's profits were down.

Three years previously, with the clinic purring and money pouring in faster than

he'd ever deemed possible, he'd fanta-
sized about retiring to play golf, write a
novel that would become a movie, date
beautiful women, and generally relax. With
that goal in mind, he'd started a search for
a younger man to take the day-to-day reins
of his booming business. Serendipitously
he'd found an eager individual fresh from
an infertility fellowship at an institution
where Spencer had lectured; he'd seemed
heaven-sent.

With the business taken care of,
Spencer turned his attention to where he'd
go. On the advice of a patient who had extensive experience with Florida real estate,
he found a condominium on the west coast
of Florida. Once the deal had been con-
summated, he'd headed toward the sun.

Unfortunately, reality did not live up to
his fantasy. He was able to play a lot of
golf, but his competitively busy mind found
it less fulfilling than he would have liked
over the long haul, especially since he
could never rise above an irritating level of
mediocrity. Spencer considered himself a
winner and found losing intolerable. Ultimately he decided there was something
basically wrong with the sport.

And the idea of writing turned out to be even more of a bust. He discovered it was harder work than he'd envisioned, and it required a degree of discipline he did not have. But worse yet, there was no immediate positive feedback like he'd gotten seeing patients. Consequently and rather quickly he gave up the novel-movie idea as not suitable for his more active personality.

The social situation was the biggest disappointment. Throughout most of his life, Spencer had felt he'd had to sacrifice experiencing the kind of lifestyle his looks and talents should have provided. He'd married in medical school, mostly out of loneliness, a woman whom he came to recognize as beneath him both intellectually and socially. Once the children, which had come early, were off to college, Spencer had divorced. Luckily it had been before the Wingate Infertility Clinic had taken off. The wife had gotten the house, which had been no great shakes, and a one-time payment.

"Dr. Wingate?" the pilot called over his shoulder. "Should I radio ahead for ground transportation?"

"My car should be there," Spencer yelled back. "Have them bring it out on the tarmac."

"Aye, aye, sir!" the pilot answered.

Spencer went back to his musings. Although there'd been no dearth of beautiful women in Naples, he had trouble meeting them, and those he did meet were difficult to impress. Although Spencer thought himself rich, in Naples there was always someone a quantum leap ahead in both wealth and the trappings that came with it.

So the only part of Spencer's original retirement dream that had come to pass was the opportunity to relax. But even that had become old after the first season, and hardly fulfilling. Then came the news beginning in January that the clinic's profits were falling. At first Spencer thought it was surely an aberration or an accounting trick of writing off a major liability in one month, but unfortunately, it continued. Spencer looked into it as best he could from afar. It wasn't that revenues had dropped. Quite the contrary. It was because the research costs had skyrocketed, suggesting that

Spencer's on-site leadership was sorely needed. Back when Paul Saunders had first come on board, Spencer had told him that he encouraged research, but obviously things had gotten out of hand.

"They tell me your car is already in front of the JetSmart Aviation building," the pilot called back to Spencer. "And buckle up. We're beginning our final approach."

Spencer flashed the pilot a thumbs-up sign. His seat belt was already fastened. Glancing out the window as they came in for the touchdown, he saw his burgundy Bentley convertible gleaming in the morning sun. He loved the car. Vaguely he wondered if he shouldn't have taken it to Naples. Perhaps with it he would have had better luck with the ladies.

Spring was a season which Joanna had always loved with its flowers and with its promise of warm, soft summer evenings to come. Spring had always arrived early in Houston with an avalanche of color that overnight transformed the dull, flat landscape into a fairyland of azaleas, tulips, and dogwoods. As she drove northwest out of Boston on the way to Bookford she tried to concentrate on such happy re-membrances and the euphoria they engen-dered, but it wasn't easy.

First of all there were few flowers in evi-dence and hence not much color save for the green grass and the light green of the budding trees. Second of all she was irri-tated at Deborah, who was sitting next to her and happily singing along with the ra-dio tuned to soft rock. Although her room-mate had promised *I'm not going to go that far* with her disguise, in Joanna's estima-tion she'd gone beyond the pale. Her hair was now strawberry blond, her lips and augmented nails a bright crimson, and she was attired in a décolleté, miniskirted dress combined with a padded Miracle Bra and high-heeled shoes. The final touch was dangling earrings and a tiny rhinestone-studded heart necklace. In sharp contrast, Joanna had on a dark blue mid-calf-length skirt, a buttoned high-necked white blouse, a pale pink, cardigan sweater also buttoned up to the top, and clear-plastic-rimmed glasses. Her hair was dyed a mousy brown.

"I seriously doubt you are going to get a job," Joanna said suddenly, breaking a long silence. "And maybe I won't either because of you."

Deborah switched her attention from staring out the windshield to her roommate's profile. Although she didn't say anything immediately, she leaned forward and switched off the radio.

Joanna's eyes diverted briefly to Deborah's, then back to the road ahead.

"Is that why you're so quiet?" Deborah asked. "You've not said boo practically since we left this morning."

"You promised me you wouldn't turn this into a joke," Joanna said.

Deborah looked down at her pantyhose-covered knees for a moment. "This is no joke," she said. "This is called taking advantage of an opportunity and having a bit of fun."

"You call it fun, and I call it a study in bad taste."

"That's your taste," Deborah said. "And, ironically, mine too. But not everybody would agree with you, particularly not the male population."

"You don't seriously think men are going to be turned on by your appearance, do you?"

"Actually, I think they will be," Deborah said. "Not all men, mind you, but a lot. I've watched men react to women dressed like this. There's always a reaction, perhaps not for reasons I care about, but nonetheless a reaction, and for once in my life I'm going to experience it."

"I think it's a myth," Joanna said. "I think it's a female distortion similar to men's idea that women are turned on by brawn and big muscles."

"Nah! I don't think it's the same at all," Deborah said with a wave of her hand. "Besides, you're speaking from your old traditional female upbringing with dating serving as a prelude to marriage. Let me remind you yet again that men can look at women and dating as being a game or even a sport. They see it as entertainment, just as, I'd also like to remind you, the modern twenty-first-century woman can."

"I don't want to get into an argument about this issue," Joanna said. "The problem is, we've an appointment with a woman, and I doubt that she is going to be amused with your appearance. The bottom line is that I don't think you will get a job, pure and simple."

"I disagree on that regard as well," Deborah said. "The personnel director is a woman, I grant you that. But she's got to be a realist about recruitment. I'm applying for a job in a laboratory, not out in the front meeting patients. Besides, they saw fit to hire that redhead receptionist who was almost as provocatively dressed as I am."

"But why even take the chance?" Joanna complained.

"The worry was, as you voiced it yourself, whether or not we'd be recognized," Deborah said. "Trust me! We're not going to be recognized. On top of that we're having a little fun. I'm not going to give up trying to loosen you up and keep you from having a social relapse."

"Oh, sure!" Joanna said. "Now you're going to try to convince me that your dressing up like a tart is for my benefit. Give me a break!"

"All right, mostly for me, but a little for you too."

By the time they got to Bookford and drove through town, Joanna had reconciled herself to Deborah's appearance. She imagined that the worst-case scenario would be for Deborah not to get a job, but there was little reason that Deborah's difficulties would affect her chances. Deborah's not getting a job would hardly be a disaster. After all, Joanna had originally planned to go to the Wingate Clinic by herself. It was Deborah who'd insisted on coming along.

"Do you remember where the turnoff is?" Joanna asked. On the previous visit she'd not been driving, and whenever she was the passenger she had difficulty remembering landmarks.

"It will be on the left just after this upcoming curve," Deborah said. "I remember it was just beyond this barn on the right."

"You're right; I see the sign," Joanna said as she straightened the car after the turn. She slowed and pulled off onto the gravel road. Ahead they could see the stone gatehouse. Nosing into the tunnel beneath the house and barring their way was a line of trucks. The uniformed guard could be seen, clipboard in hand, apparently conversing with the driver inside the cab of the first truck.

"Looks like delivery time for the farm," Deborah said. The back of the last truck said WEBSTER ANIMAL FEED.

"What time is it?" Joanna asked. She was concerned about the time since they'd ended up leaving the apartment twenty minutes later than intended, having had to wait for Deborah's nails to dry.

"It's five before ten," Deborah said.

"Oh great!" Joanna commented despairingly. "I hate to be late for appointments, especially if I'm applying for a job."

"We can only do the best we can," Deborah said.

Joanna nodded. She loathed patronizing comments like that, and she knew Deborah knew it, but she didn't say anything. She didn't want to give Deborah the satisfaction. Instead she drummed the steering wheel.

Minutes ticked by. Joanna's drumming picked up its pace. She sighed and glanced up into the rearview mirror with the intention of checking how her hair had weathered the trip. Before she could adjust the mirror she caught sight of a car turning off Pierce Street onto the gravel road. While she watched, the car drove toward them, slowed, and stopped immediately behind.

"Do you remember that Bentley convertible we saw in the clinic's parking lot the last time we were here?" Joanna asked.

"Vaguely," Deborah said. Cars had never interested her other than to get from point A to point B and she could not distinguish between a Chevy and a Ford or between a BMW and a Mercedes.

"It just drove up behind us," Joanna reported.

"Oh," Deborah commented. She turned and looked out the back of the car. "Oh yeah, I remember it."

"I wonder if it's one of the doctors?" Joanna said while continuing to eye the burgundy vehicle in the rearview mirror. With the glare on the windshield, she could not see the interior.

Deborah checked her watch again. "Gosh, it's after ten. What's the deal? That stupid guard is still talking with that truck driver. What on earth could they be talking about?"

"I guess they're careful who they let on the grounds."

"That might be the case, but we have an

appointment," Deborah said. She un-latched the door and slid out.

"Where are you going?" Joanna asked.

"I'm going to find out what's going on," Deborah said. "This is ridiculous." She slammed the door, then rounded the front of the car. Teetering on her toes to keep her narrow heels from penetrating into the gravel, she started forward toward the gatehouse.

Despite her earlier irritation, Joanna had to laugh at her roommate's gait until she noticed that Deborah's short skirt was hiked up on her backside thanks to static cling with her panty hose. Letting down the window, she leaned out.

"Hey! Marilyn Monroe! Your rear end is hanging out!"

Using the knuckles of both index fingers, Spencer rubbed his eyes briefly to bring them into better focus. He'd pulled up behind the nondescript Chevy Malibu, feeling irritated that now that he was finally here, his way was blocked by a mini traffic jam. He'd seen the two heads in the car in front but had thought nothing of them until one of them had gotten out.

For Spencer it was like seeing a mirage. The woman appeared like the person he'd been searching for and not finding the entire time he'd been in Naples. Not only was she attractive with a slim, athletic body, but she was dressed in an alluring style the likes of which he'd not seen except on rare visits to Miami's South Beach. To make the unexpected situation even more provocative, the woman's dress was pulled up in the back exposing a near-naked, pantyhose-clad derriere.

Emboldened by a sense of being on home turf, Spencer did not hesitate like he would have had he still been in Naples. He opened his door and got out. He'd heard the yell from the woman's companion, and now the skirt was down where it was supposed to be, yet it still hovered above mid-thigh, and being made of a synthetic, clingy fabric, it undulated sensuously as the woman unsteadily walked over the gravel drive.

Launching himself forward in a jog, Spencer headed toward the gatehouse in hot pursuit. As he passed the women's

Malibu he caught a fleeting glimpse of the companion, which was enough to tell him she was of a totally different ilk. Slowing to a walk, he passed the first truck and approached the woman whose back was to him. She was arguing, arms akimbo, with the guard.

"Well, have them back up the damn trucks and let us go by," Deborah was saying. "We have an appointment with Ms. Masterson, head of personnel, and we're already late."

The guard with his clipboard was unintimidated. His eyebrows were raised and he had a smirk on his face as he peered down at Deborah through his aviator sunglasses. He started to respond to her suggestion, but Spencer interrupted him.

"What seems to be the problem here?" Spencer questioned in the most authoritarian tone he could muster. Unconsciously mimicking Deborah's stance, he put his hands on his hips.

The guard glanced at Spencer and told him in no uncertain terms it was none of his business and that he should get back in his vehicle. He used the words *please* and *sir* but obviously intended them as mere formalities.

"These feed trucks are not on his list," Deborah explained contemptuously. "They're acting like this is Fort Knox, for crying out loud."

"Perhaps a call down to the farm will clear things up," Spencer suggested.

"Listen, sir!" the guard said, pronouncing *sir* as if it were an epithet. He pointed toward Spencer's Bentley with the clipboard with one hand while resting the other on the top of his holstered automatic. "I want you back in that car ASAP."

"Don't you dare threaten me," Spencer growled. "For your information, I'm Dr. Spencer Wingate."

The guard's menacing expression quavered as he stared Spencer in the eye. It appeared as if he were having an internal debate as to how to proceed. Deborah's attention switched from the guard to Spencer with his surprising announcement. She found herself looking up into the face of the stereotypic soap-opera doctor: tall, slender, angled face, tanned skin, and silver-gray hair.

Before anyone could verbally respond,

the heavy windowless black door opened. A muscular man emerged, dressed in a black knit shirt, black pants, and black cross-trainer shoes. His dirty-blond hair was cropped short. He moved as if in slow motion, closing the door behind him. "Dr. Wingate," he said calmly. "You should have warned us you were coming."

"What's with these trucks sitting here, Kurt?" Spencer demanded.

"We're waiting for Dr. Saunders's okay," Kurt responded. "They were not on the manifest, and Dr. Saunders likes to be informed of irregularities."

"They're feed trucks, for chrissake," Spencer pronounced. "You have my okay. Send them down to the farm so we can get in here."

"As you wish," Kurt said. He took a plastic card from a pocket and swiped it through a card swipe mounted on a pole near the first truck's cab. Immediately the heavy chain-link fence began to squeak open.

In response to the gate's movement, the driver of the lead truck started his diesel engine. In the confined space within the gatehouse tunnel the noise was considerable as were the fumes. Deborah quickly moved outside as did Spencer.

"Thank you for solving that problem," Deborah said. She noticed that the doctor's eyes, which were darting up and down her frame, were almost the same blue as those of the security man in black.

"My pleasure," Spencer said. To his despair his voice cracked as he tried to camouflage a surge of nervousness talking with Deborah directly. Up close, with the amount of cleavage visible, he could tell that her dark olive skin wasn't tan as he'd originally assumed. It was her normal coloring. He also noticed her eyebrows were dark, as were her eyes. Combining it all with the blond hair gave him the impression she was a wild and sensual free spirit.

"Well, see you around, doctor," Deborah said. She smiled and started back toward the car.

"Just a moment," Spencer called out.

Deborah stopped and turned.

"What is your name, if I may ask?"

"Georgina Marks," Deborah responded. She felt her pulse quicken. It was the first time she'd used the alias.

"Is it true you have an appointment with Helen Masterson?"

"At ten o'clock," Deborah answered. "Unfortunately we're late, thanks to that security fellow."

"I will give her a call and let her know it was not your fault."

"Thank you. That's very kind of you."

"So you are looking for work here at the clinic?"

"Yes," Deborah said. "My roommate and I are both interested. We plan to commute together."

"Interesting," Spencer said. "What kind of work are you looking for?"

"I've a degree in molecular biology," Deborah said, being purposefully vague about the level. "I'd like to work in the lab."

"Molecular biology! I'm impressed," Spencer said sincerely. "From what school may I ask?"

"Harvard," Deborah said. She and Joanna had discussed this issue when they'd filled out the E-mailed employment applications. Since they were concerned about being recognized from the Harvard association, they'd considered naming a different school. But they'd decided to be truthful to be able to field any specific questions about their college training.

"Harvard!" Spencer responded. He was momentarily nonplussed. Molecular biology had been enough of a surprise. Harvard only made it worse, suggesting that Deborah might not be quite as much the free spirit he'd originally taken her to be and perhaps not so easily impressible. "What about your roommate?" he asked to change the subject. "Is she looking for lab work as well?"

"No, Prudence—Prudence Heatherly— would like to work in the office," Deborah said. "She's skilled in word processing and computers in general."

"Well, I'm sure we can use both of you," Spencer said. "And let me make a suggestion: Why don't you and your roommate come to my office after you see Helen?"

Deborah tilted her head to the side and squinted her eyes as if she were assessing Spencer's motives.

"Maybe we could have a coffee or something," Spencer suggested.

"How would I find you?" Deborah asked.

"Just ask Helen," Spencer said. "As I

said, I'll be giving her a call about you, and I'll mention we'll be getting together."

"I'll do that," Deborah said. She smiled, then turned around and headed back toward the car.

Spencer watched her go. He couldn't help but notice the voluptuous way her buttocks moved beneath the silky synthetic fabric of her skirt. Although he could tell it was an inexpensive garment, he thought it was erotically flattering. "Harvard," he marveled to himself. He would have thought his old high school alma mater, Sommerville High, more likely and ultimately more promising.

"How can anyone walk around in shoes like this all day?" Deborah questioned as she climbed back into the car.

"You should see yourself," Joanna laughed. "It's hilarious!"

"Careful!" Deborah warned. "You're going to undermine my self-esteem."

Joanna restarted the car as the truck in front began to move. "I noticed you were talking with that gentleman with the Bentley."

"You'll never guess who he is," Deborah said coyly.

Joanna put the car in gear and began to move forward slowly. To her chagrin Deborah, as usual, was making her ask. Joanna resisted for several beats, but her curiosity prevailed. "All right, who is he?" she questioned.

"Dr. Wingate himself! And contrary to your concerns, he was titillated by my outfit."

"Titillated or contemptuous? There's a big difference, although it might not be apparent."

"Without doubt, the former," Deborah said. "I have proof: We're invited for coffee after we see the personnel director."

"Are you joking?"

"Absolutely not," Deborah said triumphantly.

Joanna nosed the car into the tunnel. Spencer was still there between the man in black and the uniformed guard. Although the gate was open, it started to close with the distance Joanna had allowed to develop between herself and the truck. Spencer motioned to Joanna to stop. She did and rolled down the window.

"I'll be looking forward to seeing you ladies later," he said. "Enjoy your interviews." From his wallet he pulled a blue plastic card similar to the one the man in black had used earlier, and ran it through the card swipe. The gate stopped, lurched, and then began swinging open again. Spencer motioned for them to drive on with a gracious welcoming gesture.

"He's rather distinguished-looking," Joanna said as she motored out of the tunnel.

"I should say," Deborah agreed.

"Strangely enough, he bears a strong resemblance to my father."

"Now you're the one joking," Deborah said. She looked over at Joanna. "I don't think he looks like your father in the slightest. To me he looks like a doctor on a soap opera."

"I'm serious," Joanna said. "He has the same build and the same coloring. Even the same cold aloofness."

"You have to be reading the aloofness into him," Deborah said. "With me he was anything but aloof. You should have seen the gymnastics his eyeballs were doing thanks to the cleavage my Miracle Bra has created."

"You don't think he looks a little like my father?"

"Nope!"

Joanna shrugged. "That's strange, because I do. Maybe it's something subliminal."

The car cleared the stand of evergreens just beyond the gatehouse, affording the women the first full view of the old Cabot building.

"This place is even grimmer than I remembered," Deborah said. She leaned forward to get a better look through the front windshield. "I don't even remember those stone gargoyles on the downspouts."

"There's so much Victorian decoration it's hard to take it all in at once," Joanna said. "It's certainly easy to see why the employees call it the monstrosity."

The curving driveway bore them up to the parking area on the south side. Just as they broached the top of the hill, the smokestack could be seen off to the east. As was the case when Deborah saw it previously, it was belching smoke.

"You know," Deborah said, "that chimney reminds me there was something about this place I forgot to tell you."

Joanna found a parking spot and pulled in. She turned off the ignition. Silently she counted to ten, hoping that for once Deborah would finish one of her delayed thoughts without Joanna having to ask. "I give up," she said at length. "What did you forget to tell me about?"

"The Cabot had its own crematorium as part of its power plant. It gave me a queasy feeling when I was told about it, wondering if some of the inmates' remains back then could have been used to heat the place."

"What a ghastly thought," Joanna responded. "Why on earth did you think that?"

"I couldn't help it," Deborah said. "The crematorium, the barbed-wire fence, laborers they must have had for the farm—they made me think of Nazi concentration camps."

"Let's go inside," Joanna said. She wasn't about to grace such a thought with a response. She opened the car door and got out. Deborah did the same on her side.

"A crematorium would also be a handy way to cover up any mistakes or mischief of any sort," Deborah added.

"We're late," Joanna said. "Let's get in there and get these jobs."

nine

The odor was warm, moist, fetid, and offensively feral. Paul Saunders was wearing a surgical mask but not for antiseptic purposes. It was purely because he found the smell intolerable in the sow's birthing stall. He was standing with Sheila Donaldson and Greg Lynch, the powerfully built veterinarian he'd been able to entice away from the Tufts University veterinary program with a high salary and the promise of stock options. He and Sheila had surgical gowns over their street clothes and were sporting

rubber boots. Greg had on a massive rubber apron and heavy rubber gloves.

"I thought you said this birth was imminent," Paul complained. He had his arms
crossed and his hands in surgical gloves.

"All indications are that it is," Greg said.
"Besides, we're at day two hundred and
eighty-nine in this pregnancy. She's long
overdue." He patted the pig's head, and
the animal let out a loud prolonged squeal.

"Can't we induce her?" Paul said, winc-
ing at the high pitched shriek. He looked
over the stall's railing at Carl Smith as if to
ask whether Carl had brought any oxytocin
or any other kind of uterine stimulant. Carl
was standing by the anesthesia machine
they'd purchased for the farm. He was
there in case of an emergency.

"It's best we just let nature take its
course," Greg said. "It's coming. Trust me."

No sooner were the words out of Greg's
mouth than a shower of amniotic fluid
sprayed out over the straw-covered floor
accompanied by another ear-splitting
squeal. Both Paul and Sheila had to leap
out of the way to avoid being drenched by
the warm fluid.

Paul rolled his eyes once he'd regained

his footing. "The indignities I have to bear in the name of science!" he complained. "It's unreal!"

"Things are going to happen pretty quickly now," Greg said. He positioned himself behind the animal, vainly trying to avoid stepping in the feces. The animal was on her side.

"Not soon enough to suit me," Paul said. He looked at Sheila. "When was the last ultrasound?"

"Yesterday," Sheila said. "And I didn't like the size of the umbilical vessels I was able to visualize. You remember I told you, right?"

"Yes, I remember," Paul said, shaking his head dejectedly. "Sometimes the failures we have to endure in this business get to me, especially in this part of the research. If this batch is again all stillborn, I'm going to be at a loss. I don't know what else to try."

"We can at least try to be optimistic," Sheila suggested.

A phone rang in the background. One of the animal handlers watching from the sidelines ran to get it.

The pig squealed again. "Here we go,"

Greg said. He thrust his gloved hand inside the animal. "She's dilated now. Give me some room."

Paul and Sheila were more than happy to move as far out of the way as the stall would allow.

"Dr. Saunders, I'm supposed to give you a message," the animal handler said. He'd returned from answering the phone and had come up to Paul's right side.

Paul waved the man away. The first of the litter was crowning amid squeals from the mother pig. The next instant, the first-born was out. But it did not look good, and the dusky blue creature made only feeble attempts to breathe. The umbilical vessels were huge, more than twice the normal size. Greg tied them off and then got ready for the next.

Once the births had started, they happened in rapid succession. Within minutes the entire litter was lined up on the stall's straw-covered floor, bloody and unmoving. Carl had made a motion to pick up the first one to try to resuscitate it, but Paul told him not to bother because there was obviously too much congenital malformation. For several minutes the group silently

stared at the pitiful newborns. The sow instinctively ignored them.

"The idea of using the human mitochondria obviously didn't work," Paul said
breaking the silence. "It's discouraging. I
thought my idea was brilliant. It made so
much sense, yet you can tell just by looking at these creatures they all have the
same cardiopulmonary pathology as the
last group."

"At least we're getting them to go to
term consistently," Greg said. "When we
started we were dealing with first-trimester
miscarriages every time."

Paul sighed. "I want to see a normal off-
spring, not a stillborn. I'm long past seeing
them getting to term as any sign of success."

"Should we autopsy them?" Sheila
asked.

"I suppose, to be complete," Paul said
without enthusiasm. "We know what the
pathology is because it's obviously the
same as last time, but it should be docu-
mented for posterity. What we need to
know is how to eliminate it, so it's back to
the proverbial drawing board."

"What about the ovaries?" Sheila asked.

"That goes without saying," Paul said. "That's got to be done now, while they're still alive. The autopsies can wait. If need be, after the ovaries are taken, you can put these creatures in the cooler and autopsy them when convenient. But once the autopsies are done, incinerate the carcasses."

"What about the placenta?" Sheila asked.

"That should be photographed along with the sow," Paul said. He gave the bloody mass a nudge with his rubber boot. "It should also be autopsied. It, too, is obviously abnormal."

"Dr. Saunders," the animal handler said. "About that phone call . . ."

"For chrissake stop pestering me about the phone!" Paul yelled. "Because if it's about those damn feed trucks, I don't care if they sit out there for twenty-four hours. They were supposed to have arrived yesterday, not today."

"It was not about the trucks," the animal handler said. "In fact, the trucks are already here at the farm."

"What?" Paul cried. "I specifically said

they were not to come in until I gave the okay, and I did not give the okay."

"They got the okay from Dr. Wingate," the animal handler said. "That's what the phone message was about. Dr. Wingate is here at the clinic and wants to see you over at the monstrosity."

For a moment the only sounds in the vast barn were the occasional distant moos of the cows, squeals of the other pigs, and the barking of the dogs. Paul and Sheila looked at each other with surprise.

"Did you know he was coming back?" Paul asked Sheila eventually.

"I had no idea," Sheila said.

Paul looked over at Carl.

"Don't look at me," Carl said. "I didn't have any idea, either."

Paul shrugged. "Just one more challenge, I suppose."

"Well, there you have it, Miss Heatherly and Miss Marks," Helen Masterson said, concluding her canned preemployment monologue. She leaned back in her desk chair with her palms and fingers pressed together as if praying. She was a husky woman with a ruddy, fleshy face, dimpled chin, and a short no-nonsense hairstyle. When she smiled her eyes were reduced to mere slits. Both Joanna and Deborah were seated in front of her on the other side of the woman's cluttered desk. "If the conditions, rules, and salary that I've laid out are acceptable, we here at the Wingate Clinic are pleased to offer you women employment."

Joanna and Deborah briefly looked at each other and nodded.

"Sounds good to me," Deborah said.

"To me too," Joanna agreed.

"Wonderful," Helen said with a smile, making her eyes all but disappear. "Now do you have any questions for me?"

"Yes," Joanna said. "We'd like to start as soon as possible. In fact, we were hoping tomorrow could be our first day. Is that possible?"

"That's rather difficult," Helen said. "It doesn't give us time to process your applications." She hesitated for a moment before continuing: "But, I suppose, that shouldn't necessarily restrict us, and frankly we're expanding so quickly we can use the help. So, if we can get you to be seen today by Dr. Paul Saunders who insists on meeting all new employees, and get you processed by security, why not?"

"What does it mean to be processed by security?" Joanna asked. She exchanged glances with Deborah.

"That's really just to get you an access card," Helen said. "It gets you in the front gate and allows you to log on to the computer at your workstation. It can do more than that, of course, depending on how it's programmed."

Joanna's eyebrows raised at Helen's mention of the computer. It was a gesture unnoticed by the personnel director but seen by Deborah.

"I'm curious about your computer setup," Joanna said. "Since I assume I'll be doing a lot of word processing, I'd like to learn more about it. For example, I assume your system has multi-layered authorization levels."

"I'm no expert in the computer arena," Helen said with a nervous laugh. "I'll have to refer you to our network administrator, Randy Porter, for definitive answers. But if I understand your question, the answer is certainly yes. Our local area network is set up to recognize various groups of users, each with distinct access privileges. But don't worry, both of you will certainly have appropriate privileges for your designated work if that's your concern."

Joanna nodded. "It is my concern, especially since the system sounds sophisticated. Would it be possible for me to see the hardware itself? I imagine that would give me a good idea about what to expect."

"I don't see any reason why not," Helen said. "Any other questions?"

"I have a question," Deborah said. "We ran into Dr. Wingate at the front gate. He said he was going to get in touch with you about us? Did he?"

"Yes, he did," Helen said. "Which was a bit of a surprise. And I'm to take you to his office when you are finished with me. Any other questions?"

Joanna and Deborah looked at each other before shaking their heads.

"Then I have some questions of my own," Helen said. "I know you are planning on commuting back and forth to Boston, but I'd like you to think about the very nice accommodations we have here on the premises, which we encourage our staff to utilize, since we prefer our employees to live here. Would you be willing to see the units? It would only take a few minutes. We have a golf cart out back to take us over there."

Joanna started to decline, but Deborah overrode her by saying it might be interesting to see the apartments if they had time.

"Well, that leads me to one final question," Helen said. She looked at Deborah. "I don't know how to word this, Miss Marks, but do you always dress so . . . so flamboyantly?"

Joanna suppressed a giggle as Deborah stumbled over an explanation for her style of dress.

"Well, perhaps you could tone it down a tad," Helen said, trying to be diplomatic. "We're health-care professionals, after all." Without waiting for a response from Deborah, Helen picked up her phone and dialed an extension. The ensuing conversation was short. She merely asked if "Napoleon" was in, listened for a moment nodding her head, and then said she'd be over straightaway with two new recruits.

Helen stood up and the women followed

suit. As they did they could see over the tops of the dividers that separated the large, high-ceilinged former ward into individual work spaces. They were in the administration area located on the second floor and where Joanna was slotted to work. The windows of those cubicles which had them looked out over the front of the building, affording a commanding view to the west. Few heads were visible in the maze of work spaces. It was as if most everyone were on a coffee break.

"Come with me," Helen said, stepping out of her cubicle. She started off down the central aisle while talking over her thick shoulder. "We'll have you meet Dr. Saunders. It's a pro forma exercise, but we should have his imprimatur before proceeding any further."

"You remember who he is, don't you?" Joanna whispered to Deborah as they followed a few steps behind the personnel director. Helen wended her way out into the corridor which separated the administration area from the laboratory located on the east side of the wing.

"Of course I remember," Deborah said.

"It will be the first test if we're going to get away with this."

"I'm not concerned about him," Joanna said. "It's Dr. Donaldson that I'm worried about. Dr. Saunders didn't look at my face long enough to remember me, at least not while I was awake."

"He looked at me long enough," Deborah said, "and he was not a happy camper, as I told you."

Helen suddenly stopped by a door that had a NO ADMITTANCE sign posted on it. "Why not?" she said after a beat and without explanation. She opened the door, which was unlocked, and passed through. The women followed. The twenty-foot-long corridor beyond dead-ended at a blank second door. Helen tried the door, but it was locked. She took out her wallet and extracted a blue swipe card similar to the one Spencer had used to open the outside gate. Careful to keep the magnetic strip properly oriented, she passed the card rapidly through a card swipe attached to the wall next to the door. There was a click. When she retried the door, it opened.

Helen pushed the door wide open and stepped to the side. She looked back at

Joanna. "This is our computer server room. There's our equipment. Beyond that I can't tell you very much."

Joanna's eyes swept the windowless room whose floor had been raised eight inches to conceal the wiring. There were four large vertically oriented electronic units and a small bookcase filled with manuals. More importantly, there was a server console with a keyboard, a mouse, and a monitor displaying an active screen saver. Golden sting rays and blue-gray sharks endlessly swam to and fro. A single empty ergonomic chair sat in front of the console.

"Very impressive," Joanna said.

"I wouldn't know," Helen admitted. "Have you seen enough?"

Joanna nodded. "Will I have access to this room with my card?" she asked.

\ Helen regarded her as if she'd said something inordinately stupid. "Of course not! Clearance for spaces such as this is reserved to department heads only. Why would you want to come in here anyway?"

Joanna shrugged. "Only if I were having a problem I couldn't rectify from my workstation keyboard."

"For that kind of a problem, you'll have

to see Randy Porter, if you can find him. I have to admit, he's fairly elusive if he's not in his cubicle." Helen closed the door, and it locked with a resounding click.

"On to see our fearless leader," Helen said. She retraced her steps back to the main corridor and set out again. Acting as if the slight detour to see the server room had caused them to be late, she upped her pace. Joanna and Deborah had to hurry to keep up. Deborah's heels striking against the terrazzo floor made loud cracking noises like automatic-rifle fire. The vaulted ceiling magnified the sounds by producing multiple echoes.

"What do you think?" Deborah whispered between breaths.

"If we don't luck out and get the access we need to our files, then I'll have to get into that room for about ten or fifteen minutes."

"Which means we'll need a blue card that will open the door. Apparently ours won't. How are we going to manage that?"

"We'll have to be creative," Joanna said.

"I'm sorry to have to hurry you like this," Helen called back to the women from where she was holding open a heavy fire door leading from the building's south wing into the central tower. "Dr. Saunders can be hard to corner. If he leaves his office before we arrive, we could have trouble finding him, and if you don't get to see him, you will not be starting work tomorrow."

Joanna and Deborah passed through the fire door which Helen let close behind her. The women found themselves in a dramatically different environment. Instead of terrazzo the floor was oak, and instead of tile, plaster, or exposed brick, the walls were paneled mahogany. There was even a threadbare oriental runner extending down the long hallway.

"Come on!" Helen urged. She led the women down the corridor and through a doorway into an outer office. A secretary sat at a desk behind which were two doors: one closed, the other ajar. There were several couches and a coffee table.

"Don't tell me we missed Dr. Saunders?" Helen inquired of the secretary.

"He's still here," the woman said as she gestured over her shoulder at the closed door. "But he's engaged at the moment."

Helen's face registered understanding. She knew full well whose office was behind the closed door. Lowering her voice, she said: "I was shocked to learn Dr. Wingate was here."

"You and everyone else," the secretary whispered with a nod. "No one expected it. He arrived this morning unannounced. There's been a bit of fireworks as you well can imagine."

It was Helen's turn to nod. Then she shrugged. "It will be interesting to see what happens."

"That's the truth," the secretary said. "At any rate I'm sure Dr. Saunders will be out shortly. Perhaps you and your applicants would like to make yourselves comfortable." She smiled graciously at Joanna and Deborah.

Almost simultaneous with the group taking seats, the closed office door opened and banged against its stop. Paul Saunders's short frame filled the doorway, but his attention was directed back into Spencer's office. His face was flushed and his hands were balled into tight fists.

"I can't sit in here the entire day and argue about all this," Paul spat. "I've got patients to see and work to do even if you don't."

Spencer's form materialized behind Paul and crowded him out of the doorway, forcing him to take a step back into the anteroom. Spencer was almost a foot taller and his tanned skin made Paul look paler than usual. His eyes blazed with an intensity equivalent with Paul's. "I'll excuse that kind of impertinence as a product of the heat of the moment," he snapped.

"That's very big of you considering it's true."

"I have a fiduciary responsibility to this clinic and its stockholders," Spencer hissed. "And I want you to understand that I intend to carry out that duty. The Wingate is primarily a clinical organization, and we've been that way from day one. Our research is to support our clinical efforts and not vice versa."

"That's a Luddite attitude if I've ever heard one," Paul shot back. "Research is an investment in the future: short-term sacrifice for long-term benefit. We're positioned to be at the cutting edge of stem-cell research which has the potential of being the basis of twenty-first-century medicine, but we have to be willing to forfeit some profit and take some risks in the short run."

"We'll revisit this discussion when you have more time," Spencer stated flatly. "See me after your last patient!" Abruptly he stepped back into his office, grabbed the edge of his door, and slammed it shut with a resounding bang.

Paul took another step backward as if blown by wind from the slamming door. Furious at being dismissed when it had been his intent to walk out, he spun around. He took a single step toward his office when his eyes caught sight of the un-expected audience. Like the turret on a battleship, his head pivoted in a staccato fashion as his gun-barrel eyes took in each individual in turn. They stopped on Deborah. His expression softened.

"Ms. Masterson has some recruits for you to interview," the secretary announced.

"So I see," Paul said. His tightly fisted hands relaxed, and he gestured toward his open door as his eyes took in Deborah's high-heeled shoes, short skirt, and plung-ing neckline. "Come in, come in!" he said. "Gladys, did you offer our guests some-thing to drink?"

"It didn't occur to me," Gladys admitted. She furrowed her brow.

"We'll have to rectify that," Paul said. "How about some coffee or a soft drink?"

"Not for me, thank you," Deborah said, struggling to get to her feet. It was an effort in the high heels since the couch was inordinately deep. Paul responded by bounding around Gladys's desk to offer a hand, but Deborah made it upright without assistance. She pulled her miniskirt down, which had the effect of lowering her already low neckline.

Paul glanced at Joanna.

X"Nothing for me either," Joanna said. She felt like the poor relation when Paul immediately switched his attention back to Deborah and then made a point of graciously guiding her into his office. Joanna and Helen followed.

Paul added a third chair to the two facing his desk and gestured for everyone to sit. He went around behind his desk and sat himself. Helen proceeded to introduce the two women with their aliases and mentioned their respective Harvard undergraduate degrees along with which departments they hoped to work for.

"Excellent," Paul said with a broad smile, revealing his small, square, widely spaced front teeth which were in concert with his wide, squat nose. "Bloody excellent, as they say in Merry Old England." He laughed. Without taking his eyes off Deborah he added: "It appears, Miss Masterson, you've found us several more fine prospective employees. You're to be congratulated."

"So we should continue with the employment process?" Helen questioned.

"Certainly. By all means."

"They have expressed an interest in starting as early as tomorrow," Helen said.

"That's even better," Paul said. "Their zeal should be rewarded since we're in dire need of help, particularly in the lab. You'll be very welcome, Miss Marks!"

"Thank you," Deborah said, mildly self-conscious about the attention she was getting at the expense of Joanna. "I'm looking forward to using some of that superb equipment you have." No sooner had the statement left her mouth than Deborah felt her pulse quicken and her face redden. It had belatedly occurred to her that she had yet to see the lab on this trip. Luckily the only person who seemed to realize the blunder was Joanna. Paul continued the conversation without so much as a beat.

"Let me ask you something about your lab experience, Miss Marks," Paul said. "Have you ever done any nuclear transfer?"

"I haven't," Deborah stammered. "But I can certainly learn."

"We do a lot of nuclear transfer," Paul said. "It's an integral part of our research efforts. Since I spend a lot of time in the lab, I'll be happy to show you the technique personally."

"You'll find me a willing and hopefully apt pupil," Deborah said, having regained her composure. Out of the corner of her eye she caught Joanna briefly rolling her eyes.

"Well, then," Helen said after a brief silence gripped the room. She stood. "I think we'd better get to it if we're going to have Miss Heatherly and Miss Marks working tomorrow."

The women stood, as did Paul.

"I'm sorry about the verbal exchange you people inadvertently witnessed earlier," Paul said. "The founder of the clinic and I have an occasional minor disagreement, but it's more about style than substance. I hope the little episode doesn't adversely color your impression of the institution."

Five minutes later Helen was leading the women back through the fire door into the south wing of the building.

"I gather that Dr. Wingate doesn't come into the clinic often," Joanna said to Helen.

"Not over the year and a half," Helen said. "We all thought he was permanently retired and living in Florida."

"Is there some problem about him and Dr. Saunders getting along?" Deborah asked.

"I wouldn't know anything about that," Helen said vaguely. As she'd done previously, once in the football-field-length south-wing corridor, she bustled ahead. Mostly due to Deborah's high-heeled shoes the younger women lagged behind.

"That was a strange interview," Joanna said in a hushed voice. "That man is weird which, of course, we already knew."

"At least he didn't recognize us," Deborah said.

"True, but no thanks to you."

"What is that supposed to mean?" Deborah demanded in a forced whisper between breaths.

"I don't think you should be coming on to these men like you are."

"Get out of here! I'm not coming on to anyone. They're coming on to me!"

"Well, you're not helping. This is supposed to be a quick, clandestine operation, not a drawn-out parody."

"You're just jealous."

"That'll be the day. I don't want men staring at me like that."

"I'll tell you what I think all this proves," Deborah said, but then didn't finish her thought.

"Tell me," Joanna mockingly pleaded after a brief silence.

"We blondes certainly have more fun!"

Joanna swiped at Deborah playfully, but Deborah avoided the blow. Both laughed briefly. Ahead they could see Helen standing at a doorway and looking back at them impatiently.

"What did you think of that little verbal set-to between the two chiefs?" Deborah asked while they were still out of earshot of Helen.

"There're obviously some interesting management issues here," Joanna said. "I couldn't help but notice how Helen referred to Dr. Saunders as 'Napoleon' when she was on the phone and how she called him 'our fearless leader' when talking with us. That doesn't imply a lot of respect."

"I agree," Deborah said. "I also didn't buy her disclaimer about having no knowledge of a problem between the two."

"Well, it's not our concern."

"That's for sure," Deborah agreed.

The next step in the women's preemployment process was a visit to security. Contrary to Joanna's earlier concerns, it was an easy procedure. The location was one of the cubicles in the administration area manned by a guard wearing the same uniform as the individual with the clipboard at the front gate. He took Polaroid photos of both women and created laminated plastic Wingate Clinic ID cards which the women were instructed to have on their person at all times while on the premises.

The second part of the security process involved the blue entry cards. The guard produced these by entering the women's predetermined level of access, obtained from material given by Helen, into a form displayed on his workstation monitor. It took a moment because he typed with only two fingers. Once the typing was completed, the cards were extruded automatically. He handed them over and told the women to be careful with them.

The next step was computer access. That involved going to a different cubicle where the women were introduced to Randy Porter. According to Helen they were lucky to have caught him at his workstation. Randy was a sandy-haired, slightly built fellow who looked like he was still in his teens. He explained to the women that when they sat at their workstations for the first time and swiped their blue cards through the slot on the top of their keyboards, a prompt would pop up asking them for a password. He said they were to select NEW and then provide a secret word which only they would be apt to know and which they could count on remembering.

"Should the password be a specific number of letters or digits?" Joanna asked.

"That's up to you," Randy said. "But it is best if it is six or more alphanumeric ciphers. Just be sure it's something you can remember, because if you forget your password, you have to come to me, and that can take some time."

Helen gave a short, corroboratory laugh.

"Any other questions?" Randy asked.

"What kind of a system is it?" Joanna asked.

"The operating system is Windows 2000 Data Center Server."

"And the hardware?"

"It's an IBM Server xSeries 430 with a Shiva firewall," Randy said. "Is that what you're asking?"

"Thanks," Joanna said simply.

"It's all Greek to me," Helen said. "Is that it?"

"That's it from my end," Randy said. "Unless there are more questions."

As they left the network administrator's cubicle Helen checked the time. It was almost one o'clock in the afternoon. She hesitated in the aisle.

"I'd like to introduce you to your respective department heads," Helen said. "But it is lunch time. Perhaps I could invite you to have something to eat in our dining hall. Gauging from Dr. Saunders's response, I'm certain he would not want you to go hungry."

Joanna started to decline the invitation but Deborah interrupted her by saying, "Lunch sounds good to me."

"Wonderful," Helen said. "I know I'm famished."

The dining hall was located on the second floor of a two-story, curved pavilion attached to the back of the central section of the building. Helen led the women back on the same route they'd used to get to the directors' office, but after the fire door they took a right instead of a left.

"Damn it! Why did you have to agree to eat here?" Joanna whispered sotto voce to Deborah when she was confident Helen had gotten far enough ahead so she could not hear.

"Because I'm hungry," Deborah said flippantly.

"The more we do here today and the longer we stay the greater the chance we'll be recognized."

"Oh, I'm not so sure about that," Deborah said. "Besides, the more we learn about this place, the greater chance we'll have succeeding tomorrow when we're here in earnest."

"I wish you'd take this more seriously."

"I'm taking it seriously!" Deborah blurted.

Joanna shushed her as they came up to Helen, who'd waited for them.

The dining room was semicircular in shape with windows looking out the rear of the building. With the ground sloping downward, the view to the east was expansive. Deborah recalled that the lab had a similar view although from smaller windows and hence it was not quite as dramatic. The roof peaks and chimneys of some of the living quarters could be seen sticking up above the budding trees as could the much larger chimney of the power station. Also, the red top of a silo was just visible between the power station and the living quarters.

Helen restrained the women at the threshold while she scanned the diners, obviously searching for someone in particular. The room was large, and like the rest of the building it had numerous Victorian details, including a central, period crystal chandelier. Considering its size, the room was hardly crowded. Only thirty to forty people were sitting at widely separated tables. Their voices caused only a soft murmur.

Joanna stiffened as she caught sight of Dr. Donaldson sitting with five other professional-appearing colleagues. Turning her back in the doctor's direction, Joanna grabbed Deborah by the upper arm and motioned with her head. Deborah immediately comprehended.

"Relax, for goodness' sake!" Deborah said. Joanna's anxious paranoia was getting on her nerves.

"Is something wrong?" Helen asked.

"No, nothing," Joanna said innocently. She gave Deborah a dirty look.

"There they are," Helen said, pointing off to the right. "There's Megan Finnigan, the laboratory supervisor, and Christine Parham, the office manager. Conveniently enough, they're sitting at the same table. Come on, let me introduce you!"

Joanna cringed and tried to keep her back toward Dr. Donaldson as she followed Deborah, who'd fallen in behind Helen. Helen was leading them toward one of the tables near the window. To Joanna's dismay, the sound of Deborah's heels on the aged parquet floor combined with her tawdrily provocative outfit had caught the attention of every one in the place, including Dr. Donaldson.

Deborah was unconcerned about the stir she was causing. Her attention had been absorbed by a table of Spanish-speaking diners she'd passed near the dining room's entrance. They were all young, compact, darkly complected women who Deborah guessed were South American or Central American natives. What caught her attention was that they all appeared to be pregnant—and all of them seemed equally far along.

Following the introductions to the two department heads who had finished their meals and were about to depart, Helen took Joanna and Helen to a separate table. There they were served by another woman who, like the young women they'd seen on the way in, appeared to Deborah like she was from South or Central America. She, too, was pregnant to the same degree as the others.

Once the lunch was served, Deborah's

curiosity got the best of her, and she asked Helen about the women.

"They are Central Americans," Helen said corroborating Deborah's impression. "They're from Nicaragua. It's an arrangement that Dr. Saunders has made with a colleague in that country. They come for a number of months on a work visa, and then return home. I have to say, they have solved a big problem for us by providing kitchen, cleaning, and serving help, which we were unable to find in this area."

"Do they come with their families?"

"No, just by themselves. It's a chance for them to make a serious amount of money, which they send back home."

"But they all look pregnant," Deborah remarked. "Is that some kind of coincidence?"

"No coincidence at all," Helen said. "It's a way for them to earn extra money. But listen, eat up! I really would like to show you the living quarters which I hope we can talk you into taking advantage of. I know you'll be pleased with the rents. They're shockingly reasonable, especially compared to those in Boston."

Deborah looked at Joanna to see if

she'd been listening. For most of the meal
Joanna had been preoccupied by Dr.
Donaldson's presence and the supposed
need to keep her back to the table where
the doctor had been sitting, but Dr.
Donaldson had now left, and it was apparent to Deborah that Joanna had heard
what Helen had said about the women laborers. Joanna returned Deborah's stare
with a look that was a mixture of dismay
and disbelief.

ten

MAY 9, 2001
2:10 P.M.

After lunch Helen managed to get the two women into the golf cart despite Joanna's reservations. Once the tour began, even Joanna found it interesting. The size of the property was impressive, and most of it was covered with dense, old-growth forest. The residences of the upper-echelon personnel like Wingate, Saunders, Donaldson, and a few of the others, were detached homes similar to the gatehouse in style although with white trim instead of black, making them significantly more appealing.

Even the average workers' housing was

charming. The buildings were two-story row houses grouped together in a fashion reminiscent of a rural English village. The two-bedroom unit Helen showed the women was quite homey. Its front windows looked over a small, cobblestoned central square, while its larger rear windows faced south, affording a view over the millpond. Equally attractive was the rent: eight hundred dollars a month.

At Deborah's insistence, after leaving the apartment Helen took them on a short loop around the farm and even around the power plant before bringing them back to the main building. The only downside of the entire excursion was that Joanna and Deborah were never out of Helen's earshot and had no chance to speak privately. It wasn't until Helen deposited them back in the anteroom of Wingate and Saunders's office to wait for Dr. Wingate that they had their chance to talk.

"What was your take on those pregnant workers in the dining room?" Deborah asked in a whisper to keep Gladys, the secretary, from overhearing.

"I was blown over," Joanna said. "I can't believe they have a whole group of migrant women who are being paid to become pregnant!"

"Do you think it is some kind of experiment?"

"Heaven only knows," Joanna said with a shudder.

"The question is, What are they doing with the children?"

"I should hope the children are going back with the mothers to Nicaragua," Joanna said. "I don't even like to think of any other possibility."

"The first thing that comes to my mind is that they are selling them," Deborah said. "Surrogacy doesn't seem likely since they are all so equivalently far along. Selling them could be quite a lucrative business on the side. Being an infertility clinic they certainly have the appropriate clientele, and when we were here a year and a half ago you were impressed with the money this place was seemingly raking in."

"I was impressed with the money they have to be generating from the infertility business," Joanna said. "With the numbers they're obviously doing here, they don't have to be in the baby business to make ends meet. It doesn't make sense! Selling babies is against the law, pure and simple, and Helen Masterson was so upfront about it. If they were doing something against the law, she certainly wouldn't have been so forthright."

"I suppose you're right," Deborah said. "There has to be some reasonable explanation. Maybe they are women suffering from infertility themselves. Maybe helping them get pregnant is part of the deal to get them to come."

Joanna treated Deborah to a look of disbelief. "That's even less likely than surrogacy and for the same reason."

"Yeah, well, I can't think of any other explanation."

"Nor can I," Joanna agreed. "I'm going to be happy to learn about my eggs, and then turn my back on this organization. I felt uneasy about this place the first day we came here to donate, and today has just underlined that impression."

The door to Dr. Wingate's office opened and the doctor emerged with narrow-rimmed reading glasses perched on the end of his nose. Clutched in his hand were balance sheets, which he continued to examine intently up until the moment he placed them on the secretary's desk. He didn't appear to be pleased.

"Call the accountants," he muttered to Gladys. "Tell them I want to see all four quarters of last year."

"Yes, sir," Gladys said.

Spencer gave the balance sheets a final knock with his knuckle as if he were still mulling over their contents before looking in the women's direction. He took a fortifying breath and then walked over to where they were sitting. As he approached his expression softened and a tentative smile appeared.

"Good afternoon, Miss Marks," he said, reaching out to shake Deborah's hand, which he held for an extra moment as he locked eyes with her. Then turning to Joanna he said: "I'm sorry, but I don't remember your name. Georgina mentioned it, but it's slipped my mind."

"Prudence Heatherly," Joanna said. She shook Spencer's hand and stared up into his face. Deborah had been right; the man didn't look like her father, yet there was something about him that was similarly superficially appealing.

"I'm sorry to have kept you ladies waiting," he said, switching his attention back to Deborah.

"We've been enjoying a chance to sit and relax," Deborah said. She could tell the good doctor was having trouble keeping his eyes off her crossed legs. "Miss Masterson has kept us on a busy schedule."

"I hope your visit has been successful."

"Very much so," Deborah said. "We'll be starting work tomorrow."

"Excellent," Spencer said. "Excellent indeed." He rubbed his hands restlessly and looked back and forth between the two women as if he were trying to make up his mind about something. He pulled a chair over and sat down across from them. "Well," he said. "What can we get you: coffee, tea, or a soft drink?"

"Some sparkling water would be nice," Deborah said.

"Same for me," Joanna said reluctantly. She felt like the odd man out. She hadn't particularly wanted to come to Wingate's office, and now that she had, it was painfully obvious the man was unabashedly interested in Deborah. As far as Joanna was concerned, the way he was

looking at Deborah bordered on disgusting.

Spencer told the secretary to get the
cold drinks. While she was doing so, he
made small talk about the clinic. When the
secretary returned it was with only two
small bottles of San Pellegrino.

"Aren't you having anything?" Deborah
asked.

"No, I'm fine," Spencer said. But he
didn't seem to be. He crossed and un-
crossed his legs several times while the
women poured their drinks. He was obviously nervous about something.

"Are we taking too much of your time?"
Joanna inquired. "Perhaps we should go
and let you get back to your work."

"No, don't go," Spencer said. "Timewise
I'm fine. What I would like to do, Miss
Marks, is have a word with you in private."

Deborah took the glass from her lips and
stared at Spencer. The question was so unexpected she wasn't sure she'd heard cor-
rectly.

Spencer pointed toward his office. "If we
could just step into the other room for a
moment, I would be appreciative."

Deborah looked at Joanna, who

shrugged, suggesting it didn't matter to her, although Deborah could tell she was not amused about the whole situation.

"All right," Deborah said, redirecting her attention back to Spencer. She put her glass down on the coffee table, and with a muffled grunt got herself to her feet. Following Spencer's lead she entered the office. Spencer came in behind her and closed the door.

"I'll come right to the point, Miss Marks," Spencer said. For the first time he avoided looking at her by directing his attention out the giant window. "I've encouraged an un-spoken policy here at the clinic discourag-ing social liaisons between management and employees. And since you will techni-cally not be an employee until tomorrow, I was wondering if you would consider hav-ing dinner with me tonight." The moment he got the last word out, he turned from the window and regarded her expectantly.

Deborah was rendered momentarily speechless. She'd been enjoying the part she was playing, but she hadn't anticipated attracting anything more than a second look. She hadn't expected to be asked out by the head of the clinic—a man who she'd assumed was married and who was at least twice her age.

"There's a quaint restaurant not too far out of town," Spencer said as Deborah hesitated. "I don't know if you've been there yet. It's called the Barn."

"I'm certain it's charming," Deborah managed, finding her voice. "And it's awfully nice of you to think of me, but there are some logistical problems. You see, my roommate and I don't live out here. We live in Boston."

"I see," Spencer said. "Well, perhaps I could talk you into an early dinner. I believe they open as early as five-thirty, which isn't very long from now. That way you could be on the road back to Boston as early as seven or eight o'clock."

Instinctively Deborah checked her watch. It was almost four in the afternoon.

"I certainly enjoyed our little chat this morning," Spencer added encouragingly. "I'd love to continue it and learn more about what aspect of molecular biology captures your fancy. I mean, we obviously have common interests."

"Common interests," Deborah scoffed to herself while she stared into the man's blue eyes. She sensed a touch of desperation in this successful—and reasonably attractive—physician. Deborah decided to test the water. "What would Mrs. Wingate say about this idea?"

"There is no Mrs. Wingate," Spencer responded. "Unfortunately my wife divorced me a number of years ago. It was unexpected. In retrospect I suppose I was too dedicated to my work and neglected my marriage."

"I'm sorry," Deborah said.

"It's all right," Spencer said, lowering his eyes. "It's a cross I've had to bear. The good side is that I've finally come to terms with the situation, and I'm ready to get out there and socialize to some extent."

"Well, I'm flattered that you have thought of me. But, I am out here in Bookford with my roommate, and we have only one car."

"You don't think she could entertain herself for a couple of hours?"

Deborah could not believe this guy. Did he truly believe that she'd be willing to ask her best friend to twiddle her thumbs for two hours so they could have dinner? It was so absurdly egocentric she couldn't think of an immediate reply.

"There're plenty of things she could do in town," Spencer said. "There's a nice little bar and a surprisingly good pizza place. And the local book store is a favorite hangout with an espresso bar in the back."

Deborah was about to tell the good doctor to go jump in the mill pond when she held back. A way of turning the unexpected situation to her and Joanna's benefit occurred to her like a bolt out of the blue. Instead of telling Spencer off, she said: "You know, dinner at the Barn is starting to sound very tempting!"

Spencer's face brightened. "I'm pleased, and I'm sure Penelope, or what ever her name is, will find checking out the town enjoyable. As for you, I'm sure you'll find the Barn a surprisingly good restaurant. The food is country style but tasty, and the wine list isn't so bad either."

"Her name is Prudence," Deborah said. "The deal is that Prudence comes to the restaurant as well."

Spencer's expression clouded. He started to protest, but Deborah cut him off.

"She's a great kid," Deborah said. "Don't be too quick to judgment because of her style. She might look conservative, but let me tell you, she can be a hell-raiser when she gets a few drinks under her belt."

"I'm sure she's lovely," Spencer said. "But I was hoping to have some time with you alone."

"You might find this hard to believe," Deborah said. "But we often go out on dates together with the same guy, provided the guy is willing to have an open mind." Improvising in hopes of being seductively coquettish, she winked while touching her upper lip with the tip of her tongue.

"Really?" Spencer commented as his imagination took wing. He'd never been with two women before, although he'd seen such episodes in X-rated videos.

"Really!" Deborah said, trying to make her voice huskier than it really was.

Spencer gestured with his palms up, fingers spread. "Hey, I certainly have an open mind! Let's do it!"

"Wonderful," Deborah said. "We'll meet you at the Barn at five-thirty. And do me a favor."

"Certainly," Spencer said. "What?"

"Don't work too hard the rest of the afternoon. It will be better if you're not too tired."

"You have my word," Spencer said, raising his hands in surrender.

Joanna slammed the car door and stuck the key in the ignition, but she didn't start the car. Instead, she leaned her forehead against the steering wheel while Deborah got in on her side.

"Now run this by me once more," Joanna spat. "Did you tell me that you agreed for the two of us to go to dinner with this disgusting lecher who you admit has some sort of sexual fantasy in mind? Tell me that I'm just dreaming this all up!"

"No, you got it right," Deborah agreed. "But I'm surprised at your description of the good doctor. This morning you said he was distinguished."

"That was in response to his appearance, not his behavior; and that was this morning, not this afternoon."

"Well," Deborah said. "You should have let me know you felt so strongly before I was carried off into his office."

Deborah knew she was taunting Joanna, but her roommate hadn't given her a chance to explain the situation. As they left

Wingate's office, Deborah had mentioned the evening's plans, and Joanna had immediately launched into an angry diatribe. Then, without allowing Deborah so much as another word, Joanna had stormed out of the Wingate Clinic.

"This car is going back to Boston straightaway," Joanna announced. "If you want to stay out here and get it on with that rake, that's your business, but personally I think you are crazy."

"Will you calm down!" Deborah said.

"I'm quite calm enough," Joanna said. "Now, are you getting out or what?"

"Shut up and listen!" Deborah ordered. "I had the same reaction as you when he first suggested dinner. But then it occurred to me he has something we want and need: something critical!"

Joanna took a deep breath to keep from lashing out again at Deborah. As usual Deborah was forcing her to ask. "Okay," Joanna said at length. "What does he have that we need?"

"His blue access card!" Deborah said triumphantly. "He's more than a department head, he's the founder! His blue card will certainly open the door to the server room and probably every other door in the entire place."

Joanna lifted her head from where she'd been leaning it against the steering wheel. What Deborah was saying was undoubtedly true, but what did it matter? She looked at her roommate. "He's not going to give us his access card because we go to dinner with him."

"Of course not," Deborah said. "We're going to take it! All we have to do is get him drunk, and while one of us is diverting him, the other snags the blue card."

At first Joanna thought Deborah was just being her blithe self and that she'd laugh and say she was just kidding. But she didn't. She returned Joanna's gaze with a look of self-satisfaction.

"I don't know," Joanna said. "Sounds easy on paper, but difficult to execute."

"You said yourself we were going to have to be creative to get into the server room," Deborah said. "This is creative."

"You're making a lot of assumptions," Joanna said. "How do you know he drinks? Maybe he's a teetotaler."

"I don't think that's a worry," Deborah said. "He mentioned that the restaurant where we're supposed to meet him has a good wine list. Wine and women are definitely on his mind."

"I don't know about this idea," Joanna said reluctantly.

"Oh, come on," Deborah said. "Admit it's a good idea! Have you come up with another plan for getting into that room?"

"No, but . . ."

"But nothing," Deborah interjected. "What do we have to lose?"

"Our dignity."

"Oh, please! Give me a break!"

Just then Dr. Donaldson and Cynthia Carson came out through the clinic door. Joanna suddenly scrunched down and ordered Deborah to do the same.

"Now what?" Deborah asked, mimicking Joanna and flattening herself below the level of the window.

"Dr. Donaldson and Cynthia Carson just came out of the clinic," Joanna whispered. A few minutes ticked by. The women heard car doors open and slam shut followed by the noise of the tires moving on the gravel-strewn pavement. Only then did they sit up.

"I'm getting out of here," Joanna said after making sure the coast was clear. She started the car, jammed it in gear, and backed out of the parking spot.

"So," Deborah said, "are you with me or not?"

Joanna sighed. "All right," she said. "I'll give it a try. But to get that blue card will take more than dinner. We'll have to get him to take us back to his house."

"Probably," Deborah admitted. "But we might get lucky."

"As far as the division of labor is concerned, I want to make it clear that you'll be doing the distracting and I'll be doing the extracting."

"I think we'll have to play it by ear. As I said earlier, he's expecting some kind of ménage à trois."

"Good grief!" Joanna exclaimed as she nosed the car up to the gate to get it to open. "None of my old friends in Houston would believe this!"

The women drove into town and revisited the RiteSmart drugstore to ask directions to the Barn. The pharmacist had gained a few pounds but was just as cheerful as he'd been a year and a half previously.

"The Barn is about two miles north of

town," he said, pointing up Main Street in the direction they'd come. "It's a good restaurant. I recommend you have the pot roast, double-baked potatoes, and the cheesecake with chocolate sauce."

"That sounds like nice, light fare," Joanna mocked as they returned to the street.

The women spent a half hour window shopping to pass some time before getting back into the car and driving out to the restaurant. It was a quaint establishment having been an actual barn in its previous life. Lots of old-fashioned farm equipment graced the grounds, and some was even attached to the side of the building. Inside, the animal stalls had been converted into eating areas with banquettes. The only windows were in the front creating a dark, cozy atmosphere in the interior.

"Miss Marks and Miss Heatherly?" the hostess asked before the women had a chance to say a word. When they answered yes, she motioned for them to follow. Clutching several menus, she led them to the rearmost stall. There in the dim, candlelit recess was Dr. Spencer Wingate decked out in a blazer with an ascot and matching pocket square. When he caught sight of Joanna and Deborah, he bounded out from behind the table, gallantly kissed each woman's hand, and then graciously gestured for them to sit down. The hostess placed menus in front of each woman, smiled, and disappeared.

"I hope you don't mind," he said. "I've taken the liberty of ordering some wine before you got here." He reached out and turned the labels of the two bottles sitting on the table toward the women. "A crisp white and a full-bodied red! I like my reds full-bodied." He laughed briefly.

Deborah winked at Joanna. She thought the evening was getting off to a good start.

"Would anyone like a cocktail in addition to the wine?" Spencer asked.

"We're not hard liquor drinkers," Deborah said. "But don't let that inhibit you."

"A martini would hit the spot," he said. "Are you sure neither of you ladies would care to join me?"

Both women declined.

The evening progressed smoothly. The conversation was effortless since Spencer was easily encouraged to talk about

Spencer. By the time dessert was served, the women had been treated to a lengthy and detailed history of the Wingate Clinic and its success. The more Spencer talked, the more liberally he drank. The only minor problem was that he showed no outward effect from the alcohol he'd imbibed.

"I have a question about the clinic," Deborah said when Spencer finally paused in his monologue to attack the cheesecake drenched in chocolate sauce. "What's the story about the pregnant Nicaraguans?"

"Are some of the Nicaraguan ladies pregnant?" Spencer asked.

"It seemed to us they all were pregnant," Deborah said. "And all about the same degree, as if they'd become pregnant through some airborne infection."

Spencer laughed. "Pregnancy as an infectious process! That's a good one! But it's not too far from the truth. After all, it is caused by the invasion of a few million microorganisms." He laughed again at his attempt at humor.

"You mean to tell me you are unaware of these pregnancies?" Deborah asked.

"I know nothing about them," Spencer

assured her. "What those ladies do on their time off is their business."

"Why I'm asking," Deborah continued, "is because we were told becoming pregnant for them was a way to earn extra money."

"Really?" Spencer said. "Who told you this?"

"Ms. Masterson," Deborah said. "We asked her about them at lunch."

"I shall have to ask her myself," Spencer said. A short, faltering smile appeared on his face. "I've not been as actively involved with the clinic as I should have been over the last couple of years, so there are certain details I'm not aware of. Of course I knew about the Nicaraguan ladies being with us. It's an arrangement Dr. Saunders has made with a doctor friend in Nicaragua to solve our chronic manpower problem."

"What kind of research is Dr. Saunders involved in?" Deborah asked.

"A little of this and a little of that," Spencer said vaguely. "He's a very creative researcher. Infertility is a rapidly advancing specialty whose advances will soon be making a big impact on medicine in general. But this discussion is getting way too serious." He laughed, and for the first time swayed a bit before steadying himself. "Let's lighten it up. What I propose is that we go back to my house and raid my wine cellar. What do you ladies say?"

"I say the sooner the better," Deborah responded as she covertly poked Joanna, whom she felt was being far too quiet and demure.

"I think having more wine is a terrific idea," Joanna said.

When the bill came, the women were interested to see where Spencer kept his wallet. They were both hoping it would be in his jacket pocket. But it wasn't. To their chagrin it was in his rear pants pocket where it returned once the credit card had been replaced.

As they reached the front of the restaurant and were about to leave, Spencer excused himself to use the rest room.

"You're going to have to be creative to get his pants off," Joanna whispered. They were standing near the hostess podium. Although there had been no patrons when they'd arrived, the restaurant was now almost full.

"It's surely not going to take creativity to

get him out of his pants," Deborah whispered back. "The creativity is going to come in dealing with his expectations. I'm amazed at how much he drank and how little it's seemed to affect him. He's had two martinis and two bottles of wine minus the minuscule amount you and I drank."

"He did slur his words a little during dessert," Joanna said.

"And sway a little, too," Deborah added. "But that's not much effect for that much alcohol. To be that tolerant he must be more of a lush than he appears. If it had been me with that amount of alcohol, I'd be comatose for three days."

Spencer appeared at the men's room door, smiled when he saw the women, and then proceeded to stagger on a skewed course to collide with the hostess stand. He grabbed onto it for support. The dismayed hostess came from behind the stand to help.

"All right!" Deborah exclaimed in a triumphant whisper to Joanna. "That's encouraging. It must have been some kind of a delayed reaction."

"Is he all right?" the hostess asked as

the women came up on both sides of Spencer and lent a hand.

"He's going to be just fine," Deborah said. "He's just unwinding a bit."

"Do you beautiful ladies know where my house is?" Spencer asked, slurring his words again.

"We certainly do," Deborah said. "Ms. Masterson pointed it out to us today."

"Then we'll have a race," Spencer announced.

Before Deborah could nix the idea, Spencer shook free and ran out of the restaurant.

Deborah and Joanna exchanged a startled glance before giving chase. When they emerged into the fading evening light, Spencer was already climbing into his Bentley. They could hear him laughing.

"Wait!" Deborah cried. They ran toward the car, but by the time they got to it, Spencer had the huge engine roaring. Deborah got her hand on the driver's side door handle, but the door was locked. She rapped on the glass. She started to suggest that she drive, but Spencer merely laughed harder, pointed to his ear to indicate he couldn't hear, and then accelerated out of the parking lot.

"Oh crap!" Deborah said as she and Joanna watched the red tail lights disappear into the gathering gloom.

"He shouldn't be driving," Joanna said.

"Yeah, well, he didn't give us a lot of choice," Deborah responded. "I hope he makes it. If he doesn't, let's be the first on the scene—not that that's how I planned on getting that blasted card!"

The women ran back to the Chevy Malibu. Joanna got it out on the road as fast as she could. After every curve they half expected to come across the Bentley off in one of the stubbled corn fields. When they got to the traffic light at the corner of Pierce and Main streets they began to relax, realizing that in all probability if Spencer had gotten that far, he was going to make it.

"What did you think of Spencer's response about the Nicaraguan ladies?" Deborah asked as they turned onto Pierce and headed east.

"He seemed truly surprised about them being pregnant," Joanna said.

"That was my take as well," Deborah

said. "I'm getting the impression that things are happening at the Wingate Clinic that the founder doesn't know much about."

"I'd have to agree," Joanna said. "Of course he admitted he'd not been as involved with the clinic as he should have been over the last couple of years."

They turned off the main road onto gravel and approached the Wingate Clinic gatehouse. It was dark except for a barely discernible glow of light behind one of the small, shuttered windows. As they entered the tunnel beneath the structure, the car's headlights illuminated the heavy gate and the card-swipe pylon.

"Do you think the guard will come out?" Joanna asked as she slowed the car almost to a stop.

Deborah shrugged. "My guess would be no, since it's after hours. So let's just pull up to the card swipe and try one of our new cards."

Deborah got the card out of her shoulder bag and handed it to Joanna. Joanna lowered the window, leaned out, and swiped the card. The gate responded immediately and began to swing open.

"Voilà," Deborah said. She took the card back and put it away.

Joanna followed the drive as it curved around the clump of evergreens. The main building came into view. There were only a few lights visible in the first two stories of the southern wing. The rest of the building was a black, crenelated hulk rearing up against the deepening purple sky.

"The place looks even more sinister at night," Joanna commented.

"I couldn't agree more," Deborah said. "It looks like a place Count Dracula could find inviting."

Joanna passed the parking area and entered the woods beyond. A few moments later in the deepening darkness they began to see lights among the trees, emanating from the homes of the Wingate Clinic's hierarchy. They were able to pick out a house they believed to be Spencer's and drove up its driveway. The Bentley's rear end jutting askew out of the garage told them they were right. Joanna turned off the Malibu's engine.

"Any ideas of how we should proceed from this point?" Joanna asked.

"Not really," Deborah admitted. "Except

to push the alcohol. Maybe we'd better try to find his car keys while we're at it and hide them."

"Good thought!" Joanna said as she alighted from the car.

As the women made their way up the darkened front walk, they could hear rock music playing. The closer they got, the louder it became, yet despite the noise of the music Spencer heard the bell and threw the door wide open. His cheeks were flushed and his eyes red. He'd changed out of his blazer and was wearing an elaborately trimmed, dark green velvet smoking jacket. With an exaggerated flourish requiring him to grab onto the doorjamb to maintain his balance, he invited them in.

"Could we turn the music down a tad?" Deborah yelled.

With an unsteady gait, Spencer went to the entertainment console. The women used the opportunity to survey the interior. It was decorated like a English manor house, with oversized, dark brown leather furniture, red oriental carpets, and dark green paint. Oil paintings of horses and fox hunts lined the walls, each one individually illuminated. The knickknacks were mostly riding paraphernalia.

"Well," Spencer said, returning from lowering the stereo. "What can I get for you ladies before we get down to business?"

Joanna rolled her eyes for Deborah's benefit.

"Let's explore that wine cellar you mentioned," Deborah said.

"Good idea," Spencer said barely pronouncing the *d*'s.

The basement looked as though it hadn't been touched since the midnineteenth century, save for the addition of several bare low-wattage electric lights. The exposed granite blocks that formed the foundation were dark with mold. The partitions were made of rough-hewn oak planks held together with huge, primitive iron nails. The floor was dirt. The air was clammy because of a number of muddy puddles.

"Maybe I'll wait here on the steps," Joanna said as she looked around the dimly illuminated dungeon, but Deborah forged on despite her high heels.

Deborah was fearful that Spencer would not make it in his inebriated state. On several occasions she did have to give him support to keep him from falling.

The wine cellar turned out to be just one of the many partitioned-off cubicles whose crude doors were secured with huge old padlocks. Spencer produced a key the size of his thumb from his jacket pocket and got the hasp open. Inside the compartment were a half-dozen cases of wine placed haphazardly on makeshift shelves. Spencer did not hesitate. He opened the first case and pulled out three bottles. "These'll do," he said. Without bothering to replace the padlock, he staggered back to the stairs, clutching the bottles under his arm.

"My Fayva shoes are ruined," Deborah mockingly moaned to Joanna as they climbed the cellar stairs.

In the kitchen Spencer produced a corkscrew and opened up the three bottles, all California cabernets. Spencer selected three wide-mouthed wineglasses from the cupboard, and Deborah volunteered to carry them. Spencer led the way back to the living room. He sat in the center of the couch and motioned for the women to sit on either side. Then he poured the wine and handed out the glasses.

"Not bad. Not bad at all," he said after taking a sip. "Now! How do we get started?" He laughed. "I'm new at this threesome stuff."

"I think we better have some wine first," Deborah said. "The night is young."

"I'll drink to that," Joanna said. She held up her wineglass, and everyone else did the same.

Once again the women were able to get Spencer talking by merely asking about his childhood. That simple question unleashed a long monologue with shades of Horatio Alger. While he talked, Spencer plied himself liberally with wine. As in the restaurant he seemed oblivious to the fact that the women hardly drank at all.

When one-and-a-half bottles of wine had been consumed and the story of Spencer's early life got to the college stage, Deborah interrupted to ask Joanna if she could speak to her for a moment. Joanna agreed, and the women drew to the side. Spencer's blue eyes followed them with great interest and anticipation.

"Do you have any suggestions?"

Deborah said sotto voce. With the rock music in the background, she was confident there was zero chance Spencer could hear. "The man's a sponge for alcohol. Other than his eyes and cheeks, this extra wine has had little effect."

"I don't have any suggestions except . . ."

"Except what?" Deborah asked. She was getting desperate. It was almost nine o'clock, and she wanted to get home to bed. She was exhausted, and tomorrow was going to be a big day.

"Ask him to slip into something more comfortable like silk pajamas or whatever he has. That's a stock cliché that might work, and if he bites, it will mean his pants and wallet will stay in his bedroom where I can get at them."

"Meaning I'll have to deal with him without pants," Deborah groaned.

"Do I have to remind you this was all your idea?" Joanna blurted.

"All right, all right," Deborah said. "Keep it down! But if I scream, you better get your ass down here in a hurry."

The women returned and Spencer looked up at them expectantly. Deborah tried the line that Joanna had suggested. Spencer responded with a crooked smile. He nodded and struggled to get to his feet. The women immediately came to his assistance.

"I'm all right," he protested. He got up by himself and swayed briefly. Then he took a deep breath, set his sights on the stairs, and started off. The women watched him bob and weave on his way across the living room as if he had little comprehension where the various parts of his body were at any given moment.

"I take back what I said a moment ago," Deborah announced. "The wine is having an appropriate effect after all."

Both women winced as Spencer ricocheted off a console table and sent a group of painted toy cavalry soldiers to the floor. Despite the collision he maintained his footing and made it to the stairs. With his hands on both banisters, he managed better on the stairs than he'd done on the open floor. He disappeared above.

"Let's talk about what we are going to do when he comes down," Deborah said anxiously. "Depending on what he's wearing or not wearing, he might be too preoccupied to talk about his favorite subject any longer."

"As soon as he comes down I'll excuse myself to use the bathroom," Joanna said. "You keep him occupied."

"There is a back stair in the kitchen," Deborah said. "That should get you up to the bedroom."

"I saw it," Joanna said. "I'll just make it as fast as I can."

"You'd better," Deborah warned. Instinctively she tried to pull her miniskirt down to cover more of her thigh, but that only succeeded in exposing more décolletage. "As you can well imagine, I'm feeling rather vulnerable in this outfit."

"You're not going to get any sympathy from me."

"Thanks," Deborah said. "Let's sit down, my feet are killing me."

The women sat and discussed Spencer's life story. When they exhausted that, they talked about how they would manage the following day if they got Spencer's blue access card.

"Our goal will be to get me into that server room as soon as possible so I can give us access to their restricted files,"

Joanna said. "David said it would only take fifteen minutes or so. Once it's done we can get the information about our eggs from a workstation or even from our computer at home."

"We'll bring our cell phones," Deborah said. "That way I can stand guard when you're in the server room and let you know if anybody is coming."

"That's not a bad idea," Joanna agreed.

Deborah looked at her watch. "How long has Casanova been upstairs changing into something more comfortable?"

Joanna shrugged. "I don't know. Five or ten minutes."

"I wish he'd hurry," Deborah said. "I'm so tired I could lie down on this couch and be asleep in two seconds."

"I feel the same way," Joanna said. "It's the jet lag. Our bodies are still on Italian time."

"It's also because we've been up since six."

"True," Joanna said. "Tell me! What are you going to do tomorrow in the clinic's lab while you're waiting for me to get into the server room?"

"I'm interested in finding out exactly

what they are doing with all that fancy equipment," Deborah said. "I'd like to find out the specifics about their research, which includes finding out what the real story is behind the Nicaraguans."

"You will be careful, won't you?" Joanna warned. "Whatever you do, don't jeopardize our cover until we've got the information that we're really after."

"I'll be careful," Deborah said. She looked at her watch again. "My good God! What's he putting on up there, Superman tights?"

"It is a little long," Joanna agreed.

"What should we do?"

Joanna shrugged again. "Do we dare go up and look? What if he's stark naked and lying in wait for us?"

"Good grief! What an imagination," Deborah said. "Are you really worried? What is he going to do, jump out and say *boo*? The man walked out of the room with legs that resembled wet spaghetti."

"You know," Joanna suddenly suggested, "he might have passed out."

"That's a happy thought, and I suppose it's a distinct possibility. He's now had two martinis and three and a half bottles of wine over a three-hour period."

"Let's go up and look, but you first!"

"Thanks, buddy."

The women went to the bottom of the stairs. With the music thudding away even at its reduced volume there was no possibility of hearing any noise from above. Sticking close together, they mounted the stairs and then hesitated at the top. There were a number of closed doors, although at the end of a corridor one was ajar. A bit of weak light spilled out onto the hall carpet. Other than the music from below there was no sound.

Deborah motioned for Joanna to follow, and feeling like trespassers the women headed toward the open door. When they reached the threshold they had a full view of an undisturbed king-sized bed. The only light was coming through an open door to a bathroom beyond. Spencer was nowhere to be seen.

"Where the hell is he?" Deborah whispered angrily. "Could he be playing some kind of game with us?" Joanna's earlier suggestion sprang into her mind.

"Should we look in the other rooms?" Joanna asked.

"Let's check the bathroom," Deborah said.

They'd taken no more than three steps into the room when Joanna's grip on Deborah's arm tightened suddenly.

"Don't scare me like that!" Deborah complained.

Joanna pointed toward the bed. On the opposite side just visible were Spencer's feet snagged in his trousers. With some trepidation the women went around the bed and looked down. Spencer was lying prone with his shirt half off and his pants in a bundle around his ankles. He was obviously sound asleep and breathing heavily.

"It looks like he fell," Joanna said.

Deborah nodded. "I'd guess in his haste he tripped on his pants. Once horizontal he was out cold."

"Do you think he hurt himself?"

"I doubt it," Deborah said. "He wasn't close enough to anything to hit his head, and this broadloom is two inches thick."

"Do we dare?"

"Are you kidding?" Deborah said. "Of course we dare. He's not going to wake up." She bent down, and after a brief search and a tug, she extracted Spencer's wallet. Spencer did not move.

The wallet was inordinately thick. Deborah opened it and began rifling through it. The blue access card was not immediately apparent, but she found it in one of the compartments behind the credit cards. "I like the fact that it was hidden away," she said. She handed it to Joanna, bent back down, and slid the wallet back into the pocket she'd found it in.

"Why do you care where he had it in his wallet?" Joanna asked.

"Because it means he doesn't use it often," Deborah said. "We don't want him to miss it until after we've had a chance to use it. Come on! Let's find those car keys, hide them, and get the hell out of here."

"Getting out of here is the best suggestion you've made all day," Joanna said. "As far as the car keys are concerned, why bother? He's not going to wake up for at least twelve hours, and when he does, he's not going to feel much like driving."

*   *   *

Kurt Hermann stared at the polaroid photo of the new employee, Georgina Marks. He was holding it in his rock-steady hand beneath the green-glass-shaded desk lamp. As he studied her face he recalled the appearance of her full body, with her breasts ready to spill out over the front of her dress, and her skirt barely able to cover her behind. To him she was an abomination, a direct affront to his fundamentalist mentality.

In his slow, deliberate style, Kurt laid the photo down on the desktop next to the photo of the other new employee, Prudence Heatherly. She was different—obviously a Bible-fearing female.

Kurt was sitting in his office in the deserted gatehouse where he frequently spent his evenings. Adjoining the office was a makeshift gym where he could hone his muscular, finely tuned frame. As a determined loner he avoided socialization. And living on the Wingate premises made it easy, especially since the institution was sited in a small town which had nothing to offer as far as he was concerned.

Kurt had been working for the Wingate Clinic for a little more than three years. The job was perfect for him, with just enough intrigue and challenge to make it interesting and yet not so busy that he had to work too hard. His military experience made him uniquely qualified for security. He'd joined the army directly after high school and had made it into the Special Forces, where he'd been trained for covert operations. He'd learned to kill with his bare hands as well as with any number of weapons, and he'd never been troubled by it.

Joining the army had not been the beginning of his association with the military. Having grown up as an army brat, Kurt had never known a different lifestyle. His father had been in the Special Forces and had been a strict disciplinarian who'd demanded utter obedience and perfection from his wife and child. There'd been a few ugly scenes in Kurt's early adolescence, but he'd fallen into line quickly enough. Then his father had been killed in the waning days of Vietnam in a Cambodian operation which to this day was still classified. To his horror, after his father's death his mother embarked on a series of love affairs before she wound up marrying a prissy insurance salesman.

The army had been good to Kurt. Appreciating his abilities and attitude, it had always been there to smooth over the minor brushes with the law that Kurt's aggressive behavior sometimes brought on. There were a number of things Kurt could not tolerate, but prostitution and homosexuality in any form were at the top of the list, and Kurt was not one to shy away from acting on his principles.

Things had gone well in Kurt's life until he'd been posted to Okinawa. On that rugged island, he admitted, things had gotten out of hand.

Slowly Kurt leaned over and stared again into Georgina's eyes. On Okinawa he'd met a number of women just like her. So many, in fact, he'd felt a religious calling to reduce their numbers. It was as if God had spoken to him directly. Getting rid of them was easy. He'd have sex with them in an isolated environment, and then, when they had the moral depravity to demand money, he'd kill them.

He was never caught or charged, but eventually he was implicated by circumstantial evidence. The army solved the problem by discharging him under President Clinton's government employee reduction plan which turned out to be mostly from the military and not from the bureaucracy. A few months later Kurt answered an ad placed by the Wingate Clinic and was hired on the spot.

Kurt heard the gate creak open followed by the sound of a car accelerating through the tunnel. Pushing back from his desk, he went to the window and opened the shutters. He could make out the taillights of a late-model Chevrolet as it disappeared down the gravel road. He looked at his watch.

After closing the shutters, Kurt returned to the desk. He looked down at the woman's now-familiar face. He'd seen that car come in soon after Wingate's and he'd followed it up to Wingate's house. It didn't take a rocket scientist to know what was going on behind closed doors. The appropriate Biblical passages immediately sprang to mind, and as he recited them his hands balled into tight fists. God was talking to him again.

eleven

It was another gorgeous, bright spring morning as the women sped northwest, heading back toward Bookford, which they'd left only nine hours previously. Both were exhausted. Contrary to the morning before, they'd not awakened spontaneously and had had to be dragged out of their beds by their respective alarms.

When they'd gotten home the night before, neither went to bed, much as they'd longed to. Deborah had felt impelled to clean her shoes, which had gotten muddy in Spencer's basement. She also spent some time accessorizing her outfit for the next day; she'd realized belatedly that she'd have to wear the same dress since all her other clothes were a completely different style, a fact which she felt would have suggested she wasn't whom she said she was.

Joanna had gotten on the phone with David Washburn to rehash exactly what she would do once she got into the Wingate's server room. At his insistence she even had to go over to his apartment to get some of his brute-force cracking software. He'd told her that the more he'd thought about it, the more he believed that even the server room console would require a password to get the keyboard to function. He showed her how to use the software and had her try it several times until he was confident she was familiar with it. By the time she got home it was well past midnight, and Deborah was already fast asleep.

As fatigued as they were, they drove in silence while listening mindlessly to morning talk radio. When they got to the Wingate entrance, Deborah, whose turn it was to drive, used her swipe card. The gate opened without a hitch, and in they drove. Since they were some of the first employees to arrive that morning, there were any number of parking spaces available. Deborah took one close to the front door.

"Are you worried about running into Spencer?" Joanna asked.

"Not really. With the hangover he's undoubtedly going to have, I don't think anybody is going to be seeing much of him today."

"You're probably right. Besides, he's probably not going to remember much about last night anyway."

"Well, good luck, partner," Deborah said.

"Same to you," Joanna said.

"I forgot to ask if you remembered your cell phone."

"I certainly did. And you?"

"Yup! And I even remembered to charge the battery. So let's do it!"

With a sense of purpose and not a small amount of anxiety, the two women alighted from the car and entered the building. According to instructions they'd gotten the previous day they went first to Helen Masterson's cubicle, where they completed a bit more paperwork. They were relieved that no problems with their fake Social Security numbers had emerged overnight.

From Helen's office space they split up, with Joanna heading to Christine Parham's cubicle only three down from Helen's and Deborah crossing the main hall to find Megan Finnigan's office.

Joanna wasn't sure how to get Christine's attention. The woman was at her desk, facing away from the cubicle's doorless entrance. First Joanna rapped on the partition wall, but since it was composed of a sound-absorbent material, the meager noise was not enough to rouse the office manager. Joanna resorted to calling the woman's name.

Christine had remembered Joanna from the introduction the previous day in the dining room. She also had a copy of Joanna's employment questionnaire sitting on the corner of her desk.

"Come right in and sit down, Prudence!" Christine said. She removed some folders from the chair pressed up against the side of her desk. "Welcome to the Wingate."

Joanna sat as requested and eyed the

office manager. She was a woman cast from a similar mold as Helen Masterson, with the same solid build and broad, spadelike hands suggesting her immediate forebears could have been farmers. She had a kind face with natural florid patches that appeared like dabs of rouge on her broad cheekbones.

In a no-nonsense manner Christine informed Joanna what would be expected of her and what her initial duties would be. As Joanna had anticipated, she would be doing data entry for billing purposes for the clinic side of the Wingate operation. She was told that her duties and responsibilities would be expanded in the near future if working at the Wingate continued to be mutually satisfactory.

"Any questions?" Christine asked.

"What is the office policy on coffee breaks?" Joanna asked. She smiled. "I suppose that sounds like asking about vacation on the first day, but I should know."

"It's a very reasonable question," Christine said. "We're not strict about coffee breaks, and we encourage people to do what's best for them. The important thing is to get your work done. Generally speaking, most people take a half hour in the morning and another half hour in the afternoon, either at one time or broken into several shorter periods. Lunch is also a half hour, but again, we're not sticklers for that."

Joanna nodded. She liked the idea of being able to take a half hour, especially if she were able to coordinate it with Deborah. That was when she'd try to get into the server room. If that didn't work, then she'd have to use the lunch period.

"I should remind you there is no smoking," Christine said. "If you do smoke, you have to go out to your car."

"I don't smoke," Joanna said. "No problem there."

"In your application it says you have a lot of computer experience," Christine said. "So I suppose we don't have to go over anything about our system. It is rather straightforward, and I know you have spoken with Randy Porter."

"I think I'll be fine in that regard," Joanna said.

"Well, let's get you started," Christine said. "I've got a clear cubicle for you and a full in-basket."

Christine led Joanna to a work space pressed up against the common wall with the main hall. The cubicle was as far from the windows as possible. It had a standard metal desk, a file cabinet, a desk chair, a side chair, and a wastebasket. On the desk was an in-basket which was brimming, an out-basket, a keyboard with a monitor and a mouse, and a telephone. The partition walls were completely bare.

"I'm afraid it's not very cozy, Prudence," Christine admitted. "But you are welcome to bring in any decorative items you wish to personalize the space."

"It's fine," Joanna said. She put her purse on the desk and smiled back at the office manager.

Christine then introduced Joanna to the other workers who occupied the immediately adjacent cubicles. They seemed a pleasant and hospitable group who readily reached over the chest-height dividers to shake Joanna's hand.

"Well, then," Christine said. "I think that covers the basics. Remember! I'm here to help, so just give a yell."

Joanna said she would and waved as Christine took her leave. Turning to the desk, Joanna took her cell phone out of her purse and immediately dialed Deborah's number. She got Deborah's voice mail and assumed Deborah was still going through her introduction. She left a message for Deborah to call her back whenever she had a free moment.

\ Next, Joanna sat down at the keyboard. After swiping her blue card through the slot, she got a window on the monitor requesting her to set up a new password. Joanna used the word *Anago;* it was her favorite Boston restaurant. Once on the network, Joanna spent a quarter hour checking what kind of access she had. As she had expected, it was very limited, and the donor files in which she was interested were unavailable.

At that point Joanna turned her attention to the in-basket. It was her intent to get as much of the required busywork out of the way as possible so that when she had the opportunity to get into the server room, no one would be looking for her for mundane, work-related reasons.

Joanna hadn't been working very long before she was concretely aware of how much money the clinic was able to generate, and she was looking at only a small portion of a single morning's receipts. Even without knowledge of costs, she gathered the infertility business was an enormously appealing investment.

Deborah nodded every so often to make it seem like she was listening. She was sitting in Megan Finnigan's postage-stamp-sized office just off the main laboratory room. Shelves lined all four walls and were filled with manuals, laboratory source books, and loose stacks of papers. The laboratory supervisor was a rail of a woman with gray-streaked, mousy-colored hair that continually fell into her line of sight. Every minute and a half, with metronomic regularity, she tossed her head to whip the errant strands away from her face. The tic made it hard for Deborah to keep her eyes on the woman without reaching out, grabbing her by the shoulders, and telling her to stop.

Deborah's mind couldn't help but wander as the woman gave her a canned lecture about laboratory techniques. Deborah wondered how Joanna was making out.

"Do you have any questions?" Megan asked suddenly.

As if having been caught napping, Deborah sat up straighter. "I don't think so," she said quickly.

"Good," Megan said. "If any occur to you, you know where I am. Now I'll turn you over to one of our more experienced technicians. Her name is Maureen Jefferson. She'll be training you in nuclear transfer."

"Sounds good to me," Deborah said.

"As a final point," Megan said, "I'd like to suggest you wear more sensible shoes."

"Oh?" Deborah asked innocently. She glanced down at her high heels, which looked good despite the previous day's rigors. "You have a problem with these?"

"Let's just say they are inappropriate," Megan said. "I don't want you slipping on the tile and breaking a leg."

"I wouldn't want that either," Deborah said.

"As long as we understand each other," Megan said. She glanced briefly at Deborah's skirt, which was revealing a lot of leg, but didn't say anything. Instead she stood up, and Deborah did the same.

Maureen Jefferson was a twenty-two-year-old African American woman whose color was like coffee with a lot of cream. There was a sprinkling of freckles over the bridge of her nose. She wore her hair bobbed, which showed off to maximum advantage an impressive collection of pierced earrings. Her eyebrows were quite arched, giving her an expression of continual amazement.

With the introductions complete, Megan took her leave. At first Maureen didn't say anything but merely shook her head as Megan walked back down the central aisle. It wasn't until Megan disappeared into her office that Maureen turned to Deborah: "She's a piece of work, wouldn't you say?"

"She is a bit rote," Deborah said.

"My guess is she gave you her stock lecture on laboratory cleanliness."

"I'm not sure," Deborah said. "I didn't listen to too much of it."

Maureen laughed. "I think you and I are going to get along just fine, girl. What do you go by, Georgina or what?"

"Georgina," Deborah said. Using the alias always made her pulse quicken.

"My friends call me Mare, like a female horse," Maureen said.

"Then Mare it is," Deborah said. "Thank you."

"Let's get down to business. I've got a double-headed dissecting microscope set up here so we can be looking at the same field. Let me get some eggs from the incubator."

While Mare was on her errand, Deborah pulled out her cell phone and turned it on. She saw she had a message, but rather than listen to it, she dialed Joanna's number. Joanna picked up right away.

"Did you call?" Deborah asked.

"I did, but the message was just to call me."

"How's it going?"

"Boring but tolerable," Joanna said. "The first thing that I did was try to access the donor files, but no go."

"That's not surprising."

"The plan is, I'll be taking a half-hour break at eleven. Can you meet me?"

"Where?"

"Let's say that water fountain in the main hall near the door to the server room."

"I'll be there," Deborah said. She ended

the call and slipped the phone back into her shoulder bag. While she'd been talking she'd looked around the lab. There were only five other people visible in a work space that could have supported fifty. It was obvious the Wingate anticipated growing exponentially.

Mare returned carrying a covered petri dish that contained a small amount of fluid. To the naked eye the fluid was clear and uniform but in actuality it was layered. On top was a film of mineral oil and beneath was an aliquot of culture fluid containing sixty or so female eggs.

Mare sat on one side of the double-headed microscope and motioned for Deborah to take the stool on the other side. She turned on the source light and the ultraviolet light. Then both women leaned forward to peer through the eyepieces.

For the next hour Deborah was treated to a hands-on demonstration of nuclear transfer using micropipettes. The first part involved removing the nuclei from the eggs. The second part involved putting much smaller, adult cells just under the eggs' outer covering. The process involved a certain amount of finesse but Deborah caught on quickly and by the end of the hour was doing it almost as well as Mare.

"That finishes that batch," Mare said. She leaned back from the scope and stretched her tight shoulder muscles. "I have to say, you've caught onto this more quickly than I expected."

"Thanks to an excellent instructor," Deborah said. She stretched as well. The delicate operating of the micropipettes required such strict control that all muscles were kept tense.

"I'll get you another petri dish that's been set up when I take this group we've done to the fusion people," Mare said. "I don't see any reason you can't be on your own already. Usually it takes a day or two, but you're already doing it like a pro."

"I think you are being overly generous," Deborah said. "But tell me! What kind of eggs are we working with here? Are they bovine or swine?" Deborah had seen a few female gametes of different species either in photomicrographs or in actuality in the lab at Harvard. She knew they looked strikingly similar except for size, which could vary considerably. From the size of the eggs she was working with she guessed they were swine since it was her impression that bovine eggs were larger, but it was truly a guess.

"Neither," Mare said. "These are all human eggs."

Although Mare had answered Deborah's question matter-of-factly, the information hit Deborah like a sledgehammer. In the entire hour she'd been working with the cells, the idea that she was working with human eggs had never even occurred to her. It made her tremble to think about it, especially since she'd been paid forty-five thousand dollars for one egg!

"Are you sure these are human eggs?" Deborah managed.

"I'm pretty sure," Mare said. "At least that is my understanding."

"But what are we doing here?" Deborah stammered. "Whose eggs are these?"

"That's not for us to question," Mare said. "This is one busy infertility clinic. We're helping to get the clients pregnant." She shrugged. "They're clients' eggs and clients' cells."

"But by doing nuclear transfer, we are cloning," Deborah said. "If these are human cells, we're cloning human beings!"

"Technically, perhaps," Mare said. "But it's part of the embryonic stem cell protocol. In private clinics like the Wingate, we're allowed to do stem-cell research on extra material not used for the infertility treatment and otherwise destined to be destroyed. We're not getting any government funding, so anybody who is against this kind of work doesn't have to feel they are paying for it through their taxes. And remember: These are extra gametes, and the clients who've produced these gametes have agreed for them to be used. And most importantly, the fused cells are not allowed to become actual embryos. The stem cells are harvested in the blastocyst stage before any cellular differentiation."

"I see," Deborah said with a nod, but she wasn't sure she did. It was a situation she was not prepared for, and she was troubled.

"Hey, calm down!" Mare urged. "This is no big deal. We've been doing this for several years. It's okay! Trust me!"

Deborah nodded again, although she wasn't sure how she felt about all this.

"You're not one of those religious nuts,

are you?" Mare asked. She leaned forward to look Deborah in the eye.

Deborah shook her head. At least she was certain of that.

"Thank goodness," Mare said. "Because this stem-cell research is the future of medicine. But I'm confident I don't have to tell you that." She slid off her stool. "Let me go get some more eggs," she added. "If you'd like we can talk more about it when I get back."

"Fine," Deborah said, thankful for a moment to think. With her elbows on the lab bench, Deborah cradled her head. Keeping her eyes closed, she tried to imagine how the Wingate Clinic could produce so many extra eggs. She estimated that she and Mare had already gone through four or five dozen, and the morning was young. Knowing what she did about ovarian hyperstimulation, ending up with that many eggs for research was extraordinary. Usually only ten or so eggs resulted from a stimulated cycle and most of those were used for in-vitro fertilization.

"Ah, Miss Marks," a voice said. Simultaneously there was a tap on Deborah's shoulder. She looked up, and although she was sitting, she found herself eye to eye with Dr. Paul Saunders. "I'm glad to see you, and you look as lovely as you did yesterday."

Deborah managed a smile.

"How are you finding the lab work?"

"Interesting," Deborah said.

"I understand Miss Jefferson has been showing you the ropes," Paul said. "She's certainly one of our best technicians, so you are in almost as good hands had I had the opportunity to come over first thing this morning as I had originally planned."

Deborah nodded. Such conceit reminded her of Spencer, and she found herself wondering if it were a universal character trait of infertility specialists.

"I suppose," Paul continued, "I don't have to explain to you how important this work is to our clients and the future of medicine in general."

"Miss Jefferson told me the eggs on which we'd done nuclear transfer were human eggs," Deborah said. "Needless to say I was shocked, knowing how scarce human eggs are."

"Did she say she was certain?" Paul asked. His pale face darkened.

"I think her words were *pretty sure,*" Deborah said.

"They are swine eggs!" Paul said. Absently he ran his fingers through his hair. "We're doing a lot of work with pigs lately. Do you know what the major thrust of our research is these days?"

"Miss Jefferson mentioned stem cells," Deborah said.

"That's part of it," Paul agreed. "Very definitely an important part, but not necessarily the most important. Right now my major focus involves how the oocyte cytoplasm reprograms an adult cell nucleus. That's the basis for current animal cloning techniques. You know, the way Dolly the sheep had been cloned."

"I'm aware of Dolly," Deborah said. She leaned back. As Paul spoke, his ardor magnified as evidenced by a suffusion of color in his otherwise pale cheeks. Progressively, he thrust his face toward Deborah so that she could feel the wind as he pronounced hard consonants.

"We are at a fantastic crossroads in biological science," Paul said, lowering his voice as if imparting a trade secret. "You're in luck, Miss Marks! You've joined us at a most exciting, revolutionary time. We're on the brink of a number of huge break-throughs. Tell me! Did Helen Masterson ex-plain our employee stock-option plan?"

"I don't think so," Deborah said. She was now leaning back as far as she dared without jeopardizing her balance on the lab stool she was sitting on.

"We in management want everybody to benefit from the coming gold mine this area of research is about to be," Paul said. "So we're offering stock options to all our val-ued employees, particularly those on the laboratory side of the operation. As soon as the first breakthrough occurs, and we announce, probably in *Nature,* we'll go public. Wingate Clinic will go from a nar-rowly held private company to a publicly traded one. I suppose you can guess what that will do to the value of the stock op-tions."

"I guess they'll go up," Deborah offered. Paul was now so close she could see di-rectly into the black depths of his pupils. It occurred to her why his eyes looked so strange. Not only were the irises slightly different colors, but his inner canthi covered enough of the white sclera to make him appear mildly cross-eyed.

"Through the roof!" Paul said, slowly pronouncing each word separately. "Which will mean everybody will be a millionaire; everybody, that is, with stock options. So the important thing is that it all stays quiet." Paul put a finger to his lips in the classic gesture for silence to emphasize his point. "Secrecy is of paramount importance. That's why we encourage our people, particularly our lab personnel, to live on the premises, and why we discourage loose talk with anyone outside the organization. We liken this effort to the Manhattan project when the atomic bomb was created. Am I making myself clear?"

Deborah nodded. Paul had moved back slightly although he still had her locked in his unwavering, unblinking stare. She was able to right herself on the stool.

"We're trusting you not to talk with anyone about what we are doing here," Paul continued. "It's for your own benefit." He hesitated.

"I'm a very trustworthy person," Deborah said when she sensed he was waiting for her to respond.

"We don't want another organization to beat us out," Paul continued. "Not after all this work. And there are a number of institutions working on the same problems right here in the Boston area."

Deborah nodded. She was well aware of the local biotech industry, especially since she was scheduled for an imminent interview with Genzyme.

"Can I ask a question?" Deborah said.

"By all means," Paul said. He put his hands on his hips and rocked back on his heels. The pose, combined with his shock of dark hair, reminded Deborah of Helen Masterson's nickname for him: Napoleon.

"I'm curious about the Nicaraguan workers. They all look pregnant to the same degree. What's the story?"

"Let's just say for now that they are helping," Paul said. "It's not that big a deal, and I'll be happy to explain it in more detail at a later date."

Paul broke off from staring into Deborah's eyes to cast a quick look around the lab. Reassured that no one was paying them any heed, he returned his attention to her. This time his line of sight rapidly scanned the long, hosiery-clad legs and the plunging neckline before snapping back to Deborah's face. It was a fleeting visual inquisition not lost on Deborah.

"I'm glad we've had the opportunity for this little chat," Paul said, lowering his voice. "I enjoy talking with someone with whom I feel equivalent intelligence and with whom I have strong common interests."

Deborah suppressed a sardonic laugh. Distinctly she remembered the same inane *common interests* comment from Spencer, and intuitively she sensed it was going to lead to the same end. She wasn't disappointed. In the next breath Paul said: "I'd love to have the opportunity to describe to you all the exciting research I'm doing, including the contribution from the Nicaraguans, but it would be best in private. Perhaps you'd like to have dinner tonight. Although the Wingate is unfortunately out here in the sticks, there is a fairly good restaurant you might enjoy."

"That wouldn't be the Barn, would it?" Deborah asked wryly.

If Paul was surprised Deborah knew the name of the restaurant, he didn't let on. Instead he launched into a glowing description of its food and romantic decor and how he'd enjoy sharing it with Deborah. He then went on to suggest that after dinner they could return to his house where he'd show her the protocols for some of the major breakthrough experiments he currently had underway at the Wingate.

Deborah suppressed another laugh. Being asked to Paul's house to see research protocols sounded like a variation on the come-see-my-etchings ploy. Deborah had no interest in going out with the nerd, despite her keen curiosity about the Wingate's research. She declined his invitation using Joanna as an excuse just as she'd done with Spencer the day before. To her surprise Paul's reaction was almost identical to Spencer's with the same suggestion about Joanna entertaining herself while they dined. Deborah now wondered if megalomania was a requirement to be an infertility specialist or if the job evoked it. Emphatically she declined again.

"What about later in the week?" Paul pleaded. "Or even over the weekend. I could drive into Boston."

Mare's return saved Deborah from Paul's

deepening desperation. She brought a petri dish over to the lab bench and set it in on the microscope's stage before deferentially acknowledging Dr. Saunders's presence.

"So how is our new employee doing?" Paul asked, reverting with surprising agility to his usual condescending manner.

"She's doing terrific," Mare said. "She's a natural. She's ready to be on her own as far as I'm concerned."

"That's good news," Paul said. He then asked Mare if he could have a word with her in private. Mare agreed and the two withdrew several lab benches to be out of Deborah's earshot.

Deborah pretended to be interested in the fresh petri dish but watched Paul and Mare converse out of the corner of her eye. Paul did all the talking. He was obviously agitated as evidenced by his emphatic gesticulations.

The monologue lasted less than a minute after which they returned to Deborah.

"I will talk to you later, Miss Marks," Paul said stiffly prior to leaving. "In the meantime, carry on!"

"I'll get you started with this new group," Mare said, taking the seat opposite Deborah.

Deborah put her eyes to the microscope, and for the next few minutes the women worked in tandem organizing the oocytes for Deborah to begin extracting the DNA. Moving all the eggs to one side had been the way they'd begun with the first group. Earlier Mare had explained it was to avoid missing any. When it was finished, Mare leaned back.

"There you go," Mare said, uttering the first words since Paul's departure. "Good luck! If you have any questions just yell. I'll be over on the next bench doing another batch."

Deborah couldn't help but notice the new coolness in the way Mare treated her. As the lab tech stood up to leave, Deborah cleared her throat: "Excuse me. I don't know how best to say this . . ."

"Then maybe you shouldn't," Mare said. "I've got to get to work." She started for the neighboring lab bench.

"Have I somehow put you in an awkward position?" Deborah called after her. "Because if I have, I'm sorry."

Mare turned around. Her face softened to a degree. "It's not your fault. I was just wrong."

"Wrong about what?"

"These eggs," Mare said. "They're pig oocytes."

"Oh, right," Deborah said. "Dr. Saunders already told me."

"Good! Well, I've got to get to work." Mare pointed toward the other microscope she'd set up earlier. She smiled weakly, then continued on.

\ Deborah watched the woman for a moment as she settled herself in preparation for work. Deborah then leaned her face forward to her own microscope's eyepieces. She peered in at the field, whose left side was chock-full of tiny, granular circles each containing a fluorescing clump of DNA, but for the moment her mind wasn't on the task at hand. Instead she was thinking about the eggs' species. Despite Paul and Mare's allegations to the contrary, Deborah believed she was looking at a mass of human oocytes.

A half hour later Deborah had enucleated more than half the eggs beneath her microscope's objective. Needing a rest from the intensity of the work, she leaned back and rubbed her eyes forcibly. When she opened them, she started. With her degree of concentration she'd not heard anyone approach and was surprised to find herself staring up into the contrite face of Spencer Wingate. In the background she could see that Mare had looked up as well, and her face registered similar surprise.

"Good morning, Miss Marks," Spencer said. His voice was more gravelly than it had been the day before. He was dressed in a professorial long white doctor's coat, a crisp white dress shirt, and a demure silk tie. The only outward evidence of the previous night's inebriation was red, road-map eyes.

"Could I speak with you for a moment?" Spencer asked.

"Certainly," Deborah said with a degree of uneasiness. Her first concern was that he'd come to ask about his blue card, but she instantly dismissed the idea as unlikely. She slid off the stool, assuming that Spencer meant for them to step away. A glance in Mare's direction revealed the woman was watching them with rapt attention.

Spencer pointed toward one of the windows, and Deborah walked over to it. Spencer followed.

"I want to apologize for last night," Spencer said. "I hope I wasn't too much of a bore. I'm afraid I don't remember too much after we got to my home."

"You certainly weren't a bore," Deborah said with a forced laugh, trying to make light of the situation. "You were very entertaining."

"I'm not sure that's a compliment," Spencer said. "Of course, the worst part from my perspective is the lost opportunity."

"I'm not sure I follow."

"You know," Spencer said lowering his voice even more, "with you and your roommate, Penelope." He winked suggestively.

"Oh, right!" Deborah said, realizing he was making reference to the ridiculous ménage à trois fantasy. All at once she felt as put-off with Spencer as she'd felt earlier with Paul, but she held her tongue. Instead she said: "Her name is Prudence."

"Of course," Spencer said while tapping his forehead with the palm of his hand. "I don't know why I have so much trouble remembering her name."

"I don't know either," Deborah said. "But thank you for the apology for last night, even though it wasn't necessary. Now, I better get back to work." Deborah took a step back to her seat, but Spencer moved into her path blocking her progress.

"I thought we could try again tonight," he said. "I promise to be more sensible with the wine. How about it?"

Deborah looked up into the man's blue eyes. She sought for an appropriate response, which was difficult to find given the lack of respect she had developed for him. Considering the disagreement she'd witnessed the day before between Spencer and Paul, she had a sudden desire to say she'd just been asked out by his apparent rival in an attempt to fan intramural discord. Under the circumstances she thought it would be the quintessential putdown. But she held herself back. In view of what she and Joanna were trying to do, making an enemy of the founder was hardly prudent.

"No sense in taking two cars," Spencer added when Deborah hesitated responding. "We could all meet in the parking lot around five-fifteen."

"Not tonight, Spencer," Deborah said in as sweet a voice as she could force herself to assume.

"Tomorrow then?" Spencer suggested.

"Let me get back to you on it," Deborah said. "Joanna . . . I mean Prudence and I need to catch up on our sleep." Deborah felt a warmth wash over her and knew that she was blushing. It had been her only name slip, but it was a bad one in front of the clinic's founder.

"Maybe on the weekend," Spencer suggested, apparently unaware of Deborah's blunder. "What do you think?"

"That's a distinct possibility," Deborah added quickly, trying to sound positive. "Partying for us is far better on a night when we don't have to get up early the next morning."

"I couldn't agree more," Spencer said. "Then we could all sleep in."

"Sleeping late sounds heavenly," Deborah agreed generically.

"My direct dial number is triple eight," Spencer said with another lascivious wink. "I'll wait to hear from you."

"I'll be in touch," Deborah responded, although she had no intention of actually doing so.

Spencer walked out of the lab. Deborah watched him go, then switching her attention to Mare, noticed the lab technician was still staring at her. Deborah shrugged as if to say there's no accounting for the management's behavior. Reclaiming her stool, she checked her watch. Thank goodness there wasn't long to wait before she'd be meeting up with Joanna, and they could get on with what they were there for.

twelve

As eleven o'clock neared, Joanna had considerably more respect for people doing office work. Although it was true she'd been working particularly hard to get the maximum amount done, data entry was more tiring than she'd imagined. The concentration necessary to keep from making a mistake was intense, and doing it day in and day out for three hundred sixty-five days a year was difficult to imagine.

At exactly five minutes before eleven, Joanna stood up and stretched. She smiled at her neighbor in the immediately adjacent cubicle to the south who'd stood up when she heard Joanna's chair roll back. The woman proved to be rather nosy and had made it a point to look in on Joanna periodically throughout the morning. Her name—Gale Overlook—seemed fitting to Joanna.

Joanna had given a lot of thought to her plan; she knew what she would do first. With the scheduled rendezvous time with Deborah imminent, Joanna grabbed her purse, which contained the brute-force cracking software, her cell phone, and Wingate's blue card. She headed down the aisle between the cubicles. Her destination was the computer network administrator's work space. Her hope was to find him in his cubicle and for one simple reason: if he was in his cubicle he couldn't be in the server room.

Earlier, in the midst of a minor anxiety attack about being caught in the server room, it had dawned on Joanna that probably the only person who ever went in there was Randy Porter. Consequently, if he was in his cubicle, she'd have little to fear.

A wave of relief spread through her as she passed his cubicle. He was at his keyboard. Turning left, she headed over to the main corridor. Deborah was there, at the designated rendezvous. About twenty feet beyond was the door to the hallway leading to the server room with its cardboard NO ADMITTANCE sign.

"I hope your morning was as interesting as mine," Deborah said as Joanna came up and took a sip from the drinking fountain.

"Mine was about as interesting as watching paint dry," Joanna said. She looked up and down the hall to make sure no one was paying any attention to them. "Nothing happened, but then again I didn't want anything to happen."

"We got asked out to dinner at the Barn twice more," Deborah said proudly.

"Who asked you out this time?"

"Spencer Wingate for one. And he asked us out, not just me."

"Did you see him in person?"

"I most certainly did. He came by the lab to apologize for passing out last night and then pleaded for a rematch. I told him I was busy but you were available."

"Very funny!" Joanna said. "How did he look?"

"Not bad, considering," Deborah said. "I don't think he remembered much."

"That's understandable," Joanna said. "I trust the blue card did not come up in your conversation."

"Not a word."

"Who else was hitting on you?"

"The second invitation was from Paul Saunders! Can you imagine going out with him?"

"Only in a fit of self-loathing," Joanna said. "But I don't believe for a minute I was included in that invitation, not from the way he was looking at you yesterday in his office."

Deborah didn't deny it. She glanced briefly up and down the corridor to make certain no one was paying them any attention. "Let's get down to business," she said, speaking more quietly. "Do you have any particular plan for our server room incursion or what?"

"I do," Joanna said. She, too, lowered her voice and went on to tell Deborah her thoughts about Randy Porter.

"Great idea," Deborah said. "To tell the truth I was concerned about how I was going to stand watch for you. Without a back exit from the server room, even if I let you know someone was coming in, there'd be no way for you to get out."

"Precisely," Joanna said. "Now all you have to do is let me know if Randy Porter leaves his cubicle. The moment he does, press TALK on your cell phone which you'll set up dialed to mine. If my phone rings, I'll get out of the server room right away."

"Sounds like a good plan to me," Deborah said. "Should we try it now?"

"I think so," Joanna said. "If it doesn't work for whatever reason, we can try again at lunch. If that doesn't work, we'll have another chance in the afternoon. Otherwise we'll have to come back tomorrow."

"Let's think positively," Deborah said. She punched in Joanna's number on her cell phone's keypad. "I'm not wearing this dress another day in a row!"

"I checked on Randy Porter just before I came to meet you," Joanna said. "He was in his cubicle. I think he was on the Internet, which should keep him occupied."

"Do you have what you need?"

Joanna patted her purse. "I've got the software, David's instructions, and Wingate's blue card. Let's hope the card works or we're back to square one."

"It should work," Deborah said. "I'll head down to admin now, and you just hang out right here. If Randy Porter is still sitting on his duff in his office, I'll call you and let it ring twice. That'll be the green light, and you go do your thing."

The two women grasped hands for a moment. Then Deborah set briskly out walking down the corridor. When she reached the entrance to the administration area, she paused and looked back. Joanna was still at the water fountain leaning against the wall with her arms crossed. She waved and Deborah returned the gesture.

Deborah couldn't remember exactly where Randy Porter's cubicle was in the gridlike maze that filled the old hospital ward. After a quick search of the area where she thought it would be and not finding it, she began a more systematic search. Eventually she found it and was happy to see Randy still sitting in front of his monitor. Deborah didn't allow herself much of a look, but her impression was that he was playing a video game.

Deborah reached into her purse and pulled out her cell phone. With Joanna's number already dialed, she pushed the TALK button. Holding it up to her ear she listened for two complete rings, then pressed END. She replaced the phone in her bag.

Keeping one eye on Randy Porter's cubicle, she made her way over to the main corridor. There was no perfect spot where she could stand and not cause attention. Consequently, she had to keep moving.

Joanna switched her cell-phone mode from ringer to vibration the moment she'd gotten Deborah's signal. The noise made her jump even though she'd expected it. Clearly she was on edge.

After a furtive, final glance up and down the corridor to make sure no one was watching, she passed as quickly as possible through the NO ADMITTANCE door into the short hall beyond. As the door closed behind her, she found she was breathing heavily, as if she'd run a hundred yards. Her pulse soared. She was a little dizzy. All at once the reality of being an intruder enveloped her in a paralyzing rush. Belatedly

Joanna realized she was not cut out for tasks like breaking into computer server rooms; actually doing it was far more psychologically demanding than planning it.

With her back against the door to the main hall, Joanna took a number of deep breaths. Combining the controlled respiration with a short reassuring soliloquy, she was able to calm herself down enough to proceed. Tentatively she moved forward, slowly at first but then gaining confidence when her dizziness faded. She reached the server room door. After one last look back at the door to the corridor, she reached into her purse and pulled out Wingate's blue access card. Quickly she swiped it through the card swipe. Any residual concern she'd had about whether the card would work was dispelled with the mechanical click. She opened the door. In the next instant she was inside, hurrying over to the server console.

What Randy Porter liked most about computers was the games. He could play them all day and yearn for more when he got home at night. It was like an addiction.

Sometimes he wouldn't go to bed until three or four in the morning because with the World Wide Web someone was always up and willing to play. Even at 3:00 or 4:00 a.m. he hated to give up and only did so because he knew he'd be a total zombie at work the following day.

What was so good about his job at the Wingate Clinic was that he could indulge himself during office hours. It had been different back when he'd first been hired straight out of the University of Massachusetts. He'd had to put in long hours getting the Wingate local area network online. And then there'd been the demand for the best security available. That had required extra work and even some outside consulting. And finally there'd been the web page: that had taken a number of months to set up and then modify until everybody was happy. But now everything was humming along just fine, which meant there was little for him to do except be available for the occasional software or hardware glitch. Even those problems were usually because the individual involved was so *dorky* that they didn't realize they were doing something incredibly stupid. Of course, Randy didn't tell the individual that. He was always polite and pretended it was the machine's fault.

Randy's normal day began at his keyboard in his cubicle. With the help of Windows 2000 Active Directory, he checked to make sure all systems were running normally and all terminals were in a locked position. That generally took him about fifteen minutes.

After a coffee break he'd return to his cubicle for his morning gaming. To avoid being caught by Christine Parham, the office manager, he'd frequently move around to various workstations that were not in use. That made him hard to find on occasion, but that never led to any trouble since everybody thought he was off fixing someone's computer.

On May 10th at 11:11 in the morning Randy was locked in mortal combat with a slippery, talented opponent with the moniker of SCREAMER. The game, *Unreal Tournament,* was Randy's current favorite. And at that moment he was locked in a tense standoff in which he or SCREAMER would imminently be killed. Randy's palms were damp from anxiety, but he pressed on, fully believing that his experience and expertise would give him the upper hand.

There was a sudden unexpected beep. Randy reacted by practically leaping out of his ergonomic chair. At the bottom right-hand corner of his screen a small window had popped up. Within the window the words *SERVER ROOM BREACHED* were blinking insistently. Before Randy could respond to this prompt, he heard a fateful zapping noise that yanked his attention back to the main window. To his chagrin the view was a virtual ceiling. A second later his adversary's face appeared, peering down at him with a gloating smile. It took less time than a Pentium 4 processor for Randy's brain to compute that he'd been killed.

"Crap!" Randy muttered. It was the first time he'd been killed for over a week, and it was a letdown, big time. Irritably he looked back at the blinking window responsible for distracting his attention at such a critical juncture. Someone had opened the server room door. Randy didn't like anyone going into the server room and monkeying around. He considered it his domain. There was no reason for anybody to be in there unless it was IBM servicing the equipment, and if that happened it was his responsibility to be in there with them.

Randy exited from *Unreal Tournament* and pushed his joystick around behind the monitor so it was less obvious. Then he stood up. He was going to see who the hell was in the server room. Whoever it was, was responsible for getting him killed.

When the cell phone's vibration went off, Joanna's heart leaped into her mouth. She'd been struggling with her anxiety from the moment she'd come through the outer server room door. She'd found herself clumsy at the keyboard. It took her longer to carry out simple tasks, which only made her more anxious—and worse still at the keys.

Assuming the call was Deborah, Joanna knew she had only seconds to get out of the server room before Randy Porter appeared. Still all thumbs, she began exiting the system. All she had to do was cancel out the windows she'd brought up onto the screen, but it seemed to take forever since her movement with the mouse was so jerky. Finally the last window disappeared, leaving the screen blank. Quickly Joanna tossed the cracking software back into her purse; she'd had yet to insert the CD into the drive. Her phone had gone off only minutes after she'd sat down at the server-room console, and she had only been in the initial stages of giving herself access.

Frantically she snatched her purse from the desktop and dashed over to the server room door. But the second she opened it she heard the telltale sound of the outer door opening. In total panic, Joanna let go of the door she was holding and took a step backward. She felt desperate and completely trapped. With no other choice, she darted back around the vertically oriented electronic units each about the size of a shallow, four-drawer file cabinet. Scrunching down in a tight ball behind the farthest unit, she tried to make herself as small as possible. It was hardly a hiding place, but she had no other choice.

Joanna's heart was beating so hard she was certain that whoever was coming would be able to hear it. It was literally pulsing in her ears. She could feel perspiration appear within her clutched fists, which were pressed against her cheeks.

She tried to prepare herself for being discovered by thinking of what she would say. The problem was, there was absolutely nothing that she could say.

From the moment Randy had left his cubicle en route to the server room, he'd been silently venting his anger. He was upset more for having been interrupted and subsequently killed than for someone going into his server room. By the time he arrived on the scene, he was thinking more of getting back to Unreal Tournament and rechallenging SCREAMER than yelling at the person who'd violated his domain.

"What the blazes?" Randy questioned when he came on the open server-room door and the empty room beyond. He looked back at the outer door to the corridor which he'd left ajar, wondering how whoever had been in the server room had gotten out. His eyes then breezed around the inside of the server room for a second time. All was in order. He looked at the server room console. It too was as he'd left it, with the monitor displaying its screen saver. Then he grasped the door and swung it back and forth on its hinges. What had suddenly occurred to him was the possibility that when he'd last been in the room, he'd not closed the door completely, and it had just swung open.

With a shrug, Randy pulled the door closed. He heard the reassuring click and then tried to push it open again. It stayed firmly locked. With a final shrug, he turned around, and with the intent of getting back to his cubicle and SCREAMER, he hurried back out into the hallway.

"It's okay, it's okay!" Deborah repeated in a soothing voice. She was holding Joanna by the shoulders, trying to calm her down. Joanna was trembling with an occasional sob. They were in the lab, standing next to the window where Deborah had spoken with Spencer earlier that morning. Mare had seen them come in, but she'd apparently noticed Joanna's distress, and respecting their privacy, she'd not come over.

Deborah had called Joanna's cell phone the moment she'd seen Randy's head suddenly pop up above the room partition just prior to his dashing from his cubicle. Deborah had to make the call on the run because Randy was moving quickly. Her worst fears were realized when Randy made a beeline for the main corridor and turned in the direction of the server room. The other problem was that she didn't see Joanna, and her intuition told her that there'd not been enough time for Joanna to have gotten out.

When Randy had gone directly to the server room's outer door and immediately gone in, any minuscule hope Deborah had entertained that he was heading elsewhere than the server room was dashed. Coming up to the door herself, she hadn't known what to do. Unable to make up her mind, she'd done nothing.

Agonizing minutes had passed. Deborah had debated whether she should go in and try to defuse whatever situation had developed. She had even envisioned charging in, grabbing Joanna, and bolting for the car. Then to her utter surprise, Randy Porter had reemerged, alone and seemingly calmer than when he'd gone in.

Deborah had quickly bent over and taken a drink from the water fountain to avoid the impression she was loitering. Randy had passed behind her, and she'd sensed his pace slowed. But he had not stopped. When she'd righted herself, Randy had been a distance away. He'd been heading back down the corridor in the direction he'd come but with his upper torso twisted to keep Deborah in sight. When he'd caught her eye he'd given her the thumbs-up sign. Deborah had blushed as it had dawned on her that a significant portion of her derriere had most likely been exposed when she'd bent over the relatively low water fountain.

"I'm not cut out for this!" Joanna said angrily in response to Deborah's attempts to calm her, although whom she was angry at was not immediately clear. She pressed her lips together, but they quivered as if she might cry again. "I'm serious!"

Deborah shushed her.

"I'm not cut out for this," Joanna repeated, lowering her voice. "I fell apart in there. I was pathetic."

"I beg to differ with you," Deborah said. "Whatever you did, it worked. He didn't see you. Ease up! You're being too hard on yourself."

"You really think so?" Joanna took several uneven breaths.

"Absolutely," Deborah said. "Anyone else, including myself, would have blown it. But you pulled it off somehow, and here we are, ready to give it another college try."

"But I'm not going back in there," Joanna said. "Forget about it."

"Are you really ready to give up after all the effort we've been through?"

"It's your turn," Joanna said. "You go in the server room. I'll stand guard."

"If I could, I would," Deborah said. "The trouble is I don't have the facility you have with computers. And you could tell me what to do until you're blue in the face, and I guarantee I'd screw it up."

Joanna stared back at Deborah as if she were angry with her.

"I'm sorry I'm not a computer nerd," Deborah said. "But I don't think we should give up. We both want to find out what happened to our eggs, and now I have a new interest."

"I suppose you're going to make me ask what it is," Joanna muttered.

Deborah glanced over at Mare to make sure she wasn't trying to overhear their conversation. Then she lowered her voice and explained to Joanna the human eggs versus swine eggs episode that had occurred that morning. Joanna was immediately intrigued despite her distress.

"That's strange," Joanna exclaimed.

Deborah's expression suggested she hardly considered *strange* to be a strong enough word. "Incredible is more like it," she said. "Think about it! They spent ninety thousand dollars for a half-dozen eggs from us and then have several hundred for me to screw around with today. I mean, I'm an amateur with this nuclear-transfer stuff. That's more than strange."

"All right, it's incredible," Joanna said.

"So we have even more reason to create ourselves a pathway into their computer files," Deborah said. "I want to find out what kind of research they're doing and how they're getting all these eggs."

Joanna shook her head. "That may be an appropriate motivation, but I'm telling you: I don't think I'll be able to convince myself to go back in there."

"But we're better off than we were before," Deborah said.

"I can't see how," Joanna said.

"As near as I can tell, Mr. Randy Porter leapt up out of his seat simultaneously with your opening the server room door. That tells us he's got it wired to pop up on his monitor. I mean, it stands to reason. The timing couldn't have been a coincidence."

"I suppose that seems like a reasonable assumption," Joanna agreed. "But how does that help us?"

"Simply because it means we have to do more than watch him sit in his cubicle," Deborah said. "We've got to lure him out and keep him occupied."

\Joanna nodded as she thought over what Deborah was saying. "Am I to believe you have some plan to do this?"

"Of course," Deborah said with a sly smile. "When he passed me a few minutes ago in the hall while I was bending over the water fountain, he practically got torticollis. Judging from that reaction, I'd be very surprised if I couldn't corner him in the dining room at lunch and have a chat. I trust I'll be able to keep him interested. Then, when you're finished in the server room, you can give my cell phone a call to rescue me."

Joanna nodded again, but she didn't totally agree, not right away.

"Here's how it is going to work," Deborah said, sensing Joanna's lingering doubt. "Go back to administration and make sure Randy Porter is in his cubicle. Then go to yours. I don't care if you work or not, it really doesn't matter. What matters is for you to watch for Randy Porter to leave for lunch. The moment he does, call me. That way maybe I can even intercept him on his way to the dining room, which might be easier than if I get there when he's already sitting. As soon as I make contact and it's working, I'll call you. That's when you duck back into the server room and do what you have to do. The more I think about it, the more convinced I am that it's far better to be doing it over the lunch hour. It makes a lot more sense. When you're finished, come directly to the dining room. You can rescue me and have lunch at the same time."

"You make it sound so easy," Joanna said.

"I honestly think it will be," Deborah said. "What do you think?"

"I suppose it sounds like a reasonable plan. But what if you start a conversation, and he breaks it off? You'd let me know?"

"Of course I'd call you instantly," Deborah said. "And remember! If he's in the dining room you'll have plenty of time to get out. It's not the same as when he's sitting in his cubicle."

Joanna nodded several times in a row.

"Do you feel better now about going back in there?"

"I guess," Joanna said.

"Good!" Deborah said. "Now, let's get the ball rolling. If perchance Mr. Porter is not in his cubicle when you get over there, you'd better call me. We might have to adjust the plan if we can't find him."

"All right!" Joanna said, trying to bolster her courage. She clasped hands with Deborah briefly and then turned to leave.

Deborah watched Joanna go. She knew her roommate had been seriously upset, but she also knew Joanna to be resilient. Deborah was confident that when the chips were down, Joanna could be counted on to pull through.

Deborah went back to her microscope and tried to go back to work. But it was impossible. She felt far too jazzed up for such a painstaking task as enucleating oocytes. She was also on edge in case Joanna called indicating that Randy Porter was not in his cubicle. After five minutes had passed without a call, Deborah pushed back from the lab bench and wandered over to Mare's station. The woman looked up from her microscope's eye pieces when she sensed Deborah's presence.

"I have a question," Deborah said. "Where do these eggs we're working on come from?"

Mare hooked a thumb over her shoulder. "They come from that incubator way down there near the end of the lab."

"And how do they get into the incubator?"

Mare gave Deborah a look that wouldn't have qualified as a dirty look, but it wasn't all that friendly either. "You ask a lot of questions."

"It's the sign of a budding researcher," Deborah said. "As a scientist, when you stop asking questions it's time to retire or find another calling."

"The eggs come up in a dumbwaiter inside the incubator," Mare said. "But that's all I know. I've never been encouraged to ask, nor have I been inclined."

"Who would know?" Deborah asked.
"I imagine Miss Finnigan would know."

With his hands on both arms of his chair, Randy slowly raised himself to provide a progressively more expansive view of the administration area. He wanted to see if Christine was in her cubicle without her knowing he was checking. If he stood up all the way she could see him, but by doing it slowly he could stop when he just caught sight of the top of her sizable, curly-haired head. Bingo! She was there, and Randy lowered himself back down.

With the knowledge the office manager was nearby Randy lowered the volume on his computer speakers. Although when he was home he let the sound effects roar at full volume, when he was in the office he was a realist, especially with Christine only a few cubicles away.

Next Randy pulled out his joystick. When he got that in the exact position he preferred, he adjusted his rear end in the seat pan of his chair. To game at the full level of his abilities he needed to be comfortable. When all was set to his liking, he

gripped the mouse in preparation for log-
ging onto the Internet. But then he paused.
Strangely enough another thought occurred to him.

Randy had not only programmed the
server room door so that he would be
alerted when it was opened, he'd also programmed it so that the card swipe that
opened the door would record the identity
of the individual.

With a few rapid clicks of the mouse
Randy brought up the appropriate window.
What he expected to see was his name last
on the list from when he'd gone to check
the room after Helen Masterson had gone
in. That would have confirmed his suspi-
cion that the door had just opened on its
own accord from his having not shut it
properly. But to his surprise his name
wasn't last. The last name was Dr. Spencer
Wingate, the heralded founder of the clinic,
and the time was 11:10 that very morning.

Randy stared at the entry with a mixture
of confusion and disbelief. How could that
be, he wondered. Since he was serious
about his computer-gaming prowess, he
kept an accurate log of his triumphs and
even his rare failings. After minimizing the

current window, Randy brought up his *Unreal Tournament* record. There it was: He'd been killed at 11:11.

Taking a deep breath, Randy rocked back in his chair, staring at the computer screen while his mind recreated his recent dash back to the server room. He estimated that it took him only a minute or two to get from his cubicle to the server room, meaning he'd arrived there about 11:12 or 11:13. If that were the case, where the hell was Dr. Wingate, who'd entered at 11:10? And if that weren't enough of a conundrum, why did the doctor leave the door ajar?

Something very strange going on, Randy thought, especially since Dr. Wingate was supposed to be semiretired even though rumor had it that he was around. Randy scratched his head, wondering what to do, if anything. He was supposed to report any security lapses to Dr. Saunders, but Randy wasn't sure there had been a lapse. As far as he was concerned, Dr. Wingate was the highest honcho in the whole organization, so how could anything that concerned him be a security lapse?

Then Randy had another idea. Maybe he'd say something to weird Kurt

Hermann. The security chief had had Randy program his computer so it, too, recorded any and all openings of the card-swipe doors. That meant that Kurt already knew Dr. Wingate had been in the server room. What the security chief didn't know was that the doctor had only been in there for two minutes and had left the door open.

"Oh crap!" Randy said out loud. Worrying about all this was as bad as work. What he really wanted to do was get back on line with SCREAMER, so he tipped forward and grabbed his mouse.

"Miss Finnigan!" Deborah called out. She was standing in the laboratory supervisor's doorway. She'd knocked on the jamb, but the depth of Megan Finnigan's concentration on her computer had precluded her from responding. But Deborah's voice had penetrated, and the woman looked up with a startled expression. She then hastily cleared her screen.

"I'd prefer it if you knocked," she said.

"I did knock," Deborah responded.

The woman tossed her head to rid her

face of her bothersome strands. "I'm sorry. I'm just very busy. What can I do for you?"

"You encouraged me to come to you if I had any questions," Deborah said. "Well, I have a question."

"What is it?"

"I'm curious about where the eggs come from that I've been working on. I asked Maureen, but she said she didn't know. I mean, it's a lot of eggs. I just didn't realize they were available in such numbers."

"Availability of eggs has been one of the major limiting factors in our research from day one," Megan said. "We've devoted a lot of effort to solve the problem, and it has been one of Dr. Saunders and Dr. Donaldson's major contributions to the field. But the work is as of yet unpublished, and until it is, it is considered a trade secret." Megan smiled patronizingly and gave her head another one of her signature tosses that so annoyed Deborah. "After you've worked here for some reasonable period, and if you are still interested, I'm sure we can share with you our successes."

"I'll look forward to that," Deborah said.

"One other question: What species are the eggs I've been working on?"

Megan did not answer immediately but rather returned Deborah's stare in a manner that made Deborah feel as if the lab supervisor was gauging Deborah's motives. The pause was long enough for Deborah to feel uncomfortable.

"Why are you asking this?" Megan questioned finally.

"As I said, I'm just curious," Deborah responded. Megan's responses to her simple questions were answers in themselves. Deborah felt she was not going to get a straight answer and at that point wanted to leave. She had the sense that her further questioning would only draw unwanted attention.

"I'm not immediately sure which protocol Maureen is working under," Megan said. "I'd have to look it up, but at the moment I'm too busy."

"I understand," Deborah said. "Thank you for your time."

"Don't mention it," Megan responded. She smiled insincerely.

Deborah was relieved to return to her microscope. Going to the supervisor's office had not been a good or particularly productive impulse. Deborah went back to work but had managed to enucleate only one oocyte when her curiosity, heightened by her short conversation with Megan, got the best of her again. Merely looking at the mass of oocytes in the microscopic field begged the question about their origin, especially if they were human eggs as Deborah suspected.

Leaning back, Deborah gazed over at Mare, who was ignoring her as she'd essentially been doing since the verbal skirmish with Paul Saunders over the eggs' identity. A quick glance around the huge lab convinced Deborah that none of the dozen or so people toiling away were paying her any heed either.

Grabbing her purse as if she intended to go to the ladies' room, Deborah slid off her stool and headed out into the main corridor. Believing she'd only be working at the Wingate for that one day, she decided the eggs' origin was too much of a mystery to ignore. She didn't know if she could sleuth it out, but she thought she'd learn what she could while she had the chance.

Deborah walked down the corridor in the

direction of the central tower until she reached the last of the three doors leading from the corridor into the lab. Leaning into the lab, she could see Mare a good distance away, hunched over her scope. To Deborah's immediate right was the walk-in incubator where Mare had been going for the petri dishes full of eggs. Deborah went to its glass door, slid it open, and stepped inside.

The air was warm and moist. A large wall-mounted thermometer and humidistat indicated it was exactly 98.6°F with one hundred percent humidity. Shelves for the petri dishes lined both sides of the narrow room. At the rear was the dumbwaiter, but it was a far cry from its initial incarnation when it had served to bring food up to the wards from the institution's basement kitchen. It was made of stainless steel instead of the usual wood, with a glass door and glass shelves. For a dumbwaiter it was large, about the size of a highboy chest of drawers. It also had its own auxiliary heat and humidifying source to make sure it, too, stayed at the proper temperature and humidity.

Deborah pushed on the dumbwaiter to

see if it would move enough to give her a view down the shaft, but it was rock solid. It was obviously a highly engineered piece of equipment. Deborah stepped back and eyed the unit. She guessed the back of the shaft was common with the wall of the main corridor.

Leaving the incubator, she went back out into the main hall and gauged where the dumbwaiter shaft was located. Then she paced off the distance to the stairwell near the fire door to the central tower. Using the old metal stairway, she climbed up to the third floor. When she opened the door she was surprised.

Although she vaguely remembered Dr. Donaldson saying the vast old institution, save for the small portion occupied by the Wingate, was like a museum, she was unprepared for what she was looking at. It was as if sometime in the nineteen-twenties everybody, professional staff and patients alike, had just walked out leaving everything behind. There were old desks, wooden gurneys, and antique-appearing wheel chairs lining the dark hall. Huge cobweblike strands hung like garlands from Victorian light fixtures. There were even old, framed Currier and Ives prints hanging askew on the walls. The floor was covered with a thick layer of dust and pieces of plaster that had fallen from the shallowly vaulted ceiling.

Superstitiously Deborah covered her mouth and tried to breathe shallowly as she paced off the distance from the stairwell. She knew intellectually that any of the tubercular organisms and any of the other miasma that had at one time roamed the halls were long gone, but she still felt vulnerable and uneasy.

Once she had an approximate fix on where the dumbwaiter shaft was, she entered the nearest door. Not unexpectedly, she found herself in a windowless room which had served as a butler's pantry complete with cupboards full of institutional dishes and flatware. There were even some old warming ovens with their doors ajar. In the semidarkness they looked like huge dead animals with their mouths open.

The dumbwaiter shaft's doors were where she expected them to be. They were designed to open vertically like a freight elevator, but when Deborah pulled on the frayed canvas strap, it was obvious there was a fail-safe mechanism to keep them locked until the dumbwaiter itself had arrived.

Brushing her hands free of the dust, Deborah retraced her steps back to the stairwell and climbed to the fourth and top floor. She found the situation the same as on the third floor. Returning to the stairwell, she descended to the first floor.

When Deborah emerged from the stairwell, she knew instantly that the eggs did not come from there. The first floor had been renovated even more dramatically than the second floor to house the Wingate Clinic's clinical operations, and at that time of the morning it was in full swing with a constant flux of doctors, nurses, and patients. Deborah had to step to the side to allow an occupied gurney to go by.

Dodging the crowd, Deborah paced off the distance from the stairwell to where she guessed the dumbwaiter shaft was, behind the corridor wall. Leaving the corridor, she found herself in a patient-treatment area. Where the dumbwaiter shaft's doors should have been located, she was confronted by a shallow linen closet. It was immediately obvious to her that there was no opening for the dumbwaiter on the first floor.

A simple process of elimination left only the basement as the eggs' origin. Deborah headed back to the stairwell. To get down there she had to descend three flights instead of the two that had separated each of the upper floors. This suggested to her that the basement would have a higher ceiling, but it turned out not to be the case. There was a mezzanine floor of sorts between the basement and the first floor, composed of a myriad of piping and ductwork.

The basement had the appearance of a dungeon with infrequent bare-bulb lighting. The walls were exposed brick with arched ceilings, and the floor, granite slabs. The unease Deborah had felt up on the third and fourth floors was magnified in the gloomy basement. It, too, contained a multitude of mementos of its mental-institution/TB-sanitarium past, but here they were more decrepit as if abandoned in dank, shadowed recesses. Deborah's immediate feeling was that if there were any of the old infectious agents lingering in the building, this was where they'd live.

Girding herself against the power of her own imagination, Deborah proceeded to pace off the distance from the stairwell as best she could. The floor plan did not have the simple central corridor like all the floors above. It was considerably more mazelike, requiring her to be more creative in judging the distance while proceeding in a zigzag course around massive supporting piers.

As she passed through an archway and skirted a large kitchen with spacious metal countertops, huge ovens, and soapstone sinks, Deborah confronted something she'd not expected: a blank, modern, metallic door with no handle, hinges, or even lock.

Tentatively Deborah reached out in the semidarkness and lightly touched the shiny surface. She guessed it was stainless steel. Curiously, however, it was not cold but rather felt comfortably warm to her touch. She glanced around in the half-light at all the old kitchen equipment, then back to the shiny door. The incongruity was startling. Placing her ear against the door, she could hear the hum of machinery within. She listened for several minutes, hoping to hear voices, but she didn't. Moving back from the door, she caught sight of a card swipe just like the one outside the server-room door. At that moment she wished she had Wingate's card.

After a moment of indecision and a brief argument with herself, Deborah reached out and knocked on the door with her knuckle. It resonated solidly as if thick. She wasn't entirely sure she wanted anyone to answer, and no one did. Gaining in confidence, she pushed against the door, but it was immovable. Using the heel of her fist, she hit around the periphery of the door just to see if she could determine where the latch was. She couldn't.

Shrugging her shoulders in the face of such an impenetrable barrier, Deborah turned and retraced her steps back to the stairwell. It was almost noon, and time to return upstairs to wait for Joanna's call. Deborah had learned little on her foray, but at least she'd tried. She thought that maybe, if all went well, she could come back in the afternoon with Wingate's card. The stainless-steel door and what might be behind it had definitely piqued her curiosity.

thirteen

MAY 10, 2001
12:24 P.M.

Earlier in the day, Joanna had developed
more respect for data-entry-level office
workers. Now she had significantly more
respect for thieves. She couldn't imagine
doing anything like what she was currently
doing for a living. Deborah had talked her
into returning to the server room with a
compelling argument and plan that
seemed to have worked. Joanna had been
in the server room now for almost twenty-
two minutes and no one had bothered her.
Her biggest enemy had been herself.

The immobilizing panic she'd felt on the

first visit had come back with a vengeance the moment she'd come through the outer server-room door and had let up only enough to allow her to function, although not all that efficiently. The worst part of the whole episode had been the agonizing wait for the brute-force cracking software to come up with a password to unlock the server keyboard. While it ran, Joanna had been reduced to a pathetic, quivering mass of anxiety beset with intermittent jolts of fear from constantly hearing noises that were either innocuous or completely fabricated by her overwrought brain. She was actually surprised at herself. It had been her misconception that she would be a cool person under the kind of stress she was experiencing.

Once she'd gotten into the system, her terror had been ameliorated a degree just from the mere fact of doing something rather than just watching. The main trouble had then become her tremor. It had made operating the mouse and the keyboard difficult.

As she had progressed, Joanna had silently thanked Randy Porter. The man had made her job significantly easier by not hiding what she was searching for too deeply within subfolders. From the very first window Joanna had brought up, she found a server drive named *Data D* that sounded promising. Opening that drive presented her with an array of folders conveniently named. One of them was called *Donor.* Right-clicking on the folder and selecting *Properties,* she saw that access was extremely limited. In fact, besides Randy as the network administrator, only Paul Saunders and Sheila Donaldson were authorized entry.

Confident she'd found the correct file, Joanna went through the process of adding herself as a user. That required merely typing in her user account designation plus her office domain. Just as she was about to click the *Add* button she heard a door open somewhere in the distance that caused her heart to leap in her chest and a new batch of perspiration pop out on her forehead.

For several seconds Joanna was unable to move or even breathe as she strained to hear the telltale sounds of footsteps in the server-room corridor. But she didn't. Still she expected someone was behind her.

Slowly she turned. A modicum of relief coursed through her veins when she saw an empty server-room doorway. Standing up and taking a few steps back, she looked down the server-room corridor to the outer door. It was closed.

"I've got to get out of here," Joanna moaned. Quickly she returned to the keyboard and, with a trembling hand, clicked to add herself to the donor file access list.

As rapidly as she was able Joanna went back through the windows she'd progressively opened to return the server monitor to its desk top and ultimately to its password demand. She snatched up her purse and was about to flee when she remembered the cracking software still in the CD drive. Shaking worse than ever now that she was within seconds of success, she managed to get the CD out and in her bag. Finally she was able to leave.

She closed the server-room door and then ran the few steps to the outer door. Unfortunately there was no way to anticipate if it was a good time to emerge into the main corridor or not. It all depended on who happened to be out there. She just had to take a chance and hope for the best. In one motion she opened the door and stepped out, pulling the door closed behind her. Trying not to panic, she avoided looking up and down the corridor but rather went immediately to the water fountain. It wasn't that she was thirsty although her mouth was certainly dry. She just wanted something to do rather than look like a thief making her escape.

Joanna straightened up. It had been encouraging while drinking not to have heard any voices, and now that she looked it seemed she'd selected a particularly opportune moment to emerge. It was one of the few times Joanna had seen the corridor completely deserted.

Eager to see if she had been successful and also to take a quick look inside the folder even if Deborah was not with her, Joanna hurried back to her cubicle in administration. Since it was the middle of the lunch hour, the administration area was all but deserted, which was fine with Joanna. She dashed into her cubicle, tossed her purse on the desk, and sat down. She unlocked her workstation. With dexterity somewhat improved above what she'd had to deal with in the server room, Joanna quickly mapped a network drive to the donor folder. As she clicked for the command to take effect, she held her breath.

"Yes!" Joanna hissed loudly through clenched teeth. She was into the folder's directory. She felt like cheering, but held herself back, and it was a good thing.

"Yes, what?" a voice asked. It was halfway between a demand and a question. "What's going on?"

Feeling an iota of the same terror of discovery she'd experienced in the server room, Joanna raised her eyes and looked up and to the right. As she'd feared she would when she'd first heard the voice, she found herself gazing up into Gale Overlook's pinched face.

"What'd you do, win the lottery?" Gale asked. She had a way of speaking that made anything she said seem derogatory.

Joanna swallowed. She had another cruel instantaneous realization. Although she considered herself reasonably witty and as capable of repartee as any of her friends, feeling anxious and guilty, which she did at that moment, caused her mind to go blank. Instead of words, a kind of stuttering emerged from her mouth.

"What'd ya have on your screen?" Gale asked, becoming even more interested in the light of Joanna's apparent distress. Gale bobbed her head around trying to see the screen through the reflected glare.

Although Joanna was momentarily speechless, she did have the presence of mind to close the computer window, bringing her screen back to its desktop.

"Were you on the Net?" Gale asked accusingly.

"Yes," Joanna said, finally finding her voice. "I was checking some stocks to see what they're doing."

"Christine's not going to like that," Gale said. "She frowns on people going on the Net for personal reasons during working hours."

"Thank you for telling me," Joanna said. She stood, smiled stiffly, grabbed her purse, and left.

Joanna walked swiftly. Anger at herself for acting so suspiciously and irritation at Gale Overlook for being such a meddler had the beneficial effect of focusing her rampant anxieties. As she headed toward the dining room, she actually began to feel better. By the time she got to the fire door leading into the tower portion of the building, she had recovered enough even to feel mildly hungry.

Hesitating on the dining room's threshold, Joanna scanned the room for Deborah. It was significantly more crowded than the day before, when Helen Masterson had brought her and Deborah. Joanna's eyes stumbled onto Spencer Wingate. Quickly she moved them away. She was not in the mood to make eye contact with the man. She saw Paul Saunders and Sheila Donaldson at another table and looked away equally quickly. Then she saw Deborah sitting at a table for two with Randy Porter. They appeared deep in conversation.

Joanna made her way over to Deborah, attempting to keep her face away from Sheila Donaldson as much as possible. It wasn't until Joanna was standing at the table side before Deborah was aware of her and looked up.

"Hello, Prudence, dear!" Deborah said lightly. "You remember Randy Porter, I'm sure."

Randy smiled shyly and shook hands but didn't stand. Joanna wasn't surprised.

She'd long since become accustomed to the fact that a lot of men raised above the Mason-Dixon Line had little schooling in the social graces.

"Randy and I have been having an interesting discussion," Deborah said. "I didn't know the world of computer games was so intriguing. It seems we've been missing something, big time. Am I right, Randy?"

"Absolutely," Randy said. He leaned back with a self-satisfied smile.

"Well, listen, Randy," Deborah said. "I tell you what! I'll come by your workstation later and you can show me *Unreal Tournament.* How does that sound?"

"Sounds good to me," Randy said. He was rocking forward and backward slightly as if constantly agreeing with himself.

"I'm glad to have had this opportunity to talk with you, Randy," Deborah added. "It was fun." She nodded and grinned, hoping Randy would take the hint. But he didn't.

"I have a couple extra joysticks in my car," Randy said. "I can have you ladies set up to play in no time at all."

"I'm sure we'd appreciate that," Deborah said, losing patience. "But right now Prudence and I have some things we'd like to talk about."

"Hey, that's okay by me," Randy said. But he didn't budge.

"We'd like a little privacy," Deborah added.

"Oh!" Randy said. He looked back and forth between the two women as if confused, but then finally got the message. He then fumbled with his napkin before standing. "I'll see you guys around."

"Right!" Deborah said.

Randy left and Joanna took his seat.

"He's not well trained in his social cues," Joanna commented.

Deborah gave a short, mocking laugh. "And you probably believe you had the worst part of the deal going in the server room."

"Was it that bad?"

"He's a total computer nerd," Deborah complained. "He couldn't talk about anything else. Absolutely nothing! But that's water over the dam." She cleared her throat, leaned forward, and in an excited but lowered voice, asked: "Well, what happened? Did you do it or what?"

Joanna leaned forward as well. Their faces were only inches apart. "It's done."

"Fantastic! Congratulations! So what did you learn?"

"Nothing yet," Joanna said. "Other than I checked from my workstation, and what I did in the server room worked. I was into the proper folder. I even saw your name in the directory."

"So why didn't you learn anything?"

"Because my nosy neighbor interrupted me," Joanna said. "She's like a jack-in-the-box whenever I say or do anything out of the ordinary. I thought she'd be at lunch when I got back there, but unfortunately I was wrong."

One of the Nicaraguan waitresses came over and Joanna ordered a soup and salad. The food choice was Deborah's suggestion. She said it would be the fastest.

"I can't wait for us to get back to your workstation," Deborah said once the waitress had left. "I'm really psyched about all this. And strangely enough, at this point I'm as interested in finding out about the research around here as I am about our eggs."

"That's going to be a problem," Joanna

said. "First of all we have to worry about my nosy neighbor. I think it might be best if we wait until she leaves her cubicle before we go back into the donor folder."

"Then let's do it over in the lab," Deborah said. "There're a lot of available workstations that will be private enough. We won't have to worry about someone looking over our shoulders."

"We can't use a workstation in the lab," Joanna said. "The access I created is via the office domain only."

"Good grief!" Deborah remarked. "Why does this all have to be so complicated? But, all right! So we use yours. But I think we should just ignore your neighbor. Hell, I can stand between her and the screen. As soon as you've eaten, let's go and do it."

"There's another problem," Joanna said. "The only access I created is into the donor folder. There were other folders in the same drive, such as *Research Protocols* and *Research Results,* but I didn't give myself access to them."

"Why the hell not?" Deborah questioned. She furrowed her brows.

"Because I was too afraid to take any more time," Joanna said.

"Oh! For chrissake!" Deborah complained. "I don't believe this! You were right there with the files staring you in the face. How could you pass it up?" Deborah shook her head in irritated amazement.

"You don't understand how nervous I was," Joanna said. "I'm lucky I was able to do anything in that room."

"How much more time would it have taken?" Deborah questioned.

"Not long," Joanna admitted. "But I'm telling you I was terrified. It's been a hard lesson, but I've learned that I'm lousy at committing felonies. You understand what we are doing is a felony, don't you?"

"I suppose," Deborah said absently. She was clearly disappointed.

"If worse comes to worst, and we are caught," Joanna said, "at least if we can prove we were just after information about our own eggs, I think we'd be treated leniently. But we certainly wouldn't be if we were caught breaking into their research protocols no matter what the rationalization."

"All right, maybe you have a point," Deborah said. "Anyway, I've another plan. Give me the Wingate blue card!"

"Why?" Joanna asked. She eyed her roommate questioningly. She knew Deborah could be impulsive.

Before Deborah could respond Joanna's food arrived. The waitress served it and left. Deborah leaned forward again and told Joanna the story of her search for the eggs' origin by investigating the dumbwaiter shaft. She told about finding the blank, highly polished, stainless-steel door, completely out of place in the decrepit, antiquated basement kitchen. When she was finished she said simply: "I want to see what's behind that door."

Joanna finished chewing her mouthful of salad and swallowed. She gazed at Deborah with exasperation. "I'm not going to give you the Wingate card!"

"What?" Deborah blurted.

Joanna shushed her before looking around to see if Deborah's outburst had attracted any undo attention. Luckily it hadn't.

"I'm not going to give you the Wingate card," Joanna repeated in almost a whisper. "We're here to find out about our eggs. That has been the goal from the beginning. No matter how compelling you believe finding out what they're doing around here is, we can't afford to put what we're here for in jeopardy. If that door down in the basement has a card swipe like the server-room door and you go in there, there's a good chance someone is going to be alerted just like with the server room. And if that happens my intuition tells me that we'll be in deep trouble."

Deborah returned Joanna's stare irritably, but as the seconds ticked by her expression softened as did her indignation. Although she didn't like to hear it, what Joanna was saying had the ring of truth. Still Deborah felt frustrated. A few minutes earlier she had thought she had two equally promising avenues of approach to what she thought was an important mystery. Her intuition was loudly proclaiming that at best, the Wingate Clinic was involved in ethically questionable research, and at worst it was breaking the law.

As a biologist who was aware of many of the biomedical issues of the day, Deborah knew that fertility clinics like the Wingate operated in a medical arena without oversight. In fact, the desperate clients of such clinics frequently begged them to try untested procedures. In such an environment no patients minded being proverbial guinea pigs, and they blithely dismissed possible negative consequences for themselves or society in general as long as there was the slightest possibility of producing a child. Such patients also tended to put their doctors on a pedestal that encouraged the doctors to believe, in a kind of intellectual conceit, that ethics and even laws did not apply to them.

"I'm sorry I didn't do more," Joanna said. "I suppose I let you down. I wish I hadn't been such a basket case in the server room. But I did the best I could under the circumstances."

"Of course you did," Deborah said. Now she felt guilty about having gotten upset at Joanna who actually had accomplished a rather heroic task. For all of Deborah's bluster, she sincerely questioned if she'd have been able to do what Joanna had done even if she had the computer know-how. Entertaining Randy had been a nuisance, not a stressful challenge.

"What we should really be discussing is where we should access the donor folder,"

Joanna said, taking another bite of her lunch.

"Explain!" Deborah said.

"I'd really be more comfortable doing it from home tonight via the modem," Joanna said. "It would be safer, but there are problems."

"Such as?"

"If our download of a secure file is detected, they could trace it back to our computer through our Internet provider."

"Not good," Deborah said.

"There's also the chance that if we wait, my access could be discovered and eliminated before we take advantage of it."

"Now you tell me," Deborah complained. "This I wasn't aware of. What are the chances of it happening?"

"Probably not terribly high," Joanna admitted. "Randy would have to have some reason to look for it."

"Sounds like we have to do it here," Deborah said.

"I agree," Joanna said. "Sometime later this afternoon. But I think we should plan on leaving immediately afterward. If Randy detects the download and figures out it is coming from within the network, he'll find the pathway. Then it wouldn't take him long to trace it to Prudence Heatherly's workstation."

"Which means we have to be long gone," Deborah said. "All right, I get the picture! Now, are you finished eating?"

Joanna looked down at her half-eaten soup and salad. "Are you in a rush?"

"I can't say I'm in a rush," Deborah said, "but the entire time I've been here, including the half an hour or so with my new friend Randy, the security chief has been staring at me."

Joanna started to turn around but Deborah quickly reached out and gripped her wrist. "Don't look!"

"Why not?"

"I don't know exactly," Deborah admitted. "But he gives me the creeps, and I'd rather not even acknowledge that I've noticed he's been looking at me. For all I know it's this damned dress again. What was a lark initially has become a pain in the ass."

"How do you know it is the security chief?"

"I don't know for certain," Deborah admitted. "But it stands to reason. Remember yesterday when we were trying to get in and the trucks were in the way? It wasn't until he came out and ordered the uniformed guy to let them in that the Mexican standoff was resolved. When we drove in he was standing next to Spencer. Do you remember him?"

"Not really," Joanna admitted. "Remember, my attention was taken by Spencer at the moment, when I had the distorted idea he reminded me of my father."

Deborah chuckled. "Distorted is right! But we're getting away from the issue. What about your food? You haven't taken a bite for the last five minutes."

Joanna tossed her napkin onto the table and stood up. "I'm ready! Let's go."

Except for frequenting the dining room, Kurt Hermann seldom went into the Wingate Clinic proper. He preferred to remain in the gatehouse, or on the extensive grounds, or in his apartment in the staff village. The problem was, he knew some things went on in the clinic that he did not countenance, but thanks to his military training he could compartmentalize his thinking. By not going into the clinic, it was like out of sight out of mind, and he just didn't think about it.

But there were occasions when entering the main part of the clinic was required, and his current preoccupation with Georgina Marks was one of them. Using his contacts and the few facts from her employment application form plus the registration of the car she drove, he'd put out requests for information about her. What had come back so far was confusing if not intriguing. He had originally intended to approach her in the dining room during lunch, but he had changed his mind. It had been obvious that she'd set her talons on the adolescent computer fellow with whom she'd arrived, and the last thing Kurt wanted to weather was a rejection from the kind of person she was.

Then the situation had abruptly changed. Georgina's girlfriend had shown up, and from afar it appeared as if the computer whiz had been summarily canned. Kurt needed to know why.

"He's not in his cubicle?" Christine Parham, the office manager, asked.

Kurt looked away for a moment to keep

from lashing out in response to such an inane question. He'd just finished telling the woman that Randy Porter was not at his desk. Slowly Kurt returned his glaring eyes to Christine's. He didn't have to respond.

"Would you like me to page him?" Christine asked.

Kurt merely nodded. For him, the less said the better. He had a counterproductive penchant for telling people what he thought of them when irritated and Georgina Marks had him irritated.

Christine put in the call. While she waited for a response, she asked Kurt if security was having computer problems. Kurt shook his head and checked his watch. He'd give this mission another five minutes. If Randy Porter had not been found by then, he'd leave instructions for the twerp to come to the gatehouse. Kurt didn't want to be away from his office for too long. With the number of feelers he had out about Georgina Marks and the calls he expected in return, he wanted to be available to take them in person.

"Nice weather we're having," Christine commented. Kurt didn't respond, but she was saved from having to come up with any more small talk by her phone's insistent jangle. It was Randy, who reported that he was working on someone's computer in accounting but could come by immediately if needed. Christine told him the chief of security was there to see him so he'd better come right over.

"I'll meet him at his desk," Kurt said before Christine had hung up. She relayed the message.

Kurt wended his way to the network administrator's cubbyhole. He sat in the second chair and gazed around contemptuously at the science fiction artwork gracing the cubicle's walls. He took in the joystick foolishly pushed behind the monitor as if to hide it. Kurt thought the kid could use a few months of boot camp, which is what he thought of all young people who'd not experienced it.

"Hello there, Mr. Hermann," Randy said breezily as he swooped into the room. His insouciant attitude around people like Kurt belied a wariness like a dog around an unpredictably cruel master. "Is something amiss with one of the security computers?" He threw himself into his desk chair as if it were a skateboard, requiring him to grab onto the edge of the desk to keep from rolling into the wall.

"The computers are fine," Kurt said. "I'm here to talk to you about your lunch date."

"Georgina Marks?"

Kurt looked away for a moment, like he'd done recently with Christine. He ruminated why everybody had to answer his questions with essentially the same question. It was maddening.

"What do you want to know about her?" Randy asked brightly.

"Did she come on to you strong?"

Randy wagged his head. "So so," he said. "More so in the beginning. I mean, she initiated the conversation."

"Did she proposition you?"

"What do you mean?"

Kurt looked away again briefly. It was trying talking to most of the staff, particularly Randy Porter, who looked and acted like he was still in high school. " 'Did she proposition you' means: Did she offer sex for money or services?"

Randy had had the distinct impression that the security chief was a weird dude, but this question out of the blue took the cake. He didn't know what to say since he sensed the man was angry and wound up tight like a piano wire tuned to high C.

"Would you mind answering the question!" Kurt growled.

"Why would she be offering me sex?" Randy managed.

Kurt looked away yet again. Another question generating a question, which unhappily reminded him of the compulsory chats with a psychiatrist he'd been ordered to have prior to leaving the army. Taking a breath, he then repeated his question slowly and threateningly.

"No!" Randy barked. Then he lowered his voice. "Sex didn't come up. We were talking about computer games. Why would she bring up sex?"

"Because sex is what that type of woman does."

"She's a biologist," Randy said defensively.

"It is a strange way for a biologist to dress," Kurt said mockingly. "Do any of the other biologists look like her?" At this point in his investigation Kurt wasn't sure Georgina was a biologist or that her name was Georgina, but he did not mention his suspicions. He didn't want them getting back to the woman and alerting her until he'd finished his inquiries. It was his current belief that she was at the Wingate for some ulterior motive, and dressed as provocatively as she was, prostitution was high on his list. After all, it had been his original assessment, and she'd already apparently scored with Spencer Wingate the same day she'd met him at the gate.

"I liked the way she was dressed," Randy said.

"Yes, I bet you did," Kurt snapped. "But why did you leave so abruptly this afternoon? Were you turned off for some reason? Is that when she asked you if you were interested in a trick?"

"No!" Randy protested. "I'm telling you, sex wasn't involved. We'd had a nice conversation, but she wanted me to leave. Her friend had appeared, and they wanted to talk, so I left."

Kurt stared at the skinny computer kid. From Kurt's interrogation experience, he sensed the fellow was telling him the truth. The problem was that what Randy was saying didn't jibe with any of Kurt's current beliefs about this new employee. She was becoming more of a mystery rather than less of one.

"There is something I'd like to talk to you about," Randy said, eager to get the conversation away from Georgina Marks. He went on to tell Kurt about the strange episode involving Dr. Wingate and the server room.

Kurt nodded as he absorbed the information. He didn't know what to make of it nor what to do about it. For the last several years he'd answered to Paul Saunders, not Spencer Wingate. As a military man, he loathed situations with a blurred hierarchy.

"Let me know if it happens again," Kurt said. "And let me know if you have any more interaction with Georgina Marks, or her friend for that matter. And it goes without saying that you're to keep this conversation just between you and me. Do I make myself clear?"

Randy nodded immediately.

Kurt stood up and without another word walked out of Randy's cubicle.

Deborah gave up trying to work. With her mind churning, it was impossible to con-

centrate, and since she and Joanna would
soon be departing the scene, it was a
sham anyway. She'd been waiting over an
hour for Joanna's call to say that her nosy
cubicle neighbor was gone, clearing the
way for them to access the donor file, but
it had never come. Apparently the neighbor
wasn't going anyplace soon.

Deborah drummed her fingers on the
counter top. She'd never been particularly
patient and this unnecessary waiting was
pushing her beyond her limit.

"Screw it," she said suddenly under her
breath. She pushed back from the microscope, grabbed her purse, and headed for
the door. She'd kowtowed to Joanna's ap-
prehensions and paranoia about her neighbor long enough. After all, what did it
matter? As soon as they got the information, they were out of there. Besides, as
Deborah had suggested, she could block
the screen with her body so the neighbor
couldn't see anyway.

Avoiding looking in the direction of the
few lab people she'd met, Deborah headed
out into the hall once again as if she were
on her way to the ladies' room. A few min-

utes later she slipped into Joanna's cubicle. Joanna was dutifully working.

Without sound Deborah mouthed the question, "Which direction is Gale Overlook?"

Joanna pointed to the partition to the right.

Deborah stepped over to it and looked over. It was a cubicle the mirror image of Joanna's. Interestingly enough it was not occupied.

"There's no one here!" Deborah reported.

Adopting a questioning expression, Joanna looked as well. "Well, I'll be darn," she said. "She was here two minutes ago."

"How convenient," Deborah said. She rubbed her palms together excitedly. "How about doing your sorcery right this minute. Let's get the information about our progeny and fly the coop."

Joanna stepped over to the opening of her cubicle and looked in both directions. Satisfied, she came back and sat down at her keyboard. Hesitantly she looked up at Deborah.

"I'll keep a lookout," Deborah assured

her. Then she added, "And after all this effort, this better be good."

With a few rapid keystrokes and clicks of the mouse Joanna pulled up the first page of the directory for the donor file. There amongst other names at the beginning of the alphabet was Deborah Cochrane.

"Let's do you first," Joanna said.

"Fine by me," Deborah said.

Joanna clicked on Deborah's name and her file popped up. Both women read over the material which included background and baseline medical information. At the bottom of the page was an underlined, boldfaced notation that she'd adamantly insisted on local anesthesia for the retrieval.

"They certainly took that anesthesia question seriously," Deborah said.

"Have you finished with this page?" Joanna questioned.

"Yeah, let's get on to the good stuff!"

Joanna clicked to the next and what turned out to be the final page. At the top was the notation NUMBER OF EGGS RETRIEVED. Next to it was a zero.

"What the hell?" Deborah questioned.

"This suggests they didn't get any eggs from me at all."

"But they told you they had," Joanna said.

"Of course they did," Deborah said.

"This is strange," Joanna said. "Let's check my file." She returned to the directory and scrolled through until she got to the M's. Finding her name, she clicked on it. For the next thirty seconds they read through the material, which was similar to what they'd read for Deborah on her first page. But on the next page they were in for a larger surprise than the one caused by Deborah's zero eggs. In Joanna's file it said that 378 had been retrieved.

"I don't know what to make of this," Joanna said. "They told me they'd gotten five or six, not hundreds."

"What's after each egg?" Deborah asked. The type was too small to read.

Joanna enlarged the view. After each egg was a client's name along with the date of an embryo transfer. After that was Paul Saunders's name, followed by a brief description of the outcome.

"According to this, each one of your eggs went to a different recipient,"

Deborah said. "Even that's strange. I thought each patient would get multiple eggs, if they were available, to maximize the chances of implantation."

"That was my understanding as well," Joanna said. "I don't know what to make of all this. I mean, not only are there too many eggs, but none of them was successful." With her finger she ran down the long list where there was either a notation about implantation failure or a miscarriage date.

"Wait! There's one that was successful," Deborah said. She reached out and pointed. It was egg thirty-seven. A birth date of September 14, 2000, was indicated. It was followed by the name of the mother, an address, a telephone number, and the notation it was a healthy male.

"Well, at least there was one," Joanna said with relief.

"Here's another one," Deborah said. "Egg forty-eight with a birth date October 1, 2000. It was also a healthy male."

"Okay, two," Joanna said. She was encouraged until both she and Deborah had gone through the entire list. Out of the 378, there were only two other positives, egg 220 and egg 241 both having been implanted that January. Each of these was followed by the notation that the pregnancies were progressing normally.

"How could they have implanted this so recently?" Joanna asked.

"I suppose it means they're using frozen eggs," Deborah said.

Joanna leaned back and looked up at Deborah. "This is hardly what I expected."

"You can say that again," Deborah responded.

"If this is correct, that's a success rate around one in a hundred. That doesn't speak well for my eggs."

"There's no way they got almost four hundred eggs from you. This has to be some kind of research fabrication for God knows what reason. Almost four hundred eggs is about as many as you'll produce during your whole life!"

"You think this is all made up?"

"That would have to be my guess," Deborah said. "Weird things are going on here, as we both know. In that light, a bit of data falsification wouldn't surprise me in the slightest. Hell, it happens in the best of institutions much less in an isolated place like this. But I'll tell you: now that we're confronted with this mishmash, I'm even more disappointed we can't get into their research files."

Joanna turned around to the keyboard and started typing.

"What are you doing now?" Deborah questioned.

"I'm going to print the file out," Joanna said. "Then we're going to take it and leave. I'm crushed with these results."

"You're crushed!" Deborah said. "They have me down for no eggs whatsoever. At least they thought enough of you to attribute some live kids."

Joanna glanced up at Deborah. As she suspected, her roommate was smiling. Joanna had to give her credit. Thanks to her mischievous personality, she could find humor in most any circumstance. For her part, Joanna was not amused at all.

"One thing I do notice," Deborah said. "With each egg entry of yours, the sperm donor is not mentioned."

"I would assume it was the woman's husband," Joanna said. She finished setting up the printing command and clicked on the *Print* button. "Now that's going to take a few minutes with the size of the file.

If there's anything you want to do, do it now, because once we have the file, I want to leave."

"I'm ready now," Deborah said.

"What a day," Randy lamented. He was thankful to have gotten rid of Kurt Hermann but disgruntled he'd had to have such a weird conversation in the first place. The man was like a caged tiger with his quiet demeanor and the slow way he moved and spoke. Randy shook himself as if having had a wave of nausea just remembering talking with him.

Randy was on his way back from fixing the workstation in accounting which he'd had to put on hold when he'd been called to have the chat with the security chief. It was going on two in the afternoon, and he was looking forward to getting back to his cubicle. Putting up with Kurt hadn't been the worst part of the day: that was reserved for having lost to SCREAMER, and Randy was aching for a rematch.

Arriving in his cubicle, Randy went through his usual trick to see if Christine was around. He was glad to see she wasn't, which was typical for that time in the afternoon when she had her department-head meetings. That meant he could allow a little more sound. Sitting down, he pulled his joystick from behind the monitor. Next he typed in his password to unlock his keyboard. The moment he did so, he saw the same pesky prompt flashing in the lower right-hand corner of his computer desktop that had been responsible for his death that morning. Somebody had been in the server room again!

With angry strokes, Randy brought up the appropriate window. Sure enough, the door had been opened at 12:02 P.M. and left open until 12:28 P.M. which meant that whoever had gone in there had remained for twenty-six minutes. Randy knew that a visit of twenty-six minutes was not like someone popping in for a peek, and it bothered him considerably. In twenty-six minutes someone could cause a lot of trouble indeed.

Next Randy called up the appropriate folder to see who it had been. He was shocked to find that once again it had been Dr. Spencer Wingate! Randy sat back and stared at the founder's name while trying to decide what to do. He'd told Kurt about the first incident, but the security chief had hardly seemed impressed although he had asked to be informed if it happened again.

Randy tipped forward again. He decided he'd call the security chief but only after seeing if he could find anything in the system that had been changed. What first came to mind was a change in user levels. With rapid strokes and movement of the mouse, he accessed his Active Directory. After only a few minutes he had the answer. Dr. Wingate had added Prudence Heatherly to the access list for the *Donor* folder in the server's data drive.

Randy tipped back in his seat again. He asked himself why the founder of the clinic would add the name of a new employee to a secure file that even Dr. Wingate didn't have access to. It didn't make a lot of sense unless Prudence Heatherly was working for him in some undercover capacity.

"This is unreal," Randy said. In a way, he was enjoying himself. It was something like a computer game where he was trying to figure out his opponent's strategy. It wasn't as exciting as *Unreal Tournament,* but then again, little was. He sat and pondered for a number of minutes.

Without coming up with a plausible explanation, Randy reached for the phone. He wasn't looking forward to talking with Kurt again, but at least it was by phone, not in person. He also decided to tell the man just the facts and none of his supposition. While he dialed the extension he noted the time. It was two o'clock on the button.

fourteen

MAY 10, 2001
2:00 P.M.

Joanna tried to act normally despite a creepy feeling she was being watched as she descended the steps at the Wingate Clinic's entrance and started down the walkway toward the Chevy Malibu. Deborah was already in the car, and Joanna could see her head silhouetted in the driver's seat. Since the workday was hardly over, they had decided that it would attract less attention if they left separately than if they walked out together. So far it seemed to have worked. Deborah had apparently made it safely, and no one had confronted Joanna.

Joanna had her purse over her right shoulder. In her left hand she was carrying a thick envelope containing the bulky print-out of the donor file. As she walked she had to fight against the urge to run. Once again she felt like a thief making her get-away, only this time she was carrying the stolen goods.

She got to the car without incident and went around to the passenger side. As quickly as she could she climbed in.

"Let's get the hell out of here!" Joanna proclaimed.

"Wouldn't this be a good time for the car not to start?" Deborah joked as she reached for the ignition.

Joanna swatted her playfully, giving vent to the tension she felt. "Don't even suggest it, you tease! Move it!"

Deborah leaned away from Joanna's slap, got the car going, and backed out of the parking space.

"Well, we did it, for whatever it was worth," Deborah said as she maneuvered the car to begin the descent of the long, curving drive. "I guess we should give ourselves credit for that, even if the payoff was a big disappointment."

"We didn't do it until we get out of the gate safely," Joanna said.

"I suppose that's technically true," Deborah said. She pulled up to the gate, stopping at the indicated white line.

Joanna held her breath during the short interval before the gate began its long, slow swing open.

A moment later Deborah powered the car through the tunnel beneath the gate-house and into the clear beyond.

Joanna visibly relaxed, and Deborah noticed.

"Were you really worried there?" Deborah asked.

"I've been worried all day," Joanna admitted. She opened the envelope and extracted the heavy printout.

Deborah glanced at Joanna as she made the right turn onto Pierce Street to head into Bookford. "What are you going to do, a little pleasure reading on the way home?"

"Actually, I had an idea," Joanna said. "And a pretty good one as I'm sure you'll agree." She began shuffling through the pages, looking for two in particular while being careful to keep them all in order. It took her several minutes.

"Are you going to clue me in, or is this great idea of yours a secret?" Deborah asked finally. She was mildly miffed at Joanna's continuing silence.

Joanna inwardly smiled. She realized by not completing her thought she'd unconsciously subjected Deborah to the same irritating speech foible Deborah was forever pulling on her. Enjoying her revenge, Joanna didn't answer until she'd isolated the proper pages and put the rest of the file on the backseat.

"Voilà!" Joanna said. She held the sheets up so Deborah could look at them.

Deborah took her eyes off the road long enough to see that the papers Joanna was holding were those giving the details about the two children that had supposedly been born from her eggs. "Okay, I see what you've got there. So what's the big idea?"

"Both these children would be about seven to eight months old," Joanna said. "That is, if they exist."

"Yeah, so?"

"We've got names here, addresses, and

phone numbers," Joanna said. "I suggest we call them up and if they're willing, pay them a visit."

Deborah gave Joanna a fleeting glance with an expression of total disbelief. "You're joking," she said. "Tell me you are joking."

"I'm not joking," Joanna said. "It was your suggestion that this list was a fabrication. Let's check it out. At least one of these addresses is right here in Bookford."

Deborah pulled over to the side of the road. They were in sight of the public library at the corner of Pierce and Main. She put the car in park and turned to look at Joanna. "I hate to disappoint you, but I don't think visiting these people is a good idea at all. A call, okay, but not a visit."

"We'll call first," Joanna said. "But if the children exist, I want to see them."

"That was never part of our plan," Deborah said. "We were just going to find out if children had resulted. We never talked about a visit. It's not healthy, nor do I think the parents would appreciate it."

"I'm not going to tell them I was the donor," Joanna said. "If that's what you are worried about."

"I'm worried about you," Deborah said. "Knowing a child exists is one thing, seeing him in reality is another. I don't think you should put yourself through such a situation. It's asking for emotional heartache."

"It's not going to cause any emotional heartache," Joanna said. "It will be reassuring. It will make me feel good."

"That's what the addict said with the first dose of heroin," Deborah said. "If these children exist, and you see them, you'll want to see them again, and that's not fair to anyone."

"You're not going to talk me out of this," Joanna said. She took out her cellular phone and began punching in the number for Mr. and Mrs. Harold Sard. She looked at Deborah as the call went through. The fact that it was ringing meant it was a real number and not a made-up one.

"Hello, Mrs. Sard?" Joanna questioned when the phone was answered.

"Yes, who's this?"

"This is Prudence Heatherly from the Wingate Clinic," Joanna said. "How's the little one doing?"

"Jason is doing just fine," Mrs. Sard

said. "We're quite excited. He's just starting to crawl."

Joanna raised her eyebrows for
Deborah's benefit. "He's starting to crawl
already! That's terrific! Listen, Mrs. Sard,
the reason I'm calling is that we'd like to do
some follow-up on Jason. Would it be all
right if myself and another Wingate Clinic
employee came by for a brief visit with the
boy?"

"Of course!" Mrs. Sard said. "If it weren't
for the hard work you people do, we
wouldn't have this bundle of joy. He's such
a blessing. We've wanted a child for so
long. When would you like to come by."

"Is the next half hour or so convenient?"

"That would be perfect. He's just awakened from his afternoon nap, so he should
be in good spirits. Do you have the address?"

"I do, but I could use some directions,"
Joanna said.

The directions turned out to be simple.
They involved merely turning left on Main
Street, heading into town, and then taking
the first left after the RiteSmart pharmacy.
The house was a sixties-style split-level
with its faux brick disengaging from its

front facade and its trim sorely in need of a paint job. In contrast a brand-new child's swing set stood gleaming in the afternoon sun at the side of the modest house.

Deborah pulled into the driveway behind a vintage Ford pickup. She spotted the swings. "A new swing set for a six-month-old! I'd wager that means an eager dad!"

"The woman did say they've been wanting a child for some time."

"It doesn't look like a house belonging to people able to pay the money the Wingate requires."

Joanna nodded. "It makes you wonder where they found the money. Infertility makes couples desperate. They often re-mortgage the house or just borrow the money, but looking at this house doesn't suggest either of those avenues as possibilities."

Deborah turned to Joanna. "Which means they've probably ended up with little money for the financial burden of raising a child. Are you sure you want to go through with this? I mean, it might be rather bleak in there, and upsetting. My advice is we just turn around and leave, no harm done."

"I want to see the child," Joanna said. "Trust me! I can handle it." She opened the door and got out. Deborah did the same on her side, and the two women headed up the front walk. With her high heels Deborah had to walk with particular care to avoid the many cracks in the concrete. Even so she lost her shoe, requiring her to bend over to extricate it.

"Do me a favor and bend your knees when you do that," Joanna said. "I can see why you caught Randy's attention back at the water fountain."

"Your jealousy has no bounds," Deborah teased back.

The two women climbed the front steps.

"Are you ready for this?" Deborah asked with her finger poised over the doorbell.

"Ring the darn bell!" Joanna said. "You're making this into such a big deal!"

Deborah rang the bell. It could be heard chiming within. The chiming went on for several seconds as if playing a tune.

"That's a nice touch," Deborah said sarcastically.

"Don't be so judgmental!" Joanna complained.

The door opened and through the dirty

glass of the storm door the women could make out a moderately obese woman in a house dress carrying a baby with a shock of black hair. When the storm door opened to provide an unencumbered view, both women's mouths dropped in astonished dismay. Deborah even staggered back in her high heels, and only by grabbing onto the railing was she able to maintain her balance.

Paul Saunders had more important things to do than meet with Kurt Hermann. He'd even had to postpone the autopsy he was going to do with Greg Lynch on the sow's newborns down in the farm autopsy room. But Kurt had said it was crucial they speak right away, and Paul had reluctantly agreed, especially when Kurt had insisted they meet in the gatehouse away from other ears. Paul knew that meant trouble, but he wasn't concerned. He was confident in Kurt's abilities and discretion for which he was paid a lot of money . . . a very lot of money!

As Paul neared the squat structure he recalled the last time he'd been there. It had been well over a year before when there'd been the anesthetic disaster. He couldn't help but remember how efficiently and with what aplomb Kurt had handled that crisis, and the memory contributed to Paul's composure.

At the door Paul kicked off the mud his shoes had picked up on his walk down the moist lawn that was still recovering from the previous snowy winter. Once inside, he found his security chief at his desk in his ascetic office. Paul grabbed a chair and sat.

"We have a major security problem," Kurt said with his characteristic equanimity. He had his elbows on the desktop with his clasped hands in the air. He pointed his steepled index fingers at Paul to emphasize his point but otherwise there was no sign of emotion or panic.

"I'm listening," Paul said.

"Two new employees started today," Kurt said. "A Georgina Marks and Prudence Heatherly. I assume you interviewed them as you normally do."

"Absolutely," Paul said. In his mind's eye he immediately pictured Georgina and her curvaceous body.

"I've been doing some investigating. They are not who they said they are."

"Explain!"

"They've used assumed names," Kurt said. "Georgina Marks and Prudence Heatherly were from the Boston area, but they are both recently deceased."

Paul swallowed in an attempt to relieve a suddenly dry mouth. "Who are they?" he asked. He cleared his throat. "Do we have any idea?"

"We know the name of one of them," Kurt said. "It's Deborah Cochrane. The car they were driving is registered to her. The other name is as of yet unknown, but that will soon change. The address they gave is incorrect, but we have a real address, at least for Deborah Cochrane, and at this point I'm assuming it's the correct address for both."

"Congratulations on finding this out so soon," Paul said.

"I don't think congratulations are in order just yet," Kurt said. "There's more."

"I'm still listening," Paul said. He fidgeted. He was momentarily concerned that as good as Kurt was, perhaps he'd discovered that Paul had asked the woman using the Georgina alias out to dinner and had been turned down.

"Randy Porter has discovered that the woman calling herself Prudence Heatherly has managed to download and print out one of your sensitive files. It's a file called *Donor.*"

"Good God!" Paul blurted. "How could that have happened? I was assured by that computer prick that my files were secure."

"I'm not as computer-savvy as I ought to be," Kurt said. "But Randy implied that she had help from Dr. Spencer Wingate, who I believe they seduced."

Paul had to steady himself by grabbing the sides of the chair. He knew Spencer was disgruntled, but this was going too far. "How did he help her?"

"By adding her name as a user of the file," Kurt said. "I had to practically beat that information out of Randy, but that was what he said."

"All right," Paul snapped, feeling his cheeks redden. "I'll talk to Spencer and get to the bottom of it from his end, although I might need your help with him, too. In the meantime, you handle the women and be as thorough as you were with that unfortunate anesthetic death, if you catch my drift. I don't want those women to leave the premises under their own power and preferably not at all. And I want the file that was printed out." By the time he was finished he was practically yelling.

"Unfortunately the women are gone already," Kurt said, maintaining his calmness despite Paul's mounting fervor. "As soon as I learned all this I immediately tried to track them down to detain them. Apparently, once they got the file, they left."

"I want you to find them and get rid of them!" Paul barked while repeatedly stabbing a finger at Kurt. "I don't want to know how you get rid of them, just do it! And do it in a way that does not implicate the Wingate. We've got to contain this!"

"That goes without saying," Kurt said. "And since I've already given it some thought, I'm pleased to say that I believe it will be rather easy. First, we have an address, which means we'll have quick access to the women. And second, the women had to know their behavior was felonious, meaning they wouldn't have been inclined to tell people what they were up to. Also, at least one of them was a donor here, which makes the motive for wanting the file personal rather than for some social crusade. All this means is that although there's been a major security breach, it is containable if we act quickly."

"Then by all means act quickly," Paul shouted. "I want this taken care of by tonight at the latest. These women could cause us a major goddamn headache."

"I've already made arrangements to head into Boston," Kurt said. He stood up, and as he did so he made sure Paul caught sight of the silenced Glock automatic pistol he pulled from the desk's center drawer. He wanted to get the credit for the seriousness he considered the situation to be. But Paul's response was different than Kurt expected. Instead of pretending he didn't see it, Paul asked if there was another one around he could borrow for the night. Kurt was happy to oblige. He was hoping Paul would solve the Spencer Wingate problem himself. After all, having two potential commanders-in-chief at odds with each other could be a messy situation.

*   *   *

Joanna was still trembling from the initial shock of the reality she was facing, and she had the sense that Deborah shared her feelings with equal intensity. Mrs. Sard had invited them into their living room and insisted on giving them coffee. But Joanna didn't touch the cup. The house was so filthy, she was afraid to. Food that resembled week-old yogurt was smeared on the couch next to where Joanna was sitting. Toys and dirty clothes were strewn about haphazardly. The smell of dirty diapers permeated the air. The kitchen, which Joanna had caught a glimpse of when they'd first come in, was piled high with dirty dishes.

Mrs. Sard had maintained nonstop chatter which mostly involved the baby who clung to her for most of the visit like a marsupial. She was manifestly pleased by the unexpected visit, giving Joanna the impression she was starved for company.

"So the baby has been healthy?" Deborah asked when Mrs. Sard paused for breath.

"Quite healthy," Mrs. Sard said. "Although just recently we've been told he has some mild, senorineuronal hearing loss."

Joanna had no idea what senorineuronal

hearing loss was, and although she'd not opened her mouth during the whole visit, she managed to ask.

"It's deafness caused by a problem with the auditory nerve," Deborah explained.

Joanna nodded but still was unsure. But she didn't pursue it. Instead she looked down at her hands. They were trembling. Quickly she covered one with the other. That helped considerably. What she really wanted to do was to leave.

"What else can I tell you about this little pumpkin?" Mrs. Sard said. Proudly she lifted the baby off her shoulder and bounced him on her knee.

Joanna thought he was cute like any baby, but she thought he would have been cuter if he'd been cleaner. The footed pajamas he was wearing were soiled in the front, his hair was dirty, and some dried cereal was tenaciously clinging to his cheek.

"Well, I think we've gotten the information we need," Deborah said. She stood and an appreciative Joanna immediately did the same.

"How about some more coffee?" Mrs. Sard asked with an echo of desperation in her voice.

"I think we've overstayed our welcome," Deborah said.

Mrs. Sard tried to protest, but Deborah was insistent. Reluctantly Mrs. Sard walked her guests out the front door and stood on the porch while they descended the walkway. When they got to the car only Deborah looked back, and when she did, Mrs. Sard was waving the baby's hand to say good-bye.

"Let's get out of here," Joanna said as soon as the doors were closed. Purposefully she avoided looking back at the child.

"I'm trying," Deborah said. She got the car started and backed out of the driveway.

They drove for a few minutes before speaking. Both were glad to be away.

"I'm horrified," Joanna said, finally breaking the silence.

"I can't imagine anyone who wouldn't be," Deborah said.

"What amazes me is that that woman acts like she hasn't a clue," Joanna said.

"Maybe she doesn't. But even if she does, she's probably wanted a child for so long she doesn't care. Infertile couples have been known to be desperate."

"Did you know immediately?" Joanna asked.

"Obviously," Deborah said. "I almost fell off the damn porch."

"What was it that made the association for you?"

"It was the whole package," Deborah said. "But if I had to narrow it down I suppose I'd have to say the baby's white forelock was the giveaway. I mean, that's pretty dramatic, especially on a six-month-old child."

"Did you notice the child's eyes?" Joanna shuddered as if chilled.

"Certainly," Deborah said. "They reminded me of a husky one of my uncles had, although the dog's were even more shockingly different colors."

"What bothers me so much is that what's probably the first human clone had to be cloned from one of my eggs."

"I can appreciate your feelings," Deborah said. "But I have to say what bothers me so much is who did it and whom he cloned. Paul Saunders is not the kind of person the world needs another copy of. Cloning himself means he's more egocentric and conceited and arrogant than I could have ever imagined, although I'll wager he'd try to argue he did it for science or mankind or some other ridiculous justification."

"At least there's none of me in that child," Joanna said. For the moment, she couldn't see beyond the personal aspect of the calamity.

"I hate to tell you this, but that's probably not true," Deborah said. "The egg contributes the mitochondrial DNA. The child has your mitochondria."

"I'm not even going to ask what mitochondria is," Joanna said. "I don't want to know because I don't want to believe there's anything of me in that child."

"Well, we now have an explanation why the success rate with your eggs was so low. Cloning by nuclear transfer is like that. On the positive side, it was better than the people got who cloned the sheep, Dolly. I think they went through two hundred attempts or so before getting one positive. You've got four positives in less than three hundred."

"Are you trying to make a sick joke?" Joanna questioned. "If you are, I'm not finding it funny."

"I'm being serious," Deborah said. "They must be doing something right. Their statistic is more than twice as good."

"I'm certainly not going to give them any kudos," Joanna commented. "The whole affair makes me sick. I wish I hadn't gone in there, that's how terrible I feel."

"I would never tell you I told you so," Deborah teased. "I'd never do something like that. It would be too cruel."

Joanna smiled in spite of her distress. It was amazing how Deborah could always buoy her up no matter what the circumstance.

"But I do have another suggestion if you think you're capable."

"I hate to ask what you have in mind," Joanna said.

"I think we should visit the second child to see if our fears are justified."

They drove in silence for a while as Joanna considered the suggestion.

"It's not going to make it any worse," Deborah said eventually. "We've already experienced the shock. It might help us to decide what we're going to do about all this, if anything. That's a conundrum we've studiously avoided."

Joanna nodded. In that regard Deborah was totally correct. Not only had they not discussed what they were going to do, Joanna herself had purposefully avoided even thinking about it. Short of just turning it over to the media who would undoubtedly implicate them, whom could they tell? The problem was, they'd gotten the information by committing a felony. Joanna didn't know a lot about the law, but she knew that obtaining evidence criminally affected its utility. On top of that she didn't even know if human cloning carried out by a private clinic was against the law in the state of Massachusetts.

"All right," Joanna said impulsively. "Let's try to see the second child. But if it's the same situation, let's not go in." She reached for the second sheet of paper and pulled out her cell phone.

The surname of the second child was Webster, and Websters lived in a town a number of miles closer in toward Boston than Bookford. Joanna placed the call. The phone rang more than five times. She was about to disconnect when the call was answered by a woman who was out of breath.

The conversation with Mrs. Webster was almost identical to the one with Mrs. Sard except for Mrs. Webster's breathlessness. She explained she'd had to run for the phone since she'd just taken Stuart out of the bath. Most importantly, she welcomed the women to stop by and gave explicit directions.

"At least the baby will be clean," Joanna said as she put away her cell phone.

A half hour later the women pulled into the driveway of a home that was the antithesis of the Sards'. The Websters' was a comparative mansion in brick colonial style with massive chimneys sprouting up like weeds in a garden. The women eyed the house and the carefully tended grounds. A rash of blooming magnolias and dogwoods graced the lawn.

"I'll have to say that Dr. Saunders is eclectic about his choice of stepparents," Deborah commented. "That is, if this child is another clone."

"Come on!" Joanna said. "Let's get this over with."

The women proceeded up the flagstone walkway with reservation. Neither was entirely sure they wanted to go through with the visit, yet both felt compelled. Joanna pushed the doorbell.

Once again both Joanna and Deborah knew instantly that the child was a clone of Paul Saunders. The baby looked identical to the Sards' child with the same white forelock, the same heterochromic irises, and the same broad-based nose.

Mrs. Webster was as gracious as Mrs. Sard without Mrs. Sard's apparent starvation for company. She invited the women into her home, but the women declined and insisted on remaining on the front stoop.

Since Joanna had had time to adjust emotionally from the initial shock, she was able to participate more in the brief conversation with Mrs. Webster than she had with Mrs. Sard. Also, confronting a clean child in an environment more auspicious for the baby's well-being made the episode more tolerable. Out of curiosity, Joanna asked if the baby had any hearing problem. She was told that he did, and it sounded equivalent to the Sard baby's problem.

After leaving the Webster house the women were silent, each absorbed in their own troubled thoughts. It wasn't until they got onto Route 2 and got up to highway speed that Deborah spoke up: "I don't mean to beat this issue to death, but you can see now why I was disappointed we couldn't get into the Wingate research files. My intuition tells me they're doing something really wrong out there and this cloning we've stumbled on is just the tip of the iceberg. With the kind of arrogance Dr. Saunders undoubtedly has, the sky's the limit."

"Cloning humans is bad enough."

"I don't think it's bad enough to get Saunders et al. closed down," Deborah said. "In fact, if it gets out in the media that they're offering cloning, there might be a stampede of infertile couples to their doorstep."

"What can I say?" Joanna muttered. "As I told you, I did the best I could in that server room."

"I'm not blaming you."

"Yes, you are!"

"All right, maybe a little. It's just so frustrating."

They lapsed into silence again. The engine droned. In the distance the Boston skyline appeared along the horizon.

"Wait a second!" Deborah blurted suddenly, causing Joanna to start. "The shock of discovering the cloning has made us forget about the eggs!"

"What are you talking about?" Joanna questioned.

"The number of eggs they supposedly got from you," Deborah said. "How could they get hundreds unless . . ." Deborah paused and stared out through the windshield with a horrified expression.

"Unless what?" Joanna demanded. Under the circumstances she found it more irritating than usual that Deborah was up to her old tricks.

"Look in the donor file," Deborah said quickly, "and see if there are any more donors who have supposedly given hundreds of eggs."

Muttering under her breath, Joanna reached into the backseat and with a grunt brought the heavy file onto her lap. She started at the beginning and didn't have to go through many pages. "There are plenty. And here's one that's even more impressive. Anna Alvarez is down for having given four thousand two hundred and five!"

"You have to be joking!"

"I'm not," Joanna said. "Here's another multi-thousand donor: Marta Arriga. And yet another: Maria Artiavia."

"They sound like Hispanic names."

"They certainly do," Joanna agreed. "Here's another, even more astounding. Mercedes Avila reputedly donated eight thousand seven hundred twenty-one!"

"Look and see if it suggests that all those eggs were individually implanted like with your eggs."

Joanna turned to the next page of Mercedes Avila's file and ran her finger down the column. "It seems to be the case."

"Then they probably were all destined to be nuclear transfer clones," Deborah said. "Are they all followed by Paul Saunders's name?"

"Most of them," Joanna said. "Although there are some with Sheila Donaldson's name as well."

"I should have guessed," Deborah said. "It means they're working together. But, tell me! When you leaf through the names, do there seem to be quite a few Hispanic names in general or was it just a fluke with the A's?"

Joanna did as Deborah suggested. It took her several minutes. "Yes, there seem to be quite a few, and all of them are listed for having donated thousands of eggs."

"I wonder if that's the Nicaraguan connection?" Deborah questioned with a shudder.

"How so?"

"Female embryos have the maximum number of eggs in their ovaries for an individual's entire life," Deborah explained. "Someplace I read that at a particular point in embryonic development, the female embryo has close to seven or eight million, whereas when it is born it's down to a million, and by puberty down to three or four hundred thousand. Some distorted souls like Paul Saunders and Sheila Donaldson might think of the female embryo as a virtual gold mine."

"I don't think I like what you are suggesting," Joanna said.

"I don't either," Deborah said. "But unfortunately it stands to reason. These Nicaraguan women could be allowing themselves to be implanted and then subjected to abortions at twenty weeks just to get the eggs."

Joanna averted her eyes and stared out the side window as she shuddered through a wave of revulsion. What Deborah was saying was as horrific as the cloning, with its implications about the role of a woman and the lack of sanctity of human life. With difficulty she suppressed a caldron of emotion that threatened to bubble to the surface. She found herself wishing she'd never had anything to do with the Wingate Clinic. Having been involved as a donor made her feel like an accomplice.

"The problem with that scenario, if it is going on, is that it's legal. It might be a PR disaster to be happening at an infertility clinic, but it would be hard for anybody to do anything about it as long as the women were not being coerced."

"Paying them is a type of coercion!" Joanna snapped. "These women are poor and come from a struggling Third World country!"

"Hey, calm down! We're trying to have a discussion here."

"I'm not going to calm down!" Joanna spat. "And what was that thought of yours that you didn't finish about my eggs? I hate it when you leave me hanging like that."

"Oh, yeah, sorry," Deborah said. "The Nicaraguan connection got me side-tracked. The only way I can imagine they got that many eggs from you is if they took your whole ovary."

Joanna swayed as if Deborah had slapped her. She had to shake her head to refocus her mind. With a tremulous voice Joanna asked Deborah to repeat herself in case Joanna had misunderstood.

Deborah took her eyes off the road to cast a quick glance at her roommate. She could hear from Joanna's voice that she was momentarily on thin emotional ice. "I'm just thinking out loud here," Deborah explained. "Don't get yourself in a dither."

"I deserve the right to get upset if you're suggesting they took my ovary," Joanna said, slowly and seemingly in perfect control.

"Then you come up with an alternate explanation for all the eggs," Deborah challenged. "This is a brainstorming session to try to make up for not having much information."

Joanna got a grip on herself and tried to think up another explanation as Deborah had suggested. With only high-school biology and girls' locker room chatter as her reproductive technology sources, she couldn't think of a thing.

"The most eggs I've ever heard of being harvested in an ovarian hyperstimulation was around twenty," Deborah said. "Retrieving hundreds suggests to me some kind of ovarian tissue culture."

"Is it possible to culture ovarian tissue?" Joanna asked.

Deborah shrugged. "You know, I haven't the slightest idea. I'm a molecular biologist, not a cellular biologist. But it sounds reasonable."

"If they took one of my ovaries," Joanna asked, "how would it affect me?"

"Let's see," Deborah said, screwing up her face as if thinking deeply. "With half your usual ovarian production of estrogen, your adrenal testosterone level would be relatively doubled. That means you'll probably grow a beard, lose your breasts, and go bald."

Joanna looked at her roommate with renewed horror.

"I'm just kidding!" Deborah cried. "You're supposed to laugh."

"I'm afraid I don't find any of this funny."

"The truth is, there'd probably be very little effect, if any," Deborah said. "Maybe there could be a slight statistical drop in your fertility since you'd be reduced to ovulating from one ovary, but I'm not even sure of that."

"Still, having your ovary ripped out is an awful thought," Joanna said, hardly mollified. "It's like rape but maybe even worse."

"I totally agree," Deborah said.

"Why just me and not you?"

"That's another good question," Deborah said. "My guess would be because I refused to have general anesthesia. To take an ovary they'd have to use a laparoscopic approach as a minimum, and certainly not just an ultrasound guided needle."

Joanna closed her eyes for a moment. She found herself wishing she'd not been such a coward about medical procedures when she'd donated. She should have followed Deborah's advice.

"I just thought of something," Deborah said.

Joanna stayed still. She vowed to herself she wasn't going to ask.

They drove in silence for almost two

minutes. "Aren't you interested?" Deborah asked.

"Only if you tell me," Joanna said.

"If we can prove they took your ovary, then we might have something. I'm not saying they did take it, but if they did, we might have some legal recourse. I mean, taking your ovary without consent is technically assault and battery, which is a felony."

"Yeah, well, how could it be proved?" Joanna said without enthusiasm. "What would they have to do, open me up and look? Thanks, but no thanks!"

"I don't think they'd have to open you up," Deborah said. "I think they could tell by ultrasound. What I suggest is that you call Carlton, explain as little or as much as you want, and tell him you need to find out if you are missing an ovary."

"It's a bit ironic for you to be suggesting I call Carlton," Joanna said.

"I'm not advocating you marry him, for goodness' sakes," Deborah said. "Just take advantage of the fact that he's a medical resident. Residents know other residents. It's like a fraternity. I'm sure he could arrange for an ultrasound."

"I've been home for three days and haven't called him once," Joanna said. "I feel guilty about calling him up out of the blue and asking for a favor."

"Oh, please!" Deborah groaned. "Your Houstonian upbringing is reasserting itself. How many times do I have to remind you that men can be used just like men use women? This time instead of using him for entertainment, you're using him to get an ultrasound. Big deal!"

In her mind Joanna went over what she thought the conversation with Carlton would be like. From her perspective it wouldn't be as easy as Deborah suggested. At the same time Joanna wanted to know whether she'd been internally violated or not. In fact, the more she thought about it, the more she had to know.

"All right!" Joanna said. She reached for her cell phone. "I'll give him a call."

"Good girl," Deborah said.

fifteen

MAY 10, 2001
6:30 P.M.

Louisburg Square was up on the slope of Beacon Hill reached by heading up Mount Vernon Street and turning left either into the square's upper roadway or lower road-way. Technically it wasn't a square but rather a long rectangle bordered by a col-lection of mostly bow-fronted, brick town houses with multi-paned, shuttered win-dows. The center of the square was a patch of anemic, trampled grass ringed by a tall, threatening cast-iron fence and cov-ered by a canopy of old-growth elms which had somehow survived the ravages of

Dutch elm disease. At either end were modest copses of shrubbery with a single weathered piece of garden statuary.

Kurt had found the square without difficulty despite his unfamiliarity with Boston in general and the profusion of one-way streets on Beacon Hill in particular. But parking was another matter. The square's parking was discreetly labeled PRIVATE with the admonition that whoever tested the ban would be towed. Kurt did not want to be towed. He was driving one of the Wingate Clinic's unmarked, black security vans with a lockable compartment in the back. In the compartment were the various and sundry things he might need, as well as ample room for uncooperative passengers.

Kurt's plan had been sketchy from the start other than knowing he'd be bringing the women back to the Wingate. He thought he'd first locate the women and then improvise, and at present he was still reconnoitering the area. It was his third pass through the square. On the first pass he'd located the building. It was the first on the upper right. He'd paused long enough to note that it was five stories tall with the top dormered and another story partially below grade. Whether there was a basement below that, he did not know. It had one entrance in the front at the top of five steps. He assumed there was another door in the back, but the first story in the back was obscured by a brick wall.

On the second pass he'd noted the degree of activity in the area. A lot of renovating was going on, so there were a number of workmen and construction vehicles. Within the square there were several children ranging in age from four or five up to eleven and twelve. A few nannies were either chatting with each other or absorbed with their charges.

Now on the third pass, Kurt was trying to decide where to put the van. Most of the construction workers had now departed, so that had freed up spaces. He decided the best was at the Mount Vernon end despite the PRIVATE PARKING sign—after all, the construction vehicles hadn't been towed— and rounding the block again, he pulled up to the fence. Turning his head to the right gave him an unencumbered view of the building in question.

By that time Kurt's only concern was

that he had not yet sighted the Chevy
Malibu. He'd memorized the license number when he'd run the trace, so he was not
worried he'd confuse it with a similar vehicle. He'd assumed he'd come across it either as he drove around the square or in
the nearby streets. But it hadn't happened.

Despite the adrenaline flowing in his
veins, Kurt maintained his calm exterior. He
knew from experience that it was danger-
ous to give in to the excitement of such a
mission. It was important to be slow and
methodical to avoid making mistakes. At
the same time he had to maintain his vigi-
lance like a coiled snake, ready to strike
when the opportunity presented itself.

Reaching round to the small of his back,
Kurt pulled out the Glock and again
checked its magazine. Satisfied, he rehol-
stered it. He then checked his knife
strapped to his calf. In his right pants
pocket he had several pairs of latex gloves,
in his left a ski mask. In his right jacket
pocket he had his collection of lock-picking tools with which he'd practiced until
he'd become adept; in his left pocket he
had several automatic injection devices
containing a powerful tranquilizer.

After sitting in the van for almost a half hour, Kurt decided the time was right. The level of activity in the square had diminished but was not so quiet he'd stand out as a stranger. Kurt got out of the van and locked it. After a final, casual glance around the area, Kurt set out for number one Louisburg Square.

With his van keys in his hand, Kurt went up the steps to the building's front door. Holding the keys as if he were having unexpected trouble with the lock, Kurt went to work with the lock-picking tools. It took him longer than he'd anticipated, but the cylinder finally yielded to his efforts. Without looking back, Kurt pushed in the door and stepped inside the building.

The squeals of the children still playing in the square died away as the door closed. Without rushing, Kurt put away his tools and started up the stairs. He knew from the doorbell panel that Deborah Cochrane and Joanna Meissner occupied the fourth floor. He assumed that Joanna Meissner was Prudence Heatherly, but he intended to confirm that assumption.

With each flight, Kurt's excitement built. He truly loved the type of action he was anticipating. In his mind's eye he could see Georgina Marks dressed in her disgustingly provocative dress. He wanted her alive for sure, and he wanted her back in his villa on the Wingate grounds.

Cresting the third flight, Kurt pulled on a pair of the gloves. He then reached around and gripped the Glock with his right hand but kept the gun holstered. With his left hand raised, he was about to knock when he heard the front door to the building open on the first floor below. Kurt did not panic as a less-experienced man might have. He merely stepped over to the railing and looked down the stairwell. He thought it might have been the women, but it wasn't. Instead it was a solitary man trudging up the stairs after a day at the office. Kurt couldn't see the individual except for his arm gripping the banister.

Kurt prepared himself for whatever confrontation was going to occur. His plan was to start down as if on his way out if the individual began to climb the third flight. But the ruse wasn't necessary. The man stopped on the second floor, keyed open a door, and disappeared. The hallway lapsed back into its sepulchral stillness.

Kurt went back to the door to the fourth-floor apartment. He knocked loud enough for the occupants to hear if they were home, but not loud enough to disturb other people in the building. He waited, but when no one responded and he could hear no sounds from within, he went back to work with his lock-picking tools. As was typically the case in Kurt's experience, the interior apartment door was more of a challenge than the outer door, mainly because it had two locks: a regular lock and a separate deadbolt.

The regular lock was easy, but the deadbolt took patience. Finally it gave way and opened. In the next instant Kurt was within the apartment and had the door closed. With speed that belied his earlier slow and deliberate movement, Kurt dashed through the apartment to make certain it was empty. He didn't want to give anyone a chance to make a 911 call. To be complete, he checked every room and every closet. He even peered under the beds.

Once he was satisfied he was alone in the unit, he checked the alternate exit. It was a fire escape that zigzagged its way down the back of the house. Its access was through the window of the rear bedroom. Walking back through the bedroom, Kurt caught a glimpse of a photo of a young couple. The woman looked similar enough to Prudence Heatherly despite the longer hair for Kurt to be certain the two women he was after were roommates and that Joanna Meissner was Prudence Heatherly.

Passing out of the bedroom and down the hall, Kurt entered the living room. Going over to the desk, he searched for any papers suggesting an association with the Wingate Clinic. He didn't find any, but he did find some material relating to the two aliases the women had used. Kurt carefully folded these sheets and pocketed them.

Continuing on, Kurt found a photo of Georgina. He preferred to relate to her as Georgina rather than Deborah. In the photo Georgina had her arm around an older woman Kurt assumed was Georgina's mother. He was astounded how different Georgina looked in dark hair and chaste attire. Her lascivious transformation was clearly the work of the devil.

Kurt put the photo down and opened up the top drawer of the bureau. Reaching in he pulled out a silky pair of lace panties. Despite the latex gloves that dampened his sense of touch, there was something about the feel of the lingerie that excited him.

Leaving the second bedroom, Kurt walked back through the living room and into the kitchen. Opening the refrigerator door, he was disappointed. He'd expected a cold beer, and the fact that there was none irritated him immeasurably.

Returning to the living room Kurt removed the Glock from the small of his back and placed it on the floor. Then he sat down on the couch. He checked his watch. It was well after seven, and he wondered how long he'd have to wait for Georgina and Prudence to return.

"It's called Waardenburg Syndrome," Carlton said. He nodded as if agreeing with himself, then sat back with a proud expression on his youthful face. He and the women were sitting at a Formica table in the middle of the MGH basement cafeteria where he'd brought them for a quick bite of supper since none of them had eaten. Carlton was on call that night and had warned them he could be paged for some emergency at any moment.

"What in God's name is the Waardenburg Syndrome?" Joanna asked impatiently. Carlton's response suggested he'd not been listening to what she'd been saying. She'd just finished describing the shock she and Deborah had had in discovering the two cloned children.

"Waardenburg Syndrome is a developmental abnormality," Carlton said. "It's characterized by white forelock, congenital sensorineural hearing loss, dystopia canthorum, and heterochromic irises."

Joanna glanced at Deborah for a moment. Deborah rolled her eyes indicating she had the same reaction. It was as if Carlton was on another planet.

"Carlton, listen!" Joanna said, trying to be patient. "We're not on hospital rounds like you've described to me in the past. We're not grading you, so you don't have to spout off with this medical minutia. It's the forest that's important, not the tree."

"I thought you'd want to know what this doctor you've described has," Carlton said. "It's a hereditary condition involving the migration of auditory cells from the neural crest. It's no wonder the cloned kids have it. His legitimate kids would have it, too."

"Are you trying to suggest that these kids we've described aren't clones?" Joanna questioned.

"No, they're probably clones," Carlton said. "With the normal genetic shuffling that would occur in a normally fertilized egg, there would be variable penetration, even of dominant genes. The kids wouldn't look exactly the same. There'd be significant variation of the same characteristics."

"Are you trying to be abstruse on purpose?" Joanna demanded.

"No, I'm trying to help."

"But you still think these children are clones, am I right?" Deborah chimed in.

"Absolutely, from how you've described them," Carlton admitted.

"Doesn't that shock you?" Joanna questioned. "We're not talking about fruit flies or even sheep. We're talking about cloning human beings."

"To tell you the truth I'm not all that surprised," Carlton admitted. He sat forward again. "As far as I'm concerned it was just a matter of time. Once Dolly was cloned, I thought human cloning would happen eventually, and it would happen in the kind of environment you've described: a non-university-based infertility clinic. Many of the infertility guys, particularly the mavericks have been bantering around about cloning and threatening to do it since Dolly was announced."

"I'm shocked to hear you say that," Joanna stated.

Before Carlton could respond, his pager went off. After looking down at the LCD display, he scraped back his chair. "Let me make this call. I'll be right back!"

Both Joanna and Deborah watched him wend his way through the mass of empty tables toward one of the wall phones.

"Your analogy about the forest and the trees is marvelously apropos," Deborah commented.

Joanna nodded. "By his own admission he's so isolated in here. With his mind cluttered up with trivia like Waardenburg Syndrome, it's no wonder he hasn't the inclination to think about what's going on in the world or about ethics. He's taking this cloning in stride."

"He wasn't even all that incensed about

what we told him concerning the Nicaraguans," Deborah said. "Or even about you
for that matter."

Joanna nodded reluctantly. Carlton had
not been particularly empathetic. When
they'd first arrived, Joanna had been concerned about his feelings and had made it
a point to apologize for not having called
during the three days she'd been in
Boston. Although Carlton had been gracious about the lack of contact, Joanna
had still felt guilty about asking him for a
favor, but that feeling had passed with
Carlton's lack of reaction to her fears.

The women had decided it best if they
told Carlton the whole story from the egg
donation onward. He'd listened with rapt
attention and without interrupting until they
got to the part where they got jobs at the
Wingate with assumed names and dis-
guises.

"Wait a second!" Carlton had asked.
He'd looked at Deborah. "Is that why you
bleached your hair, and you're wearing that
wild, skimpy dress?"

"I hadn't thought you'd noticed,"
Deborah had said, resulting in a suppressed chortle from Carlton as if not hav-

ing noticed would have been impossible. At that point Joanna had asked Carlton what he thought of her disguise. To Joanna's chagrin he'd asked, "What disguise?"

The only part of the whole story that had truly captured Carlton's interest was the egg quandary. When he learned the reputed numbers of eggs involved, his response, like Deborah's, was to suspect that the Wingate had developed a successful ovarian tissue culture technique along with the ability to maturate extremely immature oocytes. He had told the women that such an advance would be an exciting scientific development.

When the women had revealed that the reason they were there was to get an ultrasound on Joanna for fear she'd been shorn of one of her ovaries, he'd agreed to see what he could do and had made some calls. The fact that he'd not had more of an emotional reaction was a surprise to both women.

"I don't want to speak out of school," Deborah said as she and Joanna watched Carlton talking on the phone. "But I'm even gladder now than I was before that you're not still engaged to that man."

"You're not speaking out of school," Joanna assured her.

Carlton finished his conversation, hung up the phone and started back. As he approached, he flashed a thumbs-up sign. "It's a go!" he said, reaching the table. He made it a point not to sit down. "That was one of the radiology residents who is on call. She's arranged to do the ultrasound."

"When?" Deborah asked.

"Right now!" Carlton said. "The machine's all fired up and ready to rumble."

The two women got to their feet and gathered their belongings.

"I've never had an ultrasound," Joanna said. "Is this going to be an ordeal? I'm sure I don't have to remind either one of you, I hate needles."

"You're not going to mind it at all," Carlton assured her. "There are no needles involved. The worst part is the gel, but that's only because it's a bit messy. The good part is that it is water-soluble."

They crowded into the elevator and rose up to the radiology floor. Carlton held the door to allow them to exit and pointed in the proper direction down the hall. After making a series of turns in the mazelike department, they came to the ultrasound unit. The waiting room was deserted. A janitor with a power buffer was doing the floor.

"Should I wait out here?" Deborah questioned.

"No, not at all," Carlton said. "The more the merrier."

He led them back behind the check-in desk into a hall with numerous doors lining both sides. Each door opened into a separate, unoccupied, and darkened ultrasound unit. The women followed Carlton almost to the hall's end where a light spilled out from one of the side rooms.

Inside, a woman in a short white coat stood up and introduced herself before Carlton could do the honors. Her name was Dr. Shirley Oaks. She had bobbed hair not too dissimilar from Joanna's both in style and color. In contrast to Carlton she was sympathetic about the potentially missing ovary and said so.

Joanna thanked her but then cast a concerned look at Carlton. She'd urged him to be as discreet as possible.

"I didn't tell the whole story," Carlton

said in his defense. "But I had to say what we were looking for."

"Nor do I want to know the whole story," Shirley said. She patted the ultrasound couch to encourage Joanna to climb onto it. She'd covered it with fresh paper from a roll of paper at the head. "We've got to be expeditious about this," she added. "I've got another procedure I was about to do, plus I could get called away for an emergency at any moment."

Joanna started to comply but Shirley restrained her. "It might make it considerably easier if you slip off your skirt and unbutton your blouse."

"Sure," Joanna said.

"I'll wait outside and give you some privacy," Carlton said.

"It's not necessary on my behalf," Joanna said as she slipped out of her skirt and passed it into Deborah's waiting hands. "There's nothing you haven't seen before."

Joanna climbed up onto the couch and Shirley exposed her lower abdomen by pushing away her shirttails and lowering the top edge of her panties. The three tiny

puncture sites from the egg retrieval laparotomy were just barely visible.

"Do these scars appear normal for a
laparotomy?" Shirley asked Carlton as she
prepared to put on the ultrasound gel.

Carlton bent over and took a closer look.
"They sure do. They're the usual size, and
they've healed normally."

"Could an ovary be delivered through
such a small incision?" Shirley asked.

"Certainly," Carlton said. "Young,
healthy skin like Joanna's is surprisingly
elastic. It wouldn't be any problem at all."

"Let's get this over with," Joanna said.

"Of course," Shirley agreed. She
squirted out a generous dollop of the gel
onto Joanna's bare abdomen.

"Ahhh! That's cold!" Joanna cried.

"Oh, yeah, sorry," Shirley said. "I forgot
we usually warm this stuff, or at least the
nurses and the technicians do."

Shirley turned the lights out with a foot
pedal and applied the probe to Joanna's
abdomen. The monitor was on an arm, and
it was positioned so that everyone could
see, including Joanna.

"Okay, there we go!" Shirley said, speaking to herself. "There's the uterus. It looks good and completely normal."

Both Joanna and Deborah marveled how anyone could make anything out of the squiggly white lines on a dark background.

"Now we'll move laterally," Shirley said. "We can see the ligaments and the tubes and there! There's the left ovary."

"I see it," Carlton said. "It looks normal."

"Very normal," Shirley said. "Now let's move back to the uterus. That's good! Now to the right."

Joanna kept watching the screen, hoping to see something she could say she recognized, but in truth she knew little about her inner workings, and she preferred it that way as long as everything functioned normally.

Shirley moved the ultrasound probe around in a tight circle in Joanna's right lower abdomen. Then she began to press in on it to the point of discomfort.

"Ah," Joanna complained. "That's starting to hurt!"

"Just a second more," Shirley said. Then she stopped and straightened up and looked at Carlton. "Well, as near as I can tell the right ovary is not there."

"It couldn't be retroflexed or anything like that?" Carlton asked.

"It's not there," Shirley said. "I'd be willing to put money on it."

"Is it all right if I get up?" Joanna asked.

"Oh, of course," Shirley said. She gave Joanna some tissues to help wipe up the gel from her abdomen. Shirley lent a hand as well.

Joanna slid off the couch and buttoned her blouse.

"What are the chances that Joanna only had one ovary to begin with?" Deborah asked.

"That's not a bad question," Carlton said. He shrugged. "I don't know."

"Call one of the gyn residents," Shirley suggested. "They should know."

"Good idea," Carlton said.

"If I can help any more, give me a buzz," Shirley said. "I've got to go."

The group thanked the radiology resident, who then left. Joanna grabbed her skirt and shook out the wrinkles.

"Come out to the main desk when you are ready," Carlton said. "I'll page the gyn resident from out there." He stepped out into the corridor and disappeared down the hall.

"Well, our worst fears have been corroborated," Deborah said. She held Joanna's arm while Joanna stepped into her skirt.

Now that she was alone with Deborah, Joanna felt a surge of emotion and even suffered some tears. She wiped them away with the back of her hand. "I don't know why I'm crying now," she said with a short, emotional laugh. "I guess it's just that I've had a long, intimate relationship with that ovary, and I didn't even know she was gone."

Deborah smiled. "I'm impressed you can find humor in this!"

"As tired as I am, laughing seems easier than crying."

"Well, I'm mad!" Deborah said. "The nerve of Paul Saunders and Sheila Donaldson and whoever else is in on all this." Using her fingers to count, she said: "Consider what they are apparently doing: one, stealing ovaries from unsuspecting women; two, cloning themselves to beat the band; three, impregnating poor Nicaraguan women and aborting them for eggs.

And that's only what we suspect! We have to do something about this."

Joanna adjusted her skirt and her blouse and slipped into her shoes. "I know what I'm going to do. I'm going to go home and go to bed. After ten or eleven hours of sleep, maybe I'll be able to think up something appropriate for the Wingate Clinic."

"Do you know what I think we should do?" Deborah said.

Joanna picked up her purse. She was in no mood to play Deborah's game and didn't respond. Instead she walked out of the room.

Deborah followed. "I'll tell you what we should do, even if you don't want to hear it. I think we should go back out there to the Wingate Clinic tonight and see what's in that egg room. There could very well be incriminating evidence in there. Hell, we might even find your ovary. And if that doesn't work, we can get you back into the server room and get the research files. At this time of night we won't have to contend with Randy Porter."

Joanna stopped and turned around. "That's the craziest idea I've heard in a long time. Why in heaven's name would we go back out there tonight!"

"Because we can!"

"You must be just as tired as I am. What kind of answer is that?"

"We still have access cards," Deborah explained. "We left early today, and I'm sure they discovered it, so we're out of jobs. But knowing bureaucracies, the cards are probably still operative. That will change tomorrow, but I'd be awfully surprised if they didn't work tonight. And we still have Spencer's card, and that's not going to stay good forever, either. My only point is that if we don't go out there sooner there probably won't be a later. We've got this narrow window of opportunity that we have to take advantage of."

"I suppose you have a point," Joanna said wearily. "But we're both way too tired." She turned around and continued down the hallway. Deborah followed at her heels, trying to convince her they had a moral responsibility. When they emerged into the waiting area they were still arguing. Carlton had to quiet them so he could hear while he was on the phone.

"What are you women arguing about?"

he asked when his call was completed. Joanna and Deborah were glaring at one another.

"She's trying to talk me into going back to the Wingate Clinic tonight," Joanna explained. "She wants to break into what she calls the egg room, and she wants me to hack into their research files."

"Do you ladies want to hear my opinion?" Carlton asked.

"It depends," Deborah said. "Are you for or are you against?"

"Against."

"Then we don't want to hear it," Deborah said.

"I'd like to hear it," Joanna said.

"I don't think you should break the law any more than you already have," Carlton said. "You're lucky to have gotten away with what you did. Let professionals take over. Go to the authorities!"

"Like to whom?" Deborah challenged. "The Bookford police? What are they going to do—shoot themselves in the foot? The FBI? We don't have any evidence there's any interstate aspect to all this that would justify them getting a search warrant, and I'm sure Saunders and Donaldson have contingency plans if there are any general inquiries. Medical authorities? They're not going to do anything because they never have. For them infertility clinics are somehow beyond the pale."

"What did you find out from the gyn resident?" Joanna asked.

"Congenital absence of one ovary is a rare bird," Carlton said. "She said she's never seen it, never heard of it, and never read it, but she thought it could happen."

"They stole your damn ovary!" Deborah rejoined. "The facts are written on the wall. Hell, I'd think you should be the one trying to talk me into going back out there tonight rather than vice versa."

"That's because I apparently have significantly more sense than you do."

Carlton's pager went off. In the deserted waiting room it sounded louder than it had in the basement cafeteria. He used the phone directly in front on him.

"I don't think we should to lose this opportunity," Deborah persisted.

"All right, I'll be right down!" Carlton said. He hung up. "Sorry to break up this party, but that was the ER. There's been a pileup on Storrow Drive, and the ambulances are on their way in."

Carlton accompanied the women down in the elevator while they kept up their debate in forced whispers in deference to the other passengers. They even persisted quarreling all the way down the main corridor to the front door of the hospital.

"This is where I have to leave you two," Carlton said, interrupting the women and pointing toward the emergency department. Then, looking at Joanna, he said: "Great to see you. And I'm sorry about that ovary."

"Thank you for arranging the ultrasound," Joanna said.

"Glad to be able to help. I'll call you later."

"Do that," Joanna said. She smiled and he did the same. Then he waved self-consciously before disappearing through the swinging doors.

Deborah made the gesture she was sticking her finger down her throat to gag.

"Oh, please!" Joanna said. "He's not that bad."

"Says who?" Deborah countered. "*'Sorry about that ovary'!* What a bird-brained, insensitive thing to say! It's like you lost your pet turtle and not part of your identity as a woman."

The two women exited the hospital and headed toward the parking garage. Evening had turned into night and the streetlamps had come on. Approaching ambulance sirens could be heard screaming in the distance.

"Doctors see tragedies more poignant than losing an ovary every day," Joanna said. "He doesn't see it in the same way you and I do. Besides, you said yourself one ovary will not physically affect me."

"But you were his fiancée," Deborah said. "It's not like you're just another patient. But, you know what? Just forget it. He's your problem, not mine. Let's get back to the issue at hand. I'm going to go out to the Wingate tonight whether you go or not. I can't do anything about the computer part, but I can get in that egg room, and if there's incriminating evidence, I'm going to find it."

"You're not going out there by yourself!" Joanna ordered.

"Oh, really?" Deborah questioned superciliously. "What are you going to do, let

the air out of my tires or lock me in my bedroom? Because you're going to have to do
one or the other."

"I cannot believe you are this adamant
about such a stupid, idiotic, dim-witted
idea of yours."

"Ah . . ." Deborah cooed sarcastically.
"I'm getting the impression you're sensing
my commitment! I'm impressed. Such
clairvoyance!"

Feeling irritated with one another and
the escalating sharpness of their comments, the women lapsed into silence as
they climbed to the proper floor in the hospital's parking garage, found their car, got
in, and drove out.

The silence lasted until they were heading up Mount Vernon Street in sight of
Louisburg Square. Joanna was the first to
speak. "What about a compromise?" she
said. "Would you be amenable?"

"I'm listening," Deborah answered.

"I'll come with you, but we restrict our
sleuthing to the egg room or whatever it
turns out to be."

"What if there's no good evidence in
there about what they're up to?"

"That's a risk we'll have to take."

"What's wrong with going back into the server room if we're all the way out there?"

"Because I think Randy Porter will have already made changes in his system, which would mean going back into the server room would be a big risk with a low probability of a payoff. He'll have detected the hack into the secure files from me downloading them, and he'll figure out how I did it through the server room console. As soon as he does that, he'll beef up the security for the server room keyboard. I doubt I'd get into the system."

"Why didn't you say this earlier?"

"Because I think going out there is idiotic, plain and simple," Joanna said. "But I'm not going to let you do it alone even if it is idiotic, just like you wouldn't let me go out there and get a job by myself. So do we have a compromise, or what?"

"All right, we have a compromise," Deborah said as she eased into a parking slot at the end of the square. She cursed under her breath because the spot was so narrow she knew she and Joanna were going to have a hard time getting out of the car. The problem was a black van parked where she normally did.

"I'm not going to be able to get out of this car," Joanna said, eyeing the neighboring vehicle less than five inches away.

"I was afraid of that," Deborah said. She looked over her shoulder and backed out, giving Joanna the chance to exit unencumbered. Then Deborah eased the car back into the slot but even tighter to the passenger-side vehicle. Opening her door against the pesky black van, she was able to squeeze herself out.

sixteen

Kurt felt a renewed squirt of adrenaline course through his body when he caught sight of an auspicious-looking car coming up Mount Vernon Street.

As the time had dragged on he'd become concerned that he'd made a false assumption about the women returning directly to their apartment. By nine-thirty he'd been concerned enough to pace the room, an activity that was foreign to his usual practiced serenity. If he'd been able to read, the wait would have been more tolerable, but he dared not turn on the light.

Ultimately Kurt had been reduced to looking out the front window at the gaslit square, wondering what the women's absence meant and how long he should wait before coming up with an alternative plan. He'd only been at the window for five minutes when a Chevy Malibu had appeared and then nosed into a parking place right next to his van.

Kurt was quite confident it was the women, but he became certain when the car backed up to let off the passenger before nosing back into the slot. The woman who emerged was Prudence Heatherly, the chaste one. Kurt had gotten a fleeting but good look at her face from the glow of the gas lamp on the corner almost directly below him. Then he saw Georgina squeeze herself out between her car and the van. In the process one of her breasts spilled out. Kurt could see her laugh as she readjusted herself.

"Whore!" Kurt whispered to himself with disgust. The woman was shameless in his mind, but he would soon be showing her the consequences of such lewdness. But what Kurt did not allow himself to acknowledge was that the brief flash of carnality had sexually excited him.

Kurt was about to leave the window to finalize his preparations for the women's arrival when his attention was drawn back to the scene below. Instead of advancing toward the door, the women had become engaged in a discussion that quickly escalated in its intensity. Even from as far up as he was, and even with the glass in between, he could hear bits and pieces of their conversation. It had definitely become an argument.

Fascinated by this unexpected turn of events, Kurt pressed his nose against the glass to give a fuller view of the scene. Georgina had come halfway from the car to the house, but Prudence was remaining by the car and pointing to it repeatedly.

Suddenly Georgina threw up her hands and returned to the car. With as much difficulty as she'd evinced getting out of the car, she got back in. Kurt watched with growing concern as the car backed out. When Prudence climbed back in, he inwardly groaned. And then, when the car took off down Mount Vernon Street, he swore.

Kurt returned to his pacing. A mission he'd assumed would be easy was proving not to be and was now threatening to get out of hand. Where could these women be going at almost ten o'clock at night? He suggested to himself that they could be going out to dinner, but then dismissed the idea, thinking dinner had probably been part of what had kept them away for so long. And how long would they be away? And would they come back alone? The last question was a particular concern.

Kurt had no answers, and the minutes ticked by. He went back to the window. The only people in sight were a few dog walkers with their pets. The Chevy Malibu was nowhere to be seen.

Kurt pulled out his cell phone. Although he was embarrassed not to be able to report success, he felt it best to apprise the commander of the current situation. Paul Saunders answered on the second ring.

"Can you speak freely?" Kurt questioned.

"As much as can be expected on a cell phone."

"Roger!" Kurt said. "I'm in my clients' home. They returned briefly moments ago but drove away without coming in, destination unknown."

Paul was quiet for a moment. "How difficult was it to get into the clients' home?"

"Easy," Kurt reported.

"Then I want you back here," Paul said. "You can go back for the women later. Spencer is the problem at the moment. I need your help."

"I'll be there straightaway," Kurt said, not without disappointment. It meant that dealing with Georgina would have to wait.

Kurt then thought he'd spend a little time looking for a spare set of keys. When he returned he wanted to be able to get in faster than he had earlier.

"I still don't know why you won't let me go up in the apartment and change," Deborah complained. "It would only take me five minutes." She and Joanna were standing in one of the aisles of the twenty-four-hour CVS, which was more like a mini-mart than a drugstore. Drugs were only a small part of the merchandise available, which ran from car products to industrial cleaning agents.

"Oh, sure, five minutes!" Joanna said sarcastically. "When was the last time you changed clothes in under a half hour? And it's already after ten. If we're going back to the Wingate, I want to get it over with."

"But I don't relish stumbling around in these high heels while we do our detective work."

"Then put on your sneakers," Joanna said. "You admitted your workout gear is in the trunk of your car."

"I'm suppose to wear sneakers with a minidress?"

"We're not going to a fashion show! Come on, Deborah! Have you gotten what you wanted here? If so, let's get on the road."

"I suppose," Deborah said. She was holding several flashlights, batteries, and a disposable camera. "Help me! Is there anything else we should take? I can't think."

"If they sold some common sense, perhaps we should take whatever they have."

"Very funny," Deborah said. "You're being a brat, you know. All right, let's go."

At the checkout register, Deborah grabbed a pack of gum and a few candy bars when she paid for her items. Soon they were back in the car and on their way out of town.

Having spent themselves arguing for the previous half hour, they drove mostly in silence. With no traffic, they made the trip in slightly less than half the time that previously it had taken. Bookford appeared deserted as they drove up Main Street. The only people they saw were two couples outside the pizza place. The only other sign of activity was the floodlights over the Little League field behind the municipal building.

"I'm kinda hoping our cards will no longer work," Joanna said as they neared the turnoff.

"Such a pessimist," Deborah responded.

They drove up to the gatehouse which looked as dark and unwelcoming as it had the night before.

"Which card should we use?" Joanna asked. "One of ours or Spencer's?"

"I'll try mine," Deborah said. She eased the car up to the card swipe and ran her card through. The gate opened immediately. "Just as I suspected: no problem with the access cards. The ironic thing is that I never thought I'd be appreciative of bureaucratic inefficiency."

Joanna was not appreciative in the slightest. After they'd driven onto the Wingate grounds and started up the driveway, she turned around and forlornly caught a glimpse of the gate closing. Now they were locked in, and she couldn't shake the feeling they were making a big mistake.

When his cell phone rang, Kurt had been engrossed in his thoughts, and the sound startled him. He'd involuntarily jerked the van's steering wheel and for a brief moment had to struggle to get the vehicle straightened out. He was traveling close to eighty miles an hour, heading northwest on Route 2 and closing in on the turnoff to Bookford.

With the van under control, he fumbled unsuccessfully for his phone in his jacket pocket while its insistent ring continued. Hastily he undid his seat belt. At that point he was able to get the phone out and establish a connection.

"We have a contact," a voice said.

Kurt recognized the voice. It was Bruno

Debianco, Kurt's number-two man who served as the evening-shift security supervisor. He'd been in the Special Forces at the same time as Kurt and, like Kurt, had been discharged under less-than-honorable circumstances.

"I'm listening," Kurt responded.

"The Chevy Malibu with the two women just came through the gate."

A shiver of excitement passed down Kurt's spine. The mild despondency he was feeling at having been ordered back to the compound to deal with Spencer Wingate vanished in a split second. Having the women on the grounds would make apprehending them as easy as a turkey shoot.

"Do you copy?" Bruno questioned when Kurt hadn't immediately responded.

"I copy," Kurt said matter-of-factly to cover his excitement. "Follow them, but do not make contact. I want the pleasure. Do I make myself clear?"

"Ten-four," Bruno answered.

"There's one proviso," Kurt said as an afterthought. "If they try to meet up with Wingate, detain them and keep it from happening. Is that understood?"

"Perfectly," Bruno said.

"I should be there in another twenty min-utes," Kurt added.

"Ten-four," Bruno said.

Kurt disconnected. A smile spread across his face. The evening that had started out so promising but had turned bleak had become rosy again. Now it was a given that within the hour both women would be locked in the holding cell he'd had constructed in the basement of his liv-ing quarters, and they would be tantaliz-ingly at his disposal.

Keeping one hand on the steering wheel, Kurt used his speed dial to call Paul.

"Good news," Kurt said when Paul came on the line. "The women have returned to base on their own accord."

"Excellent!" Paul said. "Good work!"

"Thank you, sir," Kurt said. He was willing to take credit if Paul was willing to offer it.

"Handle the women, then we'll face the Wingate problem," Paul said. "Call me when you are free!"

"Yes, sir," Kurt said. Like a conditioned Pavlov dog, Kurt felt the almost irresistible urge to salute.

*   *   *

"This is not what I suspected," Deborah said.

"I didn't know what to suspect," Joanna said.

The women were sitting in the car in the Wingate Clinic's parking area. The vehicle was pointing toward the butt end of the building's south wing with its engine still running. The parking spot was slightly east, affording a view along the building's rear. All the second-story windows of the rear of the wing were ablaze with light.

"The whole lab is lit up," Deborah said. "I thought the place would be like a graveyard after hours. I wonder if they are working around the clock."

"In a way it makes sense," Joanna said. "If things are going on out here they don't want people to know about, it would be best for them to be happening when the crowds of clinic patients aren't here."

"I guess," Deborah said.

"Well, what are we going to do?"

Before Deborah could respond, both women saw car lights appear at the base of the driveway and start up.

"Uh-oh," Deborah said. "Here comes company!"

"What should we do?" Joanna demanded in a minor panic.

"Stay calm for one thing!" Deborah said. "I don't think we should do anything for the moment other than scrunch down as best we can."

Bruno saw the car he knew to be the women's even before he could tell it was a Chevy Malibu. It was parked in a spot pointing toward the clinic entrance. What had caught his attention was that although the front lights were out, the brake lights were still on. Someone was sitting in the car with their foot on the brake.

As Bruno's black security van crested the lip of the parking area and his headlights strafed the car in question, he was able to make out the tops of two heads in the front seat. Bruno didn't even slow, much less stop. He continued across the parking area and descended the road on the other side as if he were on his way to the living quarters of the compound.

As soon as he knew he was out of sight,

Bruno pulled to the side of the road, killed the headlights, turned off the engine, and jumped out. Dressed in black like Kurt, he was invisible in the darkness. He sprinted back up the road, then skirted the edge of the parking area. Within only a few minutes he had the Chevy Malibu in sight, and he could make out that the two women were still in the front seat.

"I'm a nervous wreck," Joanna admitted. "Why don't we just leave? You admitted yourself that you didn't expect this place to be in operation like it is. Now we're bound to run into people if we go in there. What are we going to say?"

"Calm down!" Deborah ordered. "You're the one who insisted on coming along. That was only a van that passed by. It didn't stop; it didn't even slow down. Everything's cool."

"It's not cool," Joanna said. "Now we're trespassing to add to our list of offenses. I think we should go."

"I'm not leaving until I have something concrete on this place," Deborah said. "You can stay in the car if you want, but I'm going in, although first I'm putting on my sneakers."

Deborah opened the door and stepped out into the crisp night air. She went around to the trunk, got out her workout shoes, then returned inside the car.

"I just saw someone at one of the second-story windows," Joanna said nervously.

"Big deal," Deborah said. She pulled on her sneakers and laced them up. "This is going to look hilarious with this short skirt, but who cares?"

"I can't believe you're not worried about running into someone," Joanna said.

"Enough of this!" Deborah snapped. "Are you coming or not?"

"I'm coming," Joanna said reluctantly.

"What do you think we should take with us?"

"As little as possible," Joanna said. "Considering we might have to make a run for it. Maybe we should turn the car around so that at least we could get out of here fast if need be."

"I suppose that's not a bad idea," Deborah said.

She restarted the car, did a three-point

turn, then backed back into the spot. "Happy?"

"Saying I was happy would be a gross exaggeration."

"Let's just take the flashlights, the access cards, and the disposable camera," Deborah said.

"Fine," Joanna said.

Deborah reached around and got the bag from the drugstore off the backseat. She gave one of the flashlights to Joanna and kept the other for herself, plus the disposable camera. "Ready?"

"I suppose," Joanna said without enthusiasm.

"Wait a minute," Deborah said. "I just got an idea."

Joanna rolled her eyes. If Deborah expected her to guess what was on her mind under the circumstances, she was insane.

"You don't want to know what my idea is?"

"Only if it's something like you think we should leave."

Deborah flashed Joanna an exasperated expression. "No, smart aleck! The first time we came out here to donate, we left our coats in a cloakroom. There were long white doctors' coats in there. I think we should borrow a couple. It will make us look more professional, especially me with this miniskirt."

Finally the women got out of the car and hurried up the walk. They were mildly surprised to find they needed an access card to get into the building, but like at the gate, the card worked fine. Inside they found the large reception area dark and deserted. They ducked into the cloakroom, and once the door was closed they turned on the lights.

Deborah's memory had served them well. There were plenty of white doctors' coats although few in small sizes. It took a few minutes to find two that were reasonably appropriate. They used the pockets for the flashlights, access cards, and disposable camera. Thus equipped, they turned out the light and reemerged into the reception area.

"I'll follow you," Joanna whispered.

Deborah nodded. She skirted the empty receptionist's desk and started down the darkened main corridor, passing the patients' changing room on the left, where a year and a half earlier they'd donned hospital johnnies prior to their egg-retrieval procedures. Deborah's destination was the first stairwell, and they made it without encountering anyone. The only noise they heard was their own footfalls.

Both breathed a sigh of relief once inside the stairwell. It felt safer than the open hallway, at least until they got down the three flights and opened the fire door into the dark, dank basement.

"No lights!" Deborah said. "It's a good thing we're prepared." She pulled out her flashlight and switched it on.

Joanna did the same, and the moment she shined it into the mausoleum-like basement hallway she caught her breath.

"What's the matter?" Deborah questioned.

"My God! Look at all the old, creepy hospital paraphernalia!" Joanna said. She shined the light over a profusion of disabled wooden wheelchairs, dented bedpans, and broken hospital furniture. An antiquated portable X-ray machine with a bulbous head stood out in Joanna's flashlight beam like a prop for an old Frankenstein movie.

"Didn't I mention this stuff?" Deborah asked.

"No!" Joanna said irritably.

"You don't have to get mad about it," Deborah said. "It seems that the whole rest of the building is filled with all sorts of gear from its previous mental-institution/ TB-sanitarium days."

"It's spooky-looking," Joanna complained. "You could have at least prepared me for it."

"Sorry," Deborah said. "But Dr. Donaldson told us about it back when we first came out here. She said the place was a museum of sorts. Remember?"

"No!" Joanna said.

"Well, come on anyway," Deborah said. "It's just a bunch of trash." She led the way out into the corridor and headed north. Almost immediately the corridor twisted to the right and then turned again. Smaller arched openings led off on either side.

"Do you know where you are going?" Joanna questioned. She was following close behind Deborah.

"Not really," Deborah admitted. "The stairway we came down wasn't the one I came down earlier today. But I know we're at least going in the right direction."

"Why did I allow myself to be drawn into this?" Joanna mumbled just prior to letting out a muffled scream.

Deborah wheeled around and shined her light into Joanna's face. Joanna averted her gaze from the glare and got her hand between Deborah's light and her face. "Don't shine that thing in my eyes!"

"What the devil is the matter?" Deborah demanded angrily through clenched teeth once she'd seen Joanna was in one piece.

"A rat!" Joanna managed. "I saw an enormous rat with bright red eyes right over there behind that old desk."

"Jeez, Joanna!" Deborah complained. "Get ahold of yourself! This is supposed to be a clandestine exercise. We're trying to be stealthy here!"

"I'm sorry. I'm on edge in this junkyard dungeon. I can't help it."

"Well, pull yourself together. You scared me half to death." Deborah set out again but only managed a few more steps when Joanna reached out and grabbed her, pulling her to a stop.

"What now?" Deborah complained.

"I heard something behind us," Joanna said. She shined her light back the way they'd come. Expecting to see the rat again, she saw nothing but the junk they'd just passed. For the first time she looked up into the tangled mass of pipes and ducts.

"We're going to be here all night unless you cooperate," Deborah said.

"All right!" Joanna snapped back.

They walked for another five minutes along the twisting corridor before coming to a large, old-fashioned kitchen mixer attached to its own wheeled stand. It was covered with a layer of dust. A few assorted kitchen implements stuck out of the mixing bowl. The top of the mixer was tilted back and the beaters pointed off at a forty-five-degree angle.

"We must be getting close," Deborah said. "The door I'm looking for was on the other side of the kitchen, and we must be close to the kitchen now."

Rounding the next bend proved Deborah to be correct. Soon they were passing through the old kitchen. With the help of her flashlight Joanna gazed into the yawning, filthy ovens and the huge soapstone sinks. Overhead the light played against a line of blackened and dented pots and skillets hanging over the counter-top.

"There it is," Deborah said. She pointed ahead. The stainless-steel door stood out in the dark, dingy environment as if it were glowing. Its polished surface reflected back most of Deborah's flashlight beam.

"You were certainly right when you de-scribed it as out of place down here," Joanna said.

The women moved over next to the door. Deborah placed her ear against it as she'd done earlier. "Same sounds as I heard before," she said. She then told Joanna to put her hand against the door.

"It's warm," Joanna said. She then handed Spencer Wingate's access card, which she'd been carrying, to Deborah.

"My guess is that it's somewhere close to ninety-eight point six degrees Fahrenheit," Deborah said. She took the card but did not run it through the card swipe.

"Well, are we going in or what?" Joanna asked. Deborah was just looking at the door.

"Of course we're going in," Deborah said. "I'm just trying to prepare myself for what we're going to find." Finally, after taking a fortifying deep breath, she ran the card through the swipe. There was a slight delay followed by the sound of air escaping as if the space beyond was at a slightly higher pressure. Then the thick, heavy door began slowly to recede into the wall.

seventeen

MAY 10,
2001 11:05 P.M.

Cursing under his breath from having smacked his shin against an unknown metal object, Bruno stumbled back along the corridor in the darkness using his fingers against the brick wall to guide him. He tried not to trip over any more of the trash cluttering the floor but it was impossible, and he winced every time he collided with something, more from the sound it made than from any pain it caused. As soon as his fingers detected a corner, he eased himself around it. Only then did he venture a look back the way he'd come. In the distance the stainless-steel door of the culture room suddenly snapped back into place a hundred times faster than it had opened. But in the brief interval Bruno was able to catch sight of the two women standing within the lighted space beyond.

Quickly Bruno got out his flashlight, switched it on, and stuck it in his teeth to hold it. He directed the beam into the recess he'd eased into rather than back out into the corridor. He didn't want the women to suddenly look back and see the light if they happened to open the door. Next he struggled to get his cell phone out of his pocket. As quickly as he could, he used the phone's internal directory to find the culture room number. The moment it popped onto the screen, he pressed the talk button.

Although cell-phone reception in the Wingate's basement was not good, he could hear the phone ringing through static. "Come on, answer!" he urged out loud.

Finally a voice came on the line: "Culture room, Cindy Drexler speaking."

"This is Bruno Debianco. Can you hear me?"

"Just barely," Cindy answered.

"Do you know who I am?"

"Of course," Cindy said. "You're the security supervisor."

"Then listen up!" Bruno said, talking as loudly as he dared. "Two women have just come into the culture room. How they got an access card I have no idea. Do you see them?"

There was a pause. "Not yet," Cindy said coming back on the line. "But I'm nowhere near the entrance."

"This is important," Bruno continued. "Keep them occupied for fifteen or twenty minutes. Be creative! Tell them whatever they want to know, but keep them there. Do you understand?"

"I guess," Cindy said. "Tell them everything?"

"Anything and everything; it doesn't matter," Bruno said. "Just don't alarm them. Kurt Hermann is on his way, and he'll personally be taking them into custody. They are unauthorized intruders."

"I'll do what I can," Cindy said.

"That's all I ask," Bruno said. "We'll be in there as soon as he gets here."

Bruno disconnected from Cindy, then

speed-dialed Kurt's number. There was even more static when Kurt answered than when Bruno had spoken with the culture-room technician.

"Can you hear me?" Bruno asked.

"Well enough," Kurt answered. "What's going on?"

"I'm outside the culture room in the Wingate basement," Bruno said. "The women had a card to get them inside. I called the technician and told her to keep them in the room. You'll be able to nab them with ease."

"Did they see you?"

"No, they're unsuspecting."

"Perfect! I'm just entering Bookford. I'll be there in ten minutes, fifteen tops. Do you have handcuffs with you?"

"That's a negative," Bruno said.

"Get some from the gatehouse!" Kurt ordered. "And meet me at the gate! We'll grab the women together."

"Ten-four," Bruno said.

For several minutes the women stood still, absorbing the surroundings. In keeping with the starkly modern door they'd just passed through, both had expected a futuristic netherworld. Instead they were in a maze of rooms with the same general decor as the rest of the basement, separated from one another by the same brick archways. The difference was the bright light coming from banks of newly installed fluorescent fixtures, the ambient temperature, and the contents. Instead of discarded hospital and kitchen material, the room they were in and the others they could see were filled with modern-appearing laboratory equipment, mostly in the form of large incubators brimming with tissue culture dishes. Most of the incubators were on wheels.

"I expected something a bit more dramatic," Joanna said.

"Me too," Deborah said. "It's not even as impressive as the lab upstairs."

"It feels like the tropics. What do you think the temperature is?"

"Close to body temperature," Deborah said. She turned back to the stainless-steel door. A laminate box was mounted on the wall just to the right of the door. The box had a central protruding, red panel. On the panel in block letters were the words OPEN/CLOSE.

"Before we take a tour I want to make sure we can get out of here," Deborah said. "The way this door snapped shut, I want to reassure myself it's going to open again." She pushed the red panel.

The door slid open just as it had a few moments before. Then when Deborah pushed the panel again, the heavy, insulated door closed in the blink of an eye, and its silence was as impressive as its closing speed.

Deborah was about to comment about the door when Joanna frantically grabbed her arm and blurted out in a whisper, "We have company!"

Deborah's head snapped around in the direction Joanna was looking. In one of the archways stood a smiling, middle-aged woman with a narrow, deeply tanned face displaying prominent crow's feet and smile creases. She was dressed in a super-lightweight white cotton outfit. Her hair was contained in a hood of the same material. A surgical mask was tied around her neck and hung down over her chest.

"Welcome to the culture room!" the

woman said. "My name is Cindy Drexler. And what might your names be?"

Joanna and Deborah exchanged a brief, confused, and panicky glance.

"We're new employees," Deborah managed to say after a few false starts.

"How nice," Cindy said. She came forward, hand outstretched, and shook hands with each of the women. "And your names?" she repeated, looking directly at Joanna, whose hand she'd just shaken.

Joanna stuttered for a moment, desperately searching for some rational way to decide whether to use her real name or her alias. "Prudence," she blurted out, remembering they were trespassing.

"Georgina," Deborah quickly mimicked.

"Nice to meet you two," Cindy said. "I suppose you've come for a tour?"

Joanna and Deborah exchanged yet another rapid glance although now out of auspicious surprise rather than panic.

"We'd love a tour," Deborah said. "We were so mesmerized by the door, we had to see what was in here." Deborah gestured self-consciously at the stainless-steel door.

"I'm not accustomed to giving tours,"

Cindy said with a self-deprecating laugh, "but I'll give it my best shot. Here, in this room, which, by the way, was the old pantry for the kitchen back in the Cabot days, we have the eggs ready for nuclear transfer tomorrow. They will be going up to the lab in the dumbwaiter which is just around the corner. They're in the incubators with the red tags. We use a color-coding system down here. The incubators with the blue tags are the fused cells which will be going back into the embryo room."

"What kind of eggs are they?" Deborah asked. "I mean, what species."

"Human eggs, of course," Cindy said.

"All of them?"

"Yes, the animal eggs are handled in the animal culture room down at the farm."

"Where do so many human eggs come from?" Deborah asked.

"They come from what we call the organ room," Cindy said.

"Can we see?" Deborah asked.

"Of course," Cindy said. "Just follow me!"

Cindy gestured toward the archway through which she'd arrived and motioned for the women to follow. Joanna and

Deborah fell in behind her. "What luck to run into her," Deborah whispered, leaning her head close to Joanna's. "This is almost too easy."

"You're right!" Joanna whispered back. "It is too easy. She's being too gracious. I don't like it. If it were up to me, we'd leave now!"

"Oh, for God's sake," Deborah complained. "Always the cynic! Let's enjoy our good fortune, find out what we can, and then split."

After passing through several rooms of proportions and contents similar to the first room, they came to a room considerably larger. Behind a row of incubators was a bank of more than fifty aged wooden doors, each about three feet square with heavy latches like meat refrigerators. Deborah hesitated. "Excuse me, Cindy." She pointed toward the timeworn doors. "Are these what they look like?"

Cindy stopped on her way into an even larger room beyond. She followed Deborah's pointing finger. "Are you asking about those old ice compartments?"

"Was this area the morgue in the building's former life?" Deborah asked.

"It was indeed," Cindy said. She walked back and with a bit of effort rolled one of the large incubators to the side to expose the doors. She opened one and slid out the wheeled, stained wooden tray. "It's interesting, isn't it? They had to load the ice in the other side. I wouldn't have wanted to be down here if they ever ran out of ice. Can you imagine?" She laughed uneasily.

Deborah and Joanna looked at each other. Joanna shuddered. "Let's get this visit over with."

"Would you like to see the rest of the morgue?" Cindy asked. "The old autopsy theater with a grandstand is still intact. Back in the nineteenth century it must have substituted for entertainment out here in the sticks." She laughed again, this time more hollowly than anxiously. "In those days it took a whole day to get to Boston by carriage, and there wasn't much for the staff to do when off duty. Let me show you."

Cindy took off in a direction opposite to the way she'd originally been heading. Deborah followed after her vainly trying to get her attention. Joanna took up the rear, not wanting to be left behind.

"Cindy!" Deborah called, quickening her pace. "We'd really rather see the organ room!"

Undeterred, either not hearing or just ignoring Deborah, Cindy continued on to a set of leather-covered double doors with small oval windows. Pushing one open, she leaned into the darkness and snapped on a light switch. The sound was a low-pitched thud and large, old-fashioned kettle drum-shaped lights came on. They were high in the ceiling and acted like spotlights to illuminate an old metal autopsy table.

Joanna, who'd come up behind Deborah, took in the scene and caught her breath. The setting with the rows of spectator seats rising up into the gloom was even more like the gruesome anatomy-lesson painting than the operating room upstairs where she'd had her procedure.

"This is very interesting," Deborah said with a sarcastic overtone after taking a quick gander into the room. "But, if you don't mind, we much prefer to see the organ room."

"How about checking out the old autopsy tools?" Cindy questioned. "Myself and a couple of the other techs were joking the other day about sending them out to Hollywood for a horror movie."

"Let's see the organ room," Joanna stated flatly.

"Fine by me," Cindy said. She turned out the light and started along the hall again. She glanced at her watch, a gesture Joanna noted but Deborah didn't. It was the third time Joanna had seen the woman do it. Deborah was busy, looking back the way they'd come.

"Isn't the organ room the other way?" Deborah called out to Cindy who was a dozen paces ahead.

"We can get to it either way," Cindy said over her shoulder. "But this route is shorter."

✗ As Deborah caught up to the others she saw ahead a pair of horizontally oriented doors like dumbwaiter doors in an opening the size of a small garage. As the group walked past, Deborah asked about them.

"That's the old freight elevator," Cindy said coming to a stop. "The dead bodies used to come down in it from the upper floors."

"That's a cheery thought," Joanna commented. "Let's keep moving!"

"It's actually been handy for us," Cindy said. She tapped the doors appreciatively with her knuckle. "We've used it to get most of the equipment down here. Would you like to see how it works?"

"We'd prefer to see the organ room," Joanna said. "I think we know how a freight elevator works."

"Fine by me," Cindy said again.

After passing through a twenty-foot-long, narrow vaulted passageway which, Cindy explained, penetrated the foundation support for the building's Italianate tower, the women found themselves on the threshold of the largest room they'd seen in the subterranean complex. It was at least one hundred feet long and fifty wide. In it were row upon row of voluminous Plexiglas aquarium-like containers approximately six feet long, three deep, and two wide. Each contained multiple glass spheres approximately a foot in diameter that were submerged in fluid. From the top of each sphere sprouted a tangle of tubes and electric leads. On the surface of the fluid floated a continuous layer of tiny glass spheres.

For a moment the women just took in

the spectacle. Although the walls of the room were still exposed brick, the scene was more like what they had expected when they'd first passed through the stainless-steel door. Even the ceiling was higher in this space than in the other rooms due to an absence of the overhead piping and ductwork. The lighting was also less harsh, but with the addition of an apparent ultraviolet component.

While Deborah was transfixed by the vista, Joanna caught Cindy again checking her watch. What made the repeated gesture remarkable to Joanna was the woman's otherwise apparent hospitality. If she were so concerned about the time, as suggested by her constantly looking at her watch, why was she spending so much of it with them? It was a question for which Joanna had no immediate answer, but it progressively bothered her.

"What exactly are we looking at here?" Deborah asked.

"This is the organ room," Cindy explained. "These tanks are constant-temperature water baths. The small floating spheres are to keep the bath water from evaporating. The larger spheres hold the ovaries."

"So," Deborah commented, "you're able to keep entire ovaries alive by, I assume, perfusing them etcetera."

"That's pretty much the story," Cindy said. "We've mimicked their accustomed internal environment with oxygen, nutrients, and endocrine stimulation. Of course removing waste products is also important. At any rate, when we do it right, the ovaries are constantly ovulating mature oocytes."

"Can we see closer?" Deborah asked.

Cindy gestured ahead. "By all means."

Deborah walked down an aisle between two rows of the tanks and stopped to gaze within one of the spheres. The contained ovary was about the size of a flattened walnut with a ragged, pock-marked surface reminiscent of the moon. Tiny perfusion cannulas were connected to the major ovarian vessels. Various sensing wires were attached at other points on the small organ.

"We have more traditional cell cultures of oogonia as well," Cindy said. "I can show you them if you'd like."

"Some of these spheres contain two ovaries rather than one," Deborah said.

"That's true, but most are single, as you can see. How about we move on to the oogonia room?"

"What does it mean when there are two ovaries?" Joanna asked.

"That's Dr. Donaldson's department," Cindy said. "I'm just one of the many technicians who monitor and take care of them."

Joanna and Deborah exchanged one of their signature glances. As familiar as they were with each other, each generally could tell what the other was thinking.

"I see each sphere is labeled alphanumerically," Joanna said. "Does that mean you know the origin of each ovary?"

For the first time during their visit Cindy appeared clearly uncomfortable with the question. She hemmed and hawed and again tried to change the subject back to the oogonia cultures, but Joanna was insistent.

"We have a vague idea of each ovary's origin," Cindy admitted finally.

"What does *vague* mean?" Joanna persisted. "If I were to give you a name of an ovarian donor, could you locate the ovary?"

"I believe so," Cindy said evasively. She looked at her watch and switched her weight from one foot to the other.

"The name I'm interested in is Joanna Meissner," Joanna said.

"Joanna Meissner," Cindy repeated. She glanced around the area as if unfamiliar where things were located. "We'd need a computer workstation."

"There's one right behind you," Joanna said.

"Oh, indeed!" Cindy said as if surprised. She turned, unlocked the keyboard with her password, then typed in Joanna's name. The screen flashed back "JM699." Cindy scribbled the code on a scrap of paper and then set off. The women followed behind. Two rows over and two tanks down she stopped and pointed. JM699 was written on the glass sphere's surface with an indelible marker.

Both Joanna and Deborah stared in at the small organ. It was significantly more pockmarked than the first one they'd seen, and Joanna asked about it.

"It's one of our older specimens," Cindy

explained. "It's nearing the end of its useful life."

"I have a donor's name," Deborah said. "Kristin Overmeyer."

"Okay," Cindy said agreeably, as if reconciled to the situation. She retraced her steps back to the computer workstation having recovered her previous poise. She typed in the name without hesitation, and the computer immediately produced the code: KO432.

"This way," Cindy said, waving for the women to follow. She skirted the periphery of the room before turning into the first row. Joanna held Deborah back and whispered: "I know what you are thinking. It's a good thought!"

Deborah merely nodded.

"Here we are," Cindy said almost proudly, stopping at a specific tank. She pointed at the middle glass sphere. "KO432. It's a double specimen."

"Interesting," Deborah said after a quick glance. "The specimen has a lower number than the previous one, but looks younger. How can that be?"

Cindy glanced in at the two ovaries. It was apparent she was flustered again. She stuttered a moment before saying: "That's something I know nothing about. Maybe it has to do with the way the specimens are taken, but I really don't know. I'm sure Dr. Donaldson would be able to explain it."

"I have one more name," Deborah said. "Rebecca Corey."

"Are you sure you people wouldn't like to see the oogonia cultures?" Cindy asked. "We feel that's the arena where we have made the biggest advances. The oogonia cultures are soon going to make these full ovary cultures passé."

"This is the last name," Deborah promised. "Then we'll move on to the oogonia cultures."

After another check of her watch, Cindy repeated the procedure for getting the code number. She then led them to the tank immediately adjacent to the one containing Kristin Overmeyer's ovaries and pointed at the appropriate sphere. Once again it was a double specimen.

Both Joanna and Deborah peered in at the ovaries which, like Kristin's, appeared younger than Joanna's. Both women trembled with the realization that they were looking at the ovaries of a woman who was

supposed to have disappeared along with
Kristin Overmeyer after picking up a hitchhiker.

"The oogonia culture room is immediately adjacent," Cindy said. "How about
we head over there?"

Joanna and Deborah simultaneously
raised their eyes from the ovaries and
looked at each other. The horror reflected
in their eyes made it instantly apparent
they shared the same thoughts. They had
uncovered significantly more than they'd
envisioned, and it was terrifying as well as
horrifying.

"I think we've already taken too much of
your time," Joanna said. She gave Cindy a
crooked smile.

"It's true," Deborah chimed in. "It's been
interesting, but it's time we moved on.
Maybe you could point us in the right direction toward the entrance, and we'll get
out of your hair."

"I've plenty of time," Cindy said quickly.
"It's no problem, trust me! I've enjoyed the
break in my routine, and I think you should
see the whole setup before you go. Come
on! We'll see the oogonia cultures." She

tried to take Deborah's arm, but Deborah pulled free.

"We want to leave," Deborah said more emphatically.

"You'll be missing the most significant part," Cindy said. "I have to insist!"

"Like hell you'll insist!" Deborah spat. "We're outta here!"

"We'll find our own way," Joanna said. She started back the way they'd come. Although she knew it might not be the shortest route from what Cindy had said earlier, she didn't care. At least she'd be passing recognizable landmarks.

"I can't let you wander in here by yourselves," Cindy stated. "It's against the rules." She grabbed Joanna's arm with more force than she'd used with Deborah, pulling Joanna to a stop.

Joanna looked down at the woman's hand clasped around her arm. "We're leaving," she said assertively. "Take your hands off me!"

"I can't let you be in here unattended," Cindy repeated.

"Then take us to the exit!" Deborah snapped. She snatched Cindy's hand from Joanna's arm and pushed the woman back where she stumbled against one of the Plexiglas containers. The slight jolt set off a beeping alarm along with a flashing red light at the tank's control panel.

When Cindy reached for the button to disengage the alarm, Joanna and Deborah took off, running as fast as the narrow row between the tanks would allow. When they broke free of the tanks, Deborah's athleticism came to the fore, and she passed Joanna, urging her on. Behind they could hear Cindy cry out for them to stop.

"I knew we shouldn't have come in here!" Joanna panted, trying to keep up with Deborah.

"Shut up, and run!"

They ran through the arched tunnel, past the old freight elevator and darkened autopsy pit, and into the series of rooms with the incubators. Suddenly Deborah stopped. Joanna had all she could do to keep from bumping into her.

"Which way?" Deborah demanded.

"I think that way," Joanna said, pointing due south through a succession of archways.

"I hope you're right," Deborah said. They could hear the echoes of Cindy approaching and calling their names, but the echoes made it impossible to tell the direction. A second later she appeared at a run from around an archway and collided with them. She grabbed onto Joanna's and Deborah's clothes as best she could.

"Good God, woman!" Deborah cried. With significant force she ripped herself free of the woman's grasp only to have the woman use both hands to clench Joanna. Deborah swung around behind Cindy and, grabbing her around the chest, pulled her free from Joanna. Then, with a slight twisting motion, she threw Cindy to the floor where the woman hit up against one of the incubators. The unmistakable but muffled sound of breaking glass came from within.

Without waiting to check on the woman's condition, Deborah grabbed Joanna's hand and dashed in the direction Joanna had suggested. To their relief, after they'd passed through several arches they caught sight of the stainless-steel door. Quickly running up to it, Deborah slapped the OPEN/CLOSE panel. The door began its painstaking glide to the left. Both women glanced over their shoulders in fear that Cindy was on her way, and she was.

Turning back to the door, Deborah tried vainly to speed its movement with muscle power. The moment the gap was wide enough to squeeze through, Deborah propelled Joanna to the opening so that Deborah could deal with Cindy.

"Oh no!" Joanna cried as she pulled back after starting through the widening crack of the door.

Deborah, who'd momentarily turned to check how close Cindy was, spun around to see what had caused Joanna's cry and halted her progress out of the room. What she saw over Joanna's shoulder brought an involuntary cry to her own lips. Two large, smirking men dressed in black were coming toward them through the dilapidated but now lighted kitchen. They had handcuffs in one hand, guns in the other. The blond man in the lead, seeing the door opening and seeing the women, had started to run. Deborah recognized him. It was the man who had been leering at her in the dining room and who she assumed was the security chief.

eighteen

MAY 10, 2001
11:24 P.M.

Deborah responded by instinct, again slapping her hand against the raised open/close button, closing the heavy steel door in the face of the onrushing men. At the same time she was assaulted by Cindy from behind, who grabbed her around the neck and tried to pull her away from the door. Deborah resisted, keeping the button depressed.

"Get this banshee off me!" Deborah cried. Cindy was screaming that the door had to be opened.

Joanna peeled Cindy's fingers from

around Deborah and shoved her stumbling backward. But the woman quickly recovered and lunged back at Deborah.

"Joanna, hold the damn button," Deborah yelled while fending Cindy off with one hand.

As soon as Joanna had the panel depressed, Deborah brought both hands to bear on the persistent technician. Although Deborah had not hit anyone since clocking a bratty male fellow fifth-grader, she hauled off and punched Cindy on the left cheek. After four years of varsity lacrosse, Deborah was significantly stronger and more of an aggressor than she'd been in the fifth grade, and the blow stunned Cindy into sudden silence and immobility. A second later she sagged to the floor in slow motion, first sinking to her knees and then sloshing prostrate like a melting ice cream cone.

Deborah cried out from the pain in her hand, which she flapped wildly for a moment. Forcing herself to regain control, she grabbed the nearest incubator and rolled it over to the door. Joanna immediately comprehended what Deborah had in mind and helped guide the incubator so that its weight continued to depress the button, which both women recognized was keeping the door closed. To be sure the incubator wouldn't move, Joanna and Deborah continued to hold on to it to maintain its position.

"What's your plan?" Joanna demanded in a panicked, forced whisper.

"The only way out is the dumbwaiter or the freight elevator! What do you think?"

"The freight elevator!" Joanna said. "We know exactly where it is, and we know we'll fit."

A few paces away, Cindy pushed herself up into a uncertain, semi-sitting position. She had a blank, unfocused expression in her eyes like a boxer hit too many times.

"All right!" Deborah said after casting one last glance Cindy, who was now struggling to get to her feet. "Let's do it!"

Both let go of the incubator in unison and made a dash back through the maze of rooms. Unfortunately they made a wrong turn and ended up in a blank room. They had to retrace their steps before getting back on track. Behind them they heard the unmistakable sound of an incubator clunking up against another followed by deep-throated shouts by the men.

"Heaven help us if that freight elevator is not running," Deborah managed between gasps.

They rounded the final bend, ran past the doors to the autopsy theater, and literally collided with the freight-elevator doors. A heavy canvas strap protruded through the chest-high horizontal gap. Deborah grabbed it first, but Joanna lent a hand as well. With their combined weight, the doors gave way, with the lower door opening downward while the upper door rose. When the gap between the two doors was large enough, the two women climbed in.

The elevator itself was a heavy wire-mesh cage eight feet square. To the right at chest height was a control panel with six buttons. The floor was made of rough wooden planking. Above, the supporting cables disappeared up into blackness; the only light was coming from the hallway through the open doors. In the near distance heavy footsteps could be heard running toward them and closing quickly.

"The doors!" Deborah yelled as she reached up and grabbed the canvas strap attached to the inside edge of the upper door. Joanna reached up and grabbed it as well. Once again with their combined weight the women succeeded in getting the heavy doors to move. Slowly at first and then with increasing speed they began to close, but before they did, the men arrived outside. A hand was thrust between the narrowing gap and grabbed a handful of Deborah's doctor's coat, yanking it back through just as the doors came together and thrust the women into blackness. With her hands still grasping the canvas strap, Deborah felt herself roughly hauled against the door.

"Hit one of the buttons!" Deborah screeched to Joanna without taking her weight off the strap. She could feel someone outside was now trying to open the doors, but to do so they would have to lift Deborah in the process.

Like a blind person, Joanna groped for the control box she'd caught a glimpse of before the closing doors had extinguished the light.

"Hurry! God damn it!" Deborah yelled. She could feel herself being lifted off the planking.

Frantically Joanna widened her blind search over the surface of the wire mesh. Finally her hand knocked against the control box. In the blackness she pushed the first button her fingers encountered.

A high-pitched screeching sound erupted, like chickens being tortured, and with a lurch, the old freight elevator began to rise.

Deborah let go of the strap she'd been gripping, and falling to her knees and twisting, she managed to yank her arms free of the doctor's coat, which was still caught between the closed freight elevator doors. A second later, with an agonizing tearing and crushing sound, Deborah felt the coat disappear into the narrow gap between the front lip of the rising elevator and the stone elevator shaft wall.

"What the hell was that noise?" Joanna demanded through gasps for breath.

Deborah shuddered in the darkness. She knew the crushing sound could have been her body had she not gotten out of the coat. She, too, gasped for breath. "It was my flashlight and car keys being crushed in my doctor's coat."

"We've lost our car keys?" Joanna moaned with her chest heaving.

"That's the least of our worries at the moment," Deborah managed. "Thank God this elevator worked. Those men almost got us. I mean, that couldn't have been any closer."

Joanna's flashlight snapped on. She shined it at the control box. The button that was depressed was the third floor.

"What should we do?" Joanna asked tensely. "We're heading for the third floor. Should we see if we can change that?"

"This is hardly a high-speed elevator," Deborah complained. "The third floor is probably better than certainly the first and maybe even the second. I don't want to run into those men again."

"Obviously," Joanna said. With her breathing coming under a semblance of control, it was her turn to shudder. "Now we have proof this place is capable of murder, and they probably know we know. And that Cindy bitch knew the men were coming the whole time we were in there. That's why she was being so nice to us. We should have suspected something was wrong the minute she offered a tour. What's wrong with us?"

"That's all easy to say now," Deborah said, still panting. "We were under the delusion they were violating ethics here, not commandments. Murder for eggs makes this a completely different ball game."

"We have to get out of here!"

"True," Deborah said. "But without car keys we're not driving anyplace, at least not in our own car. I think our best bet is to get to a telephone in the Wingate Clinic on the first or second floor."

"The problem is, that's probably what they are expecting," Joanna said. "At least that's what I would expect if I were them. What do you say about hiding for a time to give ourselves a chance to think what we should do and come up with a plan?"

"Maybe we should hide until morning," Deborah suggested. "My guess would be that a very small minority of the people who work here know what they are really doing, and if they did, they'd be as horrified as we are. We could approach someone for help."

"My guess is that they are going to

search until they find us tonight. We've got to get out of here."

"But how? Those men had guns, for chrissake!"

"That's why we have to find someplace to hole up. We have to think. We can't be rash."

"The one thing in our favor is the size of this building and the fact that it's so cluttered with stuff," Deborah said. "There's got to be safe places to hide for a time. Unless they call in a lot of help, it's going to take them most of the night to search with any thoroughness."

"Exactly," Joanna said. "My guess is that they'll do a rapid, superficial search, and if that proves futile, they'll go back for a complete one. By then we have to be out of here or we'll be caught."

Deborah shook her head and took an uncertain breath. "I'm sorry I brought us out here. It's all my fault."

"This is no time for recriminations," Joanna said. "And just for the record: You didn't make me come here. I came here on my own accord."

"Thanks," Deborah murmured.

Joanna switched off the flashlight. "I

think we'd better let our eyes adjust to the darkness. We can't be running around with the light on."

"You're right," Deborah managed, trying to get ahold of herself.

A few minutes later, with a final jolting screech, the elevator stopped. Pure silence returned in a smothering rush. The women leaped to the door. As quickly as they could they got it open, only to be confronted by an impenetrable wall of darkness.

"There's no choice; I've got to turn on the light," Joanna said. The click sounded loud in the silence. She rapidly ran the beam around the small, windowless room. It was the freight elevator vestibule with a wide double door.

"They'll quickly figure out the elevator is here on the third floor," Deborah said. "So they'll be here soon. Let's find a stairwell and get up to the top floor. That's where we should find a place to hide until we figure out what we're going to do."

"Agreed!"

Deborah pulled open one of the doors to the corridor, and Joanna stepped through. Quickly Joanna beamed the light up and down the hall. Even though she was now forewarned about all the medical paraphernalia cluttering the old hospital, she was still taken aback by the scene. She hadn't expected to see framed prints still on the walls, nor a laundry cart with folded sheets still on its shelves. "It's like there was a fire drill and everybody ran out and then never came back," she said.

"There's an exit sign," Deborah said, pointing toward the south. "That must be a stairwell. Let's go!"

Joanna kept her hand over the flashlight lens. She wanted to limit the light to just what she and Deborah needed to avoid the gurneys, supply carts, and old wheel chairs. They moved quickly. Arriving at the stairwell, Deborah cracked open the door. For a second they listened. All was quiet.

"Come on!" Deborah urged pushing into the stairwell.

They started up the stairs at a run but slowed immediately because of the noise they were making. The stairs were metal and reverberated like kettle drums in the confined space.

They got only as far as the intermediate landing before both women froze in place.

They'd heard a door somewhere below burst open and slam against the wall. Joanna recovered enough to switch off her flashlight.

In the next instant, booming footfalls resounded against the metal treads, accompanied by a flickering glow that filtered up the stairwell. One of the men was running up the stairs clutching a flashlight.

Joanna and Deborah edged to the rear of the landing and pressed themselves up against the bare brick as the sounds and the light rising from below rapidly reached a crescendo. Simultaneously one of the men in black appeared on the third-floor landing no more than twenty feet away. He was so close to the women that his labored breathing was clearly audible. Luckily, he did not look up but rather concentrated on getting into the third-floor corridor and down to the freight elevator as quickly as possible.

The instant the stairwell door closed behind the man, Joanna and Deborah restarted their climb to the fourth floor. Too scared to switch on the light, they had to move slowly by feel while they struggled against succumbing to their renewed panic. The fourth-floor landing was particularly difficult to navigate in the darkness due to stacks of empty cardboard cartons.

Once they were in the fourth-floor corridor, Joanna again switched on the light. Keeping her hand over the lens, they started out, heading north and moving as fast as the cluttered hall allowed. Both instinctively felt that the farther they were from the part of the building occupied by the Wingate Clinic, the safer they would be. They also tried to be as quiet as possible on the aged wooden flooring in deference to the man searching for them on the floor directly below.

They reached the fire door leading to the tower. Without discussion they traversed the tower and passed through the opposite fire door into the north wing. Except for an occasional creak of a floorboard, they were silent, each consumed by her own fears.

The wards in the north wing were a mirror image of those in the south wing, arranged lengthwise along either side of a central corridor. Each ward was separated from its immediate neighbor by side rooms, and each ward had twenty to thirty beds. Most of the beds were covered with bare mattresses although a few also had moth-eaten blankets.

"Any ideas about where we should hide?" Joanna whispered nervously.

"Not yet," Deborah said. "I suppose we could climb into cabinets in one of the many storage rooms, but that might be too easy."

"We don't have a lot of time."

"Unfortunately I think you're right," Deborah said. She directed Joanna to shine the light into the room between the last two wards on the northwest corner of the building. Instead of being a storage room like most of the others, it had been set up as a minor procedure room with an iron examining table and a sink. The opposite wall had a large, glass-fronted instrument cabinet. Pushing through a connecting door they found a small storage room for linens and dressings along with a large, old-fashioned sterilizer.

Deborah quickly went over to the sterilizer, and while Joanna held the light on it, she pulled its door. It resisted at first, but then slowly creaked open.

"What about this?" Deborah asked.

The sterilizer was about three feet in diameter and about five feet deep. Joanna shined the light inside. There were a number of stainless steel boxes sitting on a metal grate. "Only one of us would fit even if we took the stuff out," Joanna said. "And even that would be a squeeze."

"I guess you're right," Deborah said. She let go of the sterilizer and hurried over to the connecting door leading to the end ward. Joanna followed her with the light, continuing to keep the lens mostly covered. When Deborah pushed open the door, Joanna turned out the flashlight. A meager amount of moonlight filtered in through the windows, enough to illuminate the larger objects in the room.

The ward was the same size and decor as the others but differed by having in it a six-foot-long, horizontal cylinder mounted on legs. It stood about waist height in place of one of the beds lining the interior wall of the room.

"Now there's a possibility," Deborah exclaimed.

"What?"

"That cylinder," Deborah said, pointing at the large object. "I remember reading about them. They were called iron lungs and were used for people who couldn't breathe, like patients in the nineteen-fifties with infantile paralysis."

The women walked as quickly as they could through the dark ward and approached the old-fashioned ventilator. It had appeared light gray, but as they got closer they could tell it was yellow. Along its sides were small, round, glass viewports. The end facing out into the ward was hinged and contained a central, black rubber collar to fit around a patient's head to make a seal. Just above the collar was a small mirror oriented at a forty-five-degree angle. Below the collar was a platform for the patient's head.

While Deborah unlatched the front cover, Joanna nervously glanced around. She was concerned about too much time passing. They needed a hiding place, and they needed it sooner rather than later.

As Deborah pushed the iron lung's door open, it squeaked but not as loudly as the sterilizer.

"Shine the light in," Deborah said.

"Deborah, we can't be fooling around here," Joanna complained.

"Shine the light in!" Deborah repeated.

The moment Joanna did as Deborah suggested, a distant fire door banged against a wall followed by the flickering of a flashlight beam out in the main corridor.

"Oh God!" Joanna voiced. She turned off the light.

"Well, this has got to do," Deborah said. "We're hiding in here." She grabbed a side chair from between the beds and shoved it under the front lip of the iron lung. She gripped Joanna's arm. "Quick! You first, and feet first!"

The play of flickering light increased in intensity through the open doorway to the main corridor.

"Quick!" Deborah repeated.

With some reluctance but feeling she had little choice, Joanna climbed up on the chair. Holding on to the upper edge of the cylinder's rim, she got one foot inside. With Deborah supporting her backside, she got the other one in as well. She then slid her body in.

Deborah grabbed the chair and returned it to where she'd found it.

"Where are you going?" Joanna demanded in a whisper when Deborah disappeared from her view.

Deborah didn't answer but reappeared almost instantly. "I've got to get in without the chair," she said. "It would be too much of a giveaway."

Using the strut between the iron lung's two front legs as the first step, Deborah rose up so her chest was above the iron lung's top. Finding a narrow toehold in the top of the leg where it was welded to the iron lung's body, she draped herself over the top. Then by swinging around, she was able to get her feet into the cylinder's opening. But then she ran into trouble. She couldn't figure out how to get the rest of her body in without falling to the floor, even if Joanna tried to hold onto her legs.

"This is not going to work," Deborah said. She twisted to the side, and dropped back to the floor.

"You've got to hurry," Joanna rasped in a whisper. The light from the hall was brighter still and was now accompanied by voices. It was the two men coming all the way to the end of the corridor.

Deborah stuck as much of her upper body head first into the iron lung as she could. "Grab onto me, and pull," she told Joanna out of desperation.

With a little leap and Joanna's help, Deborah managed to get herself into the iron lung but not without scraping the front of her thighs and shins on the front lip of the metal cylinder. She had to claw herself into the depths. Because of the tightness of the space, the two women ended up on their sides pressed against each other head to toe.

"Try to close the door as much as you can," Deborah whispered from the recesses of the ventilator.

Joanna reached out and grabbed the rubber collar and pulled. The door slowly began to close, but as soon as it squeaked, she stopped. It was none too soon. A flashlight beam came into the room and moved about. For a brief moment the beam came directly inside the iron lung through the three glass side ports on the side facing the door. Then the beam dropped and arced around the room beneath the beds, searching out the recesses.

Both women involuntarily held their breaths. One of the men quickly walked up and down the center of the ward, passing within ten feet of the half-open iron lung not once but twice. He was bent over and swinging the light from side to side beneath the beds to illuminate their undersides, particularly up under the heads and along the sides of the intervening tables.

"See anything?" the man suddenly shouted, causing both women to start.

From the ward across the hall the other man answered with a negative.

A moment later the man who'd come into the women's ward could be heard in the connecting room rapidly slamming open cabinets and cursing loudly. The flicker of his flashlight could still be seen by Deborah through one of the viewports until he moved beyond the procedure room and on into the next ward.

Almost in unison the women let the air out of their lungs and took in deep breaths. For Deborah it was hardly fresh.

"That was almost as close as the freight elevator," Joanna whispered.

"They must be sweeping the building as you suggested," Deborah said.

"Let's stay put for a while in case he comes back," Joanna said. "And we'd better start thinking about what we're going to do to get ourselves out of here."

Time dragged by, especially for Deborah, who began to feel claustrophobic wedged down in the base of the narrow cylinder designed for one person. For her the situation was hardly conducive to thought. The smell of the old bare mattress was ripe and the dust bothersome. On several occasions it took sheer will for her merely to avoid sneezing. Eventually she began to perspire and experience a progressive shortness of breath.

After almost a half hour Deborah couldn't take it any longer. "Have you heard anything or seen any lights?" she asked.

"The only light I've seen has been some flickering through the windows," Joanna said. "There's a light outside that wasn't there before."

"Nothing inside the building?"

"Not a thing," Joanna said.

"I've got to get out of here," Deborah admitted. "Push open the door and try to do it without making any noise."

Joanna pushed on the door. It swung almost fully open without making a sound.

"I'm coming out," Deborah said. "If I put

my hand someplace you'd rather I didn't, I'll apologize in advance."

With a lot of wriggling and grunting Deborah managed to ease herself back out of the iron lung. Her eyes scanned the room, noticing that the ambient light had increased as Joanna had mentioned. Then she mopped her forehead with the back of her hand and ran her fingers through her damp, shoulder-length hair. She felt bedraggled and exhausted, yet she knew the night was still young, with more trials ahead. In her mind's eye she could picture the razor-wire-topped fence, and she knew that even if they managed to get out of the building, leaving the premises was not going to be easy.

"How about getting that chair?" Joanna said.

"Oh, sorry," Deborah said. She'd been distracted by her worries. She dragged the chair over to the mouth of the iron lung.

"Did you come up with any ideas about getting out of here?" Joanna asked as she extracted herself from the ventilator.

"I didn't," Deborah confessed. "Jammed in that tube the way I was, I couldn't think. What about you?"

"Something did occur to me," Joanna said. "The power plant could be the way to get out of this building."

"How so?" Deborah asked.

"If they're creating heat over there to heat this building, it's got to get here," Joanna said. "There's got to be a tunnel."

"You're right!" Deborah said.

"I noticed that the freight elevator control had six buttons," Joanna said. "I hadn't given it any thought until I started thinking about a tunnel. This building must have a sub-basement. Maybe that should be our goal. The more I think about our trying to get to a phone in the Wingate Clinic the more risky I think it would be."

"But I haven't seen access to a sub-basement," Deborah said. "There wasn't any in the stairwell we used tonight when we got here, or the one I used this afternoon."

"Let's check out the freight elevator," Joanna said.

"We can't use that," Deborah said. "It's too noisy."

"I'm not talking about using the elevator itself," Joanna explained. "Usually they have a ladder in elevator shafts. I don't know why, I guess for maintenance."

"Where did you learn this?" Deborah questioned. She was impressed.

"It's thanks to Carlton," Joanna explained. "Mindless action movies are his favorite, and at one time or another I've had to suffer through watching most of them. There've been dozens of scenes in elevator shafts."

"I suppose it's worth a check," Deborah said. "Do you think we've waited long enough?"

"There's no way to know for sure, but since we can't stay here all night, we have to do it sometime. Let me check the hall."

"All right, you do that," Deborah said. "I want to see what this extra light is, coming through the front windows."

While Joanna cautiously made her way over to the archway leading out into the corridor, Deborah crossed the ward. Bending over at the waist to keep her head down, Deborah approached one of the windows. Slowly she raised her eyes above the sill and found herself staring into multiple automobile headlights positioned to illuminate the building. Although the cars were at a considerable distance down the lawn, Deborah quickly ducked out of sight to be sure not to be spotted. She'd caught a glimpse of several uniformed guards silhouetted against the lights. They had large dogs on leashes. The two men in black had called in reinforcements.

Deborah quickly joined Joanna who was waiting for her at the archway and told her what she'd seen.

"Dogs are not good," Joanna said gravely. "These people really mean business."

"I think we already knew that," Deborah said.

"It also means leaving the building underground is suddenly a necessity," Joanna said. She then opened her mouth to tell Deborah the main corridor was clear when the sound of a bullhorn coming from outside startled her.

nineteen

MAY 11, 2001
12:37 A.M.

"Joanna Meissner and Deborah Cochrane!" A voice echoed against the front of the building. "There is no need to extend this charade. Don't make us come into the building with dogs, which we will do if you don't come out on your own accord. The Bookford Police are on their way. I repeat! Come out immediately."

"So much for our carefully crafted aliases," Deborah said.

"If I thought they'd turn us over to the Bookford police, I'd walk out of here in a heartbeat."

"They're not going to turn us over to anyone," Deborah said.

"That's my point," Joanna said. "Come on! Let's check out the freight elevator before I lose my nerve."

Gaining some familiarity with the building, the women retraced their route back through the fourth floor to the stairwell they'd used earlier. At first they tried to descend without turning on the flashlight but quickly realized the risk of knocking some of the unseen debris down the stairs was greater than the risk presented by the shielded flashlight. They turned it off again before they entered the third-floor corridor. While in the corridor they heard the bull-horn message again.

They had to turn the light on again in the freight elevator vestibule. The elevator was exactly the way they had left it with the doors half open. Joanna shined the light into the car. Through the wire-mesh of its back wall a ladder was visible attached to the brick of the elevator shaft.

"You were right about there being a ladder," Deborah said. "But how do you get to it?"

Joanna moved the light beam to the side

wall of the elevator. Attached to the cab's wall were ladder rungs. The rungs led up to a wire-mesh trapdoor in the elevator's ceiling.

"All we have to do is climb to the top of the elevator," Joanna said.

"Is that all?" Deborah questioned sarcastically. "Where are you finding this sudden chutzpah."

"I'm pretending I'm you," Joanna said. "So let's do it before I revert back to me."

Deborah gave a short, derisive laugh.

The women stepped over the half-open lower elevator door. Joanna held the light while Deborah climbed the ladder rungs. While holding on to the top one, she pushed up the trapdoor. Just beyond ninety degrees it hit up against a stop and stayed open.

Joanna handed up the flashlight, and Deborah placed it on top of the elevator before hauling herself up. The elevator swayed slightly when she stood up, forcing her to grab the supporting cables, which were covered with grease the consistency of petroleum jelly. A moment later Joanna came up through the hole. She stayed on her hands and knees rather than standing up.

The ladder ran along the back wall of the shaft and cleared the elevator car by only twelve inches.

"Well, what do you think?" Deborah asked.

"I think we should give it a try," Joanna said. She shined the flashlight down the shaft. It wasn't strong enough to reach the bottom. The ladder merely disappeared into a murky haze.

"You first," Deborah said. "And you keep the light."

"I'm not going to be able to climb and hold the light at the same time."

"I know," Deborah said. "But you have a pocket, and I don't."

"Okay," Joanna said with resignation. She was accustomed to Deborah's being the leader in such a circumstance. Joanna turned out the light, plunging them into utter blackness. She pocketed the flashlight, then groped for the ladder. When she got ahold of it, she had to argue with herself to abandon the relative safety of the elevator, especially when the elevator swayed slightly during the transition. Gripping the rung of the ladder tightly with both hands, she tried not to think about being suspended on a vertical ladder four stories above a black hole.

"Are you doing okay?" Deborah whispered in the dark when she didn't hear any movement.

"This is harrowing," Joanna said.

"Are you on the ladder?"

"Yes," Joanna said. "But I'm afraid to move."

"You have to!"

Joanna lowered one foot to the next rung and then the other. What she had more difficulty with was letting go with one hand. Finally she did it, and then repeated the movement with the other hand. Slowly at first, and then with building confidence she descended between the elevator and the ladder. It was a tight fit, which made the process more difficult.

"Can you give me a little light so I can see where the ladder is?" Deborah asked from above.

"I can't," Joanna said. "I can't let go for that long."

Deborah mumbled a few choice words as she reached out blindly with one hand while maintaining the grip on the greasy cable with the other. But the ladder was too far away. Eventually she had to go down on all fours like Joanna and creep over to the edge of the elevator's cab. Finally she got ahold of the ladder, transferred herself onto it, and followed Joanna down.

The women moved slowly, particularly Joanna. Although she began to build up confidence, a new concern emerged from feeling corrosion on the rungs. She began worrying that one of the rungs might have become so weakened from rust that it could give way under her weight. Before she put her weight on any rung, she kicked at it to get an idea of its integrity.

The blackness of the shaft aided Joanna, especially after passing below the elevator cab. Without being able to see, the height was only a mental problem, not a visual one.

Deborah had to slow herself down when she caught up with Joanna.

After a quarter-hour of climbing, Deborah was ready to reconnoiter. "Can you see the bottom?" she questioned in a whisper. The muscles of her arms were beginning to complain, and she imagined Joanna's were as well.

"You must be joking," Joanna answered. "I can't even see my nose."

"Maybe you should shine the light for a second. You could hook your arm around one of the rungs."

"I think I should just keep going until my foot touches the floor," Joanna said.

"Do you want to rest?"

"I really think I should keep going."

Another ten minutes passed before Joanna's outstretched foot touched litter-strewn pavement. She pulled her foot back. "We're here," she said. "Hold up!" Hooking her arm in a rung as Deborah had suggested earlier, she got out the flashlight and turned it on. The bottom of the shaft was filled with debris as if it had been a garbage dump over the years.

"Can you tell if we're at the sub-basement or not?" Deborah asked.

"I can't," Joanna said. "Come on down, and we'll see if we can get the doors open."

Joanna used her foot to push away some of the trash at the ladder's base before stepping onto the pavement. She waited for Deborah to come the rest of the way down, keeping her hand over the flashlight lens.

"Wow, it's freezing down here," Deborah said, rubbing her arms once she got off the ladder. "It certainly feels like a sub-basement."

The women gingerly made their way to the doors through the junk which was mostly paper, rags, and miscellaneous pieces of wood interspersed with a few cans. While Joanna held the light, Deborah reached up and got her fingers between the upper and lower doors. Try as she might, they wouldn't open.

Joanna put the light down on the floor and lent a hand. Still the doors wouldn't so much as budge.

"This is not good," Joanna said.

Deborah picked up the light and took a step back. She shined the light around the periphery of the doors. She stopped at a spring-loaded lever arm protruding out from the wall at the edge of the doors just above where they came together.

"That's our problem," Deborah said. "I haven't seen too many action movies, but that has to be a fail-safe mechanism to keep the doors locked until the elevator is in front of the doors."

"Meaning?" Joanna questioned.

"Meaning one of us has to hold it down while the other opens the doors."

"You're taller," Joanna said. "You get the fail-safe mechanism, I'll try the doors."

A moment later the doors cracked open, although it wasn't until Joanna leaned her full weight on the lower door that they opened fully. Deborah shined the light into the space beyond.

"It's a sub-basement all right," Joanna said. The entire floor was just intersecting supporting arches through which ran a tangle of clay sewer pipes and insulated cast-iron heating pipes. There were no doors or separate rooms. The walls were brick like the basement above, but the arches were flatter and the adjoining piers thicker.

A passageway with a vaulted ceiling higher than the rest of the sub-basement led from the freight elevator to intersect with a similar corridor that ran the length of the building. Bare electric wire looped along the peak of the vault to lighting fixtures, but they were not lit.

The women stopped at the intersection

and shined the light in both directions. In each direction the view was a study in perspective, with the arches marching off into the darkness as far as the meager light was able to penetrate.

"Which way?" Joanna questioned.

"I'd favor going left," Deborah said. "That will take us toward the tower section of the building. That's the center."

"But if we go right, we're going more in the direction of the power plant," Joanna said. "The power plant is off to the southeast." She pointed forty-five degrees off the axis of the main corridor.

"How are we going to decide?" Deborah asked, looking in both directions.

"Shine the light on the floor," Joanna said. She knelt down. The floor of the passageway from the freight elevator, as well as the main corridor, was paved in clay tiles whereas the rest of the sub-basement was paved in the same brick as the walls and arched ceiling.

"There's definitely more evidence of traffic going to the right," Joanna said. "The tile shows a lot more wear in that direction, which not only suggests to me the tunnel is to the right, but also that the tunnel was used for a lot more than just heat."

"My word," Deborah commented, looking down. "I think you're on to something. Is this another trick you learned from watching those action movies with Carlton?"

"No, this is just common sense."

"Thanks a lot," Deborah said sarcastically.

The women commenced walking rapidly to the south. Deborah kept the flashlight trained ahead. Their footsteps echoed off the concave ceiling.

"This is like a catacomb down here," Joanna commented.

"Perhaps I shouldn't ask, but what were you thinking when you suggested the tunnel was used for more than heat?"

"It occurred to me that the tunnel was probably the way they transported dead bodies from the morgue to the crematorium."

"Now there's a cheerful thought," Deborah said.

"Uh oh," Joanna voiced. "Maybe we spoke too soon. It looks like our footworn corridor is coming to an end."

About thirty feet directly ahead the flashlight beam illuminated a blank brick wall.

"We're okay," Deborah said after they'd taken a few more steps. "The trail is just turning to the left." When the women reached the wall they noticed that not only did the vaulted corridor take an abrupt left-hand turn around an arched pier, but it also fell away relatively steeply. Also joining the descending corridor was a large-diameter insulated pipe.

"Thanks to your sleuthing I think we're on our way to the power plant," Deborah said as they began their descent. "Now we just have to hope these batteries hold out."

"Good grief!" Joanna exclaimed. "Don't even suggest such a thing!"

With a new worry of being lost underground in utter darkness, the women picked up their pace to the point of practically jogging. After several hundred yards the tunnel leveled out and became significantly more damp. There were even occasional puddles and stalactitic formations hanging from the arched ceiling.

"I feel like we're halfway to Boston," Deborah said. "Shouldn't we be there already?"

"That power plant was farther away than it looked," Joanna said.

Becoming winded, the women hurried along in silence, each harboring an unspoken worry about what they would face at the other end. A locked, stout door would spell disaster by forcing them back the way they'd come.

"I see something up ahead," Deborah said. She extended the light at arm's distance as they walked. A few moments later the women found themselves at an unexpected juncture; the corridor and the heating pipe bifurcated.

The women stopped, figuratively scratching their heads. Deborah shined the flashlight into both tunnels. They appeared identical, and all three tunnels intersected at approximately the same 120-degree angle.

"I wasn't expecting this," Joanna said nervously.

Deborah shined the light at the corner between the tunnel they were in and the new tunnel to their left. Set into the brick at chest height was a cornerstone of granite. Using the heel of her hand she rubbed off

a layer of mold, beneath which were in-
cised letters.

"Okay!" Deborah said with renewed enthusiasm. "One mystery is solved: The tunnel to the left goes to the farm/living
quarters, which means the other one must
go to the power plant."

"Of course," Joanna affirmed. "Now that
I look, the pipe heading to the power plant
is definitely a larger diameter."

"Wait a second," Deborah said, reaching
out and restraining Joanna who'd already
started in the direction of the power plant.
"With a choice here, maybe we should
think for a minute which might be a better
destination. Assuming we're going to be
able to get aboveground at either location,
I think we . . ."

"Don't even suggest that we're not going to be able to get out," Joanna snapped.

"Okay, okay!" Deborah soothed. "Let's
think where we'd rather be: at the power
station or at the farm. Once we're out of
the hospital building, our problem has become getting off the grounds. Maybe being
at the farm would be the best idea. They
probably get delivery trucks there like we
saw the other day on a regular basis."

"I thought we decided we have to get off the premises tonight," Joanna said.

"That would be best, but we have to have some alternatives in case we can't manage it."

"I still think if we don't get off tonight we'll be caught."

"Do you have any ideas?"

"Considering the razor-wire fence, I think our only chance is going through the gate. If we could get a vehicle, particularly a truck, maybe we could just smash through."

"Hmm, that's an idea," Deborah said. "So where do we have the best chance of getting a vehicle with its keys?"

"I suppose I'd say the farm," Joanna said. "But it's just a guess."

"I'd guess the same thing," Deborah said. "Let's try the farm at least first."

With newly found resolve the women set out toward the farm. They moved quickly, avoiding the puddles as well as they could. The puddles had become decidedly more plentiful in this section of the tunnel. After only a hundred yards the tunnel bifurcated again. Another engraved cornerstone directed them to the right for the farm and to the left for the living quarters. The women continued on the right fork.

"Seeing the sign for the living quarters makes me think of Spencer Wingate," Joanna said. "Maybe we should give some thought to approaching him for help."

Deborah stopped and Joanna did the same. With the flashlight directed downward, Deborah looked at her roommate. Joanna's eye sockets were lost in shadow. "Are you suggesting we go to Spencer Wingate?"

"Yes," Joanna said. "We go to his house, which we're at least familiar with, and we tell him what we've uncovered here. We also tell him that the security people are trying to hunt us down and possibly add us to their ovary collection."

Deborah let out a short, scornful laugh: "This is a strange time for you to be developing a sick sense of humor."

"At the moment it's the only way I can deal with the reality we're facing."

"Are you basing this idea of putting ourselves in Spencer Wingate's hands on overhearing that argument between him and Paul Saunders?"

"That and his response to you asking

him about the Nicaraguans," Joanna said. "Neither one of us thinks Spencer truly knows what's going on around here. If he's a normal human being, he'd be as horrified as you and I."

"That's a big if, and it would be taking a mighty big risk," Deborah said.

"We've already taken a lot of risk just being here," Joanna said.

Deborah nodded and stared off into the darkness. Joanna was right; they'd taken more risk than they'd bargained for. But did that justify taking the irreversible risk of going to Spencer Wingate?

"Let's check out the farm," Deborah said. "We'll keep the Spencer Wingate idea on a back burner. At the moment finding some big truck that can take us out of here seems like the best idea to me. Do you agree?"

"I agree," Joanna said. "I just think we have to consider all our options."

To the women's relief, the tunnel entered the farm complex the same way it left the hospital building. It ran unobstructed into a basement area where the heating pipe splintered off in multiple directions before disappearing up through the ceiling. Also like the hospital, the corridor, which was continuous with the tunnel, led to a freight elevator. But the women did not try to open the elevator doors. Instead they searched for stairs. They found a flight behind the elevator shaft.

At the door at the top of the stairs, the women paused. Deborah put her ear to it and reported back to Joanna only the quiet hum of distant machinery. After dousing the light, Deborah cracked the door slowly. The fact that they were in a barn was immediately apparent from the smell. All was quiet.

Deborah eased the door open enough to get her head through and take a look around. There was a low level of illumination from infrequently spaced bare lightbulbs on the ceiling of the post-and-beam structure. Across the way, numerous stalls lined the wall three deep. To the left were a number of closed doors. In between were huge stacks of cardboard boxes, bales of hay, and sacks of animal feed.

"Well?" Joanna whispered from a few

steps down the stairs. "Do you see any-thing?"

"There are plenty of animals in the stalls," Deborah said. "But no sign of any people, at least not yet."

Deborah opened the door and stepped out onto the hay-strewn, rough-planked floor. A few of the animals sensed her presence and grunted, bringing others to their feet. Joanna joined Deborah, and the two continued to survey the scene.

"So far so good," Deborah said. "If they have a night shift they must be sleeping."

"What a smell," Joanna said. "I can't imagine how anyone could work in this kind of environment."

"I bet it's the pigs," Deborah said. She found herself looking across the room at the beady eyes of a large pink-and-white sow. The pig seemed to be regarding her with great interest.

"Somebody told me pigs are clean," Joanna said.

"They're clean if they're kept clean," Deborah said. "But pigs don't mind being dirty, and their excrement is bad news."

"Do you see what I see on the wall behind you?" Joanna questioned. She pointed.

Deborah looked over her shoulder, and her face lit up. "A phone!"

The women dashed for the phone. Deborah got it first and put the receiver to her ear. Joanna watched her with great anticipation until Deborah's expression became one of disgust, and she hit the disconnect button several times in a row. Deborah hung up. "No deal! They've turned off the phones."

"I'm not surprised," Joanna said.

"Nor am I," Deborah admitted.

"Let's look for the truck," Joanna said.

Leaving the stairway door slightly ajar, the women skirted the animal feed and the hay and walked to the nearest door. Deborah opened it and shined in the flashlight.

"My word!" Deborah exclaimed.

"What is it?" Joanna asked, trying to see over Deborah's shoulder.

"It's another laboratory," Deborah said with amazement. She had not expected a laboratory, and the transition from a barn to super high tech over a single threshold was dizzying. The lab wasn't nearly as large as the one in the hospital but appeared to be almost equally well equipped.

Deborah let go of the door and stepped into the room. Joanna followed. Deborah moved her light from one piece of equipment to another, seeing such things as DNA sequencers, a scanning electron microscope, and polypeptide synthesizers. It was a molecular biologist's dream come true.

"Shouldn't we be looking for the truck?" Joanna asked.

"In a minute," Deborah said. She walked over to an incubator and looked in at the petri dishes. They were the same as she'd been using that day in the main lab, and she gathered they were doing nuclear transfer here as well. Then her light caught a large plate-glass window dividing a separate room off from the main part of the lab.

Deborah started back toward this room. Joanna followed to avoid being left in the dark.

"Deborah!" Joanna complained. "You're sidetracking."

"I know," Deborah said. "But every time I think I have a general picture of what they are doing at this Wingate Clinic, it turns out they are doing a lot more. I didn't expect another lab here at this farm, and certainly not one this well equipped."

"It's time for professionals," Joanna pleaded. "We have enough information to justify a search warrant. What we have to do is get ourselves out of here."

Deborah put the lens of the flashlight directly against the plate-glass divider to avoid the glare while illuminating the room beyond. "And here's yet another surprise. This looks like a fully operational autopsy room like the ones they use for people but with a very small table. What in heaven's name is it doing in a barn?"

"Come on!" Joanna urged with growing irritation.

"Just let me check this out," Deborah said. "It will only take a second. There's a refrigerated compartment like in a morgue."

Joanna rolled her eyes in frustration as Deborah pushed through the autopsy room's door. Joanna watched through the glass partition as Deborah walked over to the compartment and unlatched the door. Except for the light now coming back out through the glass divider from Deborah's flashlight, Joanna was in the dark. She glanced back at the door out of the lab and briefly entertained the idea of searching for a truck on her own, but she decided it was foolish without the flashlight.

Mumbling expletives, Joanna followed Deborah into the small autopsy room with the intent of demanding that Deborah come to her senses, but that goal was quickly forgotten. Deborah had the tray in the refrigerated compartment pulled out and was transfixed by what was on it. Joanna couldn't see what it was, but she could tell that Deborah was trembling by the way she held the light.

"What is it?" Joanna asked.

"Come and look!" Deborah said in a quavering voice.

"Maybe you should just tell me," Joanna said. "Remember, I'm not a biologist like you."

"You have to see this," Deborah said. "There's no way I could describe it."

Joanna swallowed nervously. She took a breath and walked over beside Deborah and made herself look down.

"Ugh!" Joanna muttered as her upper lip

involuntarily pulled back in disgust. She was looking at five newborn infants with bloated umbilical vessels and extremely thick, dark lanugo. The faces were flat and broad and the eyes tiny. The noses were mere stubs with the nares oriented vertically. Their appendages ended in paddle-like extremities with minute digits. Their heads were crowned with a shock of black hair accentuated with minute but definite white forelocks.

"It's Paul Saunders clones again," Joanna sneered.

"I'm afraid so," Deborah said. "But with a new twist. I think what he's doing down here for his stem-cell research is cloning his own cells into pig oocytes, and then gestating them in pigs."

Joanna reached out and took ahold of Deborah's arm. She needed momentary support. Deborah had been right about the Wingate Clinic. This new discovery indicated that Paul Saunders and his team were operating a quantum leap beyond the realm of reasonable or even anticipated ethics. The egotism and intellectual conceit required were simply beyond Joanna's comprehension.

Deborah slid the tray back into the refrigerated compartment and slammed the
door. "Let's find a damn truck!"

With indignant anger helping to over-
come the shock of their recent discovery,
the women retraced their steps back into
the barn proper. Emerging from the laboratory, their presence again caused a stirring
among the animals. Previously it had been
mainly the pigs close to the stairway door
which had become aroused. Now it was
more generalized with even the cows
adding to the growing din.

The women went from door to door until they found a passageway leading to
what they assumed would be a garage. But
it turned out to be something more. With
the light from two red exit signs, they could
see it was a hangar. Bathed in the ruby
glow was an Aerospatial turbojet helicopter.

"There's our answer, if we could only fly
it," Deborah said. She stood for a moment
longingly admiring the craft.

"Come on," Joanna urged. "I think
there's a garage beyond this building."

Joanna turned out to be right, and when
they went through the next door, they were

rewarded to see a tractor and a dump truck. Both women headed for the truck.

"Keys be there!" Deborah prayed out loud as she mounted the truck's running board and got the door open. She swung herself up into the cab. Frantically her fingers searched for keys while Joanna held the light. Deborah checked along the steering column, then along the dash. She found the ignition key slot but no keys.

"Damn!" Deborah cursed and hit the steering wheel with the heel of her hand. "I suppose we could hotwire this thing if we only knew how." She glanced down at Joanna.

"Don't look at me," Joanna said. "I have no idea, not the slightest!"

"Let's go back to that office we saw in the barn," Deborah suggested. "Maybe the keys are there."

Deborah climbed out of the truck. The women retraced their steps back to the barn, giving the helicopter another longing look as they passed through the hangar.

As they came into the barn proper, the animals became even more agitated.

"They must think it's meal time," Deborah commented.

The women reached the door to the office when they heard the unmistakable sound of a vehicle pulling up outside the barn. They'd also caught a glimpse of the headlights briefly coming through the windows of the door as the car turned before coming to a stop.

"Oh no! We're going to have company!" Deborah rasped.

"Get back to the stairs!" Joanna cried.

The women bolted for the stairs, but they didn't make it. The barn door was rapidly keyed open and a figure burst within. The first thing he did was snap on the all the lights, catching the women more than twenty feet from their goal. All they could do was duck behind the cartons, hay bales, and feed sacks and hunker down while the man made his rounds among the stalls. They could hear him carrying on a continuous monologue with the animals, demanding among other things who was the culprit for getting everybody riled up.

"Do you think we should try to get to the stairs?" Deborah asked when it sounded as if the man was at a significant distance.

"Not unless you can see exactly where

he is and whether or not he's adequately preoccupied."

Slowly Deborah raised herself until she had a view of the area of the stalls. She couldn't see the man although she could still hear him talking to one of the animals. Then suddenly he stood up, and Deborah ducked back down.

"He's not as far away as I thought," Deborah said.

"Then we'd better stay put," Joanna said.

"We could cover ourselves with some of this loose hay."

"I think we should just stay still and quiet," Joanna said. "We should be okay unless he comes over here to get some of these supplies."

"If he comes over to go in the office, we might be in trouble."

"We'd just have to inch around the cartons," Joanna said. "That shouldn't be so hard, and once he was in there, we'd be able to get to the stairs."

Deborah nodded, but she wasn't so confident it would work. It was one of those things that sounded easy but would probably be difficult in reality.

Suddenly the women heard the sound of a second vehicle arriving outside. They exchanged a worried look. One person was enough of a problem, and two could be a disaster in the making.

The newcomer entered and the door banged behind him. The women cringed as they heard him yell out for Greg Lynch.

"Hey, keep it down!" Greg called from one of the stalls. "The animals are restless as it is."

"Sorry," the newcomer said. "But we have an emergency underway."

"Oh?"

"We're looking for a couple of young women. They got in under aliases, hacked into the computer files, and broke into the egg room. Now they're somewhere out here on the premises."

"I haven't seen anyone," Greg said. "And the barn's been locked."

"What are you doing down here at this time of night?"

"I've got a sow who's nearing term. Through the monitor I heard the animals getting restless; I thought maybe she was about to deliver, but she's okay."

"If you see the women when you're driv-

ing back to your place, let security know,"
the newcomer said. "They were over in the
main building to start with, but we've been
through it. They walked, but they haven't
been back through the gate, so they're hiding someplace."

"Good luck."

"We'll get them. We've got the whole security team out searching, including all the
dogs. And, by the way, the hard-wire
phone system is off-line until they're apprehended. We don't want them calling out
and causing us difficulties."

"No problem," Greg said. "I've got my
cell phone."

After the men said their good-byes, the
women heard the barn door open and then
slam shut.

"This is going from bad to worse,"
Deborah whispered. "It sounds like they
are combing the grounds."

"I don't like the idea of dogs after us,"
Joanna said.

"You and me both," Deborah said. "It's a
wonder they haven't thought of the tunnel."

"We don't know that they haven't."

"True," Deborah said. "But I have a feeling this fellow who just left would have

mentioned it. Maybe the only way to the sub-basement over in the clinic building is via the freight elevator, and they'd never guess we'd be stupid enough to climb down the ladder."

"Do we dare go back down there?"

"If they've got dogs out looking for us, I don't think we have a lot of choice."

Fifteen minutes later the women heard Greg loudly yawn and sigh. Then he spoke out as if he were dealing with a clutch of children: "All right, you guys. Knock it off! I want you all to settle down because I don't want to have to come back here tonight."

With that said, Greg began to whistle softly. The women noticed the sound began to get louder, and Deborah hazarded a quick glance.

"He's heading for the office," Deborah whispered urgently.

Following Joanna's earlier suggestion the women crabbed along the floor in an attempt to keep the stack of supplies between themselves and Greg. It was an anxious maneuver as Deborah had anticipated, since they had to do it without looking. The man was heading in their general direction.

Once the sound of the office door closing reached them, Deborah's head popped up. "Okay," she whispered when she saw the coast was clear, and the two women beelined for the stairway door.

It wasn't until Joanna pulled the door closed that Deborah snapped on the flashlight. Wordlessly they descended the stairs. When they reached the bottom Joanna motioned for Deborah to stop. Both were mildly out of breath from tension and exertion.

"We've got to decide what we are going to do," Joanna said, speaking softly.

"I thought we were going to the power station."

"My vote is to go to Spencer Wingate," Joanna said. "There were no keys in the truck here at the farm. If there were a truck out at the power station, there's little guarantee there'd be keys. In fact, common sense would say there wouldn't be, and each time we poke our heads above ground we take the risk of being caught. I think it's time to take the chance with Wingate."

Deborah shifted her weight uneasily and chewed the inside of her cheek as she mulled over Joanna's suggestion. She hated making decisions that left no alternative available. If Spencer Wingate were in cahoots with the current Wingate Clinic hierarchy, she and Joanna would be sunk. It was as simple as that. Yet their situation had become desperate the moment they'd originally been chased back in the egg room and was now rapidly becoming untenable.

"All right!" Deborah said suddenly. "Let's throw ourselves at Spencer Wingate's mercy, for better or for worse."

"You're sure? I don't want to feel as if I've talked you into this."

"I'm not sure of anything other than the fact that I'm still exercising my free will." Deborah stuck out her hand and Joanna decisively slapped it. "Onward and upward," Deborah added with a crooked smile.

The women returned into the heating tunnels with the unspoken concern that they could run into their pursuers at any moment. But they reached the branch to the living quarters without incident other than noticing that the flashlight beam was noticeably dimmer.

Approximately a hundred yards beyond the fork they encountered another. On this occasion there was no cornerstone to direct them.

"Cripes!" Deborah complained. She shined the failing light into both tunnels. "Have any ideas?"

"I'd say we go left. We know that the village is between the detached housing and the farm, so the village would have to be to the right."

Deborah looked at Joanna with puzzlement. "You're impressing me again. Where has this resourcefulness come from?"

"From my traditional Houstonian upbringing that you've so shamelessly berated."

"Yeah, right!" Deborah said scornfully.

After another five minutes of walking the women came to a series of bifurcations all in a row.

"I'd guess each of these tunnels are going to individual houses," Deborah said.

"That would be my guess as well," Joanna added.

"Do you have any strong feeling which we try first?"

"I don't," Joanna said. "Although it makes some sense to take them in order."

The first basement the women peered into after opening a simple paneled door clearly wasn't Spencer's since it had been renovated to some degree. Both women clearly remembered Spencer's basement from when they'd accompanied him down to his wine cellar. Backtracking, they took the next tunnel. This one terminated in a crude, rough-hewn oak door.

"This looks more promising," Deborah said. She shook the flashlight to encourage the brightness of the beam. She'd had to do it occasionally over the previous few minutes.

She handed the light to Joanna before giving the door a push. It scraped on its granite threshold. Instead of just pushing, Deborah tried lifting the door first. It then opened with minimal sound. Deborah took the light back, and after giving it a shake, shined the faltering beam into the basement beyond. The dim light revealed the wine cellar door with its lock still hanging unclasped.

"This is it," Deborah said. "Let's do it!"

The women navigated the muddy floor to reach the basement steps. Up they climbed with Deborah in the lead. At the top of the stairs they hesitated. A crack of light showed under the door.

"I'm thinking we have to play this by ear," Deborah whispered.

"We don't have any choice," Joanna said. "We don't know whether he's even awake. Do you have any idea of the time?"

"Not really," Deborah said. "I suppose around one."

"Well, a light is on. I suppose that suggests he's still awake. Let's just try not to scare him too much. He might have an alarm that he could push."

"Good point," Deborah said.

Deborah listened through the door before turning the door handle slowly, and cracking it open. When there was no untoward response, she slowly pushed it open, revealing progressively more of the kitchen.

"I hear classical music," Joanna said.

"Me, too," Deborah said.

The women ventured out into the darkened kitchen. The light they'd seen beneath the cellar door was coming from the chandelier in the dining room. As quietly as they could they moved down the hallway toward the living room and the music. With a view of the foyer directly ahead, they could see that the corps of toy cavalry soldiers Spencer had knocked off the console table the evening before in his drunkenness had been carefully replaced.

Deborah was in the lead with Joanna directly at her heels. Both women were intent on the living room, which opened up to the left off the hall and where they expected Spencer to be. By happenstance Joanna glanced to the right as they passed a dark, intersecting corridor leading to a study. There in the distance was Spencer Wingate, sitting at his desk in a puddle of light from a library lamp. He was facing away from the women, studying blueprints.

Joanna tapped on Deborah's shoulder. When Deborah turned, Joanna frantically pointed toward Spencer's hunched figure.

Deborah looked at Joanna and silently mouthed the question, "What should we do?"

Joanna shrugged her shoulders. She had no idea, but then thought it best if they called out to the man. She gestured by touching her mouth and then pointing toward Spencer.

Deborah nodded. She cleared her throat. "Dr. Wingate!" she called, but her voice was tentative, and it blended seamlessly with the chorus of Beethoven's Ninth Symphony emanating from the living room.

"Dr. Wingate!" Joanna called more decisively and loud enough to compete with the music.

Spencer's head popped up and shot around. For a moment his tanned face blanched, and he stood up so quickly his desk chair tipped over with a crash.

"We don't mean to frighten you," Deborah called out quickly. "We were hoping we could have a word with you."

Spencer recovered rapidly. He smiled with relief when he recognized the women, then waved for them to join him as he bent down to right his desk chair.

The women started for the room. Both were acutely sensitive to Spencer's reaction to their presence, which so far was auspicious. His initial fear had changed to surprise with a hint of reassuring delight. As they approached, he slicked back his

silvered hair and adjusted his velvet smoking jacket. But as the women came into the
light his expression changed to puzzlement.

"What happened to you two?" Before
the women could respond he asked: "How
did you get in here?"

Joanna started to explain about coming
in through the basement while Deborah
launched into a capsule of their evening.

Spencer raised his hands. "Hold up! One
at a time. But first, do either of you need
anything? You look terrible."

For the first time since the ordeal
started, the women looked at themselves
and at each other. Their appearance
brought expressions of embarrassment to
their faces. Deborah had fared the worst
with her minidress torn and tattered and
abrasions on her thighs and shins from the
lip of the iron lung. One of her dangling earrings was gone and her tiny heart necklace
had lost all its rhinestones. Her hands were
black from the elevator cable grease, and
her hair was a tangled mess.

Joanna still had on the doctor's coat,
which had protected her clothes to a large

degree. But the coat itself was a soiled mess, particularly from crawling prostrate on the barn floor. A few stalks of hay protruded from the pockets.

Deborah and Joanna then exchanged one of their knowing glances. The combination of their appearances and anxieties brought forth a fit of laughter which took them by surprise and a moment to recover. Even Spencer found himself smiling.

"I wish I knew exactly what you women are laughing at," Spencer said.

"It's a combination," Deborah managed. "But probably mostly tension."

"I think it's mostly relief," Joanna said. "We were hoping you'd be here and unsure if you'd mind if we dropped by."

"I'm pleased you came by," Spencer said. "What can I get you?"

"Now that you ask, I could use a blanket," Deborah said. "I'm freezing."

"How about some hot coffee?" Spencer said. "I could make it for you in a moment. Even something stronger if you'd like. I could also get you a sweater or a sweatshirt."

"Actually, we'd like to talk right away,"

Joanna said. "There's some urgency involved here." She laughed nervously again.

"This blanket right here will do,"
Deborah said. She picked up a tartan
throw from a velvet couch and tossed it
around her shoulders.

"Well, sit down," Spencer said. He gestured toward the couch.

The women sat. Spencer grabbed his
desk chair and pulled it over. He sat across
from them.

"What's the urgency?" Spencer asked.
He leaned forward, glancing from one
woman to the other.

The women looked at each other.

"Do you want to talk, or do you want me
to?" Deborah said.

"I don't care," Joanna responded. "It
doesn't really matter."

"I don't care either," Deborah said.

"Of course you know the biology better
than I," Joanna said.

"True, but you can explain about the
computer files better."

"Wait, wait, wait!" Spencer said, holding
up his hands. "It doesn't matter who does
the talking. Someone start."

Deborah pointed to herself, and Joanna nodded.

"Okay," Deborah said. She looked Spencer in the eye. "Do you remember last night when I asked you about the pregnant Nicaraguan ladies?"

"I do," Spencer said. Then he laughed self-consciously. "I might not remember too much else about last night, but I remember that."

"Well, we think we know why they are pregnant," Deborah said. "We think it's to produce eggs."

Spencer's face clouded. "They're pregnant to produce eggs? I think you have to explain."

Deborah took in a lungful of air and gave her explanation. Following that explanation which she admitted was supposition, she went on to say that the Wingate Clinic was definitely obtaining eggs by an even more unethical and even unlawful manner. She explained that the clinic was removing, without consent, the entire ovaries of unsuspecting women who thought they were only donating a few eggs. Finally Deborah said that at least two women had been murdered because both ovaries had been obtained, and the women had never been seen again.

Spencer's mouth had slowly dropped open during Deborah's monologue. When she finished, he sat back, clearly horrified by what he'd heard.

"How did you learn all this?" he asked with a raspy voice. His throat had gone dry. Before either woman could respond, he added: "I have to get a drink. Can I get anything for anyone else?"

Both Deborah and Joanna shook their heads.

Spencer stood up on mildly unsteady legs and got himself over to a built-in liquor cabinet. He opened it and poured himself a splash of neat scotch. He tossed off a portion of it before returning to his chair. The women watched him intently and noted the tremor in the hand holding the tumbler.

"We're sorry to have to tell you all this," Joanna said, speaking up for the first time. "As the founder of this clinic to help infertile couples, it must be disturbing to hear what has been going on."

" 'Disturbing' is putting it mildly," Spencer said. "You have to understand that this clinic has been the culmination of my life's work."

"Unfortunately there's more you should know," Deborah said. She went on to describe the cloning and how once again unsuspecting women were being exploited. Then she told in graphic detail about the chimeric infants being gestated in pigs in the farm which she and Joanna had just discovered. After this final piece of shocking information, Deborah fell silent.

The women watched Spencer. He was clearly distraught, running his fingers repeatedly through his hair and unable for a time to make eye contact. He polished off the last of his scotch in a single toss and winced.

"I appreciate your coming to me," Spencer managed. "Thank you."

"Our motivation wasn't entirely altruistic," Joanna said. "We need your help."

Spencer lifted his face and stared at Joanna. "What can I do?"

"You can get us out of here," Joanna said. "The Wingate Security force is searching for us. They have been chasing us since we managed to get into the egg room. They have a pretty good idea what we know."

"You want me to get you off the premises," Spencer said.

"Exactly," Joanna answered. "We've got to get out through the gate."

"That won't be difficult," Spencer said. "We'll drive out in the Bentley."

"We want to make sure you understand exactly how much they want to catch us," Deborah said. "I mean, this is a very serious situation. We cannot be seen. I'm sure they'd stop even you if they suspected."

"I imagine you are right," Spencer said. "To make sure there will be no problem, you two can squeeze into the trunk. It's not going to be comfortable by any stretch of the imagination, but it would only be for about five minutes, or ten at the most."

Joanna looked at Deborah. Deborah nodded. "I've always wanted to ride in a Bentley; I suppose the trunk will do."

Joanna rolled her eyes. She couldn't understand Deborah's motivation for joking at that point. "I could deal with being in the trunk. In fact, under the circumstances I'd probably feel safer in the trunk."

"When do you want to do it?" Spencer

asked. "Sooner is probably better than later. I've been known to go out for late drives on occasion, but anything after two A.M. would be suspicious."

"I'm all for sooner," Joanna said.

"I'm ready right now," Deborah added.

"Let's go," Spencer said. He slapped his thighs as he got up.

Spencer led the women back through the kitchen where he picked up his car keys off the countertop before entering the garage. He went directly behind the Bentley and keyed open the trunk.

The women were surprised at the small size.

"It's because of the storage for the automatic convertible top," Spencer explained.

Deborah scratched her head. "I guess we'll have to spoon."

Joanna nodded. "You're biggest, so you get in first."

"Thanks a lot," Deborah said. She climbed in headfirst and rolled onto her side. Joanna followed suit bending her body to fit in against Deborah's. Spencer slowly closed the lid to make sure there was no problem with arms and knees, and then raised it again.

"It's actually more comfortable than the iron lung," Deborah commented.

"What iron lung?" Spencer asked.

"That's another story," Deborah said. "Let's get this current chapter over with."

"All right, let's go!" Spencer said. "Now don't panic. I'll stop and let you out as soon as it's reasonable. Okay?"

"Button it up!" Deborah said cheerfully, trying to make the best of a bad situation.

The trunk lid came down with a thud and an expensive-sounding click. Once again the women were thrust into darkness. The next thing they heard was the garage door retracting, followed by the car engine starting.

"I guess we should have thought about coming to Spencer earlier," Deborah said. "We could have saved ourselves some grief."

The women felt the car back out of the garage, do a three-point turn, and then motor down the driveway to the street.

"This is an ignominious way to be leaving this place," Joanna said.

"At least we're leaving."

"I felt rather bad for the good doctor," Joanna said after they'd driven for a while.

"What we told him certainly took him by surprise."

They drove in silence for the next few minutes while the women tried to guess where they were. Eventually they felt the car come to a stop with the engine still going.

"We must be at the gate," Deborah said.

"Shush!" Joanna said.

The trunk lid was so well insulated that the women couldn't hear anything until the engine revved again, and even then it was more vibration than noise. After they'd driven a short distance they could tell they were on gravel. A few minutes later the car stopped again, only this time the engine was turned off.

"You'd think he would have driven a bit farther away from the gatehouse," Joanna said.

"I was thinking the same thing," Deborah said. "But hell, at least we're outside the gate, so we might as well ride in style."

They heard the welcome sound of the key in the trunk lock, followed by a popping-up of the trunk cover. Joanna and Deborah looked up, and their hearts leaped in their chests. Spencer was nowhere to be seen. Instead they were looking up into the sneering faces of the Wingate security chief and his henchman.

epilogue

MAY 11, 2001
9:35 A.M.

Spencer looked out from his office window at the expansive, verdant lawn. Beyond were the spire of Bookford's church and a handful of chimneys sticking up through the budding trees. It was a pleasant sight, and it helped to a degree to calm his roiling emotions. He couldn't remember the last time he was quite so overwrought. To make it worse, he'd not slept in more than twenty-four hours and was still recovering from his recent alcoholic debauchery.

Spencer cleared his throat. "What concerns me is not just what the women knew, but how they found out." Spencer turned from the window and faced Paul Saunders and Sheila Donaldson, who were calmly sitting in armchairs in front of his desk. "I mean, I was blown away when those two women showed up inside my house, especially since you supposedly had a small army looking for them. If that doesn't smack of incompetence, I don't know what does. But more important, if those two could find out in one day everything that you people have been doing around here, so could someone else."

"Spencer, calm down," Paul urged. "Everything is under control."

"'Under control,'" Spencer repeated sarcastically. "If this is under control I can't imagine what things would have to be like to be out of control." He returned to his desk chair and sat down heavily.

"We're in full agreement," Paul said calmly. "We know we must find out exactly how the women managed to find out what they did."

"They knew about gestating human clones in pigs," Spencer said. "You didn't tell me about that last night. For chrissake, what's that about anyway?"

"It's to rid us of dependence on the Nicaraguan women," Paul said. "As soon as we've perfected the technique, that will be a major source of new eggs apart from the oogonia cultures."

"Well, how the hell did they learn about it?" Spencer roared.

"We'll find out," Paul said. "Trust me!"

"How can you be so confident?" Spencer demanded. "Kurt Hermann and his bozos have been grilling those women down in the gatehouse since three A.M., and you admitted yourself five minutes ago, they've learned nothing."

"I beg to differ," Sheila said. "I've been doing the debriefing so far, not Kurt, and it's not true we've learned nothing."

"You've been talking with the women?" Spencer questioned.

"Absolutely," Sheila said. "It was under my specific orders that I be paged the moment they were apprehended. As we're trying to tell you, we're just as concerned as you about uncovering their methods. And we are making progress. For instance, we've learned that it was your access card which got them into both the server room and the egg room."

"Oh, I see," Spencer said, glaring back at his two supposed subordinates. "So I'm to blame for this debacle."

"Allotting blame is not our intent in the slightest," Paul said.

"That's not a lot of information after six hours," Spencer said.

"They are extremely intelligent women," Sheila explained. "They recognize that the information they have is important. They are not pushovers by any stretch of the imagination, but I'm being patient."

"We're using the *good cop, bad cop* routine," Paul explained.

"Exactly," Sheila said. "Obviously, I'm the good cop. While we're having our meeting, Kurt is having his first go at talking with them. He's the bad cop. As soon as we finish here, I'll go back down and intervene. I'm confident we'll have all we need to know by noon at the latest."

"Once we have the information," Paul said, "we'll make the appropriate operational changes. We've already started in regard to computer security. From now on, access to the server room will be limited to Randy Porter alone."

"We should look at this whole unfortunate affair as a learning experience," Sheila said.

"Precisely!" Paul chimed in. "And we should look at it as a further stimulus for us to move the entire clinic, research labs and all, offshore like we discussed last evening. By the way, Spencer: What did you think of the plans I gave you last evening for the Bahamian Center?"

"The plans looked good," Spencer admitted reluctantly.

"And your response in general to the idea of moving offshore?" Paul asked.

"I must admit I like it," Spencer said. "I like the idea of having even less regulation than we've had to deal with here, even if that hasn't been that much of a bother."

Spencer nodded. "Let's get back to the women. What's to happen to them after their debriefing?"

"I don't know," Paul answered.

"What do you mean you don't know?" Spencer demanded, feeling his ire rise again.

"I don't want to know," Paul said. "I leave that kind of problem up to Kurt Hermann. That's what we pay him for."

"You leave the problem to Kurt Hermann

and yet retain the ovaries," Spencer sneered. "Is that what you are telling me?"

"Harvesting the ovaries was a mistake we made in the past," Sheila interjected. "There's no doubt we shouldn't have done it. We realize it now, and it will not be repeated. As an explanation, it happened back when we were struggling with a critical egg shortage."

"A shortage which we no longer have," Paul added. "With the Nicaraguan connection plus the progress we've made with our oogonia culture technique, we now have at our disposal an almost unlimited egg supply. Hell, we can probably supply the cloning needs for the whole country."

"Are you two trying to suggest to me that you are not disturbed by this episode?" Spencer asked.

Paul and Sheila exchanged glances.

"We certainly take it as a serious event," Sheila said. "It's a learning experience as we said. But it has been contained just like the episode involving the anesthetic catastrophe. Even if this episode with these two meddling women had not ended so auspiciously, we would have been able to cope."

"Listen, Spencer," Paul said. He leaned

forward and rubbed his hands together, and then held them up in a conciliatory gesture. "Like I said last night during our discussion, researchwise we are sitting on a virtual gold mine. With what we are learning from our cloning work in terms of generating stem cells, we will be the biotech leaders of the twenty-first century. Cloning and stem cells are going to revolutionize medicine, and we're going to be at the forefront."

"You make it sound so rosy," Spencer said.

"That's exactly the same adjective I use to describe it to myself," Paul said. "It is rosy! Very rosy!"

The latch on Spencer's office door clicked loudly. Spencer, Paul, and Sheila turned to look. All were taken aback by the interruption. The secretary's face appeared around the door.

"What is it, Gladys?" Spencer demanded. "I said we were not to be disturbed."

"It's Mr. Hermann," the secretary said meekly. "He needs to speak to Dr. Saunders. He said it was an emergency."

Paul stood up. A questioning expression

clouded his face. He excused himself and followed the distraught secretary out of the room. One look at Kurt caused a meltdown of all the nonchalance and composure Paul had been studiously maintaining.

"We've got a major problem," Kurt sputtered.

"Why are you out of breath?"

"I've run all the way up from the gatehouse."

Paul snapped open the door to his office and motioned Kurt inside. Paul closed the door behind them. "Well?"

"There's a United States attorney down at the gatehouse," Kurt blurted, running his words together.

"Slow down!" Paul ordered. "What's he doing here?"

"He's got a search warrant, and he and some federal marshals are going through the gatehouse. Plus they're demanding entrance onto the grounds."

"How the hell did he get a search warrant?" Paul was stunned.

"I asked. Apparently it was due to a complaint by a doctor by the name of Carlton Williams."

"Never heard of him."

"His father is some Texan big shot with connections to the Justice Department. The problem is, this Carlton Williams knows the women were here last night and didn't return home."

"Shit!" Paul snapped. "Where are the women now?"

"They're still in the gatehouse basement."

"Has the U.S. Attorney found them?"

"I don't know. I ran up here as soon as I was able to put them off for five minutes. They're threatening to bring in a SWAT team if we don't cooperate."

"Threatening is good," Paul said, regaining some composure. "At least they didn't show up with a SWAT team. That gives us a good half hour, minimum. Let's activate a code red. You get to Randy Porter. Have him put everything onto ZIP discs and then erase all the hard drives. Then get yourself and Randy to the hangar and rev up the chopper. I'll get Dr. Wingate and Dr. Donaldson down there after we shred paper files here in the office and have the egg room destroyed. Okay?"

"Roger!" Kurt said. He saluted before dashing out of the office and running full tilt down the corridor toward the fire door. Paul watched him until he disappeared. Paul then took a couple of breaths to bolster his gaining equanimity. When he felt he'd pulled himself adequately together, he returned to Spencer's office. Spencer and Sheila looked at him expectantly the moment he appeared.

"Well," Paul said. "It appears that we're going offshore sooner than we expected . . ."